Praise for
Will Davenport's

PAINTER

"THE PAINTER is as deft a piece of historical
fiction as the most demanding reader could ask for,
bringing together past and present in a puzzle about the
mysterious origins of art itself.
As with the great painting he describes, the author
skillfully works together the known and familiar with the
unknown and unexpected, leaving us with the surprise of
a freshly envisioned world."

—Laurie R. King
Nationally Bestselling Author of *Justice Hall*

"All the juicier thanks to the serenely manipulative
Amelia . . . Davenport does right by Rembrandt and his genius—
and that gives his fantasy a glow of its own."

—*Kirkus Reviews*

WILL DAVENPORT

the PAINTER

BANTAM BOOKS

THE PAINTER
A Bantam Book / May 2003

Published by
Bantam Dell
A Division of Random House, Inc.
New York, New York

Cover images: *The Woman with the Arrow,* 1661 (etching) by
Rembrandt Harmensz, van Rijn (1606–69): Fitzwilliam Museum,
University of Cambridge, UK/Bridgeman Art Library; *Henriette
de Kerouaille, Countess of Pembroke* by Sir Peter Lely (1618–80):
Collection of the Earl of Pembroke, Wilton House, Wilts,
UK/Bridgeman Art Library

Book design by Laurie Jewell

Material has been used from *The Life and Times of Rembrandt* by
Hendrik Willem van Loon. Liveright Publishing Corporation,
New York. Copyright © 1930 by Horace Liveright.

Library of Congress Cataloging-in-Publication Data
Davenport, Will.
The painter / Will Davenport.
p. cm.
ISBN 0-553-38206-3
1. *Rembrandt Harmenszoon van Rijn, 1606–1669—Fiction.*
2. *Marvell, Andrew, 1621–1678—Fiction.* 3. *Dutch—England—Fiction.*
4. *Painters—Fiction.* 5. *Great Britain—History—Charles II, 1660–1685—
Fiction.* 6. *Hull (England)—Fiction.* 7. *Netherlands—Fiction.* I. Title

PR6062.O5123 P3 2003   2002034255
823/.92 21

Manufactured in the United States of America
Published simultaneously in Canada

RRH 10 9 8 7 6 5 4 3 2 1

THIS BOOK IS DEDICATED
TO THE MEMORY OF THE
REMARKABLE PLYMOUTH PAINTER
ROBERT LENKIEWICZ,
WHO WAS A SOURCE OF INSIGHT
AND INSPIRATION TO ME.

ACKNOWLEDGMENTS

I would like to thank my excellent editor, Samantha Bruce-Benjamin, for holding my feet to the fire with forceful and creative patience. Sam Boyce, as ever, encouraged me throughout. Many people helped with my research. Mark, Paul, and Tina Riley of Coombe Farm Studios in Dittisham, Devon arranged for my portrait to be painted or drawn by three diverse artists, Robert Lenkiewicz, Xanthe Mosley, and Simon Drew. They were all generous and helpful with their explanations. Robert Lenkiewicz's deep insights into Rembrandt as a man and as a painter were inspirational. The Hull Local Studies Library enabled me to search for Rembrandt's faint footprints in their archives while Ann Bukantas, at the Ferens Gallery, opened up her own surprising collection of material on the subject. Among Rembrandt's many biographers, I would particularly like to acknowledge Christopher White and Gary Schwartz. George Speake always seems to be expert on any subject I write about and this was no exception. Pippa Collin and Ralph de Rijke helped me navigate through seventeenth-century Dutch expressions. My wife Annie kept my spirits and body alive throughout the long and sometimes testing process.

the
PAINTER

ONE

I PAINT WHAT I SEE.

If people don't like that they can shove their eyes up their arses. It's all the same to me, so long as they pay.

I must say, in mitigation of the circumstances I now find myself in, that on a number of occasions in the past forty years, I have been described by men who love art as one of the greatest painters of all, and it is not for me to disagree with such experts.

Honesty is everything. I paint what I see and I paint it in the only way I can. If my style has gone out of fashion, then the fault lies with fashion, not with me. A rich client tests the honesty of any painter. To the world, the man in the chair may look like a frost-nipped turnip, but what is he to himself? When he looks in the glass, does a demigod look back? I don't paint to flatter. I paint to infect the canvas with the exact humanity of my vision; turnip or no turnip.

There is a lesson in this. Paint too many honest turnips and your studio will soon fill up with orphan canvases. That way lies the road to starvation and the perpetual sideways lookout for the money-lender's men—the way my own life has gone in the last five years. Riches to rags.

I had been slow to attention with that wary sideways look, so now I was at sea for the first time in my life, unable to even contemplate the waves.

The captain was standing near the wheel and my eyes feasted on his face as soon as I saw him. His hand rested on the compass housing, and the lantern light reflecting from the brass ring around it warmed the color of his wrist so the skin shone against his dense black sleeve.

He looked at me with distaste and addressed me in English, a language I have never seen any reason to learn.

A seaman tugged at my arm. "He says who are you?"

"My name is van Rijn."

"He says do you make a habit of stowing away?"

"I did not stow away," I said indignantly.

"You were hiding on board when we cast off. What would you call it?"

I ignored the minion and spoke directly to the captain, drawing myself up to my full height, which was still far short of his.

"I am a gentleman," I said. "I wish to be treated as a gentleman."

He surveyed me with contempt. I was wearing my shirt of the best silk, one of a dozen given to me by the Cloth-Makers Guild in the forlorn hope their commission might jump the queue. A little stained with paint certainly, a little torn and stitched here and there, but the quality was undeniable. My trousers of the finest Flemish cloth, bought with Don Antonio's gold from the philosopher's portrait. I hadn't noticed until now how they had begun to age and fray. My cloak best of all, a noble velvet gown bought for a great deal of money at auction and said to have belonged to the King of Bohemia. But where was my cloak? Was it still in the bowels of the ship? Had I lost it during the evening's chase?

"I have no wish to be on your ship," I said to deflect his unnerving, unimpressed eye. "It is a mistake. Can you please turn round and take me back?"

My request was translated, and all at once he was Neptune and I was some ignorant mollusk. I could tell his tone was incredulous; the seaman preserved that tone in his interpretation.

"The captain says you know sweet sodding nothing of ships if you think he will turn round and miss this tide. He says you are coming with us, you damned van Rijn, and you can bloody well pay for your passage as well as the bottle of his good claret wine you drank before we found you."

"I am a bankrupt," I said, playing with the word as I said it. It was still a new idea to me, and whereas before the event it had seemed like a nightmare, now it rang out and surrounded me in chain mail.

The captain frowned and barked at his man. "An Amsterdam bankrupt?" the seaman said. "The captain says we will see how well that stands you in Hull."

"Where is Hull?" I asked.

TWO

Sunday, April 8, 2001

AMY DALE HAD MADE IT A GUIDING PRINCIPLE OF HER LIFE THAT she would never go to Hull, but she abandoned that principle the moment she saw the hitchhiker. At twenty-five, Amy believed that you are always closer to the essence of life by being on the move. She was driving south with no particular destination in mind, her sweater still caked in drying paint, wondering if the castanet rattle from the Ford's ancient engine was significant. Her car was more of a hindrance than a help to travel, but assistance was never far away because Amy had slim-blonde helplessness down to a fine art when it suited her. For brief periods and specific purposes only.

Amy aspired to be rootless, disdaining her true roots entirely. To push herself in that direction, she adhered to self-invented auguries. Five miles back, she had decided that if one of the next ten trucks she saw was yellow, she would sleep somewhere comfortable tonight. If not, she would sleep in the car. Her decision to head south on the main road had been settled by seeing a cow before she saw a sheep, though, not wanting to head north, she might well have looked the other way if the wrong animal had appeared first.

Eight trucks, all the wrong color, had come and gone, when a flash of yellow up ahead caught her eye. It wasn't a truck; it was a yellow plastic duck. The old man was standing beside the road, juggling three ducks, sticking his thumb out for a moment at a time then whipping it back just in time to catch the next descending duck. The cardboard sign propped against his bag said "HULL (or thereabouts)" in big blue letters, and she suddenly thought, well, why not?

"Didn't your mother tell you not to pick up strange men?" he said when he stuck his head in the door.

"For God's sake leave my mother out of it," said Amy. "Anyway, you're too old to be dangerous."

"Don't say that," he said. "That's cruel. I'm well dangerous, me."

"Get in," she said, "but if you dare mention my mother again, you're straight out, got it?"

"Fine woman," he said, chucking his bag into the back and looking for a way to strap himself in. "My lips are sealed. Have you been storing cheese in this car by any chance?"

She looked at him, considering. He was a shocking sixty or a reasonable seventy or anywhere on the sliding scale in between. Silver hair, mustache stained nicotine-yellow, and a spectacular twinkle in both eyes. "Yes, I have," she said. "A dog ate the seat belt."

"Fair enough. I didn't want to live much longer anyway. What are you going to Hull for?"

"I'm taking *you* there, aren't I?"

"Apart from that."

"Nothing. I'm just . . . wandering. Hull's as good a place as any."

"That's a funny thing to say about Hull. You might say it's as good as Goole or even Scunthorpe if you were pushing your luck, but it's not a patch on anywhere else."

"I wouldn't know," she said. "I've never been there yet."

"So what's this wandering in aid of, then? Man trouble?"

"Balls. Job trouble, that's all, leading to 'no-job' trouble."

"Get sacked, did you?"

"I quit."

"When?"

"So recently I'd have to check my watch to tell you for certain."

He snickered. "What was the job?"

"I'm a painter."

"House painter?"

"Houses, portraits. You name it. I do it."

"So why did you quit?"

"I was doing murals for a fat git who owned a nightclub. Every time he came by, he'd cop a feel, so I tipped two and a half liters of Azzurro Blue eggshell over his head."

He examined the evidence smeared across the sleeve of her sweater.

"Nice color for heads. I hope you used a good primer first. Was that before you quit or after?"

"During. What do you do?"

"Plastering. Fancy stuff."

"In Hull?"

"No, on walls. Anywhere. Outside Hull right now. Big place. Big job. Lots of money. Living in. That's the way I like it."

"So you're not a juggler?"

"I juggle, therefore I'm a juggler. *Jugglo ergo sum,* you might say. Only when I need a lift and the ducks get restless."

"Stop it. You're sounding like my mother again."

"She's a juggler?"

"No, she thinks she's a philosopher. *Cogito ergo sum.* That's her favorite. I think therefore I am. What she really means is I think therefore I'm right."

"How come you're allowed to mention your mother and I'm not?"

"Driver's privilege. Long story. More to the point, do they need any painters at your place?"

"Well, now, they might. They just might. Foreman likes a pretty face."

"Is he a groper?"

"Nah. He's the foreman. He's got people to do stuff like that for, him."

"Will he be around today?"

"Maybe. He doesn't get out much."

A yellow truck shot past in the other direction. Amy cursed under her breath. She hadn't been looking. Had there been more than ten?

"I'll deliver you to the door," she said. "Oh, I'm Amy by the way."

The old man broke into song: "From Hull and Halifax and Hell, Good Lord deliver me." He held out a hand, "Dennis the Menace."

"What was that?"

"Just an old song. Now what's this long story about your mother?"

Amy started to brake, then laughed. "You came close there. I try not to think about her. It's just that she spent years trying to get me to go to Hull."

"I call that a remarkably small ambition to have for your daughter."

"Oh, no, it's not. Believe me it's not. We were a great family once, you see. Nothing semidetached about the Dales, no, no. We're a cut above the rest if you think the way my mother does. Blood will out. That's one of her favorite sayings."

"Only if you cut yourself."

"My mother sees the world through class-tinted spectacles. We come from splendid stock in her eyes, you see, old-fashioned gentry from a great house on the banks of the Humber. Paull Holme Manor is the living proof of the former glory of the Dale family. I had it thrown at me every day of my childhood: *They wouldn't have held their knife like that in Paull Holme Manor. They wouldn't come down to supper at Paull Holme Manor with dirty jeans on. They would* never *use a disgusting word like that in Paull Holme Manor.* That's exactly why I never want to go there."

"You better drop me off, then. You won't want a job at my place."

"Why not? What do you mean?"

"It's Paull Holme Manor. That's where I'm working."

The Fiesta snaked violently as Amy threw back her head and roared with laughter.

"Come on, Fate," she cried, "give me a break!"

"So?" said Dennis, "Are you up for it?"

Amy hadn't been home in two years, had only phoned once in six months. That phone call had moved from Happy Christmas to a blistering critique of her whole lifestyle in two sentences. She had treated her parents' house in Surrey as if it had a fifty-mile exclusion zone surrounding it, but Paull Holme was nowhere near Surrey. Paull Holme was a mythical place, a concept. Amy loved irony.

"Maybe," she said. "What are the others like? Are they all guys?"

"Oh, yes."

"Are they *nice* guys?"

Dennis considered her question for a moment.

"Define nice?"

"Good looking, tough, fit, caring, sensitive, and artistic."

He shook his head. "No, sorry."

"Any of those? Three out of six?"

"Two, tops."

"Two's enough."

He looked at her appraisingly. "There could be trouble," he said.

"Sounds good," she said and, foolishly, she meant it.

They laughed most of the rest of the way until they got to Hull. Then Dennis directed Amy down the back roads past a maze of car lots and welding sheds to the back of the docks where, for the first time, she saw the great expanse of water, wide enough to give a hint of the earth's curve, which is the River Humber.

"There you are," said Dennis as Amy pulled over and stared across the vast rough river to the far shoreline of Lincolnshire, a mile and a half away. "Never seen it before? A mud-shifting, iron-rusting brute. England's Mississippi."

They got out into a searing wind that carried a faint smell of gas.

"I know that color," said Amy, looking at the water. "That's the color chocolate milkshakes used to be, before they tasted of chocolate. Light brown with a sickening touch of pink and orange."

"Drink that and die," said Dennis. "What you're looking at there is the Yorkshire Dales being flushed out to sea. There's no arguing with the Humber."

"It's certainly got a hungry look."

"Hungry? I should say so. It ate a whole town once." He pointed off to the left toward the North Sea. "Ten miles down there. Ravenser. Great big place, the main port round here once upon a time. Then one day the Humber said, I'll have you for my breakfast, and that was it, gone. Just a mud bank out in the river, that's all that's left of it now."

"When was this?" asked Amy, trawling back mentally through half-remembered TV news stories of crumbling cliffs and storm-savaged villages.

"Oh, I dunno," he said vaguely. "Before my time—1300 or there-abouts? That's why Hull's here. All those rich merchants grabbed what they could save and came back here, so they could hide their ships in a nice little side river. That's the river Hull, you see. Too traumatized to make an honest job of it and call it Kingston upon Humber. They were trying to pretend the big, bad gobbler wasn't there anymore, so they called it Kingston upon Hull."

Amy was looking at a small orange ship butting its way upriver into the fierce wind, foam spraying over its bow. Seagulls screamed over their heads. "Oh yes," she said, "I know. My mother always insisted on calling it by its *full* name."

"Well, there's too many Kingstons, and life's too short for all five syllables, so Hull it is."

"All right then, Dennis. Let's go and confront my family heritage. Which way do we go?"

"To the lost land of Holderness. East into the setting sun."

"I'm glad I don't own *your* compass. Do you come from round here?"

"That's the most horrible thing anyone's ever said to me."

From Hull, it's another fifteen miles to the sea, where the north shore is largely uninhabited. The river effectively balanced the books on Ravenser by stranding other old harbors forever behind new mud banks so that they silted up, their quays and jetties sinking back into the soil. Paull is the only riverside village left on that entire north shore between Hull and the sea. Dennis steered Amy down a tiny side road past a chemical refinery, a sprawling intestinal jumble of pipework, polished steel flashing sunlight at them through disturbing clouds of vapor that drifted across the road ahead.

"Will it kill us?" Amy asked.

"Pedal to the metal and hold your breath," said Dennis. "Into the Valley of Death. 'Tis a far, far better thing that I do now than ... oh, we're through."

Once through the steam cloud they emerged into a different, older world. The narrow lane was perched on a dyke, raised above drainage ditches. A partridge scuttled across the road and a vast sky opened up above. Amy had a strong and oppressive sense that they were below sea level. This was lowland, reclaimed from the river long ago, and the skyline ahead seemed like a bank, holding back the water. Another mile on brought them up out of that land and into hidden Paull, the street curving gently toward the still invisible river, bordered by a line of ancient terraced houses, irregular rooflines proclaiming their individuality. The Royal Oak on the right looked almost old enough to have known

the famous tree that sheltered the Stuart King from his rebellious subjects. Two more pubs guarded the far end of that street, facing each
other, the Humber Tavern, strewn with satellite dishes, and the dour
Crown, opposite—dull ochre, giving nothing outwardly away to the
modern age. And that was where the seawall started and the Humber
opened itself to view from side to side and from here to there.

There was no choice for Amy but to get out and climb the seawall,
because here the whole thing seemed to demand inspection, insisting
she soak it up with her eyes. Wavelets fizzed on the mud beyond, siz-
zling like chip shop frying vats. The river curved away from her in both
directions like a reflection on the outside of a silver bowl. Steel buoys,
green and red, heaved slowly in the waves. Far to her right she could
see the long span of the suspension bridge reduced to a thread by the
scale of the water it crossed. In the space between, two more ships were
making their way upstream.

She loved it. The raw power and the smell of it, almost untouched
by the Lilliputian marks of man's navigation.

A hundred yards along, where the road curved inland, was a low
lighthouse attached to a Dutch-gabled house.

"Where's Paull Holme Manor?" she said to Dennis, who was smoking a roll-up. He had made it so badly that the burning part flew off in
the wind every time he relit it.

"A way along yet," he said. "Hold your horses. First there's Paull
Battery, then there's Paull Church, then if you're very, very good,
there's the old place. That's if you're sure you want to go there?"

"Of course I am. Why?"

"Ah. Well, I'm a racing man, you see, and if I saw a horse looking
at the jumps the way you're looking up this river, I would not be at all
sure that horse wanted to start the race."

"It's not that. I've had pictures of this place in my head all my life
and so far, this doesn't feel anything like it."

"What were you imagining?"

"Buckingham Palace in the country, I suppose. Thousands of acres
of lawns all trimmed with nail scissors. Deer and flamingos."

"Prepare yourself for a major disappointment. There's fourteen
hungry builders living in there. They already ate the flamingos."

"No lawns?"

"There's grass."

"Well, that's halfway to a lawn."

"Only if you think a wolf is halfway to a poodle."

They got back in the car. Amy drove on in silence past the isolated church and down the long straight road, peering ahead intently for the first glimpse of the home of her mother's forebears. Ahead was a sharp left bend. On the outside of the bend was a broken gateway where a rough track led into a small, intensely gloomy wood.

"That's it," said Dennis. "In there."

She searched inside herself for a sense of anticipation or even mild disappointment but all she found, to her intense irritation, was a rising interest in the builders, not the house. *Oh, God,* she thought, *three months since my last man and my body's on the lookout again. Stop it.* Then they bumped round the corner of the track, around the perimeter of the lit-tle wood. For the first time, she saw Paull Holme Manor, watching the river as it always did for returning ships, for news of trade or for tidings of war. It was astonishingly unlike the house she expected, yet she knew instantly that she had seen it before.

THREE

Monday, January 13th, 1662

I FIRST SAW DAHL'S HOUSE THIS MORNING AT SUNRISE, AND I THOUGHT it the oddest and most disproportionate dwelling I had ever seen, having no idea of the beauty it contained. I saw the house from his ship where I was stuck, suffering. Since I was seven years old, not one day has passed when I have not worked at my art, until now. Not one day, even when they took my house from me, even when I had the swelling fever, even when my wife died. It is unforgivable to keep me away from paint and it is the world's loss.

Of course, whatever Dahl may choose to believe, I did not board this damned tub on purpose. There are good reasons why I do not travel. I went to the docks *only* to see whether the ship just come from Livorno had brought back with it a picture returned to me by an unhappy and extremely difficult purchaser. I would have sent the boy, but I have no boy in these bare-shelved, anxious-eyed times. I would have sent *my* boy, my Titus, but he and Hennie decided between them last year that they were now in charge of my life, not I of theirs. It has led us to a strange place, that decision they made. They made it for me, I know. They made it to protect me. The *law* says they are in charge of my affairs and that shields me from my creditors, but they have come to believe it means more than that. They really do think they have the whip hand. But I am still the master of my brush and they do not challenge me if I just paint so that is what I do. I do not tell them to do anything for me anymore for fear they may say no.

Having no boy, I went myself and now, in consequence, I am here on this river, on this damned boat.

It was thoroughly dark, being late in the evening when the arrival of the Livorno ship was announced in the street, and I was glad to get out, anticipating spending a little time in gentle disputation with the Arminians on my way. They do love to discuss the finer points of their sectarian views and, these days, I value a good, logical argument with fine intellects almost regardless of the subject matter. In the dark, it seemed to me there was little chance of anyone seeing me who might be after the settlement of a bill, and I did not tell Hennie where I planned to go because she would only have tried to stop me.

I had three or four guilders in my pocket and when the ship from Livorno turned out not to be the ship from Livorno at all but merely a bedraggled pink just in from Dunkerque with horses on board, most of which appeared to be dead, I decided I would spend one of the coins on a glass or two of wine instead. No sooner had I stepped into the front room of the Egbertsz Inn when a shout of recognition went up from two men at the bar. Summons-men, both of them. I had to turn and run, which is not something I excel at. Sitting at an easel, day in, day out, does not make a man fast on his feet.

I got away initially only because of the crowd between those damned men of Vondel's and the doorway. After that, I won another few seconds respite because they naturally turned right, assuming I would be heading for home, whereas I had turned left. This was not a result of any native wit, but simply because I was in such a panic that I lost all sense of where I was.

I heard the muffled shouts from the far side of the inn when they realized their mistake. The street in which I found myself was wide and promised only instant capture if they saw me there. Capture in the past would simply have meant the serving of another writ, but now I was a bankrupt I knew it would amount to something far more physical. Vondel had warned me his men would take what they were owed out of my hide if they could not get it from my purse. My only escape lay in hiding in the narrow side alleys, the slits of darkness between the warehouses that run down to the wharves on the Amstel river. I fled to the nearest one and, in the pitch-black, ran straight into a fellow humping a whore against the wall, knocking him off his business and angering both of them considerably.

I apologized, threw my remaining coins at the man, begged them both to say they had not seen me, and made my best speed down into the darkness, arms outstretched for fear of interrupting any other amorous adventures. At the end of the alley, a dim lantern showed me a ship and an unguarded gangplank, and when the echoing noise of feet behind me in the alleyway indicated that my coins had not done their work properly, I had no option but to go up that gangway.

That got me out of an old trouble and into a new one. There were sailors on board. I could hear them working away at something down below inside the ship, where a large hatchway gaped open. An open door in the deckhouse was my only choice to evade capture so I stepped into obscurity, and fell headlong down a stairway into an erupting pile of sacks of flour. When I collected myself, I found a space behind the sacks into which I could squirm, bordered by a case of bottles.

What would you have done, stuck there, waiting for the coast to clear? Exactly. This is how I found myself on this unexpected journey. Wine led to sleep and when the ship began to rock, sleep only deepened.

The reasons why I do not travel? First and most important, it wastes time. There is a limit to the number of works I can complete in my remaining years and although it is not given that I should know that limit, it is there, like it or not. There is not one duty I owe to the world, but I do owe *myself* the duty of extending my art to the uttermost boundary of its potential and that can be done only by practicing it. As I get older I find increasingly that the white spaces in between things matter more and more. My painting is no longer about building up, it is about paring down, determining the minimum required. This is a new discovery which I must explore to its limits.

The second reason flows from the first. I have to stay at home because that is where the answers lie, inside me and in the mirror I look in, not outside my windows. It is a lifetime's work to study the thickness of the air in my studio and how the moving sun changes that thickness throughout the day. Outside there is an infinity of confusion—too much for one man to handle in a million lifetimes. A man must limit the objects of his attention if he is to approach perfection.

On this voyage I have already seen far too much, far too many possibilities. I may lose everything if I cannot get back home and find my focus once more.

The slow journey up this English river was the first and only part of the whole bloody, bloody journey I enjoyed at all. The first day, after dragging me from my sleep among the flour sacks, drenching me unnecessarily with salt water from a bucket, and hauling me before this martinet of a captain, a man I would judge to be ten years my junior and of no higher standing than me, they tried to make me *work*. It was soon clear to them that ropes and knots meant nothing to me at all, and when they tried to make me climb the rigging, I could barely get off the deck. They gave me a brush, a *scrubbing* brush, and they made me kneel down to scrub the deck. Then there was the food. Oh, God, the food. In my old house, my beautiful house on the Breestraat, we ate the finest food Amsterdam could supply. Where I am obliged to live now we no longer eat so well, but all the same we eat like royalty compared to the slop they served on the ship.

For reasons which were not at the time explained to me, but which became all too plain later, we first made passage to a harbor called Gottingbourg which is, I think, in the land of Sweden, a land from which, to the best of my knowledge, no art has ever come. There Captain Dahl would have tipped me ashore but for chance and but for a fellow passenger's piece of paper.

I saw the passenger for the first time when the crew were all busy with ropes and sails on the way into the port. He emerged from a door under the high deck and talked animatedly to Dahl, waving a sheaf of papers. His fine clothes indicated he was no sailor. If he had been a sailor, he would not have tried to grab the rail as the ship heaved with the same hand in which he held the papers, and the wind would not then have whirled them down to whatever sailors call that part of the deck where the masts stick up out of the planking. I caught four of them by sheer luck because they flew straight into my open arms while the rest of them were swept into the waves beyond. Three of the sheets were crammed full of flowery handwriting but the fourth had just one line on it and I thrust that one into my pocket before anyone could see.

The passenger's pleasure at receiving some of his pages back was overwhelmed by his sourness at the loss of the rest. He merely inclined his head toward me with a penetrating look when I climbed the ladder to return them. He was a man of some thirty years, I judged, with an alert eye. Later on, when I measured his full stature as a rival for a great prize, I found him to be a full ten years older than that, but I would have to say that everything that man did, even aging, was not what it seemed. Chin down, in half profile, I thought, a sideways look with a single bright lamp lighting the socket of the eye from below—that would be the way to get him best.

I had no pencil, but as I climbed down to a quieter corner by the masts behind a great coil of rope my eye fell on a little barrel of musket balls, tied in place in case of attack. When I rubbed a corner of the paper with one, it left a dark silver trace. When I carefully cut one with my knife, I could split it into four parts like the quarters of an apple and use them to draw after a fashion.

I should admit that I had only once tried to depict a ship in any detail, a history painting of the apostles in their storm, dramatic and reeking of the salt spray, it seemed to me. My efforts had been scoffed at by the mariners of Amsterdam who said all was afly or ahoo or aback or something else obscurely nautical and this and that were pointing in contradictory directions. They missed the whole point. I had studied boats in the docks but never before had the chance to draw one, if you like, from on board, and my whole spirit was aching for the chance to release the pressure building up in me, the pressure of unfamiliar shapes all around, shapes escaping undrawn. On the high deck above my head, the captain and the passenger were still talking and for a moment they made their own composition, as perfect as any I could have devised. From my low perspective, they towered above, facing each other, the passenger holding up his paper toward the captain, eyebrows raised, pointing at some detail, while the captain himself, exuding implacable authority in his tiny wooden kingdom, stared past him across the sea. It was gone as soon as seen, but the inner eye, that part that can understand accidental perfection and hold it, entire, for weeks afterward, had trapped it. I sketched as fast as the musket ball would allow, wishing I had a copper plate and a drypoint for my work instead of this flapping, unsupported paper. My tools were awkward, the paper bent over my knee, and the lead sometimes too hard for what I intended, but enough excuses. It took. It flowed across the paper with no need for correction.

After all the scurrying fuss that seems to accompany making any ship go where you want it to, we lay relatively peacefully, though still bobbing around, anchored at a short distance from the quay. That was when the captain leaned over the rail above me, shouted straight at me, and beckoned with his hand for me to come up. I quickly shoved my paper in my pocket. At the top of the ladder, I found myself facing the passenger and the captain together. The captain pointed at me and said something to the other that prompted a harsh laugh. The passenger smiled, but then his eyes went to my pocket and I knew, dismayingly, that a corner of the paper must be showing.

"Is that one of my pieces of paper?" he asked in perfect Dutch.

Before I could do anything, the captain reached out and snatched it from my pocket, smoothing it with his hands and tutting over the marks I had made. They exchanged incomprehensible, guttural words with each other, then the passenger took the piece of paper from him, looked at it quickly, then examined it at length.

"You did this?" he asked.

"I did."

"It is good."

"It's better than that," I said.

"Ha!" he said, and looked at it again. "Yes. I won't argue. It is su-perb. You are a maker of portraits?"

"I have been," I said.

"From Amsterdam?"

"Yes, and from Leiden before that."

"From Leiden? Really? Should I have heard of you? Are you Lievens? Are you Dou? No, they would not be stowaways, stinking of wine."

Bastard. I was not about to play his game.

"I am van Rijn," I said, and could tell immediately from his frown that he had never heard of me and that he felt diminished by that lack of knowledge. This was a man, I realized, who liked to know more than others around him.

"First name?" he said and I found myself playing the game of ad-vantage, where knowledge is a currency to be guarded. There was also the matter of the bankruptcy, whose conditions, irrelevant until then, included a ban on leaving the city. Because I didn't want to give this man who spoke such good Dutch the pleasure of knowing my official label, I gave him my patronym instead. Call it a test of sorts. . . .

"Harmenszoon."

I watched his face to see if he knew enough of Dutch custom to recognize that could only ever be a second name.

He stared again. "Harmenszoon van Rijn," he said doubtfully. "I am afraid your reputation has not reached our shores." Then he shrugged and turned away to talk to Dahl, showing him the paper, which clearly held their interest. Eventually he turned back to me.

"Do you paint as well as draw?"

"As the sun outshines the moon."

"The captain is of a mind to offer you a choice," he announced and I realized the notion amused him. "He says you owe money for your fare. He will cut his losses and put you ashore here to find your own way home or, if you prefer, you may come with us to Hull and do him a proper picture, a portrait. If it is good, he will see you get passage back to Amsterdam."

It seemed to be no choice at all. There were Hennie and Titus to consider. They would manage without me, the two of them, because they would have to. They would be worried, certainly, but they must be worried already and they would be a lot more worried if I were to die a pauper's death in this gloomy Swedish port, begging fruitlessly for rides from every passing ship. I looked across at the town. Gottingbourg had a disturbing, pagan look, ill-shaped houses painted in unlikely and unsettling colors, some oxblood, some mustard, all wrong.

"Can you get a message back to my home?" I asked. "Just a note to say I am safe and will return."

"We can leave it with the port captain," said the passenger. "Write it down."

So I said yes, I would come to Hull, and in consequence matters improved a little. I was allowed a mattress in a small cot wedged into a tiny cupboard. We lay at anchor all the rest of that day, a stone's toss from the walls of the port. A few hours passed; my note was written and, I hoped, delivered. Orders were shouted again, sails were freed from their restraining ties, and the anchor was hauled up.

The motion of the ship became quite malicious as we sailed out into the open ocean. At my successive houses I have usually had to reinforce the studio floor, because my time is spent in a precise act of creation in which the tip of the brush I am holding has to be capable of adding not one whisker more or less of paint than I intend to *exactly* the right patch of canvas. My wrist is held in precise relationship to that canvas by the solid support of my maulstick. When I first moved to our shack in the Jordaan, the whole floor would creak and sway if anyone else entered the room, so I had it taken up and rebuilt on the largest beams I could find, even though Hennie fretted at the cost. Those beams came from some old ship and though they had stood a century's storms around the globe, they were only just stiff enough to make my floor sufficiently immobile. It has always seemed very probable to me that, left to myself, I would have become a habitual drunkard. It is in my blood from my grandfather. What has prevented me, what has stopped me from anything bar occasional excess, is that one single thing frightens me more than any other: It is that I might lose that exact link between my hand and my eye. I need a still point in my universe.

SHIPS' TIMBERS MAY GIVE SOLIDITY ON LAND BUT SHIPS AT SEA ARE not for me. I took my misery to my cramped cot and lay down to cherish it all the way across the German Ocean. I stayed in it for, so far as I could tell, three days of purgatory, but woke in the early hours of this morning, at dawn's first crack, to find the ship's motion quite changed and something which could almost pass as stability restored to the world.

When I went up on deck, I thought for a moment that we had returned to my home country. We were sailing slowly into a wide estuary, which had the same look as the Dutch coast. We sailed gently onward, the sails filling and slumping and filling again with a crack as the wind puffed us along. The southern bank of this wide river was too far away to see clearly, but it was full tide judging by the way the water stood against its northern bank; beyond that bank was a landscape that looked to my eyes in no way outlandish. I had quite unconsciously expected savages. Instead, there were fields with neat drainage ditches and clumps of trees sheltering small farmhouses. There were windmills, too, just as there are at home. In fact, I come from a milling family. We are called van Rijn because my family's mill on that river was the foremost of the Rhine mills and, being the foremost, was called the Mill of the Rhine. I cast an appreciative eye over these mills. These English were perhaps not so different as I had always been led to believe.

The captain was now feeling his way close in to the edge of the shore with a sailor in the bows shouting and splashing away with a weight on a line. Squinting ahead, I thought I could see a high church spire amongst a distant cluster of masts and understood then that, far from ending, the river swung away to the left around a long, wide bend with a town on the outside, northern border of that curve. It seemed we were going no nearer this port, which still lay some way ahead. Instead, our previously inexpressive and immobile captain was waving and hallooing for all he was worth toward the shore and, looking where he looked, I saw, for the first time, the extraordinary house he was in the process of building.

Two massive towers of dark brick stood at either end of it. They had their roots in a much more ancient time, those towers, as if built entirely for defense in a hostile world. The bricks of which they had long ago been made were in two colors, red and blue in bands, and what few windows opened into those towers were the sort from which an invisible archer might give you an unpleasant surprise. Between them, a new house had been built, joining the towers together like a delicate girl with one arm round each of her hulking brothers. That this central section was new seemed in no doubt. At one end, builders were still finishing the tiling of the roof and the timbers showed through, creamy yellow, so far untouched by time. This central range had many windows, their small panes catching the rising sun as if to make up for the unperforated walls of the twin towers.

A figure appeared, a man so far as I could tell, who stared in our direction and ran inside. All hands were called and sent below, where a curious rummaging began amongst the cargo, covering some things and exposing others, preparing it seemed to me for some inspection in which it would be better if not everything was plain to see. In the midst of all this, they even set me to work again, dragging sacks from one place to another; with the end of my voyage in sight, I did it moderately willingly. After what seemed a great deal of toil, I was summoned back to the deck. A boat was lowered into the water. The passenger, standing by the ship's rail, called to me.

"Come on. You're coming with me. We have to go ashore quickly."

They helped me down into the boat, more, I think, because of the risk I would upset them into the water than for any great sudden onset of solicitude. Two seamen rowed us to the shore, where I could see a small landing stage.

The passenger looked at me. "I should explain," he said. "This is Paull Holme Manor, which is owned by Captain Dahl. It suits me to be put off here away from the questioning of the burghers of Hull. It suits the captain to put you off here for two reasons, which you must mark well. First, because this is where he wishes you to do the work you have promised. Second, and more importantly, you must be set ashore here because there are stories of the Plague in Amsterdam."

"There have been only two cases," I said, annoyed, "and those are mere supposition. The disease is half a continent away and will come no nearer, I am sure."

"Two suspected cases or two hundred proven ones, it is all the same. As soon as it spreads, there will be a fresh ban on such voyages. It may already be in force for all we know. Dahl has no intention of saying his cargo comes from there or that he has even been there. We have come from Gottingbourg only. Remember that. If you say you came aboard in Amsterdam, you will find yourself spending two months at least in the Pest House and believe me, even if you go into that place healthy, you will be lucky to come out alive. Have you got that?"

"I have."

"Now, when we arrive at the house, I will explain to the captain's wife why you are here. He will see his ship safe into Hull and when it is unloaded, he will be back here for work to start. I shall be here from time to time should you require my translation services. My name, by the way, is Marfel. I am well known in these parts."

He was looking toward the house with an expression of eagerness. "Ah!" he said all at once. "There she is at last!"

There was a figure making its way down to the jetty. I could see that she was a woman. What I could not see was that she was to become both my inspiration and my nemesis.

FOUR

Sunday, April 8, 2001

WHEN AMY DALE WAS STILL VERY SMALL AND HER FATHER'S HEAD was in the sky, offering a hand she had to reach right up to hold, there had been places he had taken her to, just the two of them together. Mostly, they were places where pictures were hung. She would stare up at the frames and he would talk about them so that the figures in them began to move for her. All those places were lost to her now, leaving only a faint general sense of stone steps too high for her legs and that strong hand from above coming to her rescue.

What she saw at the end of the track through the wood ambushed her. For one short moment, the sight of the house pulled out a matching memory from those times before the new overpowered the old. She could not be sure it was not just déjà vu, a mistake of the synapses. In either case, it marked a passage for her. There had been a mansion-shaped bogeyman in her head, full of oppressive family history. The first sight of the house wiped that away.

They came to it from behind, and saw it standing on its low hill with the land around it falling away toward the wide, wide Humber. There must once have been gardens, and no doubt there would be again, but for the present it stood in the middle of a large, grassy field, approached by a rutted track. The house was half hidden inside an en-crustation of scaffolding but its shape—a bizarre collection of three dis-parate parts—was still clear. The center section was a graceful two-story building but it was wedged between two hulking structures serving as crude bookends to what lay in between. The nearest of these was a squat, foursquare tower of dark brick. It looked medieval, much older than the central range. The farther bookend might once have been the same, but something disastrous had happened to it along the way. One wall, the wall against which the central part of the house stood, was still standing, but the rest of that structure had utterly collapsed.

Such was Paull Holme as Amy first surveyed it. All around was the chaos of a busy building site—mobile cabins, piles of timber, old caravans, and heavy machinery. If she had been here before, back in that childhood before her mother ground her father down into a withdrawn and sullen reflection of her own prejudices, she could remember nothing about it.

A large sign stood next to the track. "A Millennium Project from North-East Heritage" was etched in gold on a blue background. Under-neath, in smaller letters, it said, "supported by ..." and there was a long list of organizations.

"It's a bit late for the millennium," she observed.

"The contract didn't say *which* millennium," said Dennis. "We could still be all right for the next one."

She pulled off the track and stopped where other cars were parked on the grass.

"Might just be in for a bit of trouble now," said Dennis. "Get ready to block your ears."

"Have you been a naughty boy?" she teased.

He glanced at her and for the first time looked completely serious. "I had someone to see. Family business, you know? It mattered."

He got out of the car. Immediately a bellow erupted from the door of a nearby hut.

"GREENER! Where the FUCK have you been. One day, you said. One day meant you were due back here yesterday. Saturday not fucking SUNDAY. We're on penalties, you know that. I'm fucking docking you, right?"

"Ladies present, guv. Credit where credit's due. I've had your interests in mind."

The man on the other end of the stentorian voice stepped out of the hut. His figure was much less alarming than his voice, being so small and wiry that Amy wondered where he could possibly have stored the wind to fuel his shout. He wore bib overalls and a very old bowler hat.

"First time ever, Dennis, if so."

"You needed a painter. I got you one."

"You got yourself a fifty-quid hole where your bonus was, is what you've got. Where's this painter anyway? I already got painters."

Amy climbed out of the car.

"Not this sort, you haven't," said Dennis. "This is her, Hawk. Just what you wanted."

The man called Hawk looked at Amy and then looked quickly away as if the sight of her had burnt his eyeballs. "Bloody mad," he said. "Shark bait."

"She'll be all right," Dennis said.

"Oh, yeah? You'll be responsible, will you?"

"If you like."

Amy listened to the exchange with a growing sense of irritation.

"Hello," she said. "I am still here, you know."

"What sort of painter?" Hawk's question was addressed to the space somewhere between Amy and Dennis. *One of those,* thought Amy wearily. *They don't like looking straight at you.*

"Any sort," she said. "I paint landscapes, I paint people, I paint houses. I'll even spray your car if you want me to."

"Restoration?" asked the foreman, looking quite definitely at Dennis, not at Amy.

"Absolutely," said Dennis. "No question. Restoration through and through."

Now Hawk finally looked at her. "They need a renovation artist who can work on seventeenth-century ceiling decorations. Can you do that?"

Amy turned to the concrete mixer next to her and addressed it. "That's me," she said in tones of absolutely convincing certainty, though she had never done anything quite like that in her life before.

"Live round here?" asked Hawk.

"No," Amy told the concrete mixer.

"Why are you talking to that machine?"

"It seemed appropriate."

The foreman looked at her with deep suspicion.

"There's rooms in the roof. Got a sleeping bag?"

"I have."

"Well, you'll have to see the Heritage bloke. He's inside. If he says all right then it's eleven quid an hour plus bonuses."

"That's more than I get," said Dennis.

"You're a fucking plasterer. She's an artist. Anyway, if he hires her and she stays hired you get your bonus back so shut it. Go on. Take her inside and find Parrish for her. It's his call. Oh, yeah, Greener, fix her door up with a bolt, will you?"

"On the inside or the outside?"

"Inside. You stupid or what?"

"Might change your mind when you know her better, Hawk."

The foreman stared at Dennis blankly, lifted his bowler to scratch his head, and went back inside the hut without even asking her name.

"Nice to meet you," she said into space when he'd gone. "All right then, Dennis. Let's go. I'm right behind you."

Dennis looked troubled. "Don't mind him," he said, "he's all right. It's good working here. Good laughs, good money. You can do thirty hours overtime easy and there's bonuses for getting ahead of the schedule."

"Did he mean it about your fifty quid?"

"Yeah."

"That's not why you're so keen on me working here, is it?"

He feigned an expression of comical astonishment. "Now then, Amy. In all the long years you and I have known each other, have I *ever* done anything that would give you grounds for doubting my sincerity?"

She laughed.

"I mean it," he said. "It's good, this job. Don't bother about him. There's good blokes working here, mostly."

Blokes, she thought, and discovered that untrustworthy creature prowling through her mind again. *I am* not *on the lookout,* she told herself firmly. *I always make mistakes when I start feeling this way. Screw that.*

"Mostly?" she queried.

"That's what I said."

They climbed sloping planks that covered damaged steps to an impressive doorway surrounded by carved stonework. Inside was a long hallway with a staircase rising in a curve to a landing above. There was an infantry attack in progress somewhere above, loud hammering and two men shouting at each other in echoing tones of derision. Dennis opened a temporary plywood door on the right, looked inside, and then ushered her in. In an elegantly proportioned downstairs room, with the fresh plaster on the walls still mottled with damp islands, a man in his sixties was sitting at a table, studying a mound of drawings. He looked up and, when he saw Amy, scrambled to his feet.

"Hello. Who have we here?" he said, smiling and holding out a hand. He was tall and just a little stooped, as if life was starting to be a bit too much for him. His green tweed jacket had a splash of cream paint on the shoulder. Amy looked at it, remembering her own experience with the tin of Azzurro Blue, but he didn't look like the sort of man anyone would tip paint over on purpose.

"My name's Amy Dale," she said.

"How absolutely extraordinary," he said, clearly taken aback. "Do sit down."

That seemed an unlikely response, but she sat down anyway.

"She's here for the job," said Dennis from the doorway. "I'll leave you two together, then."

"Oh!" said the man, "I see." It didn't sound as though he did. He smiled at Amy in mystification. "I'm Peter Parrish. I'm the historical sort of liaison person, I suppose you would say. I look after the ancient architectural questions, the *history* of the place, you see? Very hot on the detail, you know, North-East Heritage. Everything's got to be just exactly as it was. That's why they're putting up the money. Good thing too, if you ask me, but it does mean constant attention. It's a funny old house, two different periods of course, thirteenth-century towers, seventeenth-century domestic range in between. You'll have spotted that, I'm sure. What's this about a job?"

"Why did you say my name was extraordinary?" she asked, perching gingerly on the rickety folding chair.

"Do forgive me. How rude I was. I was just reading an excerpt from the journal. At the moment it's my absolute bible. The best reference source one could ever hope for on a job such as this. A firsthand account of life here when the house was built. We're so lucky to have it."

He was holding in his hand a modern exercise book—hard black board covers and a red cloth spine. She looked at it and frowned.

"It doesn't look very old."

"Oh, it's not the original," he said quickly. "Dear me, no. They keep that safe in the Hull archives. We just typed up all the excerpts that mattered so we could have it on hand. You know, all the bits that touch on the house and the furnishings and so forth. It's terribly useful, do you see? She was so *involved,* such an enthusiast for what she was creating. I mean, look at this." He put on a pair of half-moon glasses and flicked quickly through the book, tilting it to the light. "This is it, January third. She says, let me see, um, *'All the morning, in the house with Maskell and his joiners to see the doorway made less wide as my husband commanded before he departed. They have made new the plasterwork and narrowed the panels of the door with great skill. I have shown them how the moulding may be relieved and cut so that the light will play upon it to full effect. I believe he will be greatly pleased.'* Wonderful stuff, you see, and so helpful. It's that very doorway right behind you. We could see it wasn't the original width. Tampered with, clearly. We might even have tried to put it back to the way it was originally but with *this* to guide us, you see, we knew straight away it was meant to be like that. Terrible tragedy narrowly averted, do you see?"

"How amazing. When was that written?"

"Didn't I say? Sorry, 1662. It's a journal, you see, kept by the lady of the house. The very first lady. Runs from the beginning of January when they had just moved in, right through to summer of the following year. All right, it's not Pepys by a long chalk, not this stuff anyway. It's very, well, *domestic,* I suppose, but it's absolute gold dust as far as we're concerned. Are you related by any chance?"

"Related to who?"

"Well, the Dahls, of course."

He'd said it in an odd way, she thought, with what sounded to her ears like an affected drawl. Perhaps that was the way they pronounced it around here.

"The Dales? Yes, I am. That's sort of why I'm here. My, er ... my parents always talked about the old family house. I mean, my great-grandfather was the last one who actually *lived* here but he was the youngest son, you see. The older son inherited it, so we're sort of cousins, I suppose."

"So you *are* a descendant." Parrish looked on the verge of bursting into applause. "Well, well. They weren't always Dales, you see. They were Dahls from Norway, before they Anglicized themselves. What a wonderful coincidence. And you're here to help us with the work, are you? We're on the homestretch now but there's still so much to be done. Did you see the advertisement?"

"No, not at all. I just happened to pick up Dennis hitchhiking, and one thing led to another."

"Dennis?"

"The man who showed me in."

"The wandering plasterer! Dennis the Menace as they call him. Now I'm with you. And he told you about it?"

"Yes."

"But you *are* an experienced restorer?"

"Yes," she lied and immediately felt terribly guilty. She hadn't been the least bit bothered when she'd made the same claim to the foreman, but Parrish reminded her of a nice old schoolmaster. "That is, I'm a very experienced artist in all sorts of different fields. What sort of work do you need?"

"I'll show you. Come and look at this," he said, and led her upstairs. On the landing, a man was at work on the ceiling coving, perched on a plank between two tall stepladders. He glanced down and she caught a quick glimpse of a dark face smiling at her in surprise before they passed out of his sight.

She heard him call out something indistinct behind her that had the quality of an alert. There were answering whistles from above and she found herself wishing for a pair of high heels. In a bedroom at the back of the house, where a newly repaired ceiling showed large patches of mostly dry plaster, fragments of old plaster had been laid out on a folding table, showing a floral border painted in faded colors.

"That's what you've got to do. We have a rough idea of what the pigments should be," said Peter Parrish. "Amelia has a list of some of them, a sort of shopping list, I suppose."

"Who's Amelia?" asked Amy, immediately worried at the idea of working to the orders of some unknown woman.

"Amelia? Oh, Amelia Dahl," said Parrish. "The first lady of Paull Holme, the writer of the journal. Bless my soul, didn't I say? That was why I was a little startled when you told me your name. I was just reading the words of Amelia Dahl and in walks her living, breathing embodiment, Amy Dale. Quite something, don't you think?"

At that moment, for the first time, Amy felt a sense of connection with this old house—more than a connection, she felt a sudden sense of pride, almost of ownership. She thought of the juggling ducks. "Well, maybe nothing happens entirely by chance," she said.

"You know, I really do think you'll have to do the job," he said. "I mean, it's too good to be true, isn't it? Amelia Dahl's descendant coming to restore things to the way they used to be. Do go and tell the foreman chap, Mr. Hawkins, that I said it was all right, then perhaps we can have a chat tomorrow about how you might go about it. We'll sort out the pigments and all that stuff. Do you have your own brushes?"

"Oh yes," she said, looking at the faint paintwork on the plaster. "I always carry those with me."

"This is the best room to start in," Parrish said as he paused in the doorway. "We're still trying to piece together the patterns in the rest of the house. We'll have to do some thinking about that."

Running halfway up each of the walls was wooden paneling, coated with old paint so thick it more or less hid the curves and channels of the moldings at the edge of each panel. He tapped the wall by the door above the paneling with his knuckles. "It's pretty sound. The ceiling was the worst but it'll be dry enough to paint tomorrow. We'll be getting to work on the panels next. It's all got to be stripped off. Three centuries' worth of paint, I should think. Do you live nearby?"

"No," said Amy. "I'll be sleeping here."

"Gosh," said Parrish. "Is that wise? I could probably find a room for you in town if you like."

Amy, sensing dangerous adventure, did not like.

Outside in his portable office, the foreman told her about the hours expected, made her sign a form about tax and National Insurance numbers, and then squinted suspiciously at her.

"Breakfast's bread and cereal. Help yourself. Food's laid on at lunchtime," he said. "Sandwich van comes round. Takes orders if you fancy something special. Supper's your business. Pubs in the village or there's a gas ring in the back pantry. Now, sleeping." He pulled a face. "We don't have no women's wing here," he said. "Only one working bathroom and that's got no lock on it. I told Greener to fix a bolt to your door. Make sure he does. Until then, you better pick a room with a door handle you can wedge a chair under. Top floor only. Should be one spare somewhere."

"I can manage," she said. "Tell me, do you *only* employ rapists?"

"Boys will be boys," he said, without looking up.

"I know," she said sweetly, "but I prefer men." Outside, she took a backpack out of her car and slung it over her shoulder. Taking her painting case in the other hand, she set off to find herself a room.

A narrow back staircase led up from the kitchens straight past the first floor without stopping and up into a corridor running along the back of the house, halfway into the roof-space so that its ceiling was cramping in with the slope of the beams. It was lit dimly by the afternoon light coming in through two very dirty roof lights. Small cell-like bedrooms led off the corridor toward the front of the house. The doors were all open, but each one she looked in was strewn with an almost identical jumble of dirty clothes, boots, overalls, and sleeping bags. There were eight of them and all were very clearly occupied. For a moment, Amy wondered whether she would have to sleep in the car after all, but then through the gloom at the far end of the corridor, she saw that behind an old blanket hanging from two nails there was a rough opening in the stonework, apparently newly made judging by the stones now stacked to one side. She lifted an edge of the blanket cautiously. Beyond it was not after all entirely dark, so she stuck her head through and found a room belonging to another age. What lay beyond the blanket was a wide hallway with a floor of rough boards. It ended at the outer wall, pierced by an arrow-slit window; she realized it had to be the top floor of the square stone tower. In the dim light from the slit she could see two doors opening off this space toward the front of the house. More rooms. Both doors were shut.

Feeling the need to tiptoe, she hesitated before tapping on the first door. The corridor back there on the other side of the wall had felt much more inhabited. People had gone on living there, moving through it and letting their life soak into its walls. This space was much older, lost to view and humanity. Medieval. She pushed the door and looked cautiously inside. It was stacked with dusty junk. Something scurried, too fast for her to identify it, into a pile of broken wooden crates in the corner, something probably too small to be a rat, but only probably.

The light filtered into the room from a Gothic arched window in the front wall, its glass panes filthy. Inside, there was a broken chair, a pair of picture frames, and a rusty hip bath, which could easily have been there for a century or more.

She went back out into the hall and turned the handle of the farther door, expecting the same. It stuck in the frame and she pushed harder so that when it suddenly opened, she was carried into the space beyond by the violence of her movement.

In that gray and ancient room Amy was confronted by a scene from a childish nightmare. A claw stretching out. Something behind it, twisted and swathed in black, eyes glaring from a distorted face, swiveling to stare at her. In the moment before her brain saw it for what it was, her mouth let her down by screaming her fear.

Frozen in the silence excavated by that scream she found, without anything changing except her perception, that she was looking at the back of a man, a man dressed in black overalls sitting on a hard wooden stool. He had been holding out a hand toward a tall mirror propped against the wall directly opposite her. The mirror was cracked and dulled around its edges, the meager remains of gilt molding clinging to its frame. When she screamed, this man had twisted round toward her to reveal his pale face, marked by a savage scar from his right temple, down past the outer edge of his eye to the point of his cheekbone, a scar still healing in shades of pink and purple. The scar dragged her gaze to it and he flinched, twisting his face away.

Worse, she now found herself staring at his hand—the hand he had been holding up to the mirror, a claw of a hand that lacked its outer edge and its two smallest fingers.

"I'm sorry," she said. "I just screamed because ..." *Because what? Because you're a sight to make anyone scream?* "Because I didn't think anyone would be in here."

"Who are you?" he said in a young man's voice. His voice sounded as shocked as she felt.

"I'm Amy," she said. "I'm going to be working here. I was just looking for a room. Can I use the one next door?"

"Next door. Here? In the tower?"

His tone implied that it was *his* tower.

"The others are full." She surprised herself by sounding ingratiating, not confrontational as was her wont when she felt cornered.

He addressed her over his shoulder.

"They're not my rooms."

"But . . . you don't mind?"

His silence showed he clearly did mind—that he had purposely sought out this isolated room on the other side of the uninviting hole in the tower wall.

"I won't bother you," she said as the silence dragged out.

"Go ahead. Do what you want," was all he said, listlessly.

She closed the door on him and stood in the gloom outside, irresolute, an intruder with no real choice. The other room or the cramped backseat of her car—those seemed to be the only options open to her. The room looked no more inviting than before when she went back in, but Amy was a born pragmatist so she started making space, dragging the junk that half filled it out onto the landing beyond, stacking the heavy wooden boxes against the back wall. They were old wine crates; rubbing away the dust, she could read the words stenciled on the end of one of them: *"Château Ponsardine. Bordeaux."* Woodworm had been feasting on them for years and three of them came apart at the joints so she stacked the remaining slabs of powdery wood against the wall. Farther down the stack she found one still strong enough to serve as an impromptu table. It still had a bottle in it, made of heavy dark green glass. Wire staples held in a cork that projected just a little from the neck. The lacy remains of a paper label still clung to it and as Amy blew away the dust, she could read *"Perrier-Jouët 1902"* and *"Épernay."* A swirl of sediment twisted through the brown liquid as she lifted the bottle to look through it against the light. The chances of any bubbles remaining in the champagne after ninety-nine years seemed extremely slim.

An hour's hard labor followed with a borrowed broom, a pile of rags, and a mop, and then she had a room of her own, with her air mattress on the floor, her sleeping bag stretched out on it, and a series of drawers retrieved from the backyard, lacking only the chest that had once surrounded them. Set on her wine-box table were the objects she had saved from the rubbish pile, a delicate porcelain cup with no handle, a very old atlas, its pages all stuck together, and a smaller wooden box, which looked as if it had once been a vanity case. Fragments of the ivory that had once covered it were still pinned to its outside but inside, there were just broken strips of wood where its compartments had been.

Eric, a shaven-headed electrician, had tried to chat her up on one of her trips downstairs and wound up running a cable into the tower room for her so she now had a naked sixty-watt bulb hanging from a nail in the wall above the air bed. A minute after Eric left, there was a tap on the door and Dennis put his head round.

"Sorry," he said. "This won't do."

"This room?"

"Yeah. I'll come in here. You have mine. Much better."

"No, I'm all right. I like it. Anyway, I've cleaned it up now."

Dennis looked uncomfortable. "Better off in the other bit, eh? People around you, you know. Better for you." He was speaking in a low voice.

"Surrounded by men, you mean? It's all right, I'm fine here."

He frowned. "I mean it. There's a good reason."

"Which is?"

He looked away for a moment, toward the wall, toward the room next door.

"I've met him," she said.

"Just trust me."

Too many older people had tried to tell Amy what was sensible and what was not. "Dennis. I'm staying here," she said.

He looked at her, and accepted the inevitable. "I'll get you a bolt, then. Remember to use it."

"Oh, stop fussing." She wanted to ask Dennis more about the man next door but he'd already turned and left.

Walking back from her car a little later, carrying a bag over each shoulder, she saw Peter Parrish waving at her.

"I was about to come looking for you," he said. "I've got to be in town tomorrow. Why don't you drop in to my office there? About nine-thirty or so? We can arrange the paint and stuff like that. Do you know your way around Hull?"

"Not at all, I'm afraid."

"My office is just a few doors up from the library. Big blue sign. Ask anyone. Here's my number just in case." He handed her a business card.

"That journal you have," she said. "Amelia's journal. Could I borrow it for the night? Just to get the sense of it all?"

"Of course," he said. "It's in the table drawer in the room where we first met. Help yourself. It's mostly just the boring bits, I'm afraid."

"That's all right."

ALMOST EVERY DAY WHEN AMY WAS A TEENAGER, HER MOTHER WOULD say, "I don't know where she gets it from." The loveless remark would be accompanied by a dismissive wave of the hand, implying that it certainly did not come from her side of the family, thank you very much. That was true. It was only on her father's side, among the Dales, that a stubborn gene cropped up from time to time, a restless, inventive, unconstrained gene as capable of causing great mischief as creating great beauty. If it had once been present in her father, then marriage had placed it under house arrest. To escape, he had turned into a compulsive joiner, signing up for membership of any organization that appeared to promise stability and lack of change, a man who marched in parades with a serious expression on his face.

When Amy burst out of that restrictive chrysalis of childhood, she left no room for half-measures in her life, becoming a fierce enthusiast for all that she liked and a sometimes-too-harsh critic of those she disliked. Her attitude was tough on men. Very few of them ever looked at her without imagining having that open-eyed gaze under that shock of blond hair turned on them and only them. The men she left behind her, which so far had been all of them, tended toward a bemused and rueful resignation after she had left, finding that although they got a lot more sleep, the colors of the world had somehow dimmed. Once a man had met her, very few other women ever reminded him of Amy. More and more, she began to seek the company of people with dangerous hungers, dangerous looks. She was aware of the effect she had on the men she met, but usually chose not to dwell on it.

As she walked back to the house, men began to emerge, their day's work done. As they came out, they stretched and shadow-boxed and lit cigarettes as if this was what they did every day at the end of work, but Amy wasn't fooled. They were trying to look casual but there was too much posturing going on, too many darting glances in her direction as she approached. The word was out. This was a stage. They were the cast and she was about to make her grand entrance. Part of her, that deceptive, untrustworthy part, began to scan them, to note the way they moved, the way they looked, and if she found herself walking a little differently, her chest pushed out in front of her and her hips swaying a little more than usual, then that was entirely because of the bags over each shoulder. Dennis appeared from amongst them and they all fell back to make space as he took the bags from her.

"Meet the blokes, Amy. Untrustworthy lot, all of them. You'll have noticed I'm the only one that's halfway good-looking."

He insisted on introducing her to each of them. There were three middle-aged joiners who could easily have been brothers: Wilks, Sandy, and Tel. Nothing of romantic interest there. There was tough, tattooed Jo-Jo, who seemed to fancy himself as a ladies' man, and his shy friend, Scotch Jimmy, with Sean Connery's voice but nothing else. There was a sinuous Jamaican with a smile that melted her knees and a name that sounded like Gengko. He was the man who had looked down at her and smiled on the landing. *Maybe it's him,* said the awakening animal inside her. *Maybe it's not,* said her brain firmly. Then there was shaven Eric, the electrician, four more who came too thick, thin, and fast for her to remember anything more than smiles, ribald comments, and some impressive physiques, and last of all, emerging from the house as if he didn't give a shit, there was Micky. Micky had it. Blue eyes, cropped hair, a fighter's build, and a fighter's swagger. He looked great coming down the steps. *It could be this one,* she thought. Then he reached the bottom, which left him looking up at her, two inches shorter. He said "Nice to meet you" in a startlingly high-pitched voice and that was the end of that thought.

"Come on down the pub, kid," said Jo-Jo. "Got some good grub there." They were clustered round and she could feel the heat coming off them. Gengko winked at her.

"I might join you later," she said. "I've got to sort out my stuff first."

"Hang on a minute," Dennis announced to her and to everyone there. "Stay for the entertainment first. I won't be long." He went back inside.

There was no sign of the scarred man in the black overalls.

FIVE

THE HAWK HAD GONE AWAY DOWN THE ROAD IN THE BIG VAN, ON what Eric said was his regular evening trip to the betting shop, and in his absence, the men standing outside began to behave like schoolboys, chanting "Den-nis, Den-nis, Den-nis."

They all turned to face the house and Amy saw a hand waving from one of the top windows. The chanting rose in volume, "Den-nis, Den-nis." A minute later, Dennis appeared at the front door dressed in a clean pair of white overalls and took a bow as the chant reached a crescendo.

"To celebrate the arrival of our new friend, Amy," he announced, "a special performance of death-defying skill by the world's only professional plank-rider, Dennis the Magnificent."

"Bloody show-off," said Tel.

"All right," Dennis answered breezily. "I don't mind. You do it."

"I *need* my legs," Tel muttered and the others laughed.

To one side of the yard, there stood a roughly constructed open-fronted shed; inside lurked a brute of a machine, a great metal saw table, ten or twelve feet long. The flat top of it was fitted with rows of rollers to speed the timber on its way to bisection by the circular saw that stuck up through the table's surface in a savage arc. Dennis led the crowd over to it.

"Just to show that absolutely no trickery is involved, kindly test the sharpness of this blade with a touch of your delicate forefinger, young lady," said Dennis. "Careful now. It'll have your hand off quicker than you can blink."

Amy touched the blade with her finger. "It's sharp," she said.

"Stand back," said Dennis. "Let the show begin. Ringmaster, throw the switch."

Eric pressed a button and the teeth of the saw blade howled and blurred into life. Dennis found a thick off-cut of wood and waved it across the blade as if any further proof were needed. It sliced it in two with a *chang* and hurled the other half away.

With Eric on the other end, Dennis took a slab of wood from a stack to one side, a slice right across the trunk of a tree with the bark still on each edge. It was eight or nine feet long and some three feet wide. They set it down on the rollers.

It was only when Dennis climbed up on the saw table that Amy began to understand why all the men were standing watching with such fixed attention. He stepped onto the plank, balancing as if it were a surfboard as the blade screamed ahead of him. Amy felt her stomach tighten. She looked away at the circle of watching faces and beyond them, up above, she saw another face, just a glimpse of a pale circle behind a window at the top of the tower. It was the window next to her own.

"Oh, come on," she said, "you're joking."

"How close, Dennis?" said Eric.

"What was it last time? Six inches?"

"Bollocks to six inches. It was only five."

"All right then. Five last time means you have to make it four inches this time."

There was a roar of approval.

Eric reached for a tape measure and marked off a cross on the board, four inches to the left of Dennis's foot.

"All right then," said Dennis, "let's go. Get further back, all of you. I don't want blood spraying all over your nice clean clothes."

He kept his left foot where it was and kicked off with his right, propelling the wood along the rollers, riding it down fast on to the saw. It looked horribly close as the smoking blade bit into the end of the plank but he looked straight ahead of him and rode it all the way without moving his foot, the blade slicing a clean edge right along the plank past his leg.

He jumped off at the far end with a triumphant shout and held the plank up for inspection. The blade had ripped through the center of the cross.

"Four inches! Yeah. Three inches next time, eh?"

They all slapped his back and Amy looked up at the tower again. The pale face had gone.

"Pub time. You're all buying me a pint for that," said Dennis. "Who's driving?"

Unusually, something made Amy think twice—a slight sense that she should take things more slowly. She knew that if she went to the pub she would certainly end up sharing their jokes and their drinks and quite possibly end up dancing on a pub table. She might even end up half in love with one of them because of the peculiarly active state of the carnal creature inside her. Above all, she knew it might be the wrong one. That wasn't enough to stop her, but it was enough to make her put the decision in the hands of destiny. She watched three crows flying in circles above her head. If one of them landed on the roof before she counted to ten, she thought, she would stay here. The test was loaded heavily in favor of the pub because there was nothing in their behavior to suggest any of them planned to land. She got to eight and two of them swooped down to perch on the chimney. *Bugger,* she thought.

In the next moment, she was surprised to find that she was grateful to the crows. She felt an intense degree of curiosity about the contents of the exercise book she had borrowed, Amelia Dahl's journal. Tomorrow she would go to the pub and maybe do all those unwise things she knew she shouldn't. Tonight she would stay behind and read her ancestor's journal.

"Coming, kid?" asked Gengko, holding open the passenger door of a rusting BMW.

"I've got a bit to do. Might come later."

"Don't stay here by yourself," urged Dennis, and his eyes slid for a moment up toward the windows in the tower. "Come and try the grub. They do a great horse burger."

"In a while. Which pub is it?"

"We have a strict rota," he replied. "It's only fair. That way they have time to repair the damage. The only thing is we can never remember whose turn it is. I tell you what, though, look for the one with us in it—that'll be the giveaway."

The last of their fleet of motley cars drove out of sight and as the house quieted down, she went searching for a place to be alone with the book, unconsciously looking for a vantage point where the composition of the landscape would work on her mental canvas. A bird was singing a spring song in the evening air. She found her place a hundred yards in front of the house, across the meadow grass toward the river, where an oak tree stood alone. Next to it, the field, which must have once been a lawn, ended in a sharp dip, dropping by about half her height to the next field beyond. The edge was a straight line, a deliberate boundary—a ha-ha, the landscape designer's device to provide an uninterrupted vista while keeping the sheep off your lawn. Was it just an old children's fantasy, or was it called a ha-ha because that was what you said when you fell down it without looking? She imagined elegant women in crinolines, strolling on hand-cut lawns. It would have been a huge expanse of grass. How *did* they cut it before there were mowers?

The oak tree grew to the left of that old bank, as she looked out toward the river. She had a sudden pang of regret at what she had just turned down, feeling too alive to be by herself in this quiet place, but then she looked at the tree again and saw that it, too, was pulsing with pent-up life. Above her head its branches were tipped with wild, green jewels glittering in the evening sunlight, waiting to pump unfolding leaves out into the springtime. She put her arms halfway round the trunk and leaned her cheek against it; the upward surge of sap beneath the bark hummed in harmony with the blood flowing in her own veins. At the foot of the tree, two exposed roots ran down the bank like rivulets disappearing into the earth below. They were polished to stained ivory by wind and rain, and between them was a soft hollow of mossy grass—a seat made for anyone watching for their ship coming in.

She nestled in, leaned back against the trunk, and stared at the wide river beyond. The hill on which the house stood was little more than a slight rise, but the land all around was flat and just high enough to give her a perspective on the view. The river's edge was only a few hundred yards away down the slope but the tide was out and a bank of sandy mud spread away from the shore toward the channel. Way out in the middle of the water, a yacht heeled over in a wind that had not yet reached this shore, slogging toward the Lincolnshire side. On that distant bank a cluster of toy chimneys, catching the sun and staining the sky with steam, betrayed the presence of another refinery and marked the grand scale of the distance between them. Amy was glad she wasn't on the boat, because the Humber seemed to be a river you could die in without anyone noticing at all. A rusty-hulled tanker was butting its way steadily toward the sea, thousands of tons of steel, puny against the sullen chocolate water. Amy had a sketch pad with her and she tried to catch it, but in black and white it came out as nothing more than a wide river. It needed color to bring out the strength and the smell of it.

It displeased her to find there was nothing in sight that she wanted to draw. She needed a reason to be here in this spot, here in this house. Could Gengko be a reason? Or Micky? No. Not Micky, she told herself firmly. She gazed at the river while the currents in her own blood gradually slowed down, hearing a clatter of birds' wings up in the tree above her head and a lone car slow down for the corner behind the house and accelerate away toward Paull.

She moved her gaze slowly down to the book in her hands and wondered if it could serve as a big enough reason. Amy longed for interesting ancestors. Twenty-five years to a generation. Three hundred and thirty-nine years would be thirteen and a bit generations. Three generations is grandmother, four is great-grandmother. Thirteen would add ten greats tacked on before the grandmother. Was that who Amelia was? She might just be a distant aunt. "Directly descended," her mother had always said, "directly descended" from the Dales of Paull Holme. Lineage, to Amy's mother, explained everything. Genes, even genes by marriage, counted for a lot. The hazy ghost of Paull Holme was her equivalent of that bumper sticker that says "My other car's a Porsche." In her suburban Surrey villa life she constantly let it be known that she herself was a Beaman (from Ascot, as she would always say—the *Ascot* Beamans, the emphasis clear to all). On the complicated snakes-and-ladders board of the English class system, she was obsessed by the question of whether she had moved sideways or upward to marry. A Dale from Paull Holme might have started higher on the ladder than an Ascot Beaman, but Amy's father's family had slid down a longer snake. Considering all that, it felt surprisingly good to be at Paull Holme.

She opened the book with a flutter of anticipation but her burgeoning sense of connection disappeared in a flash. What was inside the book was distressingly modern, sheets of word-processed paper glued into the pages of the exercise book. The typeface was ugly, and at first glance, there was no humanity in the words. Amy began to read the first page, searching for its writer's voice.

January 14th 1662 Tuesday

THIS DAY WE DID NOT STIR FAR, IT BEING A FAST-DAY DECLARED BY THE PARLIAMENT WITH PRAYERS REQUIRED TO BRING US MORE SEASONAL WEATHER. THIS LAST WINTER, AS THE WINTER BEFORE IT, HAS BEEN AS IF IT WERE SUMMER AND AS LAST YEAR BROUGHT SO MUCH SICKNESS IN ITS WAKE, THERE ARE FEARS THAT THE PLAGUE WILL RETURN UNLESS COLD WEATHER COMES. LITTLE DONE. IT HAPPENED THAT A SCAFFOLD ON THE BACK WALL FELL IN THE MORNING BUT BY GOOD FORTUNE, THE MEN STANDING UPON IT HAD COME DOWN A SHORT WHILE BEFORE AND NO HARM DONE BUT FOR THE BREAKING OF TWO BOWPOTTS BELOW AND THE RUINATION OF THE FLOWERS IN THEM WHICH WERE THE DAMASK ROSES I BROUGHT HERE FROM THE OLD HOUSE IN THE TOWN. THE LIMNER DID NOT STIR FROM HIS BED ALL THIS DAY, TO MY HUSBAND'S GREAT ANGER. I AM DISPLEASED WITH THE FORM OF THE ARCHWAY TO THE KITCHEN WALL AND WILL HAVE IT DONE AGAIN. THE MEN WILL LISTEN TO THE CAPTAIN BUT AMONGST THEM ARE THOSE WHO WILL BUT STARE AND SMILE AT WHAT I TELL THEM. I INTEND TO BOW THEM TO MY WILL. THIS HOUSE IS MINE TO SHAPE.

There was a note below, written in pencil: "Bowpotts = flowerpots. Kitchen wall arch—signs of alteration, lhs." Had Parrish written it? Probably, she thought.

January 16th 1662 Thursday

THIS DAY I HAVE SENT BY THE CARTER TO YORK TO
DISCOVER THE REASON THAT THE HANGINGS HAVE NOT
COME TO US BEFORE. THERE WAS A GREAT NOISE AND TO-
DO THIS MORNING SOON AFTER THE WORKMEN
COMMENCED, OCCASIONED BY A DISPUTE BETWEEN THE
JOYNERS AND THE MASONS AS TO WHY THE BALCONY IN THE
KITCHEN YARD IS NOT SUPPORTED BY ITS PROPS AND IN
CONSEQUENCE LEANS LIKE A DRUNKARD. MY HUSBAND IS
AWAY IN THE TOWN ATTEMPTING A SETTLEMENT WITH THE
CUSTOMS HOUSE FOR THE TRINITY ELDERS. AM DID COME
AGAIN THIS DAY. HE SAID HE WAS COME TO SHEW DRAWINGS
OF THE SPURN LIGHTHOUSE TO MY HUSBAND BUT I THINK
HE HAD OTHER FISH TO FRY. HE SPENT MUCH TIME IN
DISCUSSION WITH THE LIMNER AND, KNOWING I HAVE NO
KNOWLEDGE OF THEIR LANGUAGE, CHOSE TO MAKE LITTLE
OF HIS BUSINESS WHEN I ASKED HIM WHAT IT WAS THEY
SAID. THE LIMNER NOW COMPLAINS OF THE LIGHT AND
WOULD MOVE TO A DIFFERENT ROOM. THE MEN SAY WE
MUST FIND TWENTY YARDS MORE OF GOOD ELMWOOD
BOARDS FOR THE NORTH TOWER BUT IN TRUTH I AM NOT
SURE IT IS WORTH THE CANDLE BEING A DISMAL SPACE AND
ALWAYS WILL BE. THE DRAIN NEW DUG FROM THE HOUSE OF
OFFICE IS BLOCKED UP AND SPREADS A STENCH THROUGH
THE WHOLE HOUSE. THE MEN SAY IT IS DUG TOO SHALLOW
AT THE FURTHER END AND MUST BE REDUG TO LET ALL
FLOW FASTER DOWN IT. THIS I HAVE TOLD THEM TO DO
WITHOUT WAITING FOR MY HUSBAND'S RETURN, FOR I DO
NOT THINK HE WILL WISH TO LIVE WITH THE STINK EVEN
THOUGH IT COSTS DEAR TO HAVE THE WORK REDONE.

She couldn't read the long note scribbled below this except for the
word "drains" and also something that looked like "missing corbels."

January 24th 1662 Friday

WE HEARD THIS DAY BY THE CARTER THAT THE EXECUTION
HAS BEEN COMMANDED OF ALL OF THOSE MURDERERS OF

THE LATE KING CHARLES WHO STILL REMAIN ALIVE, BUT
FOR TWO WHO WERE FORCED TO TAKE PART IN THE PLOT
AGAINST THEIR WILLS. THE PLANKS WHICH THE CARTER
BROUGHT TO US ARE OF FINE ELMWOOD AND I JUDGE IT IS
FULL-SEASONED. THERE IS SUFFICIENT TO MAKE THE NEW
FLOORS IN THE EAST TOWER WHICH HAVE BEEN OPEN TO
THE SKY IN THEIR RUIN THESE FORTY YEARS. I WOULD THAT
I COULD SHARE FULLY IN MY HUSBAND'S PLEASURE IN
THESE TWO GREAT TOWERS. THEY DO SEEM TO ME TO BE
ANCIENT SAD PLACES, BUT I SHALL PUT THAT FROM MY
HEART AND TAKE PLEASURE IN THE FINISHING OF THEM AND
THE FINE NEW HOUSE THAT NOW STANDS BETWEEN THEM
WHICH IS THE REALIZATION OF THE PROMISE HE MADE TO
ME WHEN FIRST HE TOLD ME HIS INTENTION.
THE LIMNER IS IN AN ILL TEMPER AND COMPLAINS A GREAT
DEAL. THE BRUSHES ARE WRONG, THE PIGMENTS ARE
WRONG, HE IS OBLIGED TO MIX UP HIS OWN TINTS. HE IS A
SORRY FELLOW AND DISOBLIGING. OUR FRIEND AM HAS
BEEN AT SUNK ISLAND IN DEALINGS WITH HIS OLD
ADVERSARY AND WILL COME ON THE MORROW TO DEAL
WITH HIM IN HIS NATIVE TONGUE.

Amy put down the book and leaned back against the trunk, her
arms resting along the outspread roots. From behind her came a slam
from the front door of the house, that same house Amelia described,
now being made new again. Feet scuffed through gravel where there
should have been no feet, then fell silent when they reached the grass,
coming in her direction. She sank lower into the protective embrace of
her tree, not wanting to be found, not wanting to share this with an
uninvited guest but the slightest of sounds in the grass beyond the tree
told her the feet were indeed continuing to approach. Carefully she
craned her head just far enough around the trunk to see a man heading
for the field's edge to her right. It was the only person it could have
been, the man from the attic room, the man in the black overalls. He
was not at all as he had seemed earlier. In the room, she had seen a man
at bay, contorted around his injury, someone pitiful. The man who was
now strolling across the grass, thinking himself alone, could never be
pitied. He was in command of his world, striding through it with the

grace and the disdainful certainty of a cat. He was tall and slim and from the side she was watching, the injury she had seen earlier might never have been. He made her eyes widen, and the growing excitement she had felt since she had first driven in through the wood seemed suddenly to have found a rational explanation.

He reached the ha-ha and stood at the top of it. If he had turned to look from there, he would have seen her immediately, however far she sank down into the roots. She watched him, trapped, as he stood staring across the muddy river. He was rolling a cigarette from a decorated tin. Something irresistible inside her so badly wanted to know how he managed to with his damaged hand that she leaned forward to see more clearly.

He was all black: his clothes, his thick hair, scraped back into a long ponytail exposing a widow's peak. He lit the cigarette as she opened her sketch pad again and quickly outlined him, realizing only as she brought her artist's eye into play that he was taller than she had thought, his chest widening out to powerful shoulders. A bird burst out of the tree and buzzed past his head, and he flashed a look at it as if he might seize it from the sky.

Then, so suddenly that there seemed no transition from one state to another, he was looking right into her eyes, the fresh, healing scar standing out in startling pink.

"Are you drawing me?" He had a compelling voice. It left no room for lies.

"I was trying to."

"I don't remember you asking," he said, crushing the barely smoked cigarette under his foot and turning abruptly away. Amy watched him walk back, his head high.

Not cat, she thought. *Panther. Feral and dangerous.*

The wind which had been heeling the yacht out in the channel finally reached her, bringing with it the faintest smell of sulphur.

When she heard the door of the house slam shut again, Amy tried to read more of the book, but he had taken her peace with him. Shaken by the sight of him and the words they had traded, she closed it. It was starting to grow dark and the idea of going back to the house, back to the room next to his, was unthinkable. Whatever it might bring, the pub seemed the only alternative. She got in the car.

Amy found them all at her second attempt. Every eye swiveled in her direction as she pushed the pub door open.

"Hello, gorgeous," said Jo-Jo, "what are you drinking?"

"Thank you," she said. "Pint of Guinness, please, and the next one's on me."

The tattooed builder looked at her, surprised. "Guinness?" he queried.

"That's it. Strong black stuff, with a head on it. Like him." She nodded at Gengko, sitting at the table, and they all roared with laughter. "Is there a problem?"

"No," said Jo-Jo, "I just didn't think a hairy chest would suit you."

"Well, I suppose you could order a Babycham with a cherry in it and a little umbrella if it makes you happier, but you'd have to drink it yourself because I hate the stuff." She smiled to take any sting out of her words and Jo-Jo found he couldn't help smiling back.

Dennis was chalking the end of a cue by the pool table. "Who's next for ignominious defeat?" he asked. "Step right up. Five quid says I beat you. Doubles if you like."

"Micky and me," said Gengko. "We'll take you on."

"That's a tenner, then. Tel? Coming to give me a hand?"

Tel shook his head.

"I'll play," said Amy, taking her pint and lifting it in a thankful toast to Jo-Jo. "Here's my five." She tossed a banknote on the table.

There was a moment of silence while complicated emotions crossed Dennis's face. The bar was silent as everybody looked at him. "Oh, fine," he said in the end. "Um, let's go then, shall we?"

Micky giggled as Amy picked up a cue and looked at the chalk as if she had no idea what it was for.

"Make it twenty if you like," he said casually.

"Yes, okay," said Amy, equally casual. "I mean, it's mostly luck, this game, isn't it?"

Gengko broke, delicately bringing the cue ball all the way back down to the cushion and cutting one red out of the triangle, hardly disturbing the rest at all.

"I'll go next, shall I?" offered Dennis hopefully but Amy just shrugged.

"Is it our turn?" she asked and heard another giggle from Micky.

Dennis crashed an optimistic shot into the triangle of balls, but succeeded only in leaving a yellow ball poised over the middle pocket. Micky proceeded to pocket it, while perfectly lining up for another one, and finished his turn by leaving the cue ball snookered by another yellow.

"Oh, gawd," said Dennis. "Look, love. You can't hit that ball, you see. It's got to be a red. I think we've had it. What you could do is—"

"It's all right, Dennis," said Amy. "I have played before."

"How many times?"

Amy got down to the table, squinting at the cushions. "Once," she said. She hit the ball. With massive side spin, it cannoned off the cushion, skewed across the table, knocked a red ball into the far corner pocket, and rebounded to break up a cluster of balls, lined up perfectly for another red.

"Or twice," she added, pocketing that one, too, and following it with two more. She straightened up and surveyed the sea of astonished faces. She was delighted to see that Micky was the most astonished of them all. Only Gengko was grinning. He didn't seem to mind the imminent prospect of losing his money.

"Why are you looking so cheerful?" demanded Micky. "It might have escaped your notice but we're losing."

"Goddam," Gengko replied, shaking his head. "There's nothing I like more than a sporty woman." He pocketed another two yellows, then missed a tricky cushion shot.

Dennis potted only one more ball on his next turn and Micky, playing flashily, put his side into the lead with two more.

"Down to you, darling," he said as he made way for Amy. "Used up your beginner's luck yet?"

She smiled at him sweetly and cleared the table, ending with a stylish trick shot that sent the black ball round four cushions before it trickled into the bottom corner pocket. Everyone except Micky cheered.

"Rock on," yelled Dennis. "Paul Newman, eat your heart out."

"Paul Newman?" said Amy.

"Before your time, love. *The Hustler.* Brilliant movie. He goes round kidding everyone he can't play pool."

"What's pool?" Amy asked. "I thought we were playing snooker."

"No," said Dennis in surprise. "We ..." but she couldn't keep a straight face.

Seated in amongst them at the table, Amy knew she was an accepted member of the group now. Gengko was next to her, and she could feel the heat of the Jamaican's proud grin just as if he'd been with her on the winning side. Someone bought Jo-Jo a Babycham and they made him drink it.

"This is all of you, is it?" she asked, looking round the table. "Except for the Hawk?" She knew it wasn't.

"And Don," said Sandy, from the far end of the table. "Don ain't here."

"Well, there's a surprise," Eric said sourly.

"Leave it out," Tel muttered.

"Don," said Amy. "He must be the guy in the black overalls, right? What's his story?"

No one offered a reply but there were lots of sideways looks. In the end Sandy said, "He's had a tough time," and Tel, nodding support, added, "There's not many who'd handle it like he did."

"Did he have some sort of accident?"

Dennis snorted. "Accident?" he said. "No bloody accident. I should—"

"Shut it, Dennis," Tel cut in. "We know what you think."

"Dennis has a point." The temperature round the table was rising, but Gengko suddenly rose to his feet and slammed a fist on the table.

"Stop," he said. "We don't do this. Not after last time. We agreed not to, right? Next one says anything about it has to buy a whole round, right?"

Silence fell.

"Now," he said, turning to Amy, "let's hear how you came to be world-class with a pool cue."

She spent the rest of the evening in their midst. Even though the big Jamaican was leading the race for her immediate attention, her mind kept drifting off to the shadow of the absent man in black.

SIX

Monday, January 13th, 1662

I DO NOT UNDERSTAND WHAT THE TRICK IS BY WHICH YOU ARE meant to disembark from a small boat. In Amsterdam, the boatmen who take you across the river, which was the longest sea voyage of my life until now, do you the courtesy of holding your arm as you get in and out. I could not get my foot onto the first rung of the rope ladder, which was hung hard against the side of Dahl's ship in a way that clearly required some special knack. There was nowhere for my toe to go. Instead, the crew seized me, lashed me up with rope, and lowered me down the side like a lump of cargo into a smaller boat before soaking me with spray from the blades of the oars as they rowed me to the landing stage.

The other passenger, the Englishman, left the boat first without any assistance and made it look quite simple, but when I tried to follow his lead, the boat tilted under me and then shot backward as I lunged for the jetty, taking my feet with it, so that I pitched headfirst into filthy, muddy water.

There was someone else with the passenger on the jetty and both of them roared with laughter as I surfaced, clinging to the leg of the jetty. I let fly some fine Dutch oaths before I realized I was in the presence of a woman.

"Enough of your foul mouth," said the passenger as he helped heave me up onto dry planks.

I had learnt a lot about dignity lately, having lost so much of it in recent months, but at that moment I needed the cloak of reputation around my shoulders more than at any other time. In Amsterdam, they know my reputation. They know the reduction in my circumstances is but a temporary effect. The few who matter to me understand that my temporary fall from favor is due entirely to my artistic integrity in the face of fashion and not to any diminution of my skills. My art, my backbone, is as strong as ever and supports me in the public eye. Here on the edge of this English river, I had nothing but my sodden and filthy appearance to form an impression in these people's minds.

Unexpectedly and for the first time in a long age, I wanted to make a good impression—all because of the woman, who had stopped laughing and was now eyeing me curiously.

Do you know how it is when a new form challenges your long-held ideals of what counts for beauty? My one and only Saskia had always been my model of perfection. My poor, dead Saskia. Hennie was a later comfort, and cast in the same pure Dutch mold as Saskia. They owned a pleasing roundness in the set of their faces, the bones well buried in the flesh. The trick of painting their type of beauty is all in manipulating the curving play of light, so that the eye can make the hands feel that fleshy, cupped plumpness.

But this woman had cheekbones. In Amsterdam only the old and the poor have cheekbones, but she was neither. By God, she wore them well. They hypnotized my eye and led it down that sleek skin all the way to her mouth. I am used to lips that are cramped into a pucker by the billows of flesh around them. Her lips were full and wide, with a cat's pointed chin below. The eyes were large and wide-set and stared at me, half in mirth, half in horror it seemed. That gaze held no foolishness. This was a woman accustomed to weighing situations.

Now, I am not just an Amsterdam simpleton as some people might insist. True, I did not study in Italy when I was young, as clever people think one should. That is why I paint like me and no one else. For all that, I have studied long and hard the work of other great painters. I even owned many of those works until bankruptcy deprived me of them. It was once my great pleasure to attend the auctions and bid the price the pieces deserved, which I did for the good of painters everywhere. The public needs to be reminded what a good painting is worth. But for a long time now, it is only the wealthy who wish to have themselves painted, and in those paintings, the beauty of rounded flesh has been well explored. Only in the Byzantine tradition have I seen such tautness as I now witnessed before me in this woman's exceptional face and figure.

"Make a bow," the passenger demanded. "This is the captain's wife."

I obeyed as best I could, observing as I did so that the passenger's eyes were fixed on this unearthly woman. They conversed at length then, almost all of it incomprehensible to me. I heard "Dahl" from his lips and "Marfel" from hers and "Amsterdam" shockingly mispronounced. They ignored the fact that I was standing there dripping wet until I sneezed, at which point the woman looked round at me and said something in a tone that suggested an apology.

An hour later, I was mostly dry and swathed in the strangest of borrowed clothes. Someone, and I suspect it was one of the crew of builders and plasterers who were all around the house, had been persuaded to relinquish some itchy woolen leggings, a stained vest, and a brown, smocklike garment that covered me to the waist. They were not nearly fine enough to have belonged to Dahl and not nearly as fine as the clothes I had taken off, which only required careful washing to highlight what sort of man I truly was. Around the smock, I strapped my own belt, still damp but nowhere near as damp as my shoes. I had nothing else for my feet so I squelched along, a sensation I particularly loathe.

I was delivered to a room, if that was what you could call it. It was at least a space to myself, not under the new roof where the servants dwelt, but to one side in the ancient tower that formed the upriver end of this strange building. My chamber was high up in the roof of the tower, furnished with a rude straw mattress, a chair, and a stool. The windows afforded some light but it was never a room I would have chosen. They left me alone there, and suddenly I was overwhelmed by just how far I had fallen. My house was a fine, fine house, the envy of Amsterdam, well lit by daylight through its many tall windows. I had a

fine studio with perfect light but if I sought any other light for a particular purpose, it was always to be found somewhere in that house. I
could paint whatever I wanted there, regardless of the hour. That house
was mine by right, and to have to watch it sold from under me was
more than a man should be asked to bear. It hurts to see this place of
Dahl's, because I understand the pleasure a man takes in the daily realization of his dream, of his palace. Yet does he take such pleasure? He
seems a lumpish man to me, an authoritarian dullard. Someone must. I
could see on my way up through the house that there is an artistry at
work here. Whoever is in charge of it has an eye for form and color.
Could it be the wife? How did Dahl deserve so fine-boned a woman? I
can already see how he will wish to be painted, head thrown just
slightly back, nose held high, evidence of his status on the wall behind
or on the table at his side. Probably a gold chain around his neck and
some navigator's instrument, an astrolabe or some such, in his hand. I
could do it now without even looking at him again, except that is
something I never do.

After a time, my door opened without a knock and the passenger,
Marfel, came in.

"Are you ready?" he said.

"For what?"

"You must come with me to town. We have to purchase what you
will need. You must start work."

"I don't see how I can. My subject is not here."

The man furrowed his brow. "He will be back tomorrow or the day
after. He is a busy man. We must be ready for him. Sailors do not like
to be kept waiting."

"Is there a shop in this town of yours which can supply the tools of
an artist's trade?"

"Of that I am not sure. Tell me what you need."

"Pigments. White lead, bone black, carmine, earths of all sorts, tin
yellow, vermilion, umber, ochre, and a few more. I need brushes. I will
need palettes. Above all I need fine canvas and the size to prepare it.
Will I find that in your town?"

"I don't know."

"Are there other painters there?"

"I have never heard of any."

"Well, let us go and visit this benighted town."

"It is not benighted," he said. "It is the fine town of Kingston upon Hull and I have the honor to represent it."

What pomposity.

I followed him down the stairs and out to a yard where the builders were erecting a scaffold, lashing the poles together this way and that. One let his pole fall and it nearly brained my companion, who exclaimed and struck out viciously at him. I looked around to spot what sort of conveyance we were to ride in, with some anticipation because it is only on rare occasions that I travel in any sort of carriage. In Amsterdam I walk to those few places to which I need to go. Anyone who wants to be painted comes to me.

All I could see in the yard was a pair of horses.

"That's yours," said the passenger, pointing at a huge, black animal that was rolling its eyes at me, its ears flat against the side of its head.

"I cannot ride that," I said. "I have not ridden a horse for thirty years."

"You must be able to. It's easy," he said, dumbfounded.

"No, it isn't. It's only easy if you can do it. I cannot."

"There's no other way to get there," he said. "Come on, I'll help you up."

It took him and three of the men, one holding the horse's head and the others shoving and pushing, until I was sitting upright for a terrifying moment, a hideous distance above the ground. Then the beast shuffled suddenly sideways and I promptly fell on top of the smallest of the men, which was lucky for me and a little less lucky for him.

In the end they thought to bring me a donkey, which left my feet near enough the ground to feel safe. It took a very long time to get to the town and I should have been in no good humor at all but for the fact that I had something to occupy my mind, a shining vision and a growing ambition.

I have never wanted to paint a woman so badly before.

Dahl's portrait held not the slightest interest for me. I could do it in my sleep without testing myself or learning anything new in the process. All that was at stake was my passage home, and I already knew I did not want to leave until I had painted his wife.

Painting is a way of claiming, of making someone your own. When I shared a studio in my birth town, before I went to Amsterdam, I shared it with another such as myself who, or so he believed, was better blessed in his visage and physique than myself. The women who came to me for their portraits would sigh when he entered the room but I had the knack of seduction, whereas he did not. He would impress himself upon them and it would sometimes work. I would make them press themselves on me and it would work unfailingly.

There was a girl called Cornelia whom I will always remember. She was the young wife of a corn merchant who knew my father well, far too young to be married to such a foul old rogue. He sent her to me when Jan, who shared my studio, was away so I took my time over her. I spent the first three sittings simply painting in the ground, the dead color, so that she could see the ghost of her form appearing and no more. If you keep almost quiet but not entirely, that is if you say just enough, the studio becomes a confessional, especially with young women. They start to tell you about their lives and with Cornelia, it was not good. She had little choice in her marriage and he was cruel to her. By the fourth or fifth sitting, I was well into the face and taking care to make her even more appealing than she was. The poor girl needed reassurance so badly. At the end of the sitting, she would say, "You are too kind, I am not so fair," and I would say, "I have not yet done you justice. Give me time."

There is a look a girl gives when she starts to speculate on how a union with you might be, and it was that look I began to paint into her portrait. It would never do for her husband to see it for he would recognize it immediately, but paint is paint—the thicker the better—and I could make her chaste again long before he saw it. I painted that look and made her shape her face just so, and as she did, with her eyes wide and her mouth just slightly open, the lower lip pushed forward, so the look began to produce what should have been its cause rather than its effect.

She loved the way I was translating her to the canvas and began to wear that expression even when I did not tell her to. She started to confide in me of her bedroom fears, of how each night she prayed her goat of a husband would drink himself insensible until morning. She did not flinch in the slightest when, in the interests of fully understanding the curve in her cheek and form of her lips, I would stroke her face gently between my hands. By the time I had finished her face, she would be so eager to start our sittings that I would hear her hurrying footsteps in the street five minutes before she was due.

I had to bring things to a head because Lievens was due back in a week or two, and my secluded, private studio would once again become a place shared by two and the opportunity would be gone. Cornelia was charmingly startled when I explained that to do full justice to her superb natural form, she should change behind the screen into a thin silk robe I had hung ready for her. I explained that I would be dressing her anew with my paint, as soon as I had captured her true womanly form. For propriety, I would mask her with my brush just as the clothes masked her. Only this would really make it a true portrait of her and, oh yes, she wanted a true portrait. She looked superb in the sheer silk, but of course after a few minutes, I began to tut under my breath and wear a distracted look.

"What is it?" she asked.

"It's in the way," I said forlornly. "With other women I can do it, but with you, you approach perfection so closely that the slightest barrier, the slightest uncertainty prevents me catching the full wonder that is you."

"What shall we do?" she asked. I noted the "we" with increasing delight.

Tentatively, blushing a little, I asked if she would let me explore her shoulders with my hands just as I had explored her face.

"Oh, yes," she said.

I came close to her from behind and ran my fingers slowly round her shoulders, up to her neck and back down her forearms. She trembled uncontrollably at my touch. With huge forbearance, I returned to my easel and pretended to paint for a minute or two, then came back to her and she leaned into me as I touched her. Slowly, slowly, I ran my hands down to her breasts, and she breathed out in a low moan as the silk brushed her nipples. Still I held on to my self-control and walked with difficulty back to my easel. She was no longer in the proud pose in which I had arranged her. She was curved toward me, her head down, her eyes half closed, breathing deeply. If I could have painted her as she was then, her husband would have had me killed instantly.

I went back to her then and knelt in front of her, cupping her face between my hands and stroking my thumbs across her lips.

"I see you in my head," I said, "but to know you as I want to know you, to make the marvelous picture I want to create, I must feel you against my whole body. I must be inside you as well as outside. Is that what you want, too?" Her answer was to reach her hands up under my shirt and pull me to her, her mouth opening and devouring me as her legs rose to grip me around my back. All in the interests of Art, of course.

We had four more sessions like that, panting in passionate, groin-pounding ecstasy on the studio couch before Lievens returned from his foreign travels and by so doing, fortuitously made further assignations impracticable before her husband started to suspect anything. To tell the truth, it was not a very good picture by the time I had camouflaged her expression and her body to the point where her husband might just pay for it instead of burning it. Without the giveaway pout, she looked quite dull.

Lievens and I had to come to an arrangement after that, to the effect that one would absent himself from the studio whenever the other had reached that certain point with a new client. Looks or no looks, he had to leave the studio far more often than I.

I had plenty of time to think about the past on the way to town because my donkey saw no reason at all to hurry. The countryside we rode through was very similar to the outskirts of Amsterdam, the land flat under a huge sky, fields to each side of the road, drained by ditches. These fields however were not at all like Dutch fields. Any Dutch farmer would have hung his head in shame to be found with his land in such a state. Most of the ditches were blocked by piles of mud and debris and broken fencing so that the water built up behind these dams and spilled across the earth. This was not good husbandry, not at all the way it would be done back home, but the man on the horse must have picked up that thought because he brought us both to a halt, and looked around at the mess.

Suddenly Marfel said something in English, which sounded angry, then remembered he had an audience and repeated it in Dutch. "They've had years to clear this up and just look at the mess it's all in. Good farmland going to waste."

"What happened to it? Was there a flood?"

"A flood of their own making. The town leaders opened the sluices during the siege to wash away the king's men. Bloody mess they made of everything."

"Were you a king's man?" I asked. "We played host to many of the king's men, the new king that is, in my country in the years when he was not welcome here."

"It is better not to ask questions like that," he said shortly. "Those who rake over the coals too fiercely may singe their own hands. I serve my country now and I served it then. I serve England, whoever commands her." He looked hard at me. "Now listen. In Hull you may attract some interest, and there will be others who speak your language there."

"Really? Dutch folk?"

"Certainly. It is at least in part a Dutch town when we're not fighting you. We have Dutch seamen, Dutch builders, Dutch drain diggers. You must remember to say the right thing if anyone asks. You joined Dahl's ship in Gottingbourg where you had been for—how long shall we say? How long ago is it that plague appeared in Amsterdam?"

"Three weeks. But it's not plague. I think it is more likely to be plain hysteria."

"Never mind. People have died of hysteria before now when they've decided it was plague. To be safe, let us say three months. You have been in Gottingbourg for three months. Another thing: I was not on that ship. I simply met you at Paull Holme and came with you to town as your dragoman, your interpreter. Is that understood?"

"Why the mystery?" I said.

"I have private business," was all he would say. Then he added, "I also have ways of making your life most uncomfortable should you forget."

We plodded through a mass of hovels until we came to the foot of a beast of a wall, stretching across our path and towering over us. Our road curved inland to bring us to an even larger fort in the center of the wall. Above it, a great flag was flying.

"The royal standard," he said. "Take note of it. We're very loyal these days and have been for some time. Loyal to Parliament, loyal to Cromwell, now loyal to the king."

I looked at the river. As big as the Rhine it might be, but it was nowhere near so fine. The Rhine rarely ran quite so thickly with mud. "Do you like the Humber?" he asked.

"Humber," I said, "and its color is *omber*. The *omber* Humber."

He seemed pleased to see that so brown a flood should have such a suitable name. "It is even better in English," he said. "*Omber* is umber. The umber Humber."

After that, he kept trying to teach me a silly English rhyme he had made up: "The umber Humber never slumbers." To shut him up, I revealed the only English poetry I had ever learned by heart, saying it as carefully as I could: "Who zees God's face, that is self-life, must die. Vot a death were it then to zee God die?"

It certainly stopped him and his horse in their tracks. My donkey, who was not paying much attention, blundered into the back of his horse and got a kick for its pains.

"John Donne," Marfel said, amazed. "You know the poetry of John Donne?"

"I have read it in translation," I said. "Meinheer Huygens translates it. I painted a picture on the theme of that poem, the savior dying on the cross as the horseman watches. Those two lines are the heart of it, I think, so I learnt them in the English."

"Astonishing," he said. "Why did you *learn* it?"

"It was the very crux of the painting, more than the cross itself. I needed the words to ring in my head and out of my brush onto the canvas."

"In English? A language you do not even speak?"

"All the better. I had the sound of the words in part of my head and the image of them in another. The more I repeated those sounds, the stronger the image became."

"You like poetry, do you?" he asked. "I write poetry, you know."

I had a certain prescient fear that he might be about to offer for my appreciation reams of his own verse. " 'The umber Humber never slumbers'?" I said. "Is that a good example of your verse?"

"That is not verse," he said. "Verse can measure the weight of the human soul. It is the greatest of the arts."

"You believe you practice the greatest of the arts?" I said. "I don't think so," I continued. "Painting can change the weight of the human soul. Your verse may be misunderstood. A painting is never misunderstood. A good painting changes all who look at it."

"Only bad verse is misunderstood," he said. "Verse that is written by gentlemen and read by peasants." Such as yourself, he might have added. The words were hanging there in the air.

"A painting is a transaction between two people," I said, hoping that a resort to logic would quell my temper, because I suspected that tipping him off his horse at this stage might not be the best idea. My father was not a peasant; he was a miller. There is a world of difference. No one in Amsterdam, even these days, would describe me as a peasant. I live where I have to and I have many fascinating neighbors in the Jordaan. I may have come down in the world, but the conversation on the street where I live now is infinitely more interesting. Marfel was looking at me with an expression of incomprehension on his face. "A painting," I went on, "either has or does not have an absolute validity. It is a two-way flow between artist and sitter in which the emerging picture may find and awaken slumbering elements of the sitter. A poem is no more than an assertion, a one-way business, a claim made by the poet with no possibility of substantiation. Mere politics. That is why great art is better than great poetry."

"Don't put yourself above me," he said. "You're a high-toned man for such a draggle. I'll judge you when I see what you can do with your brush."

"And I'll judge you when . . ." I stopped, not wanting to invite a flood of poetry, but he interposed.

"You cannot judge, can you?" he said. "You cannot even read my poetry. You have not the language."

"Another proof that my art is higher," I said. "It is beyond language."

"Balderdash!" he snorted. "It has its language. I have seen painted Dutch women who may appeal to a Dutch eye but not to mine. That adds up to a different tongue."

And there, for now, I was minded for the first time to agree.

We rode inland along the wall and as soon as we rounded the end, I could understand the lie of the land for the first time. This wall we had just passed guarded another smaller river that ran behind it, heading into the Humber under its shadow. Our road crossed a bridge ahead of us. On the far side of this smaller river lay the town, with a crowd of ships tied up two or three deep at the sheltered wharves of the lesser river. Beyond that was the city, with the tall spire of a great church in the middle. We paused on the bridge, where my poet pointed to the dense mass of masts, packed tight in the river.

"This is the river Hull, our safe harbor," he said, "and those masts are its forest and we all live from the fruits of that forest."

We entered the city through a gate at its northeast corner where guards displayed extraordinary respect to my companion, as they asked him what were clearly a series of searching questions concerning myself. The street on the far side was as busy a place as I have ever seen. Alleys to our left led down the sides of great warehouses to the wharves and, my goodness, some of the grand houses were just what you might see in Amsterdam, the same decoration, the same tiles, everything. Shops sold whatever a man might need, except, it soon became clear, most of what we were in desperate need of.

It was relatively easy to buy the most basic pigments, even if the quality was far from what I am accustomed to. It was the reds and the blues, the scarcer, costlier colors, which were not to be found. A ships' chandler supplied oil and the joiners' shop next door had thin sheets of elm wood on which I marked out the shape of a palette. Under my supervision, they quickly cut and sanded me two, just as I like them to be. Two would suffice for now, I thought, though at home I would have had several palettes prepared for the different parts of a painting.

The truly bad news was that brushes were not to be had anywhere, nor canvas of sufficient quality. The brushes on sale might be adequate for painting window frames but they were no good at all for my needs. As for canvas, sail canvas was the best available, of a coarseness that would not suit at all. I solved this part of the problem by turning the clock back twenty years or more and resorting to my early practices. Returning to the joiners' shop, I selected some fine oak panels, thin and flat, prepared, I should imagine, for a furniture maker. Through my companion, I ordered them jointed together to make the size I required. I asked for three to err on the side of caution.

It was back to the brush problem after that. We found some domestic brushes, of the type with which ladies may powder their faces, but that was all. As we went from shop to shop with scant success, the poet's progress became slower and slower. Every man, woman, and child seemed to know him, and half of them sought to accost him with what sounded like demands, or, in one case, belligerence of such an extreme form that I expected them both to become involved in a brawl at any moment. His name, as I came to hear it more often, proved to have a harder sound at its heart than I had thought, and a stronger tail. He was not Marfel, he was Marvell. One of these men who stopped him, friendly in his approach, looked at me with interest and talked at length to Marvell.

"We have a chance it seems. There is a portrait maker here," said Marvell to me at the conclusion of his talk. "I have never heard of him before, but I have been abroad a great deal of late and he is come from York last year. He lives quite near my own house at the end of Salthouse Lane. Let us see if he can help."

A gloomier bugger I have seldom met than this so-called portrait painter. He met us with a scowl at the door, and although I understand completely what it is to be disturbed when the creative flow is upon you, I really could not say that the creative flow had ever trickled any-where near this wretch. Eventually Marvell prevailed on him by sheer force of will to let us inside his horrible house, whereupon he led us with bad grace into a studio that was as ill-conceived as any I have ever seen. The light came from two contrary directions, a window in the ga-ble and a large roof-light. That confusion was fully reflected in the paintings stacked around the walls, all of which I saw were painted onto wooden panels. There was a landscape or two, apparently painted of a countryside lit by at least three suns, judging from the confusion of high-lights and conflicting shadows. He knew nothing of composition, of scale, of proportion, or of the proper makeup of a palette. The colors were jar-ringly varied to a bilious degree.

He made up for that paucity of skill by his surplus of brushes, how-ever, a great pot full of them in badger hair and sable. Marvell prevailed on him to sell us six, and I pocketed three more while he wasn't look-ing. He also had carmine, vermilion, a useful tin yellow, and two blues, azurite and what he claimed to be lapis, which he sold to us for an ex-tortionate amount. Marvell paid without argument.

Before returning to collect the finished panels, we went next to a grand building which proved to be the Customs House, where Marvell sought out Dahl, who came flushed and triumphant from a noisy room full of bewigged men. They talked for such a long time that I remem-bered what it was to be a tiny child, impatient at my mother's knee, aching with the cruelty of waiting out her unending conversations with friends. After a hundred years or perhaps a little longer, they concluded their ramblings and Marvell turned to me.

"The captain will return to Paull Holme later tonight and will col-lect the panels on his way. You and I may go back now. He wishes to begin the painting tomorrow."

"He may wish it but he'll have to put a halter on his wishes," I said. "The panels have to be prepared first. That's two days' work at least. There can be no rushing these things."

The captain gave me a hard look when this was translated, so hard that I wondered for one illogical second if he could have divined my thoughts about his wife. Certainly, it was the likely form of his wife's portrait, not his own, that occupied my thoughts for all of that dull jog home.

My frolics with Cornelia were more than thirty years past. Except during Saskia's short life, there had been many, many others and sometimes still were. In Amsterdam I had the power to seduce, the power of language, the power of old reputation and, above all, the power of my brush. Even in my newly reduced circumstances, even without the patronage others so ill-deservedly received, the gold chains bestowed by grateful nobility, even with the City Fathers constantly on my back about this or about that, I was *someone,* and reputation loosens clothing faster than fingers can. Here I was nobody. Could I do it here? I knew I was going to find out, because I had to catch that catlike face. There really is only one way that I know to do that properly. . . .

SEVEN

Monday, April 9, 2001

DAWN MADE UP FOR AMY'S DISTURBED NIGHT ON THE FLOOR ON her air bed. The small creatures who lived in the recesses of the dusty tower room scuttled over her on their accustomed paths. She had no particular fear of spiders but they startled her from sleep when they ran over her face, and once in the night something that was much heavier than a spider hurtled over her feet. When the first light reached her window, she got up to look out. Amy never felt she knew a place until she had seen it all by herself, alone in the early morning, without any other humans to divert attention and break into the natural gradients of diminishing sound that give the sense of scale to a landscape. Forcing the window open on rusty hinges, she looked out across the fields. The Humber was an orange flood pouring into the sun's open mouth, gulping at the horizon. Rabbits were running and stopping and running again on the grass below the tower and pigeons clattered in and out of the trees. She soaked it up, filling her lungs with the freshest air until she heard movement in the room next door and sensed that the man next door was also looking out of his tower window. Not wanting to share the scene, she got quickly dressed, took her sketch pad, and went quietly downstairs.

She crossed the dew-soaked field to her tree, rabbits scattering at her appearance, but this time she leaned against it facing the house, drawing intently, stripping away the scaffolding and the huts and sketching in lawns, flowerbeds, and pathways to restore the status it had lost. The morning light gave it definition and detail to satisfy her pencil where the evening before there had only been indistinct shadows. Along the edge of the roof, the row of dormer windows showed the rooms where the other builders lived and from these, slowly, the sounds of awakening began to come—coughs, creaks, a burst of song, complaints. She went on drawing and was just sketching in the imagined grandeur of the front steps, flanked by stone urns, when the front door opened and a figure in black overalls, holding a bowl, came out and sat down on them, right in the center of her picture, staring across at her.

She finished her drawing, closed the pad, and walked back toward the front door, as eager to see him more closely as she was nervous at approaching him. Who was this man Don, who seemed to inspire such strong opinions among the others? She'd have to wait until she was by herself with someone, Gengko maybe, before she could ask. Don stared at her as she came nearer until she was almost close enough to see his face clearly, then he looked down at his bowl and stirred its contents around with his spoon.

She intended to pass him without a word, but he spoke to her as she came close.

"May I look?" His voice was deeper than she expected, stripped of the anger of the previous night. The walls of some cavity inside her resonated with it.

"At what?"

"Your drawing."

She opened the pad and passed it to him.

"You can see through time," he said as he looked at it, then he turned the page back to where she'd drawn him the day before. The action felt like a violation, intimate and frightening in equal quantities. Something huge hung in the balance between them as he looked. The blood in her ears deafened her, but he looked at the sketches without comment and turned another page or two.

"Who's this?" He showed her the sketch.

"Me," said Amy. "Can't you tell?"

"You? This is an old woman."

"That's how I'll look when I'm seventy," she said.

"Why do you draw yourself like that?"

"I do self-portraits when I don't have anyone else to draw."

"This isn't a self-portrait. It's not what you see when you look in the mirror."

"I'm too young to be interesting."

"I might not agree with that," he said. "Tell me what you mean."

"I mean the marks time leaves make a face more interesting. I like to imagine futures for myself and try to draw the results. This one's sad, see? I met the love of my life at thirty and I was widowed at thirty-five. Never met anyone else after that. Moved to the Pembroke coast. Not much money, trying to make ends meet, but I kept working, sold just enough paintings to get by."

"Is there another one in here?"

She took it from him, flipped through the pages and showed him a full-face portrait. "Everything went right. Museums bought my pictures. I had four kids and Richard built me the studio of my dreams on our own island. Then I forgot I had to paint. I had too much."

"Who's Richard?"

"There is no Richard." She opened the pad at the sketch she'd drawn of him. "What do you think?"

"You draw well," he said. "That's me."

"It's half of you."

"Oh, yeah? Well, double up that half, then you'll know what I used to look like." He sounded so bitter.

"Nobody's symmetrical," she said. "That's the whole point of faces."

"I wouldn't mind being symmetrical," he said.

"What happened to you?"

"An accident. Okay? With a saw."

The words came wrapped in a vivid bubble of violent noise. He kept his head down. She could have said something obvious like "you poor thing" but being Amy, she said, "Can I draw you properly?"

"Why would you want to do that?"

"You've got a great face."

"I forgot, you like the marks of time. These are just marks."

"No. You've got a great face," she insisted.

He made a derisive noise.

"You have," she said. "Maybe you just can't see it at the moment."

"I'd rather not see it," he said.

"But you were looking in a mirror in your room."

"Is that your business?" he demanded, then he softened. "That's therapy. For my hand. I only look at my hand."

There was a silence while she wondered if she could ask what he meant, but then he looked half up at her and said, "Was that Parrish's book you were reading last night? The journal? Amelia's journal?"

"You know it?"

"He lent it to you already? That's a privilege."

Normal conversation felt good. If only he would look at her. She felt something starting to build in the space between them, as if a spark might soon jump.

"It's because of Amelia," she explained. "I'm one of her family. My name's Amy Dale, you see. I think that amused him. Who are you?"

"Amelia's descendant?" Amelia meant enough to him for a sudden gleam of interest to show in his eyes. "You don't want to read that version," he said. "It misses out all the good bits. My name's Don."

She knew that but she didn't say. "Don what?"

"Don what does it matter? Gilby if it makes a difference."

It did. Don Gilby. "Have you seen it?" she asked. "The real book?"

"No, they keep it safe in the archives. It's all on microfilm in the library. I've looked at that. It's difficult trying to figure it out but at least you can see it the way it really was, the handwriting. You've read the first bit in there?"

"Yes. I want to read the full version."

"There was a painter here. She calls him a 'limner.' The one she gets annoyed with."

"I remember."

"He's not a house painter, not a decorator. He's like you. I looked it up. It's the old name for a portrait painter."

"That's a sign, then. So, can I paint you?"

"What sort of pictures do you paint, Amy Dale?"

"Not like photographs," she said. "I know I can't get inside someone else's skin. I'm here and you're over there and whatever happens when I look at you and start to paint is happening inside my head."

Encouraged by his silence, she went on. "If I know someone well enough, I close one eye so that I lose the depth. Then I feel their face very gently with my fingers all over and my fingers tell me what I can't see. Sometimes I close my eyes completely and go on feeling. I like painting myself because I know how my face feels inside as well as outside. I can feel where the bone's pushing on the skin. Do you know what I mean?"

"Degas's model said he scratched her skin because he kept measuring her with dividers."

"How do you know that?" she said.

"Get stuffed."

"I meant . . ."

"I know what you meant. You meant how does a builder know about art."

"All right. Yes, that's what I meant."

He sat down again. "I was educated," he said. "My mother saw to that. Her and Mr. Parrish."

"Parrish? The Parrish who works here?"

"Long story."

"I don't use dividers, I promise."

He almost smiled. "When you paint yourself, you're looking in a mirror, right?"

"Right."

"So what you paint is the wrong way round. A self-portrait is a lie."

"Not to the painter."

"A photograph isn't a lie, but then you say you don't paint photographs."

"A photograph *is* a lie. When do you ever see someone completely still? Only when they're dead. Look at you. Look at the way you move. If I painted you, people would look at it and know how you move."

"You like the way I move?"

SHE COULDN'T STOP THINKING ABOUT HIM ALL THE WAY INTO Hull, didn't even want to. At Peter Parrish's office there was a note for her, clipped to a street map. It said, "Amelia, Called away. Back elevenish. Take a look at the old town. I've marked it. PP." Amused by the old name he'd absently attached to her, she walked slowly down between the shops to a wide circus of grand civic buildings where a shopping mall had been built alongside the remains of docks, now full of plastic yachts rocking and jangling. The map took her east into the old town where she arrived on that same High Street van Rijn had walked down. But in the intervening three and a half centuries, the city's center of gravity had shuffled west and left it to its ghosts. Only in name was this vacant, poignant road still a High Street. A side alley between decaying warehouses took her to the old merchants' wharves, but all she saw was a handful of steel boats, barges, tugs, and trawlers tied up on the other side of the Hull river.

If she had been a well-briefed, persistent searcher she would have found that wartime bombs and postwar slum clearance had not entirely obliterated old Hull. On the day van Rijn walked past the Wilberforce house, William Catlyn, *the* builder of choice for those rich enough to afford him, had been putting the final touches to it, but now it looked too museum-clean, too immaculately restored to announce its age to her. The same Catlyn had been laying the foundations for the even newer house he was building for the merchant George Crowle, but now Crowle's house hid itself from Amy behind a charmless later façade. She walked straight past the side alley that still led to its old entrance, an untouched masterpiece of decorated brick and stone in the Dutch style that was almost exactly as Catlyn had left it.

Once, Crowle and his fellows of the merchants' guild had their treasure-house warehouses lining the river, served by their private quays, the staithes, where the cargoes came and went. Amy had only a fleeting sense of that busy past as she looked at the last derelict survivors of those warehouses. Buildings were mostly inert and unenticing objects to her. She was a people person. Paull Holme Manor had begun to speak to her largely because it spoke with Amelia's voice. The library was not far away. The library held the original copy of Amelia's journal, the spider traces of Amelia's voice. She obeyed the call.

The local-studies section lay at the top of stairs separating the lending library from its community café. The building, from the outside, was Victorian Municipal in style but inside, its builders had known that a proper place of study required polished oak, Gothic glasswork, and high ceilings to do its job and focus the attention properly. She went in thinking reference libraries were simple places where you found your book and sat down to read it, but she was proven quite wrong. At the

desk, they told her politely but firmly that special advance arrangements needed to be made before anyone could inspect Amelia Dahl's
journal. As her heart sank, they lifted it for her again by explaining
that the general public could have access to the microfilm copy of
the journal and then immediately depressed her by telling her that all the
microfilm-reading machines were booked for the rest of the day. As she
turned away, the woman added that if any of the readers finished early,
she was welcome to use the rest of their slot.

She decided to wait and they got her the roll of film in its cardboard
box just in case, so she sat anxiously watching the clock tick away the
minutes toward her appointment with Peter Parrish at eleven o'clock.
The microfilm roll in her hand was useless without the machine. For
want of anything else to do, she even tried unrolling it and holding it
up to the light but all she could see in each frame was the rough outline
of a page with writing that was far too small to decipher. Blessedly, at
quarter to eleven, the man on the end machine switched off its light,
got up, closed his notebook with an air of finality, and stalked out of
the room. It took three frustrating minutes for Amy to lace the roll of
film through the unfamiliar cogs and wheels, only to have to do it all
over again when she turned the knob to "rewind" instead of "forward"
and saw her work unravel before her eyes. The machine was a combi-
nation of microscope and magic lantern, and the dusty screen came to
life with a blurred image that proved to be turned at ninety degrees to
her when she eventually found the focus knob and pulled it into some
measure of sharpness. A harassed woman at the next machine stopped
what she was doing long enough to show her how to swivel the whole
mechanism around to make it readable, tutting faintly as though anyone
with any sense should already know how it was done.

Amy consulted her watch. Eight minutes to eleven. She didn't want
to be late. No time for more than a quick look. The screen showed a
printed introductory page: "The Journal of Amelia Dahl of Paull Holme
Manor in the County of Yorkshire. 1662–1663."

She turned the knob carefully to let the spool move on and there,
as the opening page of Amelia's carefully styled handwriting edged into
view, faint and hard to read, she met her forebear in proper detail.

JANUARY THE FIRST IN THE YEAR OF OUR LORD 1661/62,
THIS BEING THE SECOND YEAR OF THE REIGN OF OUR KING

CHARLES WHO IS RESTORED TO US. ON THIS DAY, AT THE START OF THE MONTH, I HERE BEGIN TO KEEP THE JOURNAL BOOK IN RED CALF LEATHER GIVEN ME FOR THAT PURPOSE BY MY BELOVED HUSBAND. IT IS A PROPITIOUS TIME, BEING THE START OF OUR NEW LIFE IN OUR NEW HOUSE AT PAULL HOLME AFTER THE PAST FIVE AND ONE HALF YEARS OF OUR LIVING IN THE TOWN OF KINGSTON. THE AIR HERE IS CLEAR AND FINE AND IT IS A JOY BEYOND THOUGHT THAT I DO NOT ANY MORE HAVE TO SUFFER THE RANK SMOKE FROM POPPLE'S OIL MILL. I PRAY THAT I MAY NEVER AGAIN BE OBLIGED TO SMELL THAT STINK OF BURNING RAPE-CAKE WHICH HAS GIVEN ITS ODOUR TO THE WHOLE OF MY LIFE FOR SO LONG. THIS FAIR PLACE HAS EVEN A NAME WHICH IS DEAR TO MY HEART FROM THE YEARS DURING WHICH I LIVED WITH MY MOTHER'S PEOPLE IN HER LAND OF NORWAY. THERE TOO IS A PLACE NAMED PAULL HOLME, A PLACE OF BEAUTY, AND IT EASES MY HEART IN THIS OFTEN STRANGE COUNTRY TO THINK THAT TRAVELERS FROM THAT LAND, WHICH IS HALF MINE BY VIRTUE OF MY BIRTH, DID COME HERE AND NAME THIS PLACE. THIS REGION OF HOLDERNESS IN WHICH OUR NEW HOUSE IS SITUATED IS A FINE LAND, FERTILE AND WELL HUSBANDED. THE TROUBLES WHICH HAVE LATELY FACED US IN OUR FORMER HOME IN THE TOWN ARE NO MORE THAN PASSING ECHOES HERE. IT IS MY BELIEF THAT THE PEOPLE OF HOLDERNESS CONCERN THEMSELVES WITH FEW AFFAIRS OF STATE AND THINK MORE OF THEIR FIELDS, THEIR ANIMALS, AND THEIR TABLE. IN THE PAST YEARS MY HUSBAND HAS BEEN WONT TO ANCHOR HIS SHIP HERE WHEN THE TIDE AND WIND HAVE BEEN CONTRARY. HE HAS TOLD ME THAT HE HAD STARED ON MANY OCCASIONS AT THE TWO TOWERS WHICH NOW FORM THE BUTTRESSES OF THIS, OUR HOUSE, AND BENT HIS THOUGHTS TO HOW, IF FORTUNE SMILED UPON HIM, HE MIGHT NEW-VAMP THEM TO HABITABILITY. WHEN HE AND I FIRST MADE OUR ACQUAINTANCE TOGETHER, WE DID DISCOURSE OFTEN IN THE COURSE OF THAT LONG VOYAGE HERE FROM BATAVIA OF HOW OUR LIFE MIGHT BE IN MY LAND OF ENGLAND, BUT I WOULD SAY THIS DAY THAT IT IS

THE FIRST TIME THAT I MAY ALLOW MYSELF TO FEEL ANY
CERTAINTY OF HAPPINESS. THE WEATHER CONTINUES
EXTRAORDINARILY FINE AND THE GRASS WE HAVE SOWN ON
THE EARTH BEFORE THE HOUSE SHOWS A HEAD OF GREEN
HAIR. IT IS ALTOGETHER TOO EARLY, MY MAN DOES SAY, FOR
US TO LIVE IN THIS PLACE. WE HAVE BUT TWO ROOMS NOW
READY FOR OUR USE AND A THIRD TO BE FINISHED ON THE
MORROW. HE WISHED US TO STAY LONGER IN THE CITY BUT
I WOULD NOT. THIS IS TO BE MY CREATION, MY HOUSE,
BROUGHT TO A POINT OF PERFECTION BY MY EYE AND MY
VOICE IF NOT MY HAND. IF I AM NOT HERE, THESE ROGUES
WILL PERFORM A TAWDRY WORK UPON IT AND I WILL NOT
HAVE IT SPOILED SO. I SHALL MAKE A PLACE WITH MY
CONSTANT ATTENTION TO MY ART WHICH SHALL STAND AS A
MOST PERFECT PLACE. ARRIVED TODAY BY CARRIER THE
OVERMANTEL JUST AS WE DID ORDER IT FROM BEVERLEY,
ALSO TEN CHAIRS. WHEN MY BELOVED HUSBAND RETURNS
FROM HIS VOYAGE, IT IS MY HOPE THAT HE WILL FIND THIS
HOUSE TRANSFORMED FROM THE EMPTY CONDITION IN
WHICH HE DID SEE IT BEFORE HE SAILED. IN THIS HOUSE, I
AM FREE TO EXERCISE MY ART AND SHEW WHAT I CAN DO.

There was more of the same for the next few days—domestic detail, expressions of longing for the absent Dahl—and Amy spun the
control to take her through it, scanning painfully slowly at first but then
a little faster as she learned to decipher the faint, tricky handwriting. In
Parrish's typed version, the first entry had been January fifteenth. She
stopped abruptly two days before that. The entry for January thirteenth
was different, much longer than any that had gone before. She rewound
the film carefully to the start of that day.

CALLED UP FROM MY BED BY JOHN MOLD AT 6 OF THE
CLOCK WITH THE NEWS THAT MY HUSBAND'S SHIP, THE
GODSPEED, WAS IN THE RIVER, AND LOOKED FROM THE NEW
WINDOW TO SEE HER AT ANCHOR IN THE NEAR CHANNEL
WITH NO PERSON VISIBLE ON THE DECK EXCEPTING ONLY THE
BOATSWAIN XPEFFER ELY, WHO I COULD BE SURE OF AT THAT
DISTANCE BY VIRTUE OF HIS GREAT SIZE AND ENTIRELY

HAIRLESS HEAD. I DID DRESS MYSELF AT A RUN AND GO AT
ONCE ALL AROUND THE HOUSE MAKING SURE THAT ALL WAS
IN GOOD REPAIR AND THAT THE KITCHEN DID RING OF
PREPARATION FOR HIS ARRIVAL. A LITTLE AFTER THE NEW
CLOCK HAD STRUCK SEVEN I OBSERVED ALL SORTS OF
BUSTLE ABOARD. THE BOAT WAS LOWERED AND LOADED AND
STRUCK OFF FOR THE SHORE SO THAT I DID RUN ALL THE
WAY AROUND THE NEW-SEEDED GRASS THAT WILL BE OUR
GARDEN-LAWN TO THE PATH BELOW AND THEN TO THE
LANDING, WHERE IT WAS WITH SOME CONCERN AND A GREAT
PAIN TO MY HEART THAT I SAW NO MAN IN THE BOAT WHO
RESEMBLED MY HUSBAND, WHO I HAD A MONTH'S MIND TO
SEE, BUT THEN DID SPY HIM TO MY DISAPPOINTMENT,
REMAINING STILL ON THE WHEEL-DECK OF THE *GODSPEED*.
THE BOAT CAME TO THE LANDING WITH TWO SEAMEN AT THE
SWEEPS AND WITH TWO OTHER MEN SEATED IN THE STERN.
THE FIRST OF THESE I KNEW AT ONCE FOR OUR MEMBER,
MASTER MARVELL, A MAN OF HIGH DISCOURSE AND GREAT
WIT, A PRAGMATICAL MAN THOUGH QUALITIED WHO HAS OFT
HAD BUSINESS WITH MY HUSBAND. THE OTHER WAS UNKNOWN
TO ME, A DRAGGLE OF A FELLOW OF SOME AGE, A MASTY
FELLOW WHO I SAW TO LOOK AT MARVELL IN A WAY I DID NOT
LIKE. HE PAID HIS PRICE, FOR NO SOONER HAD MARVELL
SPRUNG TO THE SHORE WITH EASE THAN THIS OTHER
FELLOW, IN ESSAYING TO FOLLOW HIM WITHOUT TAKING ANY
PROPER CARE IN THE MATTER, DID FAIL UTTERLY TO HOLD HIS
BALANCE AND SPRAWLED DOWN INTO THE MUD TO THE
AMUSEMENT OF ALL OF US EXCEPTING HIMSELF. ON RESCUING
THE FELLOW, MARVELL DID INFORM ME THAT MY HUSBAND
HAD PRESSING BUSINESS, EXPLAINING HIS CARGO AND HIMSELF
TO THOSE PRATING FANFAROONS, AS MY HUSBAND WOULD
CALL THEM, WHO DO CALL THEMSELVES THE COMPANY OF
MERCHANT ADVENTURERS AND WHO WOULD HAVE HIM
FINED FOR EVERY PART OF EVERY CARGO HE BRINGS TO
THE TOWN WHICH DOES NOT MEET THEIR PETTY RULES. IT
IS PROFOUNDLY TO BE DESPAIRED OF THAT AFTER YEARS OF
LOYAL SERVICE TO THE KING, MY HUSBAND IS CALLED AN
ALIEN BY THESE PEOPLE, WHO WERE THEMSELVES TRAITORS

TO A MAN DURING THE YEARS OF THE ROYAL EXILE AND
CHEERED AT THE KILLING OF THE LATE KING. IT IS THEY NOT
OURSELVES WHO SHOULD BE BROUGHT DOWN, NOW THAT THE
THRONE HAS BEEN RESTORED. MARVELL ASTONISHED ME WITH
THE NEWS THAT THE DAMP FELLOW NOW DRIPPING ON OUR
DOCK WAS A LIMNER OF SOME SKILL, NEWLY DISCOVERED BY
THEM ALL ADRIFT IN GOTTINGBOURG IN SWEDEN AND
BROUGHT HERE FOR NO MORE THAN THE PRIVILEGE OF HIS
FARE AND KEEP TO MAKE MY HUSBAND'S PORTRAIT. ALL THIS
TIME THIS CLOUTERLY MAN, WHO WAS NOW A SCANDALOUS
SIGHT IN HIS STINKING GARMENTS, DID SHIVER AND STARE AT
ME WITH HIS DROLL AND GOUTY FACE. I WOULD NOT FALL
FOUL OF MY HUSBAND IF THIS IS HIS WISH, BUT I WAS PUT IN
A DUMP THAT MY MAN SHOULD BE REPLACED IN MY HOUSE
THIS NIGHT BY SUCH A ONE AS THIS PAINTER. MARVELL DID
THEN TELL ME THAT IT MAY NOT BE MADE KNOWN THAT THE
BOTH OF THEM HAVE COME ASHORE FROM THE SHIP SO THAT
HE PLANS TO RIDE TO THE CITY FROM HERE AND MAKE
CLAIM TO HAVE COME BY CARRIAGE FROM LONDON WITH
THE PAINTER WHO IS CALLED VANRIN. MARVELL SHEWED ME
A LITTLE DRAWING DONE BY VANRIN ON THE SHIP, AND IT IS
TRUE THAT HE CAN MAKE A VERY CREDITABLE LINE. I WENT
IN SEARCH OF SUCH STUFF AS MIGHT PREVENT THE PAINTER
FROM TAKING HIS DEATH-CHILL.

From the present day, a cleared throat made itself heard in the seventeenth century and Amy came back some of the way to see the librarian standing at her elbow.

"I'm sorry," said the librarian. "Mrs. Shoosmith has arrived."

Amy tried to make sense of the statement and failed. "Has she?"

"She's booked on your machine. It's coming up to eleven o'clock."

"Oh, right. Sorry, I'm with you."

Peter Parrish was in his office when she arrived, out of breath and late. He was wearing different tweeds with a different color of paint splashed on them.

"Did you have a look round?" he asked genially.

"I did," she said, "and I read some more of Amelia's journal, the copy in the library."

"Good, good," he said. "Excellent. You saw the house?"

"What house?"

He looked surprised. "The Salter house? You didn't see my note?" She shook her head.

"Didn't I mark it on the map?" He took the map from her. "Yes, here it is. Oh, dear."

"What?"

"Silly me," he said. "I wrote down that I'd marked it but I didn't say what it was I'd marked."

There was a cross on the map that Amy hadn't noticed before, a small inked cross at the top of the High Street.

"That was their house, you see," said Parrish. "Their house before they moved out of Hull. At least we think so. There are documents about it which mention Dahl as a past owner, and I doubt there could have been more than one Dahl. There's not much left, only a couple of walls built into a quite horrid nineteenth-century thing, but I thought you'd like to take a look."

"I went to read the journal," she said. "I didn't have much time, though. Why did they leave the town, do you know?"

"Oh, yes," he said, as if surprised that it wasn't part of her family lore. "The Civil War. Very confusing time, of course. You know Hull was the first place to come out against the king? They barred the gates to Charles the First—1642, that was. Right old rumpus after that, Cromwellians to a man. Sieges and battles. You know what happened, of course. They cut off the king's head. All very well until Cromwell died and the whole republic idea began to fall apart. By the time it got to 1660, they'd all changed their minds—couldn't wait to get a king back again."

"But Amelia says Dahl was on the king's side."

"Daresay he was," said Parrish absently. "Odd, considering he was a foreigner. Trouble is, he was on the king's side when the rest of them weren't. Bound to cause trouble, that sort of thing. Probably a bit of a troublemaker." He exclaimed and put his hand to his mouth. "I'm so sorry. Relation of yours. How rude of me."

Amy laughed. "He doesn't mean anything to me, I promise," but she was glad he'd said it about Dahl and not his wife. "It's all very interesting, the journal I mean. I'll have to go back and read the rest."

"Really? You might be disappointed. It's better at the start. Gets a bit dry later on. What was it you liked?"

"The bit when this portrait painter arrived and falls in the mud. Stuff like that."

He frowned. "I vaguely remember that, I suppose. Haven't read the whole thing for eons to tell you the truth."

"I want to know what happens with the painter later on."

"You know, I'm sorry to say I don't think he appears in it very much at all. Certainly can't recall it if he does. Mind you, that wasn't the sort of thing I was looking for, so you never know."

"And Marvell? She mentions Marvell."

"Well, she would. He was the Member of Parliament, you know. Anyway, we'd better get started. About the house. The problem we have is producing, shall we say, a *facsimile* of the decoration without being accused of going *too far*. It's always a terrible moment, you know, when you open your work up to the critical gaze and people say you've perhaps got a little *carried away*. Now of course we are very lucky to have the traces of what is very probably the original decorative scheme in one or two rooms. They were protected under wallpaper, you see, and it's going to have to be a softly, softly approach. Now somewhere here," he looked vaguely around the desk, "we have an analysis of the pigments used, and there's not too much of a problem matching them." He waved a hand at a box in the corner. "They're all in there. Dry pigment. Powder. You mix it with an off-white base—well, it's almost a cream. Modern whites are much too bright—makes it look all wrong. The proportions are all written down. It's just a question of extrapolation. We don't have the corners, you see. You'll have to do the straight sections of the borders and then just, well, work out how they must have fitted at the corners. There are some tracings, and I've had the tiniest go myself at fitting it all together."

He found a roll of paper on the desk and gave it to her with a sudden smile. "See how it goes, anyway. I'll be out tomorrow. We'll have a chat."

On the way back to Paull Holme, with the box of paint on the backseat of the car, Amy knew she wanted an excuse to get back to the library again and read more of the microfilm roll. Amelia's journal already fascinated her.

Back at the house, she was lugging the box toward the steps when a shout from the foreman's hut stopped her.

"Is that lot booked in?" he yelled.

"In what sense?" she said sweetly.

"In the sense of is it booked in? All incoming goods go in the incoming-goods book so it balances with the materials-used book, just so no one gets any ideas about taking any of it for a walk off-site, see?"

The book he put in front of her had so few entries in it that she knew this was just his way of telling her he was in charge.

"Where you working, anyway?" he said when she'd finished.

"Back bedroom, first floor," she said.

"Which one?"

"Left at the top of the stairs. Third room along?" she said, trying to remember.

"Ceiling just been plastered?"

"Yup, that's it."

"Room one three, that is," he said. "One meaning first floor."

"And three meaning three?"

He ignored that. "You'll have Don Gilby in there later. Maybe Dennis Greener from time to time. Space for all of you. You won't have met Don yet."

She raised her eyebrows, preferring to give nothing away.

"We're all looking after him a bit. Be obliged if you did, too."

"Is he ill? Is he underage? I'm not good at changing nappies."

"He got hurt, made a mess of himself."

"What happened to him?"

"That's his business. I wouldn't go asking if I were you. Best left alone. I don't want some smart-arsed woman making it any worse for him. Understood?"

"You don't have to worry about me," she said, but as he watched her walk away he thought she might be trouble. He was a good man for all his ways and was sorry for what had happened to Don. "I don't know why I bother," he said to himself, but he did really.

The upstairs room was empty but there was a scaffolding tower in the middle of the floor and a pile of planks next to it so she tugged the tower to one corner and spent a precarious twenty minutes pushing the planks up into place on top of it until she had a working platform. She found a ladder no one seemed to be using out in the yard and when it was set up and ready, she began for the first time to consider the complete unfamiliarity of the task she had taken on with such unwarranted confidence. Peter Parrish's plans helped. They were carefully dimensioned in feet and inches, which would have been helpful if she'd had a ruler.

There was a cut-off piece of wood on the floor that looked about a foot long so, with a pencil, she began dividing it up into twelve approximately equal inch segments. When that was done, she climbed up the ladder, pencil, ruler, and plans in hand, and began the excruciatingly uncomfortable task of transferring the outline of the design to the borders of the ceiling. After five minutes, the only thing that ached more than her wrist was her neck. That was when the door opened and a man in black overalls came in: Don. He was carrying an electric sander and wearing large plastic goggles that covered his eyes and most of his scar.

"Hello," she said.

"Will it bother you if I start sanding?" he answered. "It's going to be dusty."

"No. I'm not painting. I'll be drawing out the pattern for days yet, I expect. You don't need to wear those goggles on my account." As soon as she said it she regretted it.

"I'm wearing them on my account," he said shortly. "On account of the fact that we follow workplace safety regulations round here."

"Yes, of course. Sorry."

"Speaking of which, you've got an unsafe ladder there. It should be secured to the staging."

"Oh."

"I'll do it," he said, putting the sander down and taking a length of cord from his pocket. Amy watched him take three or four turns round the ladder and the scaffold then start to tie the knot. He did it, despite his missing fingers, with the same skill he'd employed to roll his cigarette, then he turned back to examine the paint-covered paneling on the walls.

"I was in Hull today," she said. "I went to look at her journal. Amelia's journal."

He looked up at her, both eyes, full on, a bright blue double-barreled gaze. *He's back in the jungle again,* she thought, *but is he stalking prey or scenting a mate?*

"The microfilm?"

"Yes."

"Could you read the handwriting?"

"Once I got used to it. I didn't have much time."

He turned away and drowned out all chance of any further conversation by switching on the sander.

EIGHT

AMY COULDN'T HELP WATCHING DON. HE DIDN'T NOTICE HER GLANC-ing down at him from where she crouched on top of her platform. She watched how many times he took his injured hand away from the vibrating sander, moving his remaining fingers to give them some relief. The job was taking longer than it should. As her eyes once again drifted down to him, coiled down there on the floor, she began quite unconsciously to compose him into a picture, feeling the pull of the dramatic high perspective. When Amy made a picture in her head, she could break the rules of vision so that a part of her brain stepped outside the usual constraints. Now, the walls came roaring upward and outward, funneling out from this man, twisted in his stance, bent to his job, the visible side of his face tightly drawn in pain and concentration. The picture she made, a cone of pale wooden colors dragging the eye down to the darkness at its center, became as clear to her as if she had already painted it.

It carried her down that cone, plunging her all the way into him; as if he had felt something physical, Don glanced up, frowned, and turned off the sander.

"Something wrong?" he asked, sounding irritated.

"No," she said. "I was daydreaming." She turned her attention firmly back to the ceiling and he switched the machine back on. Almost immediately she heard a splintering crack and an exclamation. The sander stopped again. She had to look down. The paneling around the walls came to about chest height, and each panel was around three feet wide. Don had been using paint stripper for some of the time, scraping off successive layers of the caked, ancient paint, then sanding what remained carefully back to bare, pale wood. In the time since he had come in, he'd removed only half the paint from one panel, and now the central part of that panel was cracked and pushed inward where the pressure of the sander had proved too much for it.

"Sod it," he said.

She expected him to blame her for it—to say that she had distracted him—but he simply continued staring at the wall as if it held him at gunpoint. Climbing down the ladder, she went to his side, crouching down to feel the edge of the wood.

"It was very thin," she said, enjoying the chance to be on the same side.

"That's not going to count for anything with the Hawk."

"Hawk? The foreman?"

"He told me I'd be straight out of here if I couldn't hack it. I was rushing it. Shit."

She could feel his distress and, being Amy, she had to do something about it.

"Wouldn't someone help? One of the carpenters?"

"A chippy?" He stared at her and even through the dusty goggles, she could see his eyes were wide. "Why should they? It's not a girl's school, it's a building site. If you fuck up, you carry the can."

He turned back to the wall, shaking his head, feeling the edges of the panel with the fingers of his right hand. "If Parrish sees this he'll go ape-shit."

"I'll go and talk to them, to the chippies."

"Wilks and the other two won't touch anything without instructions in triplicate. They're no special friends of mine."

"Can I try?"

He just shrugged.

She opened the door and kind Providence brought her Dennis, walking toward her.

"You're just the man I need," she said.

He beamed at her. "So what was it made you finally realize? Was it my impressive physique or my devastating intellect?"

She beckoned him into the room, worried someone might overhear.

"Both," she said. "Dennis, I've got a problem."

"Olive oil," he replied as he came in. "It always works. Rub it in hard, then wrap your whole body in a piece of red flannel." Then he saw Don and stopped abruptly.

She closed the door behind him. "I need a friendly carpenter," she said. "It was all my fault. I distracted Don and he split a panel."

Then she sensed that the temperature in the room had somehow dropped and the two men were avoiding looking at each other.

"Yeah, all right," said Dennis. "I heard Tel downstairs singing. He's the best bet. Anything that stops Tel singing is a definite plus for the rest of mankind." His voice was flat.

Amy cast her mind back. Tel had been on Don's side in the pub, hadn't he?

"Please get him," she said.

When Tel came back in with Dennis, he pursed his lips.

"What you done now, Don boy?" he asked.

Amy had a sudden insight into the male world of teasing blame that she had introduced into the situation.

"It wasn't him," she said. "I pushed him. I tripped when I was coming down the ladder." She avoided catching Don's eye.

"Your fault, was it, darling?" said Tel, with immediate, patronizing chauvinism. "You can fall on top of me next time if you'd rather. Well, let's take a look, then. Least said, soonest mended."

"I dunno," he said when they'd shown him the panel. "You know what the Hawk's like. If he walks in, I'll get into all sorts of shit."

"I'll sort him out," said Dennis. "I've got a tip on a horse racing at Doncaster tomorrow. That'll keep him busy for a half hour. I'll tell him the nag's whole life history."

"Yeah? Worth a flutter is it?" said Tel. "Put a bet on for me and let's get on with it."

Dennis left on his mission and they watched as Tel worked some effortless magic with wood glue, drawing the pushed-in section of the panel forward with an improvised grip of canvas, pinned to it with tiny nails, to mate perfectly with the split edge.

"Hang on to that for ten minutes," he said, turning to her. "Don't let go and no one will have a clue. That's your punishment. Just pull the pins out when it's done. Twist them out carefully, with the pliers. There's a bit of wax here. Rub that in. It shouldn't hardly show. Come on, Don, mate. Got something downstairs you can do for me." He looked back at Amy. "Hey, see to it I get my pliers back."

"Thanks, Tel," she said and they both went out and left her.

She sat on the floor, holding the panel together, feeling the currents that had filled the room drain away in Don's wake. *Damn,* she thought. *It's him I want. He's not like anyone I've met before.* It didn't occur to her to question whether that was good or bad. All she suddenly wanted was to be near him again. She had no sense of time passing, of whether it had been ten minutes or an hour, but a moment came when the sun, filtering down through the fringe of the western trees, made her realize finishing time must be near and carefully, she let go of the canvas. The glued edges of the wood didn't stir, so she twisted the pins out and rubbed in the wax as Tel had said. No one would spot it. She climbed back up her ladder to start clearing up. Footsteps came; even before the door opened something rising like bubbles inside her told her it was Don.

He looked at her and then at the panel. "It's done, then," he said.

"Yes, I think so."

"It's knocking-off time."

"If you felt like saying thank you, how about letting me draw you now?"

He crossed the room to the base of her scaffolding with suddenly uncoiled energy and for a horrid moment she thought he might be about to tip her off it. He stared straight up at her but his face had a layer of fine paint dust across it, as concealing as stage makeup, and the goggles gave her no clue as to how he really looked.

"Listen to me, Amy Dale," he said. "I'm no picture, not anymore. I don't want anyone feeling sorry for me and I don't want anyone trying to make me feel better, least of all the sort of woman I might have looked at twice in the street before this happened. Do you understand?"

All she could do was freeze in the face of his controlled anger.

"Now, let me tell you how it's going to be," he said. "If we're going to work in the same room, you're going to be on your best behavior from now on. That means you're going to stop banging on about the way I do or don't look, because it's nothing to do with you. I know you think you're on some sort of mission but that's all in your head, not mine. Got it?"

She could only nod and he turned away but then, to her utter fury, that treacherous part of her emotions that had not yet reached full maturity let her down, and she let out an inadvertent sound that was half sob and half sniff. Even worse, he heard her and turned round. She blew her nose, pretending it was the sawdust.

"I should get a mask," she said, her bloody, bloody voice wobbling treacherously.

"Maybe," he said. He stood looking at her and bit his lip but whatever he was going to say never came out because Dennis came back in at that moment.

"All right, is it?" he said, looking at the panel, but Don had gone by that time, the door swinging shut behind him.

Dennis glanced at Amy and seemed to sum up the situation. "Go and get yourself cleaned up, love. I'll bring you up a cuppa."

When Amy had cleared up her paintbrushes and returned the pliers to Tel, she washed her hands and face under the kitchen tap, then trudged up to her room and stood in the middle of the floor, wishing she had a chair to sit on because the air bed looked so far down she knew she wouldn't get up again if she lay on it. There were footsteps outside and a knock. Dennis stood there with a tray.

"Here you are," he said. "This is just the stuff." He set it carefully down on the box. "Sugar?"

"One, please."

She looked at the tray. It was an ancient slab of dark brown wood with thick curving edges, and because he seemed poised to say something she wasn't sure she wanted to hear, she said, "Where did you find that?"

"Lying around. They were still clearing out the junk when we arrived."

"Anything valuable?"

He gave her a shrewd look. "Not that I was in time for. Pity. That's what I like about working in old houses. You never know."

"I found a bottle of champagne in here," she offered. "Here, look. It's too old to drink, but it's nice."

"Doesn't champagne get better with age?"

"Well, yes, but this one's way past it. It's gone all cloudy."

He was fascinated by it. "Nineteen-oh-two. Look. They did the cork differently, see? It hasn't got that mushroom bit on top, just wire clips to keep it in. Do you want it?"

"Yes, I think I'll hang onto it." The question jarred her a little.

"Was that all there was?"

"There was lots of rubbish. Nothing much worth keeping."

"I hope you're right," he said. "You can't tell with rubbish. I wish I'd seen what was in all the other rooms. The only reason no one touched these two was because there wasn't a way up, not until we opened up the hole through from the main house."

"So how did people get up here in the old days?"

"Stairs from the bottom of the tower. You can get down to the middle floor from here if you're careful, but that's as far as you can go. The bottom stairs have rotted away completely."

"So what else was there?" he asked.

"Only an old box. I think it was one of those vanity cases? You know, the sort of thing women kept their makeup in. It's pretty much ruined."

"Can I have a look?"

It was odd that she felt suddenly reluctant. She drank her tea to delay the moment then took out the little sports bag she had tucked away under her rucksack. The nylon flopped around the box as she unzipped the bag to pull it out. It was an oblong box, perhaps a foot wide and six inches high. She passed it to Dennis, who inspected it carefully. The wood was covered in pinholes; here and there rusted metal pins stuck out of it, attaching blackened shards that were all that remained of some covering material.

"Look at that. That was ivory, that was," said Dennis. "Shame it's come off. An ivory-covered box, eh? Just the thing for my lady's chamber. Oh, and see here." He rubbed a finger over one corner where a triangular piece of black metal was still attached. "That looks like silver.

Must have been quite something once, this box. Anything still inside it?"

"Not really. Open it up. The hinges have fallen apart. The lid just lifts off."

Dennis took off the lid and made a face. Inside the box there was nothing to be seen at all save for a few broken wooden slats with traces of felt still glued to them. "These must have been the partitions," he said. "One little compartment for her bracelets, another one for her nipple rings, you know the sort of thing."

"It's a bit old for nipple rings."

"Speak for yourself. I'll never be too old for nipple rings, myself."

Leaning over, Amy could see the slots cut in the inside edges where the partitions must have fitted, but now they were just dry tinder.

"It was a jewelry box, all right. Not worth anything now."

It didn't matter in the slightest to Amy whether it was worth anything. She went to take it back from Dennis, much more interested in how old it was and who it could have belonged to than in any value it might have had, but he was still looking inside it.

"The bottom's loose," he said. "Hadn't noticed that, had you?"

"No."

He took out the loose partitions, turned the box upside down, and there on his hand was the box's false floor and resting on it, like the product of a conjuring trick, was a thin book, the shape and style of an old school exercise book with a soft gray cover.

"Well, now, what's this, then?" he asked with a harder note to his voice. He put the box down and opened the book. Amy stared at it, wishing she had found it alone. She silently cringed as he roughly handled it; it was too old for that. She knew just how old it was as soon as she saw the page he opened it to, the page that had come loose from its binding. She saw the handwriting and knew immediately who had written it. A terrible desperation filled her. She wanted to get it back from him, to interrupt his interest in it.

"Well, now," he said. "This might be worth a bob or two."

"It's only an old book," she said. "It's handwritten. Not even printed."

He glanced up at her quizzically. "Old? Very old, I'd say. Must have been in that box for a long time. Someone wanted it hidden."

The same thought had occurred to Amy. "Can you read it?" she said, crossing her fingers and hoping he couldn't.

Dennis pored over it, tilting it to catch the light.

"Silly writing," he said. "I'll have to take it away and look at it with my glasses on."

"No, I'll do that. I found it, Dennis."

"Really," he said looking at her. "You found the box. I found the book."

There was an expression on his face she didn't like. "No way, Dennis. I'd have found it soon enough. That's mine."

"Yours?" he said. "It's not yours any more than it's mine."

It was just the chance of easy money to him she realized, but she knew it already meant much more than that to her.

"Come on," she said, "give it to me. Now."

"Don't shout."

"I'm not shouting. Just give it back to me."

"You still upset?"

"You're upsetting me."

"No, come on. This all started with him, didn't it? Really friendly, the man in black. You shouldn't be working with him and you shouldn't be sleeping up here next to him. I told you that before."

"Why shouldn't I, Dennis? How about some straight talk for once?"

"Because he's a fucking lunatic, that's why."

"This has nothing to do with him. It's you. I don't like the way you're behaving and I—"

The door banged open to reveal Don standing in the doorway.

"Something wrong?" he asked. "What's going on?"

"Nothing," said Dennis, handing the book quickly to Amy. He picked up the tray, pushed past Don, and was gone. Don looked after him darkly, then half turned back to Amy.

"Well?" he said.

She was glad he'd interrupted them, but she didn't want anyone else butting in. "Well, nothing. Just a difference of opinion."

Don looked at the book she was holding. "Over that?"

Amy shrugged. "Maybe."

"What is it?" he said, his eyes narrowing as he stared at it.

"Just an old exercise book." Amy wanted to be left alone in the room to look at it. "What did you want?"

"To say sorry."

"Oh, really? I thought you came in because you heard me and Dennis."

"Yeah, that too, but mostly to say sorry." He was looking at her sideways, shielding his scar, but his eyes kept returning to the book in her hand.

"Thank you, I appreciate it." She did, too. He didn't seem the sort to apologize very often.

"You can do it now if you want to."

"Your picture?" She hardly dared believe it.

However much she still wanted to be left alone with the book, this was an offer to be grabbed while it was still on the table and, as she looked at him, her body began to overrule her head. There seemed to be a small thunderstorm building in the room, an electric potential growing in the air between them.

"What shall I do? Shall I sit down?"

His eyes were on the book again.

"No, let's do it in your room. I'd rather. The light's better."

The truth was the light was fading fast, but he bought it.

"Fine," he said, turning away. She slipped the book under her sleeping bag before following him.

In his room, with the door closed, she tried to pose him, but he was sitting at an angle and whenever she glanced toward him he turned his head farther away. Those were the rules she would have to get used to, but it was hard for her. Her eyes were the mouth that fed her soul. She was used to devouring the faces of those around her, searching for the way she would capture them in paint. This was not an option with Don. She wondered what it would be like to have him look at her with both eyes, full face.

"Was that mirror here when you came?" she asked just to get him talking.

It was propped against the wall, the same mirror he had been looking in the day before, when she first arrived. Odd to think that was yesterday. She already felt she had been here for weeks.

"Yes. I use it to look at my hand."

"Why?"

"You know what phantom pains are?"

"I think so. Pains you get in part of you that's missing."

"It fools the brain. I look at my right hand and the mirror makes it look like my left hand. If I look hard enough the pain stops, because there's nothing wrong with my right hand. That's what I mean about self-portraits."

"You said they were lies."

"They must be, mustn't they? Same thing. Nobody else sees you the way you are in the mirror. That's why some people never like their photographs, so why should I like any picture you draw of me? If it's the truth for you it will be a lie to me."

"My paintings tell the truth. You'll see."

She stood at her easel and felt pure excitement swelling in her. The picture was a transaction growing between them, one that gave her more power than she had so far wielded with him.

"Face me," she said, then she touched him for the first time. She did it unconsciously, taking his shoulders with both hands and turning him toward her. A shock ran through her as she felt the warm elastic give of his muscles through his overalls. She froze for a moment, both of them staring at her left hand as a pulse that could have emanated from her or him or both of them ran through her fingers. In that moment, something that had been only potential between them turned into fact.

Letting go, she picked up the table light without taking her eyes off him, moved it to where it lit the side she wanted it to light, and left the scarred cheek in dark shadow. Fog had slid up the Humber and brought a thick yellow twilight with it. *One thing at a time,* she thought. She wanted to move him again, to touch those wide shoulders and then take his head in both hands and tilt it just so. Was that what he wanted, too? She needed him to look at her; whenever her eyes turned away, she could sense his gaze darting to her face, but if she looked back it would slide away again.

She was used to grappling with the gap between her eyes and whatever she was painting, used to the gap between her eyes and the brush she was holding, used to the further gap between the brush and the canvas. It was the uncertainty produced by all those gaps that made every painting an adventure.

Because she wanted to so badly, she took two steps toward him and reached out her hands to lift his head. She was on the same side as the light, the smooth side of his face.

"You have to look at me," she said.

He moved his head just before her hands reached him, so they just brushed his chin. Electric touch. He didn't jump. He should have jumped. She needed to know that he was feeling this, too. "Come on," she said, "I need your full attention."

He did, for all of five seconds, enough for three quick strokes of the pencil, then his chin tilted down again.

"Come on, Don, for Christ's sake *look at me.*"

Four more strokes.

The devil possessed her then. "It's a bit warm in here, isn't it?" she suggested.

"Warm? No, it's halfway to freezing."

"I'm warm," she said. "Now, let me see, what am I going to do about it?"

She was wearing a black silk shirt that had once been glamorous but now, like most of Amy's clothes, bore the marks of a hard life. She undid the top three buttons.

"That's better," she said. "Ah, that's just right. Keep looking. There, you can do it when you try."

She rotated her shoulders a little, feeling the silk sliding on the tips of her nipples and the air, cold and damp with the fog, fingering its way around her breasts. It was having the right effect. Don was certainly looking at her now. The artist in her went on turning his face into a set of planes and proportions, into lines and highlights and shadows, while the woman in her felt a warm and pulsating desire pushing sensible considerations of risk farther and farther toward the fringes of her mind. Her pencil raced around the page, choosing, modifying, defining, getting his face just as she wanted it. She drew as fast as she could, but it wasn't long before his self-consciousness began to reassert itself and she lost the pose she needed as he let his face dip again.

It was all she could do not to scream at him. Another thirty seconds and she would have been there, with enough in her sketch pad to work from. She restrained herself. Instead, she fanned herself with her sketch pad and said, "Phew, it really is hot, isn't it?" as she undid the last two buttons and let the silk shirt slip off onto the floor.

She stood in front of Don wearing only a pair of jeans, as if that was the most normal thing in the world.

"Good," she said. "Now I seem to finally have your undivided attention. Just hold it there."

The light was off to one side between them and she moved backward and forward as she worked, darting into the glow of it to check an angle, then out into the darkness before he could respond. There was no need for worry. Don sat like a statue, staring at her with an expression of wonder on his face, following her every movement as the light splashed around the curving, moving contours of her body.

When she knew that there was enough in her sketch pad, she instantly knew it wasn't a sketch that she wanted but a full portrait. It was time to turn to the palette, to find the human colors to clothe that framework. She closed the sketch pad with a snap, which brought him back from somewhere so that he frowned and seemed to move just a tiny distance farther away from her.

"Don't move," she said, reaching for her paint tubes and squeezing them onto her palette.

She looked hard at him. *Black and white,* she thought. *Those are the dominants. His skin is pale and his hair is so black, shiny black as oiled coal.* Whether his head dropped or not, the power of her position was too much. She had gone too far to stop now—could simply not imagine the anticlimax of dressing again. She put down the palette, undid the tight button of her jeans, zipped them open unnecessarily slowly, and slid them down over her hips, all the way to the floor with a controlled, sensuous wriggle, then she kicked them out of the way and started to mix the paint again.

"What are you doing this for?" he asked in a husky voice.

"For me," she said, "and for you. I'm bloody cold, though," and that was when he shook his head as if to clear it, got to his feet, and, as she dropped the palette on the floor, put his hands out to her. He didn't put them round her. Instead he stood like one amazed in front of her, feeling her neck and her shoulders with his good right hand, then slowly tracing his fingers down to her breasts and running his hand around and down her back. As his hand reached her bottom and slipped between the elastic of her panties and her skin, she stepped toward him, staring into his eyes, seeing those eyes so full of lust that they gave nothing else away. When, moments later, she was on top of him on the bed, straddling him and pumping with a desperate urgency as if she could save something by emptying him into her, only then did she see a man return into those eyes. As she was gazing at him, he reached down to the plug on the wall and turned out the light so that they lay together in the masking gloom of evening.

When it was time to talk, she looked down at the mirror leaning against the wall next to them. "That's an antique," she said. "It's quite ancient, really."

"Quite bloody battered, anyway," he said. "A mirror's a mirror. It's got a frame. It reflects. That's all it has to do. Like my mother said, you are what you are and the rest is gravy."

"What does that mean?"

He shrugged. "She used to say if you had to ask, it wasn't time for you to know. You got something going with Dennis?"

She hoped it was a joke, but his voice was sharp and it startled her.

"He's a nice old bloke. Funny."

Don shrugged. "I wouldn't say that. Don't trust him and don't listen to him."

She sat up but he traced his fingers down her spine and seemed to regret the harshness of his words.

He looked around the room. "When I arrived, this room was full of crap. They'd thrown all kinds of stuff in here over the years. It was worse than yours."

"Why didn't you take mine?"

He pointed with his good right hand at the end wall where there was a small square window. "Light on two sides," he said. "I liked that. It was worth the effort."

Amy wondered if he had wanted to put himself as far away as possible from the rest of them. "When was that?" she said.

"Eight months ago. When the job started." He seemed to read her mind. "Before ... before this happened. I've been off a lot lately."

"They kept your room for you."

"Nobody else wanted it. Too many spiders. Anyway, Mr. Parrish was looking after my interests."

"He seems a nice man."

"Yes? You'd know, would you?"

Whoops, she thought. *Careful.*

"I only got the job because of him. My mother was his secretary for a long time, you see. He's pushed me along all the way. You know, school, college and that. That's how I know about this place. She was the one who typed up the journal for him."

"Amelia's journal?"

He nodded.

It struck her that there had been a finality about the way he described his mother. "Is she dead?"

"Ellen? No, why?"

"Just the way you were talking."

"No, she's alive and kicking and still smoking forty a day."

"But she's not working for Parrish anymore?"

"That was back then. She treads a hard road, does my mother."

"What does she do?"

"Runs a shelter." Something had gone out of his voice warning her not to go further down this road.

"She lives in Hull?"

"Mum? Yes. She came up from London before I was born."

Lying there against him, skin to skin, she suppressed an urge to nuzzle her head down into his neck, knowing it would be too intimate for the moment. *How odd,* she thought. *I've just screwed a man I met yesterday and there's this weird etiquette about the way we have to lie here. I don't know any parts of him that I can snuggle up to.* For a moment, the fog parted and a last ray of the setting sun reached through the window in the western wall to paint them both gold.

"Anyway, the point is she loved Amelia's book. She used to read me bits when she was typing in the evenings."

She ran her fingers across his chest. It was smooth. "So you've known about Amelia for ages."

"Simply ages, darling." Was he mimicking her? Did she sound posh to him? Amy didn't like sounding posh.

"Cut that out," she said sharply and took her hand away.

"Look, when Parrish first hired me, it wasn't as a builder, right? I was going to do the historical stuff with him. I brushed up on the journal and all that. Then I ... then I got hurt and I blew the chance. This was all there was to do when I got back here. He'd had to do the research himself. So what I want to know is, what have you found? If it's anything to do with the history of the house, you'd better give it to me."

They all bloody wanted it. "Surely I should give anything I find to Parrish, not you."

"I know my stuff. I can tell you if it matters or not."

"I haven't had a chance to look, but I really don't think it's anything at all."

"Dennis doesn't seem to agree with you."

"Dennis thought he could make some money out of it, that's all."

"That's what he's good at." Don's voice hardened. "In this house, Amy, you can't be on both sides, right?"

Even though she was still pressed close against him, even though the smallest of movements would have brought him into her again, she felt the distance between them widen dizzyingly.

"Why is that?" she said. "I don't understand."

"You don't need to. It's him or me, that's all. You can't believe in both of us. You have to choose."

"Why?"

"I'm not going to tell you. Not now. If I do, it'll all be about facts and who did what when. It'll be about who's got the best story. You make up your mind on who we are, not what we say. Can't you see what he's like? He's seen that book you found and he wants it. Doesn't that give you a clue? If you trust me, show it to me. If not, keep it to yourself. If that's the way you want it, so be it."

Because that wasn't the way she wanted it, because she still thought she could find a way of accommodating the two men into different parts of her single universe, she got out of Don's bed, peered outside to check the coast was clear, and went to fetch the book. Getting into bed again, adding a new layer to their intimacy, Amy ran her fingers over the pale gray cover. Its texture was somewhere between thick paper and cloth, stitched along the spine to the papers inside with two loops of dark thread.

He took it from her and opened it, and she was pleased to see the care he took. "It's her, isn't it?" he said. "It's Amelia." She could hear the excitement in his voice and she thought this might have the power to bring them even closer. "Is it more of the journal? Can you read it?"

The first page began with a paragraph in thin strokes of faded ink, written in the writing she already felt she knew well.

"Read it aloud, will you?" he said, and she did, hesitating over the harder parts, straining to make out the faint lettering.

" 'THIS IS THE DAYBOOK OF AMELIA DAHL, COMMENCED IN THE YEAR OF *our Lord sixteen hundred and sixty-two and intended for her eyes only so that she entreats any other person who may come upon it to refrain from reading any further than these first words.' "*

She could have no more obeyed that ancient injunction than she could cease to breathe. "What's a daybook?" she said, but Don just shook his head. Underneath that first paragraph there was a space, then in smaller, more cramped writing, harder to read even than the dusty microfilm image from the library, the story began.

" *'January the First in the year of our Lord 1662, this being the second year of the reign of our King Charles who is restored to us. In this daybook, I will write my words in rough so that I may later write again those that are worthy of my husband's perusal in that excellent journal book which he has given me for that purpose. I must remember always his solemn instruction to choose my words carefully because once chosen, they remain upon the page until time erases them. It is a good time, being the start of our new life here in our new house at Paull Holme. The air here is clear and fine and there is no more smell of burning oil-cake. That is indeed a special joy.' "*

"It's what she really thought," Don said. "That's what it is. The journal's the prettied-up version, the one she wrote for her husband. This is the rough copy, the way she wrote it first. This is the real thing."

Amy read on as Amelia covered the same familiar ground that she had already read in the journal, the familiar Norwegian place-name, the fertility of Holderness, and the fact that the local people had more to think about than the recent civil war. Then came an unfamiliar passage:

" *'I think we came it too high in Hull once it were known General Monk would cast his lot for the return of the King. My dear husband is one to settle old scores when the chance may arise and he perhaps was too fast to cry down those who had hounded him for a King's man in the darker days. Better then to be here in the quieter land beyond the hue and cry where we can ...' "*

The page ended there.

"She cut some of that out when she wrote it in the other journal, didn't she? She thought better of letting her husband read that bit," Amy said.

"He wouldn't have liked it."

Don understood, she thought. Don was as excited as she was. They could share in this.

The bottom of the book had balled out into a swollen callus of paper. Amy tried to separate the first page so as to turn it over, but she could feel the paper start to come to pieces as soon as she applied any pressure at all.

"We need a knife," she said. "Something with a really thin blade to separate them."

"There's one in the bag."

"Will we damage it?"

"Not if we're very, very careful."

So, sealing their conspiracy, Don took the book from her, slipped the blade of the table knife carefully into the wad of paper, and began to separate the pages that would tell them what had really happened at Paull Holme Manor.

NINE

Monday, January 13th, 1662

SO HERE I WAS, LURCHING ALONG MOST UNCOMFORTABLY ON THIS donkey. The sores I had collected on the way to the city had matured nicely and it was all I could do to stop myself from crying out at each stumbling step the damned beast took.

Before I return to the main point, to Dahl's new house and the exquisite woman who lived in it, I should like to talk about God for a short while. In Amsterdam, I have known a lot of people who thoroughly believed in God with every fiber of their being and it was the oddballs who always interested me most. I have known Socinianites and Anabaptists and Jews and Mennonites of both the ordinary and the Waterland variety and even Catholics—in fact, I rather think I was married to a Catholic, though she preferred to hide that fact. It was better not to dwell on such things. Amsterdam was a tolerant city but it had changed sides abruptly thirty years ago and there were still some questions it was better not to ask.

I command the best part of a thousand guilders for a full-length portrait. Even if my customers know nothing about painting, they know which painter's name creates the right impression. Lately, the way I paint has driven that sort of customer away. They haven't the stomach for it. They haven't the patience and they don't understand what I do with the paint. Smooth, glistening garbage, that's what they want. Simple paint that a simpleton can understand. Painting shouldn't be about money. I don't give a toss for that sort of client. They're not who matter.

Politics have gone against me, too. For a long time, I was aligned with the right crowd. My patrons were Mennonites. The balance of power had tilted in their favor, which was good for business for a while, but, alas, only for a while.

Anyway, Mennonites, Anabaptists, and the rest of them still give me cause for laughter. I relish the way they all think that they own the only version of the truth and am constantly intrigued by the violent way they squabble over the tiniest differing details of their variety of God, save for the Jews, who go their own way with a becoming degree of humble serenity. What they all have in common is that they believe their God is looking after them with a benevolent twinkle in His eye, excepting again the Jews, who believe deep down that He's just as likely to be coming for them with an ax.

"Ubi deus, ibi pax" as the saying has it, "where there is God there is peace." It seems to me truer to say that where there are gods there is usually war.

We stopped for a while on the way back from the city while Marvell fiddled with something supposedly stuck in his horse's hoof, and I asked him about his God. He looked at me and said, "I am a Member of Parliament. My God is the same as the God of those who elect me," which struck me as about as honest an answer as any I have heard. Almost as cynical as well.

When he had stopped pretending to remove the nonexistent stone, he shuffled around to the matter that was clearly on his mind.

"After you have painted Dahl," he said, "I have it in mind to set you a further commission, as a test, you understand."

Arrogant sod. "What test?"

"A test to see which of our two arts can soar higher. It is a commission that will be paid in coin, not in mitigation of debts incurred."

"I thought language precluded us from comparing our skills."

"We will each perform our task in another language."

I laughed until my saddle sores hurt. "You'll write a poem in Dutch? Not so hard, perhaps. How am I meant to paint a picture in English?"

"Not in English. In the language of another country, the country the Dahls come from."

"I don't understand."

"I think you may be a jobbing painter," he said. "You know how your Dutch faces look, but can you describe a face in a different tongue? Not Dahl. Whatever remains in Dahl's face, any fineness of feature, has sadly been chased away, if ever it existed, by years of hard living and salt spray."

My God, I thought, *he has read my mind. Not just that, he wants me to do what I myself want to do more than anything. He wants me to paint Amelia for his contest.*

"Jobbing painter?" I said. "*You* dare to call *me* a jobbing painter, you umber Humber jobbing poet?"

"I am no jobbing poet," he said harshly. "I studied under John Milton's tutelage. If you know of Donne, you will know of Milton."

I shrugged. I wasn't going to show him I was impressed. I feigned misunderstanding. "Fine. I'll take your challenge. You think yourself fine-featured, I suppose. All right. I'll paint you, and my painting will leave your doggerel crawling in its wake." I knew that wasn't what he had intended at all.

Marvell looked a little startled. He made as if to reply, and then stopped himself. "Me? Yes, good. You paint me if you want. We will see how that comes out." He considered, or rather he adopted the sort of expression that was meant to tell me he was considering. "But per-haps that's not such a true test. Is one face enough, I wonder? Two might be better. Paint her as well. Dahl's wife. Let us see how well you can portray Amelia."

Oh, yes, I thought. *Perfect.*

I took up his earlier point to give me time to reflect. "You can help me paint Dahl," I said, "or at least in the way he would wish to be painted. What sort of man is he?"

"Oh, I know your game, painter," he said. "You want to know what will flatter him. I am not sure I should tell you that."

"Listen, arsehole," I said, and he jumped. "I don't give a pound of dogshit for flattery. I'm asking you who he is, that's all. I don't want to leave it to him. I'll have him posturing in front of me in no time pretending to be an admiral, and if I let him decide the way he wants to look, he'll never like it. Nobody lives up to their unfettered imagination. In Amsterdam, it is true, I have some advantage. I already know the people I paint. Every subject is different. *I* decide what they wear and how they stand and they take it or they leave it. I merely require information, so stop trying to be clever and give it to me."

I wondered if he would bother to answer, but he did.

"I like Dahl," he said in the end, "but he is a mystery. We've all had to take sides for the past twenty years. We had no choice, but he did. He arrived here when any prudent and commercial man would have thrown in his lot with Cromwell's Parliamentarians, and he did nothing of the sort. Instead he took up a fight that was not his, to support a king who was in exile. He took messages abroad for the king at some risk to himself. You might say that in the last few years that was less of a risk, with Cromwell dead—you do know about Cromwell? The man who had our king killed?"

"Of course I do, we're not entirely ignorant in Amsterdam."

His smirk infuriated me.

"With Cromwell dead and the whole republic falling to pieces, it wasn't terribly difficult to be a king's man, but even in spite of that he pushed his luck."

"So he believes in a natural order of affairs, ordained by God? He thinks that kings rule by divine right?"

"Yes, perhaps he does. Where he comes from, from the land of glaciers and fjords, they have a strange and somber relationship with their god."

"And what is he most these days, a sailor or a trader?"

"He is a good sailor but he's a better trader. Here they force him to be a sailor. The Guild does not accept alien merchants in their midst. That is why he sticks in their gizzards. He made his fortune in the East, I have heard. He met his wife out there in Batavia."

"In Batavia? Our Dutch colony?"

"Yes, I should caution you, perhaps. He affects not to understand you but I think he knows at least some words of your language."

"And the wife?"

"What do you mean, 'and the wife'?"

"Where is she from? You said they come from the same place but there is a difference, by the look of her."

"Her father was English, I believe. Her mother was from Stavanger, across the German Ocean, near to his own town, but that was pure chance. They met, as I understand it, on his ship that brought her back from Batavia, where she had been stranded by misadventure."

"Does *she* speak my language, then?"

"No. She was there but a short time and very ill throughout." He looked at me. "Her portrait would be a fine thing, were it done with skill."

I tripled the price I would ask for the portrait he intended to commission. This man wanted Amelia's image for himself and he wanted it badly. I think he realized he'd given the game away because he stopped and said, "Facts pay for facts. What of you?"

"What about me?"

"How have you come to this? Will you be missed in Amsterdam?"

"No," I said, "not if my message gets through," though I supposed Hennie and Titus would indeed be worrying. It was so entirely out of character for me to go anywhere at all that they would probably think me dead in the first instance, which was not without some advantages, though it grieved me to think of them brought to sorrow. All the more joy for them, however, when the message arrived, declaring my safety.

"Where do you live?"

As he clearly knew the city, I could not bear to tell him the recent truth. I opted for an older version of the facts.

"In the Breestraat."

"Those are fine houses." His questioning tone said he did not believe me, but it had been true at one time, and not so very long ago, either.

"And do you live by your painting?"

"I have, and by my teaching."

"So, if you don't mind my inquiring, what has happened to you that you wind up a drunk and filthy stowaway in stinking clothing?"

"Painting is not an activity for good clothes. I clean my brushes on my clothes. You came upon me in my working clothes."

"Were you working when you came on board the ship?"

"I had been."

"If drinking is working then you had been. What are you running away from? From failure perhaps?"

Failure? FAILURE? Who the hell did he think he was talking to? Fashion may have switched to sillier, smoother painters, but who gives a standing fuck for fashion. In a fairer world, I would have walked where Rubens walked. I would have sported the golden chains of royal patronage. I would have had acolytes and courtesans. Emissaries from foreign thrones would have sought me out in ever-increasing quantities. And do you know why they stopped? I told you. Because I don't paint the way everyone else paints. Failure? Bastard. I'm so far ahead of the game that there is simply no way of judging where I stand.

"I paint like no one else has ever painted before," I said stiffly. "I understand things no other painter understands. The others think that getting the paint on smoothly is all that matters. I know better. I know that the eye needs rough paint, rough surfaces to conjure depth out of flat canvas. I paint perfection, then they light it too brightly, peer at it too damn closely, and ask for their money back. They don't listen. Idiots."

"You don't like to please your customers, then," he said faintly, and I could see him wondering whether this commission was such a good idea.

"Only those who aren't worth pleasing," I said.

"Perhaps it's time we went on our way," he said, swinging up into the saddle of his horse with appalling ease. I put my foot in the donkey's stirrup but it contrived to lurch off, forcing me to fall flat on my back. He didn't notice until it caught up with him all by itself. Bloody donkeys. Bloody Members of Parliament. Bloody everything.

Oh, yes, God. What I really want to know is, where do I stand with Him? Is it reasonable to have at the back of my mind, as someone who doesn't believe in any normal idea of God, a small and disconcerting suspicion that He might nevertheless be taking a keen interest in this unbeliever's doings, despite not existing? I only ask the question because of all the ships I might have stumbled on board that night in Amsterdam, that was the one that was destined to change my life, or at the least to bring it to some crisis.

I have a favorite subject, a patient sitter, the only one who puts up with the way I paint because he knows me inside out as I know him. Stumbling onto Dahl's ship was to change the way I paint that sitter forever.

I was only fourteen when I realized I was going to become the greatest painter in the world. I knew from that moment on that I should not do what everyone else said. I should not tread the well-worn path to Italy where all the painters go to learn from the supposed glories hanging on Italian walls. Above all I learnt all by myself that I should not paint quickly. Those who commission portraits want you to hurry up and get on with it. They want the evidence that they really are as gorgeous as they think, and anyone highborn enough to pay for the product is likely to have the stamina of an inbred bullfinch. I've seen other painters practice such art, fanning their bloody sitters and bringing them sherbets and all sorts of nonsense—letting them stand up while they plump up the cushions so when they sit down the posture's gone and you have to spend five minutes tugging them back into the right position. Enquiring after their well-being as if that was what mattered and not the picture, as if their health could in some way be imperiled by the backbreaking task of keeping still. The upshot of it all is that the painter finds himself painting in a huge hurry to keep the sitter sweet and, of course, you lose the potential. It's obvious, isn't it?

To tell the truth, I have only ever had that one sitter who understood the need to sit completely still, the utter importance of a consistent posture, and the ability to wear just the right expression and to keep it in place. That sitter is me. That's why any portrait painter worth his salt paints himself as often as he can. I don't complain if it takes thirty hours painting to get the thing right. I don't come round behind the easel at the end of every session and say, "My goodness, you *have* made my nose look big" or "I'm sure my eyes are larger than that."

I know I've got a big nose. I've stared at it for years.

As a result of all that happened at Paull Holme, I see a different man when I look in the mirror now.

———

DAHL RETURNED THAT NIGHT AND THE WHOLE HOUSE SEEMED TO quail before him because he arrived in the blackest of moods from his business, swathed in a dark cloak. Marvell whispered to me that he looked like a bat come from Hull, then had to explain the joke at length because it apparently derives from some English expression concerning hell which was unfamiliar to me. I found a bottle of Genever that no one appeared to want in a cupboard and took it off to show it my room, which was very far from luxurious. The following day, when my head was thick from the assailing fumes of damp plaster on the walls, a servant was sent to bring me to the master and I found Dahl standing with Marvell on the new terrace in front of the house.

"I have got to leave shortly," said Marvell. "You have slept far too long. Mr. Dahl wishes to get started with the picture while I'm here to translate. When can you start?"

I told him what I needed to prepare the panel for paint, rabbit glue and all that, and I told him I would be ready on the morning following the next day. We discussed where the picture should be painted, which gave me an excuse to go all through that house of theirs until we found a large empty room on the first floor, with a soft light from the eastern courtyard that had a touch of north in it. This suited me perfectly.

I stewed up rabbit skins for the size and made a good attempt at gesso during the day. The day after that I carefully prepared the panels. They were nowhere near the standard I would have expected in Amsterdam, but then in Amsterdam, I wouldn't have been using wood and I wouldn't have been preparing it myself. The extraordinary and galling thing about this time was that my food was brought to me in the room where I was working.

Nobody would call me a snob. I am not highborn. My father was a miller, as I said. I am happiest with people who say exactly what they think and believe me, the poor find that much easier than the rich. However, on the rare occasions when I have painted a portrait in someone else's home, the only good thing about being away from my own studio, which is something I utterly hate, is that I am very well fed. I do not leave my studio lightly. At least, I did not when I lived on Breestraat. I could probably be persuaded more easily these days if anyone tried. In the past, I would only stir from my house for the most important sitters, or those to whom I owed a great deal of money and, as an honored guest of the household, I am accustomed to sharing their table. Mealtimes were always what made these inconvenient excursions worthwhile.

To be brought a hunk of bread, a piece of very dry cheese, and a small pitcher of the most disgusting liquid imaginable was not at all what I regard as decent treatment.

That afternoon, without even another bottle of Genever to keep me company, I gazed mournfully out of the window until the light was gone. The river could have made an etching of sorts except that nobody had thought to build anything of interest to attract the eye along its banks. There was barely a tree to be seen, or a house or a barn to punctuate the wandering horizontals. I realized I was missing my Hennie, and my Saskia before her.

In Amsterdam, I never notice the night sky. I use the daylight as ferociously as I can because there is no artificial light, however pure the oil, however costly the candle, which ever approaches the true color that the sun gives. For years, I have woken at dawn, I have slept at dusk, and in the winter I catch up on the sleep I lose in the summer. You may say you have heard I have been a night bird, too, but in those days, and even now on the odd recent occasions when desperation has driven me to some drinking den in the dark hours, I cannot say I have been aware of the stars because the air in the narrow Amsterdam streets is always thick with a foggy smoke. On this night, the west wind cleaned up the air, rolling the clouds before it out to sea and, as they disappeared, first one, then two, three, and four bright pricks of light speared out of the sky. Of course, I knew what stars were, but that is like saying a man can know what love is without experiencing it. Before the sky was fully dark, it was studded with stars and then, my God, when it did reach pitch-dark, before the moon rose, I was astonished at the vast sparkling carpet that spread across the sky.

Until that moment, I had always thought that the truest test of an artist's skill was perhaps that fine line Apelles left as his calling card when he visited Protogenes and the still finer line Protogenes then painted within it. That night I understood the reason no artist has dared to paint a truly starry sky, because it is truly the greatest test of all. The blackest black that I can mix on my palette is equally as black as the black you achieve by closing your eyes in the deepest cellar of the house. The problem lies at the other end of the scale. The brightest, whitest white, even with silver powdered into it, goes not one tiny step of the way toward the brilliance of a star. Even if it did, where would that leave you? You could not paint the dark sky first and then expect the tiniest dot of this bright whiteness to succeed in overpowering the background on which you planted it. You would have to paint the entire canvas with blazing white and then surround the million stars with perfectly controlled dark sky, which would drive any painter there has ever been to utter madness.

It was impossible.

As I pondered the problem, something even more astonishing happened. With a brilliant light so large and fast that the world seemed split by the noise it should have made, a shooting star slashed down from left to right, leaving a trail of whirling, dying sparks in its wake, and in its light I saw someone moving below on the fringes of the terrace. I knew it at once to be her. I had not seen her all day although I had heard her voice from time to time in the house. I knew it was her because in the faint light of the lamps glowing from the windows, I could see the grace with which this figure moved. It could be no other. She wore pale clothes, a long gown, and she was dancing by herself in the dark. She turned and turned, arms up high and then down low, her face flashing the palest oval of light each time it faced the house, her body swaying one way and then the other to inaudible music that might have come down from the stars solely for her ears.

It lasted only a short time, this entirely secret dance, then a door opened somewhere below me, a voice called, and she hurried in.

TEN

THE NEXT MORNING, I BEGAN THE PORTRAIT OF DAHL. HE SAT BEFORE me, as unwilling a model as any I have ever had, as if I were forcing him to miss a tide.

"Sit like this," I said and, not wanting to give away the fact that I knew he might understand my language, I twisted him into shape with my hands until he made a moderately tolerable subject.

"Chin up, head a little more straight. Hands clasped so."

I have to admit I set out to make this picture with the minimum of effort necessary. Nothing in it moved me, not even the payment due. It constituted more of a ransom than a payment, as it was quite clear he would have to ship me back home eventually if only to ease the expense on his household. There was no pleasure to be found in my palette, which was laden with a gritty, unappealing burden of paint. Wrestling it onto canvas would have been hard enough, but the "give" of canvas helps to break down any lumps you don't want. You can pummel and push them into submission. It was quite clear to me that the strange mixture of pigment available from the narrow range on sale in Hull was extremely unlikely to stand the test of time.

To tell the truth, such rude supplies concerned me little. It had to do a job, this picture, that was all; and for once, I was prepared to compromise. *I* would make up for the shortcomings of the paint. It had to look good enough to pass the test of Dahl's approval so, quite cynically, I attended to certain points in the presentation of my subject that would be likely to please him. The jaw became a shade more jutting, the jowl was diminished, the hair receded a little bit less. I turned the clock back a few years for him, seeing that perhaps the difference in age between him and his extraordinary wife might be something to which he was a little sensitive. I judged that difference to be perhaps fifteen years. That made him, shall we say, the middle point between her and me. Nobody would ever judge me by *this* picture. I wasn't going to sign the end product if I could help it unless he made me. If he *did* make me, then I would use the name I had given him. There was little likelihood that it would ever damage my reputation. Any passing connoisseur could peer at that signature for a very great deal of time and still have no idea who had painted it. The paint was likely to turn sludge-brown and peel off inside a year and, frankly, I didn't really give a toss.

To pass the time, I decided to talk to him and I watched carefully to see how much Dutch he really knew.

"It's a shame you don't understand my language," I said, "because I would like to have told you how hard I find the arrangements here."

I marked the twitch of his eyebrow.

"You take me for a street vagrant but I am highly respected—one of the most sought-out portrait painters in Holland. You sit there as if I were the servant and you were the master, but at home I have always had servants to command." Almost always, anyway.

I saw his brow furrow. He wasn't following this. I picked more simple words and I spoke in a flat voice as if to myself. "Do you know? I have never in my life been fed so badly. Your food is an insult."

He swallowed. Bull's-eye. I went on talking as if ruminating to myself. "Now I do admit that lately things at home have been more than a little awkward and a bankrupt has to accept certain compromises in his life. In my case, however, one must understand that being made bankrupt was not in any way a reflection on the quality of my art. I paint now better than I ever did before but not in the way they like, you see."

How true that was. My *Julius Civilis* for the Town Hall is magnificent. It is only the malicious pygmies of the city council who do not see that. They want me to return their paltry fee. How am I going to do that? I can't have it back. It won't even fit through the door of my damned studio now. Hennie thinks I should cut out the middle part to sell and chuck away the rest. God's unspilt blood. Am I reduced to that? Bloody hell.

All at once I was contemplating the reality of my own ruin. Nothing to do with money. What I found myself facing for the very first time was the prospect of the end of my art. If fickle fashion had passed me by, whom would I paint for? For myself? To paint in a vacuum, in a world of one, was a frightening prospect. Would my brush still want to move?

I came back to myself with a start. At some point I had completely forgotten he was there. He sat transfixed in his chair, with the expression he might wear if he were facing all the pirates of Dunkerque.

"Sorry," I said and then in English because I had heard Marvell say it several times in Hull and its meaning had been quite clear, "Dooscuze me."

I went back to work in silence and despite the terrible paints, the odd unbalanced brushes, and the forgotten feeling of wood beneath them instead of canvas, something unexpected happened. In recent years I have discovered the wonderful things that happen when you build up the paint, layer upon layer so that the light careers off its slopes and facets. It takes me days to do that normally, days of experimentation and subtle addition until finally you get to a picture you could pick up by the nose. This horrible, lumpy stuff I had mixed up, using rancid linseed oil and a whole range of substances whose identity I could only guess at, went onto the wood like plaster on a wall. I was molding it, not painting it. By the end of that first day, a blind man could have told me what it was a picture of just by feeling it.

Rather magnificent, in its own peculiar way.

I painted on until Dahl could clearly stand it no more. He got up out of the chair with a desperate look on his face and mimed eating. I think he wanted a piss but couldn't bring himself to perform that particular mime. He motioned for me to sit in the chair he had just vacated. A while later, long enough for a smoke but not long enough for a screw, as Lievens used to say, a servingwoman pushed the door open with her ample bottom and set a large square tray on the table. Cold ham, a capon's leg, pickles, and a jug of wine to wash it down. Dahl's Dutch didn't go very far, but just far enough. Life was looking up.

We painted all the rest of that short day until the light faded and I put the brush down for the last time, wiping it on my smock, which I realized from the expression on Dahl's face was in fact *his* smock, after all. He got up and came to my side to look at the picture, staring hard at it while I stared at his face.

"Not finished," I said slowly in Dutch. "More time. Tomorrow and tomorrow."

He nodded.

Got you, I thought.

Then he went to the door and called "Amelia, Amelia."

My memory of her was two days old, not counting the magical ghost dancing in the meteor's flash. In those two days I had painted her picture in my mind in a score of different ways, magnificently as Diana or Minerva, sensually as Danaë or as Bathsheba, even as Flora, though I paid for that thought with a terrible pang of guilty grief, because my Saskia had been my Flora and always would be.

Those mind paintings were nothing against the reality of the woman who came in through the door, smiling at her husband and glancing for the briefest moment at me. Simply by walking into that room, she drove the Furies back off the lawn. I knew I would paint her as herself and that painting would indeed, as Marvell suspected, challenge me to find new ways of expressing the way the flesh can make a face distinct. I didn't care who paid for the painting and I didn't care who saw it apart from her and me.

She went to the easel. I moved aside to give her space and they stood side by side staring at it, she with the tip of one delightful finger to her parted lips. I saw something there I had to catch so I went quickly to my paint, took the thinnest brush and, because I had no other surface on which to paint, I drew them in outline on the plaster of the wall. My brush moved as fast as I could make it, knowing this in- tent, natural, and sensuous pose would last only seconds. I used an ocherish brown simply because it was the nearest color on the palette and, though I say it myself, I captured them magnificently.

Well, I should say I captured her, because she was standing in front of him and all you could really see of him was his head peering past her. I roughed in the shape of the canvas and sketched him in outline, which was all he deserved.

Only when they stopped looking at the canvas did they notice what I was doing. Dahl said something angry when he saw what had happened to his wall. Amelia stopped him with a hand on his arm and a word in his ear and then a comment that sounded wondering, and I suppose he was suddenly able to see it for what it was: a finished thing in itself and of itself. I dabbed yellow on the brush and, to show off, enclosed the picture in four perfectly squared lines. Amelia laughed and, to hear that laugh again, I took more paint and turned my crude frame into something infinitely more ornate with folds and moldings and curlicues, all of brown and yellow paint. I think, as happens so often, my sense of time dissolved into the task because when I finished it, I turned to find them still standing there, watching, but shifting slightly from foot to foot.

Amelia took the final rays of sunlight with her when they left so that I wondered how I would survive the evening without her or the sun, but I did not wonder for long because the plump servant came back carrying a set of clothes and indicated that I was to put them on. She pointed downstairs and then appeared to want to assist me in the matter of dressing. She was a substantial and curvaceous piece of womanhood, not at all unlike Hennie in recent years in her general build. She was quite clearly game for whatever should ensue as she made great play of holding the clothes up against me and running her hot hands all over my chest and thighs on pretext of trying them for a fit.

At any other time in the last fifteen years, I would have had her skirts over her head in a flash and even now, half of me wanted to do that. The game of cushioned thumping was but a buckle of the knees away. The other half of me had a different idea, however, a new idea, obtained through the eyes, of what it was that fired the prick's enthusiasm. What I suddenly wanted for the first time ever was bone wrapped thinly in flesh. *Jehovah*, I thought, *I had better rid this from my system or there will be no woman in Amsterdam I shall ever want again.*

I dismissed her and she left, scolding me incomprehensibly, and then I wished I hadn't because the breeches she had brought failed to meet around my waist by half a hand-span. In consequence, I had to tie them with a kerchief and cover the dangerous gap by letting the shirttails hang loose over the breeches. With a sort of coat that bit me under the armpits and caused an unseasonable sweat in seconds, I trod cautiously down the stairs wondering if I were the butt of a practical joke. If so, the company below were too polite to draw any attention to it, although Dahl did look me up and down in a startled way as I made my entrance.

There were three people in the room. The first one on whom I fixed my eyes was Amelia. She wore a gown of the most superb blue, a lapis blue, toned down by just the slightest greening touch of yellow. Its greatest marvel was that where it hung in folds, the shadow thickened and purpled it in the most enthralling way. Her hair was long and un-contained and set a backdrop to the sheer and sculpted lines of those marvelous cheeks. Dahl hovered next to her, furtively scanning the room as though checking for loose rigging or misaligned sails. The other, inevitably, was Marvell.

Dahl cleared his throat and said something to Marvell, in which I caught the word "limner." I had heard him use this word before, always, it seemed, in connection with me.

"Ah yes," said Marvell, dragging his attention away. "Master van Rijn, how gratifying that you are able to join us."

"Will you thank my hosts," I said. "Also for the loan of this cloth-ing which, I fear, I am of the wrong proportions to do full justice to."

"Yes, of course," said Marvell, and did nothing of the sort. "Now, they have asked me to tell you that they are most impressed by the por-trait."

"How can they be? It is not finished."

"They are people of discernment and it is already clearly on the way to excellence," Marvell said smoothly. "So much so in fact that Captain Dahl is most happy that you should undertake the portrait of his wife as a companion piece on terms that you and I may now dis-cuss."

I pretended to study Amelia as if for the first time with my eye-brows raised, thinking furiously. Clearly, the competition was to remain a secret.

"There would be matters to be arranged," I said.

"Captain Dahl has anticipated that," said Marvell. "He believes a price of fifteen pounds would be possible for a work of the highest quality."

"That was not what I meant," I said. "Mistress Dahl's skin color requires an altogether more extensive palette. Impossible with the materials I have here. We must send away for them."

"I don't need to send away for special ink when I write poems," he said sarcastically.

"The words would sound the same," I said neutrally.

"I have made some enquiries already," he said. "There is a merchant in York, I believe. York is not too far to travel."

Oh, please, I thought. *Not by donkey.* He read my mind. "The carrier goes there in three days. We can ride with him."

"How much is fifteen pounds in Dutch money?" I said.

"One hundred and fifty guilders."

"Absurd. In Amsterdam, my customers line up to pay six times that."

"But you are not in Amsterdam and your customers here are not lining up, except for these two." He seemed to be considering, but I already knew what he was going to say. "I will make it more profitable for you," he said. "Just a whim as I said before, a contest. I will add another two hundred and fifty guilders in rix-dollars if you do it well enough. Does that improve your mood?"

"Three fifty," I said.

"Three hundred."

"Agreed."

He turned and announced, I am sure, my consent to paint Amelia Dahl without bothering to translate the rest of our negotiation, and we moved to the table to be met by a very acceptable meal of sturgeon followed by a powdered goose. I cherished the occasion and refilled my plate whenever the chance arose. There was a canary wine to go with it, a sweeter wine than we see at table in my own town, and from time to time, Marvell let me in on the conversation, which was all about him. They talked endlessly of his plan to set a lighthouse on the curling bank that blocked the entrance to their great river, and then even more endlessly of the potential of a very large mud bank nearby that the shifting tide was gradually drying out into good earth.

"It will be valuable to whoever grabs it for his use," Marvell remarked to me, "and I think we must try to forestall the man who has his mind bent that way at present. This Gilby, my fellow Member for Hull, has designs on it. It would make a fine site for a house and I see no reason why it should be regarded as fair game for the first to seize it."

"You want it?" I said.

"I want a house on the Humber," he said. "I want a beautiful house, a place where the Muse will feel at home, a place befitting a Member of Parliament." He was looking around him as he spoke, at the remarkable harmony of that room. It was clearly unfinished, but the walls had been colored in a deep terra-cotta, an Italian shade, and there was a scumbled gilt being applied around the window frames that set it off to perfection. Amelia saw me looking and smiled, and I realized this was her canvas, her blank sheet, perhaps the only one she was permitted. I saluted her with my glass and caught a scowl from Dahl.

"Just such a house," said Marvell, musing. It became abruptly clear to me that, Gilby or no Gilby, the new island was not the whole point. Paull Holme was the house he wanted, this house.

All good things come to an end, and the moment came when roll-tobaccos were passed around to be lit and I had hopes that our fair lady would move to play the instrument, a kind of clavier, I believe, which stood in the room.

Instead it was Marvell who took command of it and inflicted on us some dreary songs, thrown out in a wavering falsetto. I used the occasion to look after Amelia as much as I could as she and Dahl watched Marvell. I thought I was unobserved, but she caught me in the act and gave me the sudden, secret, and unexpected smile of a conspirator.

When I thought the evening could dip no further, Marvell proved me wrong; he produced some of his sheets of paper from a pocket of his coat and began to intone with the cadence of verse. I discovered what I already suspected during those next interminable minutes, that the only thing worse than bad verse is bad verse in a foreign language. The bottle of canary taunted me from just beyond my reach. At the end, the other two clapped furiously, at which point Amelia said something to Marvell, who turned to me and said, "She entreats me to translate my verse for you."

"No, no, there is no need. I caught the measure of it regardless of the meaning."

Nothing would stop him. "It is about the blessed state of nature, and I call it *The Garden*," he said. "The verses I have just written begin with, let me see now, can I make it rhyme in the Dutch? This is not a part of our contest, you understand. I will just give you the rough sense."

"Don't concern yourself, I can imagine it," I said, but he thought hard, pulling bewildering facial expressions to demonstrate his creativity, and then came up with something appalling about twines and vines and lace and place and suchlike until blessed, blessed Amelia broke in with a laugh and said something that distracted him utterly.

He answered her in an animated manner, then begged my forgiveness. "Our hostess wishes to play the name rhyme game," he said. "She begs me to enquire of you what your first name may be. Please forgive me but if you told me before, I have forgot it most utterly."

I was still damned if I was going to tell him my real name. "I did tell you before," I said. "I told you it was Harmenszoon." That was true. I had told him before, so that only made it one lie.

ELEVEN

Monday, April 9, 2001

DENNIS INTERCEPTED AMY ON HER WAY TO ONE OF THE TWO TEM-
porary showers on the top floor. Both were occupied and Dennis was
forming a one-man queue outside them with a towel wrapped round
his waist. He held up a hand to stop her in the corridor and bawled
"Ladies present," at the top of his voice.

"What's that for?" she asked, not so pleased to see him after his attempt to walk off with Amelia's book. She'd left Don studying the
book, which troubled her just as much, trapping her in an unexpected
cross fire between her heart and her head.

"I'm just going to wash," she had said as she put on the clothes
spread across his floor like the shrapnel of lust. "When I come back
we'll read some more, OK?"

Don could have said something tender then, something like don't be
long, but instead he just got out of his bed, standing there in slim,
sinewy, glorious nakedness. If a burst of noise from beyond the door, the
noise of the builders getting ready for their night's entertainment, hadn't
stopped her, she might have undressed again immediately.

"I'll just have a look at it while you're gone," was all he'd said, and in that startling intimacy created by unexpected lovers, there seemed no polite way to take the book back from him against his will. It was oddly disturbing, to know that he was back there trying to read it without her, as if he was already being unfaithful.

Now, out here, Dennis inclined his head at the door leading to the showers. "Gengko's in there. He doesn't usually bother about the finer points of concealment. Wouldn't want to frighten the horses."

"Most considerate of you."

He gave her a serious look. "You're sure you're all right up that end? My offer's still good. You can have my room."

"If Gengko wanders round here in the raw, I think I'm probably safer up there."

Dennis frowned. "I don't really know how to say this, love," and he stopped.

"Go on. You're not usually tongue-tied."

"Well, you know I'm not one of Don's greatest fans and I recognize that he's probably an attractive bloke but ... I'd just keep a bit of distance if I were you."

"You're not jealous, are you," she said in a jokey voice, feeling Don still on her and in her.

"I wish it were that simple," he said, then he gave her a strange and searching look.

"Am I saying this too late?" he said, and she wondered what was written on her face.

"Maybe just a bit too late," she replied slowly.

"Just go carefully then," he said. "People get hurt when he's ..." He stopped abruptly as Eric the electrician emerged from the farther of the two showers, then shrugged. "Go on, get in there before Gengko starts waving his pet python around."

When she came out he was still standing there, even though the other shower was empty.

"I thought I'd better stand here in case any dangerous rapists showed up," he said.

"I'm *not* a dangerous rapist."

"Damn, another dream shattered," said Dennis. "However, the crucial question facing us all tonight is whether you're coming down to the pub with the rest of us lads, on account of the fact that it's a special celebration."

"What celebration would that be?" she asked.

"The feast of Saint Reginald, patron saint of builders. Martyred on this day when a wall collapsed on him while he was taking a nap, owing to him having forgotten to stir the mortar properly. You'll ruin my reputation if you don't come, Amy. I've told everybody we're secretly married."

"You may be, but I'm not," Amy had said. "I'm not even secretly single."

"Transport's leaving straight after the show," said Dennis.

"What show?"

"My best trick yet. I call it the Death Ride. Outside, soon as we're sure the Hawk's flown."

A CROWD HAD GATHERED ROUND THE SAW BENCH. DON, STILL TRYING to decipher Amelia's handwriting, had refused to come, and Amy arrived at the same moment as Dennis, once more clad in his white overalls. The fog was blowing away but the light was fading fast and someone had switched on a floodlight so that the sharp crescent of saw blade glinted.

"For the first time, lady and not very gentlemen," he called, "I will undertake the passage of the saw bench from end to end, in the WRONG DIRECTION."

There was a collective gasp and some shaking of heads.

"What does that mean?" Amy asked Gengko.

Gengko shrugged. "It means he's a silly bugger."

"Why?"

" 'Cos that's a good way to die. You feed wood into a circular saw from that end so that the saw bites downward, right? It keeps the wood down on the table. You put it in from the other end, where the saw's spinning upwards, you're likely to go into orbit is my guess."

"Won't his weight hold it down?"

"Shouldn't think so."

Others had their doubts, too. When Dennis produced a huge slab of wood, virtually half a tree trunk, out of the stack, Eric said, "Hold on, Den, have you practiced this?"

"What, and risk it twice?" he said. "Yeah, 'course I have. Up at the crack of dawn, every morning, perfecting my art, that's me."

"I think we might all agree to let you off this one," said Eric doubt-fully, but there was a chorus of whistles and catcalls.

"Bollocks," said Dennis. "Press the button and let's get on with it."

The saw whined into life and accelerated into a screaming blur, de-signed for damage, ready to bisect anything that came near it.

"I really don't want to watch this," Amy whispered, but she couldn't turn away.

"Go on, somebody, say I'm too young to die. Please," said Dennis.

"Too daft to live, more like," said Eric. "I'm not pushing you. I'd be an accessory to murder."

"No need," said Dennis, jumping up on the saw bench. Before anybody else could object, he gave the log a mighty shove, jumped on, and rode it down the rollers toward the saw blade.

At the moment when the log reached the saw, it became immedi-ately clear that he had misjudged the whole thing badly. The saw howled and smoked for a fraction of a second as it bit into the wood, then it simply picked up the log and hurled it into the air.

Dennis fell off, straight toward the blade.

The log crashed down among the scattering builders, felling two of them. Dennis, twisting in the air like a cat, landed on his shoulders right next to the whirling blade, rolled with one leg just above the spin-ning teeth, then bounced away from it, down onto the ground. Eric rushed to kill the power and the blade slowed rapidly to a halt.

There was chaos for a few seconds as people ran to Dennis and to the other two lying on the ground, but it was soon clear that they had all got away extraordinarily lightly. The leg of Dennis's overalls was ripped and he had just the slightest graze on his skin where the blade had sliced past. Tel and Scotch Jimmy were both rubbing bruised legs where the log had knocked them over, but that was the entire sum of the injuries.

"I know what went wrong," said Dennis. "I can fix that. It'll be a bloody good trick when I get it right. Let's have another go. I'll—"

"No way, Dennis," said Gengko. "I don't care about you, mate, but I'd like to stay alive. Let's go to the pub."

"All right, then. You coming, Amy?" Tel asked.

"Yes."

"What about Don?"

"I'll see if I can persuade him," said Amy. "We'll join you down there. Mine's a pint."

The cavalcade of cars left.

Don was standing just inside the front door.

"Were you watching?" she asked, in surprise.

He shrugged. "I wouldn't mind seeing him kill himself, but I'm not about to join his fan club. Anyway, who says you can persuade me? I heard you."

"You don't have to come if you don't want to."

"I don't."

"Look, just come for a walk, with me, right? We'll go down the road."

He looked at her and with a widening of her eyes, she blew on the embers of the passion they had just shared. It reached him. "If you want."

They walked down the rutted track, through the little wood to the bend in the road, and then down it toward the village, a mile or so away. The great river glowed bronze in the low evening sun away to their left and the loom of Hull was visible far ahead. She wished he would take her hand but he seemed to think he owed her no special affection. Halfway down the road, the church stood all on its own beside the road. Don turned in through the gate, and Amy followed, sensing this was as near the pub as he was likely to get.

"Is this Paull church?" she asked.

"Yes. There's an old saying round here. 'High Paull, Low Paull and Paull Holme, there never was a fair maid married in Paull Town.' "

"That's not very polite."

"It's a joke. There never was a fair maid married in Paull Town because the church isn't in Paull Town, it's out here." He went to the porch and tried unsuccessfully to open the door. "Oh, bloody hell. It never used to be locked. Anyway, come and look at this. Where is it?"

He found it after a search, a gravestone. "See what it says?"

Amy stooped to read it in the gloom. "This one? *John, son of Johnson and Ann Millson who was drowned at Hull September twenty-first and came ashore at Paull October tenth 1872. Aged twenty-four years.*' Ugh, three weeks in the water."

"They often fetch up here. There's another one. Look. *James Palmer,*

CE in charge of Coast Guard Station Paull who was drowned by the upsetting of his boat on the Humber December the twenty sixth 1876 and interred here January the second 1877 aged forty-nine years.' It's a dangerous river." He looked at her as though that should mean something special to her.

"Right, well, let's not go sailing. How old is the church?"

"Pretty old."

"Older than the 1600's?"

"Must be. I remember Mum saying it was burnt out during the Civil War siege, then they repaired it later."

"So when Amelia and our painter were doing their thing, it might have been a ruin?"

"I suppose so."

They both looked back toward the wood, higher up the road, which masked Paull Holme Manor.

"Imagine it," said Amy. "Look hard at the church and see it with no roof, all blackened. Then see if you can see the painter wandering round it, peering at it."

"How do you know he would?"

"It's such a strong visual image, a burnt church. Any painter nearby would come and have a look."

They stood together in silence. Amy tried to visualize the painter inspecting the church but the choices were too vast. Was he young or old, short or tall, fat or thin? She thought she had no idea, little realizing that Harmenszoon van Rijn's face was almost as familiar to her as her own.

"All right," she said. "Come on, I need a drink." She wanted him to say, come back to the house, come back to our quiet room with no one else around. Come back and do it with me again. Instead he just looked toward the village and shook his head.

"Listen, Don," she said, "I want to go down there. Just to be friendly, just for a short time. I'd like you to come, too, but I can't force you."

"I'm going to sit here for a while."

"All right. You do that. If you're not there in half an hour, I'll come back here." She looked at him but he was staring at the church. "I'd really like it if you came."

AT THE OUTSKIRTS OF PAULL, WHERE THE ROAD BENT PAST THE LITTLE lighthouse to run along the seawall and the Humber rustled and splashed close to her in the failing light, she paused and looked back, hoping to see him following her down the road, but there was no sign of him. She found them, most of them, in the first pub on the right. She walked in unnoticed and saw Dennis was in the middle of the crowd performing some complicated trick, involving a lot of full glasses of alcohol. Gengko saw her and winked.

"He's showing off again. Here's your pint."

"Thanks. Where are the others?"

"Bit of an altercation," he said. "I had to send Eric and his mate out for being a naughty boy. Threatened to come to blows. I think they're sulking in the other bar."

"About?"

"Somebody."

Amy could guess who that was; Gengko's tone didn't encourage her to take it further. Then Dennis noticed her.

"Here you are, darling," he said, "just in time to witness my moment of triumph. Old Gordie here reckons he can drink these four single whiskeys before I can drink these four pints of beer."

Gordie was not one of the builders. He was a grizzled sixty-year-old with tattooed anchors on his forearm.

"So do I," said Amy. "What's the catch?"

"Have you no faith in your husband, my dear? The rules are simple. Neither participant is to touch the other person or the other person's glass, nor knock them over by any means. Loser pays for all eight drinks."

"I don't know," said Amy, putting her arm round Dennis. "Leave you alone for a moment and you're betting and boozing."

There was a raucous cheer from the others.

"Did I ever promise you anything else?" asked Dennis.

"I don't remember you promising me anything at all."

"Side bet," said Dennis. "What about a kiss if I win? We are married, after all."

"What do I get if you lose?"

"I'll use my powers of persuasion to get Gengko to buy you half a packet of cheese-and-onion crisps."

"Oh, you know how to tempt a girl, all right. Done."

"Quiet, everybody. Serious concentration. Amy, you give us the countdown."

"Five-four-three-two-one, GO."

Gordie downed the first scotch before Dennis was a third of the way through his first pint. He laughed a derisory laugh at Dennis's foolish presumption and raised the second one to his lips as Dennis passed the halfway mark of the first with three and a half more pints to go. Gordie had the second scotch empty, back on the table, and was just starting the third when Dennis came to the end of his first pint, looked at it meditatively, upended it to shake out the drops, and calmly placed it, upside down, over the last full glass of whisky on the table.

"I win," he said.

"The fuck you do," said Gordie, reaching out to remove the glass.

"No, no, naughty boy," said Dennis. "Remember the precise wording of the rules. You can't touch the other person's glass."

Gordie stared at the table, thwarted. "Buggroff," he said. "Bastard. Fucking bastard."

"Do you mind," said Dennis primly, "my wife is present."

"If she's your wife, I'm a pig's arse," said Gordie.

"So where's the rest of the pig?" Dennis asked. From the way the landlord was watching nervously, Amy wondered if Gordie's record was perhaps not a very peaceful one.

"Wife, I claim my prize. A kiss," said Dennis, puckering his lips.

"Certainly," said Amy, seizing Gordie's face between her hands and kissing him straight on his mouth.

An astonished look spread over Gordie's face.

"Hold on," said Dennis. "Not him. Me."

"No, no, naughty boy," said Amy. "Remember the precise wording of the rules. You just said a kiss. You didn't say who I had to kiss."

Everybody roared, including Gordie.

"Where's Don?" asked Gengko when the laughter died down. "Did you tell him to come?"

"Have you tried telling Don anything?" she replied. "Don does what Don wants to do."

"Probably for the best," said Dennis. "He'd only be jealous with me here. When are we going to tell your mother?"

"I told you," said Amy. "Don't mention my mother." Dennis still couldn't quite tell whether she was joking.

"Come on," said Gengko, "I'll buy you a packet of crisps anyway." She went with him to the bar.

The Jamaican was oddly hesitant. "Is Don, er ... is he all right, like?"

"God knows," said Amy. "Who can possibly tell? I know I can't."

"It's just that we're all a bit worried that ..."

"Come on, Gengko," said Amy. "I've had quite enough people telling me that Don's had a bad time and that I need to be responsible or careful with his emotions or some crap like that. I don't know why everybody thinks I'm so bloody dangerous that I can't be trusted not to screw him up. I'm not on some mad ego trip, I'm really not. What do you think I am, some leggy blond tart who wants him to fall in love with me so I can carve another notch on my ... on my ..." She couldn't think of anything suitable and saw that Gengko was watching her as if she might bite him. "... On my fanny? Is that what you think? There are two of us in this, you know. Him *and* me. I didn't plan any of this. I'm not exactly enjoying it, either. He really upsets me sometimes. I don't know who he is. Do you understand that?"

"Um, no," said Gengko, "not really, but thank you for sharing it with me. All I was going to say was some of us are a bit worried that he never comes down to the pub anymore on account of the fact that he used to be the life and soul of the party, but thanks for that. Most exciting stuff. A far fuller answer than I was expecting. I suppose that puts me out of the running, then?"

"Oh, bloody hell, Gengko," she said. "What have I said now? Come here," and she gave him a hug.

"Hang on," said Dennis coming up behind her. "You're cuddling him and you kissed that old bloke," he said plaintively. "What about me?"

"Good God," she said. "Come on, then," and she kissed him quickly on the mouth.

None of them saw Don halfway in through the door, and none of them saw him turn and leave again straight away.

TWELVE

MORE THAN HALF AN HOUR PASSED BEFORE AMY GAVE UP ON DON, not knowing he had already been, and seen, and gone away. Tel, who was going back to get his wallet, gave Amy a lift to the house and when she got out of his car she saw Don's light on in the tower. Nowhere near used to being his lover, she tapped uncertainly on his door, heard only silence and went in anyway, feeling that at least was now her right, to find him lying on the bed, his head turned to the wall and her book, Amelia's book, lying next to him.

"You didn't come," she said.

"Didn't I?"

"I waited for you."

"Was that what you call it?"

His sullen, challenging response disturbed her.

"Do you want to tell me what's bugging you?" she asked.

"You are. You and bloody Dennis."

"I have no idea what you mean."

"I came to the pub. I got as far as the door."

"Why didn't you come in? I didn't see you."

"No, you didn't. You were too busy kissing him."

The absurdity of his statement made her start to laugh.

"You stupid man," she said. "If you'd been there you would have seen what that was about. It was nothing like that. It was the end of a joke. You could have shared that joke if you'd been with us instead of lurking outside like some hurt kid. I don't need to justify what I do to you. Why don't you get your act together, Don, and grow up?"

He was off the bed in a flash with his arm raised as if to strike her, and it took all her courage to stand her ground without flinching away. She was poised to kick him as hard as she could if the punch came, then he relaxed and let his arm fall to his side.

"I couldn't go in," he said. "Half of them hate me."

"In that case half of them don't," she replied as calmly as she could. "Why don't you sit down and tell me what all this is really about?"

"Some time." His face changed and he held out his arms to her. "I'm sorry," he said.

For a moment his open arms were a trap, then the bait of his waiting body overcame her common sense and she fell into them.

The power to decide what happened next lay in her hands. She could have slid them under his shirt, run her nails up and down his back, raised her mouth to his and they would have been in bed again in a second, but the memory of how he had just been kept her still, holding him calmly for a moment more, then stepping back.

"Did you read any more?" she asked, looking at Amelia's book lying on the bed. She imagined Don deep in Amelia's words, pages on from where they had stopped, trespassing into the secrets that she had wanted for herself.

"I can't really make it out."

He couldn't read Amelia's writing. She felt an unworthy joy.

"You and me," he said. "You and me. We could puzzle it out together."

Unsure of the constant shifts in his mood, she sensed there was greater safety to be found in the act of reading than in the act of love. She sat down, set his table light to shine on the page, and pored over the faint ink.

"It starts off 'not at his ease,' then something I just can't make out. Oh, hang on, it's a name. 'Marvell.' Have you got anything to write on?"

One or two pages had come apart easily, stuck only by the butterfly pressure of time. Others were still welded together, clumped at the bottom where the pages had swollen in a thicker lump. The open page in front of her came after such a clump, perhaps nine or ten pages farther on from the opening section she had read earlier. Amelia had written on one side of the paper so the writing was only on the right-hand sheet.

"There's a pad in my bag. See? Under my camera. Should be a pencil there, too," Don replied.

Amy began to jot down words, leaving gaps, then going back to fill them in as she got into her stride and the form of the faint writing began to reveal itself. Don sat on the bed and waited patiently.

"Right," she said in the end. "I've just about got it. Do you want to hear?"

"Oh, yes."

"Like I said, *'not at his ease.'* Then *'Marvell, who had been full of the grandest accounts of his Parliamentary business, coaxed him for the sake of our game and after wheedles and inducements, he told us his given name is . . .'* I don't know. I think it's *'Harmanson,'* then it goes on. *'He was much perplexed by our game, lacking our tongue, and Marvell came near to picking a hole in his coat by rhyming on his account when it came to the limner's turn. It seemed that Vanrin formed the opinion that Marvell was scandalising him with his rhymes . . .'*"

"Rhymes?" she said. "This couldn't be Marvell the poet, could it? You know, Andrew Marvell? You've heard of him?"

"Of course I have." Don frowned. "There's a famous Marvell who was a politician round here. He was Hull's Member of Parliament I think. There's a pub named after him."

"I suppose that fits," said Amy. "She talks about his parliamentary business. Pity. Let's see, *'formed the opinion that Marvell was scandalising him with his rhymes though in truth it were only to divert us so that they broke in pieces each with the other and the limner became ill-tempered. When I saw the party was gone all to pot, I did say we would change the game and brought out the cards for gleek, which was a game the Hollander did not know. We three played the game while he did sit with his tobacco and his pitcher and observe us in what we did. I marked that Marvell did show the pigeon and the Hollander had his measure. He is not a man to be got the better of. Marvell is sometime all honey and sometime all turd. It is arranged by Marvell that Vanrin will paint* my own picture although for whose gratification that may be is not so apparent to me. They must go, they say, to York for all the best pigments because the colours they have are suited to my husband but not to me. I shall go with . . .' That's the end."

"What does all that mean? Showing the pigeon and all that?"

Amy looked down at the words. "It sounds as though she's saying Marvell chickened out and let the Dutchman win the argument."

"Let's separate the next page."

That felt like a step too far for her.

"No, I don't think so," she said. "I want to take this slowly. What do you make of it?"

"We know his name, anyway. What was it? Herman?"

"Harmanson Vanrin."

Don nodded. "I want to find out more about him. I like the sound of him."

"Why?"

"He's tough. He doesn't let people push him around."

"That's good, is it? That's what you find admirable in people?"

"I reckon. Why not? You're an artist. Have you ever heard of him?"

"It's a familiar name," said Amy. It itched at her, trying to get out. "I'll have to look him up. And Marvell. It could be the poet, couldn't it? Perhaps he was a politician, too? This one makes rhymes. Amelia says so. When *was* he, Marvell the poet, I mean? Must have been seventeenth century, surely, or was it the eighteenth?"

This wasn't the sort of conversation she would normally have with a man whose smell was still on her. Was it better or worse that their common ground had shifted from hot sweat on their skin to dry words on an ancient page? For the moment it felt safer.

"I don't know. My degree was Civil Engineering, not English Lit."

"You've got a degree?" As soon as she said it, she knew how bad it sounded.

"No, I'm lying," he said. " 'Course I haven't. I couldn't be a builder and have a degree, could I? That wouldn't fit. You'd have to build a new pigeonhole for me, wouldn't you? I'm a builder so I must be fucking stupid."

"Stop, I'm sorry. I didn't mean it like that," Amy said quickly. "My mouth sometimes says things before my brain tells it to."

"You don't have any idea," said Don. "What do you see? A bloke in overalls. An ugly bloke who gets paid cash once a week. You don't know who I am."

"That's not what I see. You have to give me a chance."

"Why? What would be the point?"

If Amy had spoken with her heart, she would have said, because you're not in the slightest bit ugly, because you're difficult and proud and dangerous and sexy and those are all the things I like. But Dennis's oblique warnings came back to haunt her and got in the way of the words.

"I don't do that with just anybody. You're different."

"What does that mean?"

"It means you're a long way from being a typical builder."

"And you're a long way from understanding that there's no such thing as a typical builder. In fact there's no such thing as a typical fucking anybody."

She took the book and left the room as he turned his back on her. She lay on her air bed in the room next door, hoping that the door would open and an ardent, apologetic Don would come to her, but eventually, fitful sleep arrived instead.

The following morning, she took her time over getting up, had toast and coffee downstairs as the house picked up the rhythms of the working day, and went upstairs to start work, wondering if Don would still be exacting a price for the previous night. He was already there, with his goggles on, sander in hand, and he was talking to Peter Parrish, who was clutching a bulging folder of papers. They broke off when she came in.

"Very nice," said Parrish, looking up at the ceiling. "Very nice indeed. You've got a lot done. There's no need to rush it, you know."

Alarmed, she inspected her work for signs of haste. "I'm not. I'm only drawing outlines at the moment."

"I was just saying to Don here that some of these panels may need to come off. The moldings need very careful stripping. That sander looks a bit of a beast. It can't get into the corners."

She kept her face strictly neutral and nodded. Then, really to change the subject, she said, "What's the room going to be used for when it's finished?"

"Mostly for paintings," he said. "We're just negotiating with the Ferens. Do you know the Ferens?"

"No."

"It's the art gallery in town," Don interrupted. Amy tried to make out his tone. It seemed no more than neutral. His body language with Parrish was odd. There was nothing in the slightest bit subservient about it, quite the reverse. When Amy had walked in, he had looked like a teenager, defying a parent.

"That's it," said Parrish. "Splendid place. We're hoping the curator might make available three or four paintings from the reserve collection. Things suitable for the period. The trouble is, of course, the room they're displayed in has to be like Fort Knox and this is the only one that seems to fit the bill. We could make it secure. The light's good in here, too. I've got my eye on a few seventeenth-century pieces that would suit the place perfectly."

"You know a bit about seventeenth-century art, don't you?" Don asked. Amy guessed what was coming next, guessed and resented it a little, him asking a question that should have been hers.

"Not to any professional degree, of course," said Parrish, "but yes, I suppose I do. I've studied the Old Masters and their life stories. It's an interest of mine. You can't really study the history of architecture and ignore the best source, can you? Interiors in paintings are such a strong part of the record."

"Well, then, do you know anything about a painter called Harmanson Vanrin?" asked Don. "He was Dutch."

Perhaps Don would lose interest, Amy hoped. If Parrish didn't know him, if he was just an unknown who had fallen into the dark hole of history, then perhaps she could reclaim Amelia for herself.

Parrish looked at him in surprise. "Is that a trick question?"

"No," said Don, equally surprised, "why should it be?"

"It just seems rather a strange thing to call the poor man."

"So you've heard of him?"

"Of course I have," Parrish said. He turned to Amy. "Miss Dale, you can tell him, surely."

"Me?" Hell, Parrish knew him. Vanrin was someone, and she knew for certain she had heard the name before. "Oh dear. His name's familiar but I can't remember why."

"Did you study art history?"

"Er, yes, I did."

"Where was that?"

"At the Slade."

He seemed to be enjoying himself. "So have you forgotten everything they taught you or are you just trying to confuse young Don here?"

"No, I'm not," said Amy, almost too apologetically.

"Well, it's not *Van*rin, not like that with the stress on the first syllable. It's van *Rijn*." He spelled it out, "R, I, J, N, and it's not quite Harmanson. His name was Harmenszoon van Rijn," said Parrish, chuckling. "Now if I were to ask you if you'd heard of a painter called Buonarroti, what would you say?"

"I would say, er . . ." A retrieved memory came to her aid just in time. "I would say that was Michelangelo's last name." Half of an enormous idea was elbowing its way out of the dusty filing cabinets of her brain, and she felt sure she was about to look rather foolish.

"Exactly. So, van Rijn was a surname, too. Born in Leiden in, let me see, 1606, I believe. Shared a studio with Jan Lievens, then he moved to Amsterdam in 1620-something and stayed there until he died around 1668. Does that ring any bells?"

Don and Amy stayed silent but Amy was watching Parrish in an agony of uncertainty. It took her all the way back to being shown up in front of a class.

Parrish looked at her expectantly, shrugged, and continued trying to prompt her. "He turned the technique of portrait painting on its head. Many people would say he was the greatest painter the world ever saw. Even those who don't agree would still put him in the top three or four."

"Why haven't I heard of him, then?" asked Don, bluntly.

"Because you haven't given the poor old fellow his first name," said Parrish. "Harmenszoon is his *second* name, his patronymic. It just means his father was called Harmen. He signed his paintings with his first name, and that is the name by which he chose always to be known once he became famous." He turned and looked at Amy. "And that name was?" he said.

"Rembrandt," she said. The word seemed to expand to fill the entire room, taking the air out of her lungs.

Don pushed his goggles up on his forehead. She managed not to look at him.

"Rembrandt?" he said in astonishment. "Did, er . . . did Rembrandt ever come to England?"

At that moment, there were footsteps on the landing and the foreman stuck his head round the door.

"Here, you two," he said, "I don't pay you to—" He saw Parrish. "Ah, didn't know you were there, Mr. P."

"That's all right," said Parrish. "Just having a little discussion about how we proceed in here. Don't worry, they'll be hard at it soon."

Hawk backed out and went to harass somebody else.

"Thanks," said Amy.

Parrish was enjoying himself too much to let work get in the way. "Did Rembrandt come to England? Ah! Well, that's quite an interesting question. Now, first of all, there's a rather silly story saying he was here in the 1630's, all because he did some etchings of St. Paul's Cathedral and one or two other English buildings, but nobody really believes it. They're not realistic. He very probably based them on somebody else's work."

"Why would he do that?"

"Money, dear girl. He was the arch capitalist. He churned out those etchings, then he'd change them a little bit and sell them to the same collectors all over again. The man was a money machine. Until later on of course, until he went bust."

Amy and Don spoke at the same time: "Went bust?" but Parrish had moved on to another thought.

"Now, I'll tell you something really odd," he said, "something I bet you didn't know. There's another story, not very widely known, which claims Rembrandt actually came to Hull later in his life. How about that?"

"Hull?" Amy beat Don to it but her voice sounded to her like someone else's, someone much younger and rather overexcited.

"If you're interested, I think I've got the details back in town, in my office. You could pop in some time and look at them."

"Today? After work?"

Parrish raised an eyebrow. "If you want. I'll probably be there until about seven."

"Good," said Don. "We'll be there."

"Now, better get on, before I bring the foreman's wrath down on you. Let's have another look at these panels. This next one's very thin." Parrish was pushing gently in the center of the panel with his hand. They watched him, worried that he might switch his attention to the repaired one next door to it. "Let's have a go at taking this one off and see if we can clean it up better. It's only pinned in, you see. If you lever the moldings off very gently, let's say here and here, you should be able to get at the main framing, do you see? I think it's too dangerous to go on sanding them *in situ,* as it were."

He left them alone after that, and when the door had closed, Don said, "God almighty, I think we're in over our heads here."

"It's too late to go back."

"Think about it. Rembrandt might have been here, in this house. Rembrandt painted the family. What the hell was he doing here?"

"I don't know, Don. Maybe we're going to find out."

"Supposing we find the paintings."

"Find them? Here?" Amy looked around at the bare walls. She could imagine what might happen if the builders got the idea something of real value might be in the house. "Sadly, I don't think that's likely. Is there anywhere in the house that no one's been?"

"No, I don't think so."

"No attics? No cellars?"

Don shook his head and, in doing so, seemed to feel the weight of the goggles up on his forehead. He brought them down over his eyes quickly.

"No cellars, definitely," he said. "I suppose there was an attic but they've taken the roof right off so they must have cleaned it out."

"Have you been in all the rooms?"

"No."

"Well, anyway," said Amy. "If we do find them, it's halves, all right?"

There was no overtime in their minds that evening. They changed quickly when work stopped and went outside.

"Your car or mine?" Amy asked.

"Yours."

"It's got very little suspension and almost no brakes."

"Well, mine's got no wheels, no engine, and no body."

This was a different Don, almost chatty.

"You mean you haven't got a car," she said.

"Not at the moment, no."

His hand, thought Amy. *That's probably why he's not driving at the moment. Stupid.*

Half an hour later, they were sitting in hard chairs facing Peter Parrish across his desk.

"Won't be a minute," he said, sorting papers into files. "Got to keep the accountants at bay, eh? Wouldn't do to spend more than we've got on the old place."

He finished, looked around the desk vaguely, and rooted through drawers until he found another fat folder.

"Shall we do this over a drink?" he said. "There's a pub I'd like Miss Dale to see."

"Please call me Amy," she said. "Miss Dale sounds like something you've done when you get a wrong number."

The White Harte pub was a ten-minute walk, tucked away down an alleyway off Silver Street and age-soaked right through its walls from the outside to the rooms within. Parrish ushered Amy in. Don hung back and peered in through the door before he stepped inside. Amy guessed it was a little too public for him.

"You see, 1600's" said Parrish. "The bombs spared it. Not a bad place, eh?" He put three beer glasses down on the table. "There's a room upstairs they used to call the plotting parlor. It's where the city officials decided to close the gates to King Charles. Did you know that was the first open act of defiance in the Civil War? Just think, if our man Rembrandt was here, he might have had a drink right here."

"*Was* he here?" Don asked. He had been jumpy all the way in from Paull Holme. There were no convenient disguises he could wear away from his work, and the injury to his face was livid.

"I don't think so," said Parrish. "He's famous for never going anywhere. Just about every other painter worth his salt did the grand tour down to Italy. Not our Mr. van Rijn. He'd hardly walk across the street unless he had to, but who knows?"

"So what's the basis for the story?"

Parrish opened the folder. "All right. I'll try to keep it simple. It all stems from a man called George Vertue who was writing about fifty years after Rembrandt died. Our friend Vertue was the first real British art historian, you might say. He was an artist himself, an engraver, but what he's famous for are his notebooks. He went round writing up all the great collections of England, describing the paintings. It wasn't exactly plain sailing. There was a lot of blatant forgery, and even the Masters themselves weren't above signing their students' pictures to squeeze out a bit more cash. The thing is, old George wasn't bad at his identification."

"So he saw pictures Rembrandt painted here?"

"No, no. Well, maybe. We can't be sure, but that's not the point. No, Vertue *met* someone. In his notebooks, he says he met an old man called Laroon, another artist. Laroon told him that when he was a small boy, he had met Rembrandt in York. Vertue's quite definite about it. This man told Vertue that Rembrandt was living in Hull, painting portraits of seafaring folk, and he even described one of the portraits. I haven't looked at the entry in the notebooks for years, but he gave quite a lot of detail about it, you know, how it was signed, what the date was, what it said on the frame, that sort of thing."

"Where are these notebooks?" Don asked.

"In London. Horace Walpole owned them, and the Walpole Society had them all copied out in about 1900 so that people could use them for research. They've got copies in the library at the Victoria and Albert Museum."

"So why don't you believe it?" demanded Amy.

Parrish shrugged. "Well, it seems so out of character for a start. I mean, the man made a whole lifestyle out of staying in one place. Why on earth would he suddenly uproot and come to Hull of all places? Then, there was something else. What was it? Oh, I know. Vertue says the dates on the portraits are 1661 and 1662. Now, it's certainly true that we don't know much about what Rembrandt was doing in '62, but we've got plenty of evidence showing he was busy in Amsterdam right through '61."

"And that's all there is to go on?"

Parrish looked at Amy. "You really want it to be true, don't you?"

"It's a great story."

"Well, no. In that case, you'll be pleased to hear that's not all the evidence." He shuffled through the papers in the folder, searching.

Amy glanced at Don, who was looking at Parrish with a curious and unsettling expression. All at once she forgot about Parrish and

Rembrandt and became poignantly aware of the table between her and Don, of the other people around, and of the simplicity of her feelings. Here he was, the first man who had ever made her whole body sing with physical yearning for what he could do to her, and yet what was between them, the bond that should have been so simple, was already so tricky. He seemed to register the movement of her eyes and his face changed.

Parrish found the piece of paper he was searching for. "There was a book written in the 1850's, I think, a history of Hull by James Joseph Sheahan. I find it very useful. Loads of detail on catastrophes, what house burnt down and when and which falling wall squashed how many people—that kind of thing. Gives you lots of evidence about the old buildings. Anyway, he also lists all the famous people who have lived in Hull. Most of their names, I fear, have not stood the test of time. However, on page seven hundred and twenty-five he says, *'Van Ryn Rembrandt, the celebrated painter and etcher, practised his art at Hull for some time. He died in 1674, aged sixty-eight.'* "

"That's all?" asked Don.

"Yes," said Parrish, "and of course it's wrong because he actually died in 1669, aged sixty-three. Bit of a pauper's death, really. Nobody made much fuss."

"It's not much to go on, is it?" said Amy. "I mean, this man Sheahan, he could have got it from the first man, the one who wrote the notebooks."

"Ah, but did he? Where's your detective instinct? Vertue's notebooks weren't made public until 1900, when the Walpole Society printed them up. Sheahan wrote his book sixty years before that. How did he know? Sounds like two separate sources, don't you think? Either that or old Laroon told his story to a lot of different people."

"So who exactly was old Laroon?" asked Don.

"Old Laroon? The man who told Vertue he'd met Rembrandt in York. He was another famous engraver, Marcellus Laroon, famous for the 'Street Cries of London' etchings? Yes?"

Amy had a dim memory of her mother's set of table mats. She nodded.

"Laroon was a Dutchman himself," said Parrish. "He could only have been nine or ten years old when he says he met Rembrandt.

That's why people tend not to believe the story, but his father was an artist, too, so they might easily have recognized each other. I say, wouldn't it be fun if it was Rembrandt who taught Laroon how to etch?"

"Yes," said Amy, a little impatiently, "but there was something else I wanted to ask you—"

She never got to ask her question. Whether Laroon recognized Rembrandt or not, at that moment, someone recognized Don.

THIRTEEN

Friday, January 17th, 1662

IN THE FINE ENGLISH CITY OF YORK, MARVELL FINALLY DISCOVERED who I really was. On the way there, a tedious journey by cart of two days, I found out a great deal more about who he really was and came to like him rather less as a result.

Amelia had seen me off, handed me a stoppered bottle and a wrapped parcel of food, and then wished me what I took to be a good journey in English, which sounded unusually delightful when spoken in the musical tones of her quite enthralling voice. The journey was meant to be over by sunset. That it took twice as long was due to neglect on the part of the cart's vile driver, a filthy old man, who let it come into violent and destructive contact with a milestone sticking out of the verge. Something crucial was broken, some part of the wheel with a very specific English name that the man kept shouting loudly, attempting to punch me each time for emphasis. In the end men with huge metal tools were summoned to set things to rights. It would have made a most engrossing scene, had I but the means to paint it. I had a powerful wish for paper, paint, or charcoal—anything to let me fill the time the way I filled it best. The worst thing, the very worst thing, about the way I had somehow kidnapped myself into this inconvenient English oblivion was the absence of all the comforts of my studio, the comforts I had taken for granted for so long. I never had to think about supplying my art. Titus and Hennie always saw that what I needed was there at hand. I have met men who depend on schnapps and men who depend on laudanum but I did not know until that moment that I depended on paint to just the same degree. Looking at the back of the men's heads as they bent over the wheel, it struck me that I had never painted myself from behind. I wondered if an arrangement of mirrors might be contrived to permit it.

Would it be worth the trouble? No. The back of the head tells you nothing. It's all in the face, of course.

Why do I paint my own face? I know what's behind those eyes of mine. I know exactly how the restless consciousness inside moves that flesh-mask. I face a more subtle task when I paint myself than when I paint any other. There's another reason, one I don't admit to anybody, and hardly ever even to myself. It makes me feel better. When I'm feeling the pinch, when I wake up at first light and the pressure of my debts hits me in the face, it is a relief to start touching in the highlights of the gold chain around my neck. When I start to worry that in another few years, the folds of my face will be taken for age, not character, then I can look at the evidence that my paintbrush has produced to reassure myself that the bull is still a bull and all the better for a bit of character.

I like the way my portraits look these days. The man who looks back at me reeks of substance and reputation. He has a presence about him. Any woman would know just what was on offer when she looked into that face.

I was still musing on that when Marvell talked to the men then turned to me.

"We will be obliged to stay the night. The town ahead is Beverley and there is a good inn."

It cannot have been much after the middle of the afternoon, but it gets dark very early at this time of year and I did not argue.

"You'll pay, will you?" I said. "I've got nothing. Until you pay for the picture, that is."

"The picture you haven't yet painted," he reminded me.

He seemed to be known at the inn, a dark place of corridors filled with the smell of old cabbage and even older beer. My expectations were low, but I have to admit that the food and wine were good. A bit too good, perhaps. With the boiled beef stew we drank a sherry wine, English style, by the bucket full. It was too sweet for my taste but I matched Marvell beaker for beaker. I had the stronger head by far, helped by my greater bulk, for there is nothing like flesh for drawing alcohol away from the brain. By the end of the meal, he had passed from arrogant disdain through mild vanity to full-blown boastfulness and now, on the third jug, I started to see the true Marvell emerge.

"See all these people?" he slurred, waving his hand around the room. "Pig-ignorant shits the lot of them. Do they know anything of me and my work? No, they do not, sir, they do not."

"Your work in the Parliament?" I said, filling his beaker again.

"My work, sir. My words. My VERSE."

He tilted the beaker to his lips, a little cocked and awry so some of it trickled down his chin. He tried to put it down on a table that was a hand's-breadth higher than he thought it was and spilt even more in the resulting collision.

"She thinks she is too good for me, you see?"

"Who does?"

"No matter. Do not ask."

"All right, I won't."

"Her, of course. You know who I mean."

"I believe I do."

He tried to wink, wagging a finger at me, but the first time both his eyes closed together and he had to try again.

"Now here is the thing," he said, "and I tell you this because you have not one hope of impressing her with your brush. Not one." He stared at me truculently, then seemed to find it hugely surprising that his hand still clasped his beaker and raised it to his lips again.

I waited until he had finished.

"What were you going to tell me?" I asked in the end.

"Ah, yes. This." He spoke with slow emphasis. "She is an artist, too. Her house is her poem."

"Or her picture."

"No. Any man must match her to deserve her."

"Dahl?"

He sneered. "Dahl was a ticket. Dahl was a ship. Dahl was a purse. Dahl's day is done."

"You want her?"

"She won't turn down my verse," he slurred and fell forward into the remains of his stew.

————————

I HAD TO SLEEP IN THE SAME BED ONCE HE HAD BEEN CARRIED TO it. I was careful to arrange myself nose to tail as it were, but when I was fast asleep, two more men woke me by clambering in, one still with boots on. Being the only one with my head at the foot end, I received several kicks in the skull before the night was over. It was still quite dark when they hammered on the door to wake us, Marvell getting to his feet with surprisingly little evidence of his excesses. All things considered, I was quite pleased to be in the cart without ever seeing much more of Beverley than two fine large churches and a host of narrow streets.

York made up for everything. What a city! The walls and the gates and the river amounted to something very much finer than Hull, and even, I have to admit, than parts of Amsterdam. We had a set-to with an official at the gate who seemed to want to know unnecessary details, about me, my origins, and my purpose, but Marvell stumped him with the production of some paper from an inner pocket.

"There are some advantages to being a Member of the Parliament," Marvell observed dryly as we passed through.

I had been watching him throughout that second day's travel, weighing the artist in him, to measure my opponent as he seemed determined to be. He seemed to have no recollection of what he had said the night before. The Parliamentarian was very strong in him to-day. He delivered high-handed horseback opinions on everything of which we spoke: of politics, of the husbandry of the countryside we passed through, even of the proper way to paint a picture. He set himself above others, did that man, for much of the time, but there was a crack somewhere in his bell that stopped him ringing quite true. He spoke of the restoration of the king as if he were the man's most ardent supporter, but I could see right through him.

I do not know what it is to write a poem but if it is an art to rival painting, then should it not have at its heart a quiet, humble study of the world? I know that you are no kind of painter at all if you do not gaze quietly for long periods at the play of light on a dress or the play of love in the eyes. You must watch and wonder, because that is what brings you nearer to truth. I never saw a moment when Marvell did either. He formed his views in a trice and the world seemed to him to be of his own making, not a place in which he was privileged to wander. I became more and more sure that his poetry would be equally as arrogant, a one-sided judgment on the world, formed too fast and instantly immutable. But I forgot what irked me in the center of York. The cathedral, called Minster, was brazen in its grandeur. The shop we found in a narrow winding street beside it made up for all the discomforts of the journey. In the front it sold hand tools for craftsmen of all types, but in the back it had properly arrayed pigment, row upon row, in the finest grades. Some was ground but some—the sort that does not keep well when reduced to powder—had rightly been left in raw lumps.

The keeper of that shop knew what he was doing. I thought there must be several other painters in York to allow him to maintain such a stock. He had good oil, brushes not far short of those I am used to and, wonder of wonders, the man even understood some Dutch. Though lacking in the niceties of grammar, he certainly knew the names of the colors. I indulged myself in my selection, adding to it some excellent paper and even pausing for a moment to consider the fine canvas he had on offer before I realized there was something about the challenge of the raw boards that had begun to appeal to me.

Then I saw them, on the side of the counter. Four copper blocks, perfectly prepared.

It was months since I had last held a needle in my hand. The light in my new studio in the damned low-built Jordaan was nowhere near as good as that huge light that had flooded into the high windows of my real house, the Breestraat house, the house that rogues had stolen from me. You need good light for that fine scratching work, especially if your eyes are growing a little weary. I had spent all my time with my brushes for months now, shunning my needles, but my hand started to twitch as soon as I saw this bounty. Marvell seemed willing to buy whatever I took a fancy to, so I added the blocks, or at least I tried to.

The man gave me to believe they were already sold to another customer. I insisted, he argued. Marvell slapped coins on the counter. The shopkeeper gave me just one block and would not relent. Without wax and acid, a copper block is a more or less useless thing for etching, but there was always drypoint, my first love, and he had a drypoint needle he could sell me.

I should explain the difference, I suppose, because it is a difference that is all about directness and mutability. In etching, you coat the copper with wax or sometimes with a varnish, though I like that less. With your needle, you make your scratches in the wax to bare the copper beneath and when done, you dip it in acid to eat away at the copper just so. The wax preserves the rest of the copper from the acid's bite.

It makes a filthy smell that creeps, curdling, into the lungs. My Saskia's lungs, I think now, were damaged forever by the savage vapor that filled our house when the plates were etching. She died of the consumption but I think that the acid prepared the way for it and I have never etched a plate again without regretting it.

The simplest way from eye to final print is to dispense with the acid altogether and use the drypoint needle on the virgin copper plate, so that no other agency except your own hand decides how deep and wide the channel for the ink should be. However you do it, this work has a remarkable power to surprise the artist. At the end of a day's scratching you have the bones of your picture on the copper plate. You think you know it. Then what happens? You ink your copper and wipe it. You wet the paper and press it as hard as it can be pressed onto the plate. Then you peel it carefully off and when you look at it something wonderful happens.

It is something you have never seen before.

It is completely familiar but also completely unfamiliar because you have stepped through the looking glass and sneaked up on the world from the other side.

Left and right are as different as dark and light, as evil and good, as hell and heaven. Do you know how people look at pictures? They start on the left, a bit above center, and their eyes travel round in a clockwise circuit of the center part, having no choice in the matter. They may be deflected and diverted by highlights and clever little booby traps which the artist has inserted but that's the way they go whether they like it or not. More than that, whatever they have just looked at alters the next thing in line. Light is lighter after dark. Dark is darker after light.

When you unpeel the print from the bed of the press and see it for the first time, you can criticize your own work without that uncertainty that is always introduced by long familiarity. Then of course, you may take up the scratching tool again and adjust it to your heart's content. You can look at *yourself* in a different way too. The first time I drew myself on a copper plate, I was appalled. It was me as I had never seen myself, the way others see me, the right way round. I was happier with my familiar image in the mirror.

Now the carter had his business to do and it seemed, to my relief, that we were to stay in this city overnight before starting back at first light. Marvell made some enquiries after some items Amelia had requested, then led me to a comfortable inn that faced the Minster. There was nothing more I wanted to do than sit down on the bench in front of the inn with a jug of wine and immediately begin rendering that great edifice onto copper before the light faded. Marvell ordered the wine and sat beside me, scribbling lines. I have no idea why he needed to be out there. As I have said, it wasn't as if his inspiration came from anywhere outside his own head. I think it was mere showmanship. He wanted people to say, "Oh, look at that clever man, writing."

I had the main proportions of the great church to my liking in minutes and was lost in a happy daze of creation, feeling with every light stroke of the tool how the ink would flow onto the paper. The first pressing or two is the best, because the edges of the copper are still rough and the ink blurs out delightfully from them. I could sense through my fingers how the great window would dominate the print and how blackly its glass would drag in the eye. Then someone said, "I know you," and they said it in Dutch.

No one knew me in York. No one who did not know me would have said it in Dutch. I looked up and saw, to my utter dismay, someone who could say that sentence truthfully. I knew him for a dangerous man, but I had to wrestle his name and the type of danger he presented from the recesses of my memory.

Laroon.

A peddler of influence as well as art, he was from the Hague, not from Amsterdam and, like so many from that place, he had the conniving practices of the Court down to an art.

Laroon, the man who had helped spread the tale of what I did to the woman Geertge far and wide without ever telling the tale of what she tried to do to me. Laroon. Most dangerously, he was a man who knew me by my first name.

"Well, now, here's a surprise," he said, and I sensed Marvell pulling himself back from whatever mawkish swamp of rhyme he had meandered into to take an interest.

"Van Rijn," I said emphatically, sticking out my hand as if he might have forgotten who I was, forestalling any need on his part to use my name.

He looked at my hand in surprise. "I know who you are. What I don't know is what you're doing here."

"That's a long story." I noticed there was a small boy peering from behind his legs. "Who's that?" I asked, to change the subject.

"Marcellus the younger," he said and I thought, *never trust a man who gives his son his own name. It is remarkably big-headed.*

"So why are *you* here?" I said.

"I might settle," he said. "Lots of work in this country. All this trouble there's been. A great number of pictures get burnt in a civil war. There's a host of bare walls needing to be filled, plus a lot of new heads of households who have lost their heads if you understand my meaning. Are you of a like mind?"

He made me sound like a low-grade opportunist. "No," I said tersely. "Can we talk later? I'm losing the light."

"Oh, yes," he said. "I'm staying here, too. I'll see you at supper, no doubt."

They departed, to my considerable relief, but Marvell gave me a suspicious look before his versifying reclaimed his attention. About a minute passed and then the kid reappeared.

"My papa said I was to stay here," he announced in the sort of piping voice that makes you ache to strangle the speaker. "He said I could watch you."

"Oh, did he?"

"He said you are a famous engraver."

"Ah." The man was not a complete blackguard then. "What else did he say?"

The boy smiled the flattered smile of a child who finds himself possessing information an adult requires. "He said you put on paint like other people shovel horseshit." He went on smiling.

"Just sit here and watch and hold your tongue."

He stopped smiling. I continued to work while he watched, but I knew I should never have begun because the incoming tide of dusk was too fast for me.

"What time are we leaving tomorrow?" I asked Marvell, who sighed the exasperated sigh of someone who, in being disturbed, has just lost the perfect line that might have secured him everlasting renown.

"First light," he said. "We have wasted enough time."

He looked down at his paper and sighed again.

"Lost it?" I said.

"I have been working on this for a year, on and off," he said. "It is for someone who does not understand how brief our time on this earth is," he said.

Did I ask? Did I?

"It is a plea to them to realize that love demands we act now to fulfill that love and that we should not have to wait until time has eaten the flesh from our bones."

I could be enjoying myself in Amsterdam, I thought, *dodging my creditors.* It was a toss-up.

"It has been in my head for years but it somehow lacked the force of reality. It was only a theoretical emotion. Now I know it has been waiting there for this moment and this person."

"A woman, is it?" I asked, as if I didn't know.

He looked at me dolefully. "As beautiful as the most beautiful woman you will ever see."

And that was when Marcellus Laroon the younger said, "Master Rembrandt? I need to go and take a piss."

Marvell was miles away still, dreaming of perfect beauty. That was close.

It didn't last. The brat came back. "Master Rembrandt, I splashed my pants." May black buboes form on his testicles.

The echo of his shrill words hung between us, and this time, Marvell looked toward me and frowned.

"Take this," I said to the kid, handing him the copper plate and the needle. I knew I would never have the chance to finish it. "You do it. See if you can."

"Rembrandt?" said Marvell. "Van Rijn? Rembrandt van Rijn?" He looked me up and down. "Now that *is* a name I have heard many times. So what are you? Are you Harmenszoon or are you Rembrandt?"

I might have braved it out, but I knew we were going to encounter the brat's father inside and it was highly unlikely I would be able to persuade Marvell, who was nothing if not acutely inquisitive, to take no further interest. Anyway, I had had enough of his high-handedness. This might make him think twice about challenging my art.

"My father's father was Gerrit, therefore he was Gerritszoon. My father was Harmen, therefore I am Harmenszoon. My first and given name is Rembrandt. Yes."

"*The* Rembrandt?"

"That depends on what you mean."

"The Rembrandt who painted *The Blinding of Samson*?"

"Every bloody painter in Holland has painted a *Blinding of Samson*."

"*The Company of Banning Cocq?*"

"Yes, that was mine."

He whistled. "Good Lord above," he said. "I had no idea. How odd life is. And I said I had never heard of you. You, painting Dahl. What in heaven's name brought you to stow away in—"

I cut him off. "Listen to me. Bullshit's best left in fields. I'm just van Rijn over here and that's the way I like it, so keep your lip buttoned, right? I don't want my name attached to anything. I want to be nobody while I'm here, understood?"

"But why? I'm sure Dahl would be delighted if you told him."

"Of course he would, but I'm not meant to be overseas, understand? As a bankrupt, I'm not allowed to leave Amsterdam. In any case, he would want my signature on his sorry portrait and he cannot have that, not with paint like dog turd to work with."

"I must tell him."

"Listen, mister poet with his private ode to someone special at Paull Holme Manor, I don't think you would want Dahl to know about that any more than I want Dahl to know who I am. Do we have a deal?"

He jumped when I said that and agreed with gratifying speed. Before I went inside I looked over the shoulder of Laroon's lad at the scratches he was making. What a waste of good copper.

FOURTEEN

Tuesday, April 10, 2001

AMY RAN OUT OF THE PUB INTO PUDDLES THAT SOAKED HER SHOES in seconds. There was nothing outside but strangers and a thin drizzle. No sign of Don. Thirty seconds before, all had been well until a large, clumsy man tripped over Peter Parrish's foot, projecting a small wave of lager over Don's jeans, and, in the middle of his apologies, said, "Hang on, I know you, don't I?"

Don had mumbled something, bending down to mop his trousers. The man, overeffusive with embarrassment, said, "Yeah, it's you, in't it? Remember me? Down at the what-do-you-call-it? The dock place? No, 'course you don't." Under a fleece jacket, his T-shirt hung outside his large belly. He turned to Amy. "I was there, you see. Delivering. It was me who called the ambulance."

"Sorry," Don had said, thickly. "Got to . . ." and he was gone.

By the time Amy reached the street he was nowhere to be seen. Left or right? Darkness was left, lights were right. She chose left and ran in her sodden, flimsy shoes until she was in the old High Street among the ghosts, and thought she saw him ahead for a moment rounding the bend. At the next corner there were three roads he could have taken, and she guessed wrong. She ran along one, then another, then the third, until she knew he had gone, then she stood in the dark, with the rain falling harder and harder until the cold and the wet and the sheer difficulty of it all drove her back to the pub again. By that time there was no sign of either Parrish or the man who had spilt the beer, so she sat there, sipping a drink she didn't want, pressed against a radiator while she tried to dry out, and all the time she was watching the door, hoping Don would walk back in through it. When that hope diminished, she drove back to Paull Holme, puzzled and worried, looking hard at every one of the few people walking in the suburbs of Hull. By the time she reached the flaring refinery she had given up, and the dark country lanes beyond it cut off the world of people and towed her out of town back to the netherworld of Paull Holme. She drove in through the trees, torn between relief and fear. As she got out of the car, she smelled tobacco smoke. There, under the canopy sheltering the saw bench, she saw two cigarette ends gleaming in the darkness, both brightening in unison as the invisible smokers inhaled.

A voice said, "Howdy-do."

It was Dennis, by himself.

"Why are you smoking two cigarettes, Dennis?" she asked.

"So that anyone lurking out there thinks there's more than one of me," he said.

"No, really."

"Because I allow myself two fags every evening."

"But why together?"

" 'Cos I'm dead weary and I want to get to bed. Anyway," he said, "you're not one to talk. You went off with two in the car and you've come back with one. Have you been careless?"

She sighed. "Something happened. We were in a pub. This guy said something to him and he just rushed off."

"Oh? He'll come back when he chooses."

"What's it all about, Dennis?"

He sang it back at her. "What's it all about, Den—nisss" on a rising falsetto. "I expect he'll tell you if he wants to."

"Why don't you like him?"

She couldn't see his face but she sensed him shifting in the darkness. "We've got a deal here, Amy. We try not to talk about it. A lot of blokes together in a small space, it's not a good idea to get all stirred up. That's when accidents happen. Anyway, somehow I don't think I'd be preaching to the converted."

"Come on. He's not here. I need to know. How did he get hurt? It was a saw, he said. Was it this saw?" As she said it, she realized it couldn't have been. The man in the pub said it was down at the docks. He'd called the ambulance down at the docks.

Dennis gave a short laugh. "You wouldn't get a little cut off this saw. Dead, that's what you'd get."

"You didn't die. I didn't like that last stunt. Why did you do it? Were you showing off because *I* was there?"

"Don't tell me how to survive, love. Construction's a hard business. I'm the court jester. That gets me through most of the time, but not always. Once in a while someone will still try to pull my head off. There's times with blokes like these when you need to earn a bit of respect, to do something they wouldn't do. Protection."

"I see. But what about Don? What sort of saw was it?"

"Chain saw. You'd be better off asking him."

"What's going on between you two? I want to know, Dennis. It matters."

"You don't want to know. Once I've told you, then you're on one side or the other. You can't be on both."

"I can try. Bloody tell me, Dennis."

He sighed. "Be it on your own head. My sister Maggie, she's got this kid, Vin. He's never been quite right. Then he started taking this and that—speed and a bit of dope, then he started using himself as a pincushion. Remember when you picked me up? I'd been over Darlington way, seeing Maggie. The boy's here, in Hull, in prison. He's on remand."

"What did he do?"

"Ah, well, that depends."

"On?"

"On whether you're on Don's side or on his side. It's Pandora's box, Amy. You sure you want me to open it?"

"Yes."

"The fact is there was Don and there was Vin and there was a chain saw."

He fell silent. Amy frowned in the darkness.

"And there was an accident?"

"Oh, no. Whatever happened, it wasn't an accident. Look, you ask Don. That's the best thing, but whatever he tells you, just do me a favor, OK?"

"OK."

"You just remember that Vin tells it differently, but Vin's a druggie, isn't he? Vin's got a few screws loose, hasn't he? No one's going to listen to Vin when there's big brave Don around."

New dimensions full of malice engulfed Amy. "Did Vin have something against Don?"

Dennis didn't reply straight away. When he did, his voice was very quiet. "He didn't even know him. All he did was try to stop him. Look, love, I can see how it is with you and Don. You're in over your head, aren't you?"

"Well, up to my knees." She tried to laugh and found she couldn't.

"Just be very, very careful. I've done my best. I can't do anything more. Me, I'm off to bed. You coming?"

"Yes," she said.

"Yippee," he said. "First time anyone's said that for three weeks."

He'd drawn a line under it. The conversation was over.

"Behave yourself," she said.

"How? Well or badly?"

Amy went to bed because there was nothing else to do. For the first part of the night she dreamed disturbing dreams. In the early hours, she got up and went to Don's door. It was open just a crack, and she listened for breathing for a long time before she risked pushing it open farther to find his bed empty. She sat down on the unmade bed for a few moments; then, remembering vividly how his body had felt the last time she was there, lay down and pulled the rug over her.

In the morning, she woke with a start, her nostrils full of the distinctive smell of Don, to find she was still alone in his bed. Downstairs, washed and dressed, she did her best to slip around the edge of the breakfasting men, smiling as she ate on her feet. She went up to the first-floor room and had just started to paint when Don walked in and put down his tool bag.

"Morning," he said as if nothing at all had happened. He was bending over the tool bag, speaking with his back turned.

"I looked all over the place for you last night. I got soaked," she said, sounding angrier than she wanted to.

"I had to go," he said.

I'm not playing that game, she thought. *I'm not going to ask him why he had to go or what the man in the pub meant or what happened with Dennis's nephew. I'll let him come to me, like taming an animal.*

"I borrowed a couple of books from a friend. Look." He rummaged in the bag. He seemed as calm as calm could be. They were books on Rembrandt; she knew they were his white flag, his bridge back to her. "We could check them out after work," he said. "If he *was* here, it's big news, isn't it?"

She could imagine sitting on the bed with him, reading. Being there with him, in a universe of two with the bed beneath them, was all she wanted at that moment.

"Maybe." She turned her attention back to the ceiling, determined to show no further signs of interest in the events of the previous evening.

He was carefully removing another section of the paneling that seemed unlikely to stand up to the sander's attentions. She could hear him working away at it, easing out the ancient fixings and cautiously parting the panel framing.

Then she heard complete silence, not just an absence of speech or an absence of manual activity but the total silence of someone who had stopped breathing. It lasted three or four seconds, then there was an exhaled "aah" and she looked down to see Don staring fixedly at the wall.

"What is it?"

"Come down and see."

Crouching side by side they stared at the exposed wall behind the paneling. Down to the top of the paneling, the wall had been covered in thick layers of cream paint. Years of redecoration had built it up so that it lipped out over the plain, ancient plaster behind the woodwork. How many years, Amy wondered, feeling the thickness of the lip. There on the pale, dusty plaster were a faint series of lines, almost obscured by a gray sheet of cobwebs. Using her fingers, trying not to touch the dry-as-dust surface of the plaster, Amy gathered the cobwebs, twining them like insubstantial spaghetti, and they pulled away, anxious to clasp her fingers.

What was underneath became clear.

It was the bottom half of a simple picture painted onto the wall. Two people from the waist down, the one in the foreground wearing a long pleated skirt, one foot splayed out to the side. Behind her, the suggestion of a man's legs, the feet very solidly on the ground. In front of them was the bottom corner of something rectangular and around it all, on the three visible sides, was a frame painted on the plaster, squared off inside and with freely drawn curlicues outside in yellow and brown. The lines had a vigor in them and even without the top half, they held the eye.

"Who are they?" Don's voice was gruff, his question a demand as if he had the right to an answer.

"It's Amelia," said Amy with complete certainty.

"You don't know that. There's not enough to tell."

"She's behind there," said Amy. "All the rest of her. Her face, everything. It's all behind there." She was pointing at the fat buildup of paint above the top line of the paneling where the infinitely thin outline, mere microns of fragile brown, was buried under fossil layers of obliteration.

"Can we get the paint off?"

"Can *we*? No. Could an expert? I don't know. I shouldn't think so."

"We'll have to show Parrish," said Don.

"I'll go and see if he's around."

He was just parking his car outside when she went downstairs. He was greatly interested in what they had found.

"Precisely datable," he said, peering at it, clutching the bulging folder that seemed to go everywhere with him. "Absolutely extraordinary. We can tell the date within *weeks*. Fascinating."

"Within weeks? How?" asked Amy.

"The journal. Amelia's journal," said Parrish. "Haven't you read it?"

"I've flipped through it."

"Would you be very kind and go and get it?" She left the room and for an unthinking moment found herself heading toward her bedroom to get her precious find. She stopped short, aghast at the thought of what would have happened if she had handed Parrish the ancient daybook when he was expecting the transcript of the journal.

As it was, he took his modern notebook from her with just as much reverence as if it had been the original and began to leaf through it.

"Here," he said. "No, it's somewhere. Where is it now? Yes, third week in January. She talks about the plastering and the limner. He must be a plasterer, I think, or perhaps a painter, using lime-wash. Perhaps it should be 'limer.' Then she says this. *'To my surprise, my husband directed the man to put into place the paneling which we did bring from the Hull house which was before that in the great room at Linscot before the fire. This to be done while we are in full course in the room. This has occasioned much choler in the limner who opines that the lightness of the room will be spoiled by it.'* There you are, you see. They put those panels in only a few weeks after they plastered the room. In fact the limer is still working in the room."

Don looked at him sharply. "My mother got it right," he said. "That's meant to be limner, not limer. A limner is an old word for a painter."

Parrish looked at the book again. "Either way, they were still decorating the room."

"No, he wasn't a house painter." Don looked sideways at Amy for a fraction of a second. "A limner is a portrait painter. That means he was painting her in here. He was painting Amelia. He must have done this painting on the wall. Maybe it was like a sketch to show her how it was going to look."

"Limner?" said Parrish, doubtfully, clearly unused to being corrected on seventeenth-century wording by Don.

"I promise," said Don. "I looked it up."

"Anyway, that proves the painting was done in 1662," said Amy. "Nobody would have moved the panels since, would they?"

"There's no reason to suppose they would."

"Could we get the rest of the paint off?"

"That would be a very expensive business," said Parrish. "I can't see the committee agreeing to *that* one. Not unless it turned out to be someone very significant. Perhaps it's your friend Rembrandt." He chuckled at his own joke. Amy and Don didn't. Instead, they stared at the lines on the wall.

"Speaking of whom," said Parrish, "I waited a few minutes when you two did your disappearing act."

"Oh, I'm sorry about that," said Amy, feeling it should really be Don apologizing.

"No, no, that's all right. You had your reasons. Anyway I had to get rid of that tiresome man who spilt his beer. He kept trying to engage me in conversation, so I went back to reading my file. Something to hide behind, you know how it is. I needed a bit of protection and while I was reading, I suddenly remembered van Loon."

"And he is?"

"A good question. Hendrik van Loon. Ostensibly, he was the great-grandson, nine times removed, of Rembrandt's doctor, one Joannis van Loon. He published a book in the 1930's, which he claimed was an account of Rembrandt's life."

"It's not authentic, I assume," said Amy, "judging by your tone."

"Who knows?" said Parrish. "It's written in mock seventeenth-century language but I don't think it rings true. Have you read Pepys's diaries?"

"No."

"You should. Marvelous stuff. Same time exactly but very different to our van Loon. Anyway, it's a clever book and it's stuffed with background details that fit the facts. Tries a bit *too* hard, you might say."

"I don't suppose it mentions Hull?" asked Don lightly.

"Ah! Well," said Parrish, and he stretched the syllable out to command their full attention. "As a matter of fact, it does, so there's a surprise. I've photocopied the page for you." He pulled a sheet of paper out of his folder. "Now, this comes from the foreword to the book, which is dated 1699. Van Loon starts off explaining that they had just buried Rembrandt the previous day. A pauper's funeral. He'd wanted to be buried in his wife's grave, poor old Saskia, but he'd forgotten that he'd sold it and the bones had already been dug up and thrown away. Anyway, then the doctor meets a poet friend of his and together they bump into a sea captain in a coffeehouse. The doctor says he's on his way back from a funeral. Now listen to this:

" *'And who might that be?' the poet asked, 'for I am not aware that anyone of importance has died.'*

" *'No,' I answered, 'I suppose not. He died quite suddenly. Yet you knew the man. It was Rembrandt van Rijn.'*

" *He looked at me with slight embarrassment.*

" *'Of course I knew him,' he said. 'A very great artist. I could not always follow him and he thought very differently from me on many subjects. For one thing, I don't believe that he was ever truly a Christian. But a great painter, nevertheless. Only tell me, Doctor. Are you sure it was not an impostor? For Rembrandt, if I recollect, died five years ago. He died in Hull in England.'* "

Amy interrupted. "Bloody hell," she said. "How do you explain that one?"

Parrish smiled. "Wait. It gets better.

" 'He died in Hull in England,' " he went on. " 'He had gone there to escape from his creditors. That is, if I remember correctly.'

" 'Hull?' interrupted the Captain. 'Hull, nothing! I know all about that fellow. It was he who had that quarrel with the dominies about his servant girl. But he went to Sweden some six or seven years ago. I have a friend who sails to Danzig and he took him to Gothenburg in '61 or '62.'

" 'Nevertheless, my good friends,' I answered, 'Rembrandt died last Friday and we buried him this morning.'

" 'Well,' said the good-natured Captain, 'we all have to die sooner or later and I'm sure there are plenty of painters left.' "

He stopped.

"That's extraordinary," said Amy. "There must be something to it."

Parrish shrugged. "Perhaps van Loon read the Vertue notebooks. Who knows? All these people could be feeding off the same ancient lie. That's the trouble with this sort of history. Perhaps old Laroon's mind was wandering. Perhaps he met an impostor who pretended to be Rembrandt. It might be as simple as that, and the consequences go on and on echoing right the way down to the present day. Anyway, the story doesn't want to go away, does it?" he said. He looked at each of them in turn with an intent gaze.

"I realize there's one thing you've managed not to tell me," he said.

"Which is?" Amy asked.

"Which is why you got interested in it in the first place. Why did you ask me that odd question about the man when you knew only the wrong half of his name? How did Harmenszoon van Rijn come into your life in such a way that you didn't recognize who he was?"

Amy realized, far too late, that while he might look like affability personified, Parrish was no fool.

At that moment, she might have admitted the existence of Amelia's daybook, but whether she liked it or not, there was someone else to consider now. The daybook was part of the thread binding her and Don together, and she didn't want to break it. In the short silence that resulted, the conspiracy was driven accidentally deeper.

"Come on," Parrish said, giving them each an uncharacteristically serious look. "You two seem to be sensible people. I wish you'd tell me what this is really all about."

The silence went on too long; she had to break it because Don wasn't going to.

"There's nothing really to tell. It's all a bit silly," she said. "If we come across anything that stands up, you'll be the first to hear."

Parrish stared at her, weighing her up under his gaze. She felt acutely uncomfortable, then he seemed to come to a decision.

"Do that," he said. "I promise not to laugh. Whatever you're up to, young Amy Dale, you don't strike me as silly, and I've known this young man here for long enough to know he's no fool. Anytime you want to talk, I'll be very happy to listen. Now you'd better get on before I get us all into trouble with the Hawk." He paused, irresolute, looking at the wall. "We'd better get some protection over that while we decide what to do. I'll sort something out."

He left the room and, to Amy's astonishment, Don rounded on her.

"I don't tell lies," he said, "and I don't like being involved in your lies."

"What lies?" she said.

He imitated her voice, higher and with what seemed to her to be an unfair parody of an affected accent she didn't think she had. "There's nothing much to tell. It's all too, too silly."

"What the fuck was I supposed to say, arsehole?" she snarled at him. "I didn't notice you leaping in with a full explanation. He's your old family friend, not mine." Once Amy got started, an intoxicating cocktail of chemicals brewed up by her own anger took over to push her ever further than she would have chosen to go. "You kept quiet. I had to say something. Anyway, I haven't noticed you being too honest lately."

"Meaning what?"

"Meaning maybe you should face up to the fact that you got hurt and it's not the end of the fucking world. You're hiding. You should try facing it, not rushing off every time anybody tries to talk to you. It's pathetic. I think you should . . ."

He didn't wait to find out what she thought he should do. She found she was talking to an open door. The chemical flood went with him, leaving a sick residue of embarrassed guilt. She stood feeling a crater in her stomach. That was territory she had told herself not to step into. She stared down at the lines painted on the wall without seeing them and then, when she did take notice of them, the appalling thought that the picture could yet be covered back up without anyone else knowing who might have painted it didn't stop her from giving the wall a vicious kick.

When the Hawk looked in half an hour later, she was up on the scaffolding, painting grimly. When he said, "Where's the lad gone, then?" all she answered was, "I don't know."

Ten minutes later he was back.

"He's nowhere in the house and Eric saw him heading out."

"Did he?"

"Strikes me you might know something about that."

"Well, I wonder why you should think that?"

"Come down here and look at me," he said.

She climbed down.

"Thing is," he said, "it was all right until you showed up. He was getting along fine. I warned you. We look after Don. He's one of us."

And I'm not, she thought. The implication was clear.

"Now, my guess is he's heading into town," said the foreman. He had a trick with his eyes that hooked you like a fish. Amy could not look away. "That means on foot. You've got your car. You'll maybe catch up with him."

"If I was going. Anyway, I might not find him. He might have got a lift."

"Oh, I reckon you'll find him."

"What about my work?"

"I'll tell you something. You're going to do this on your own time. I'll tell you something else. If you don't find him, your work doesn't matter because you don't need to bother coming back here again except to pack up your things, understood?"

In the aftermath of her anger, Amy was unable to summon up anything except dull acceptance. "But if he's not on the road, where do I look?"

"Around town," said the Hawk.

"It's a big town."

"Better get started then."

She choked off a reply that would have ended her employment there and then, and headed for the door, pushing past him. As she reached the top of the stairs, he seemed to soften a little.

"Try the Drydock," he said.

She stopped. "What's that?"

"His mum's place. My bet is big bad Don has run home to Mummy."

"Where is it?"

"Ask around. You'll find it."

She went first to the tower to change out of her overalls. Searching her pockets for her car keys, she stopped as she heard a noise in the room next door, a rustle and a thump as something fell to the floor. Was Don back? She went to his door and tapped on it. No answer, just another furtive noise. For a moment, she remembered the first time she had pushed that door open and frightened herself at the unexpected sight inside. She tapped again, but he still couldn't be bothered to respond. Annoyed, she pushed the door open, and something huge and white, horribly unexpected—something that seemed to come from a different time and from an altogether different reality—rose and came at her with formless arms outstretched. She leapt backward, slamming the door and trying to stifle a scream. It flapped behind the closed door, and once again she had to work hard to make sense in her head of what she had just seen. An owl, that was all. An owl that had come in through the open window, perhaps looking for the place it had always passed its days before these interfering humans came to steal its home.

Carefully, slowly, she pushed the door open again and found it perched on the back of the chair, staring at her, half the size it had seemed a moment before. They stared at each other, woman and owl, but it was better at staring than she was. *At least you're not like Don,* she thought, and looked quickly around the room. There wasn't much to see. Some of his clothes had gone. Worse, when she went back to her room she found he'd also taken Amelia Dahl's daybook. That added a layer of fury to her concern.

Don wasn't on the road. She stopped in Paull and tried all three pubs and the shop with no success, then she drove into Hull and found along the way that the very last thing she wanted to do was to confront Don's mother, wherever she might be. Seeing a half-familiar street, she backed into a meter space and realized that the library was only a hundred yards away. The library seemed a good place to ask about the Drydock but, to someone with no great wish to hear the answer, it was also a very good place to avoid the whole issue for a while. She needed silent anonymity and distraction, and she found her feet on the stairs up to the Local Studies section before she had consciously made any decision to go that way. Before she pushed open the swing doors she decided to leave it to Fate. If there was a spare machine, she would once more get out the microfilm and put the whole matter on hold for an hour or two. If not, she would go and find the Drydock.

She went in. All the machines were in use bar one, and when she asked if she might use it, they told her there was fifteen minutes to spare before the next booking. Amy chose to regard that as a sign. She asked for the film and was rewarded by a half-smile of recognition from the woman who brought it to her. Loading it took only half the time it had before and she spun through the roll of film until she reached late January.

A DAY MORE SUITED TO THE SEASON WITH WINDS FROM THE NORTH FINDING PLACES WHERE OUR ROOF IS NOT YET SEALED QUITE TIGHT. UP BETIMES BEFORE THE SUN ROSE, SETTING BASINS IN PLACE TO SAVE THE FLOOR FROM THE DRIPS THEN, BEING FAR FROM THE POSSIBILITY OF RENEWED SLEEP I DID SET MYSELF TO BRING ORDER TO THE DISARRAY OCCASIONED BELOW. ON THROWING OPEN THE KITCHEN DOOR I DID FIND TO MY SURPRISE, THE LIMNER ALREADY ABROAD AND EMPLOYING MY LARGE PESTLE TO GRIND HIS DYE-STUFF. I DID GIVE HIM THE OLD MORTAR INSTEAD TOGETHER WITH AN ACCOUNT OF MY DISTRESS AT SEEING MY PESTLE GIVEN ME BY MY MOTHER SO STAINED AND SPOILED BUT THE MADDENING FELLOW WILL BUT SMILE WHEN I SPEAK WHATEVER IT IS THAT I SAY.

IT IS TODAY THAT HE WILL START WITH ME AND I CONFESS THAT I AM NERVOUS OF HOW IT WILL BE DONE AND OF, BY NECESSITY, BEING SO LONG IN HIS PRESENCE, WHICH I FIND IS NOT AT ALL AN EASY NOR A PLEASANT BUSINESS DUE TO HIS HABITS. MY HUSBAND IS TO THE TOWN AGAIN TO SPEAK WITH THE ELDER BRETHREN OF HIS DIFFICULTIES AND MARVELL HAS GONE TO BEARD GILBY IN HIS DEN FOR

HIS EFFRONTERY IN SEEKING TO CLAIM SUNK ISLAND FOR
HIS OWN.

Gilby? Amy wondered if there could be any connection. Did Don
have ancestors in this story as well?

MARVELL DID SAY HE WOULD RETURN TO TELL ME WHAT
THE LIMNER SAYS. WE STARTED UPSTAIRS THIS NOON-TIME
AFTER THE LIMNER WAS SATISFIED WITH HIS PREPARATION,
HAVING SPILLED MUCH VENICE TURPENTINE ON THE NEW
BOARDS. I DO NOT KNOW IF I WILL STAND THE WHOLE OF
IT. IT IS A VEXING BUSINESS AND HE WILL TALK SO.

The next day's entry was very faint, and whoever had transferred it
to microfilm seemed not to have understood the finer points of focus-
ing. Amy chafed at the waste of time and went backward and forward
through it, trying to make sense of it. The section began with a long
account of a dispute with a farmer about a boundary fence, and a complaint about the difficulty of getting the workmen to listen to her instructions in the absence of her husband. Then it turned again to the
limner.

TO THE DUTCHMAN AGAIN AND MUCH VEXED BY THE
TENDENCY OF HIS CHATTERING. HE WILL SEIZE WHATEVER
MATERIALS HE FEELS HE MAY NEED WITHOUT SEEKING
APPROVAL FOR IT. MY BEST LINEN CLOTH IS UTTERLY
SPOILED BY HIS WIPINGS. HIS WORK IS NOT PLEASING BUT
MARVELL WHO IS HERE AGAIN SAYS IT IS BUT GROUND
WORK AND WILL BE ALL THE BETTER FOR IT WITH DUE TIME.
MY HUSBAND DID RETURN TOWARD THE EVENING OF THE
DAY. TO MY SURPRISE, MY HUSBAND DIRECTED THE MEN TO
PUT INTO PLACE THE PANELING WHICH WE DID BRING FROM
THE HULL HOUSE WHICH WAS BEFORE THAT IN THE GREAT
ROOM AT LINSCOT BEFORE THE FIRE. THIS TO BE DONE
WHILE WE ARE IN FULL COURSE IN THE ROOM. THIS HAS
OCCASIONED MUCH CHOLER IN THE LIMNER WHO OPINES
THAT THE LIGHTNESS OF THE ROOM WILL BE SPOILED BY IT.

Amy made a note to show Parrish that Don had been right; it was "limner" in the original. But before she had the chance to read anywhere near enough, time had run out and the next person was standing at her shoulder waiting for her to vacate the machine. She handed the roll of film back at the desk and said to the man who took it, in that hushed voice that libraries command, "Do you know a place called the Drydock? It's some kind of shelter."

"It's across the river," he said.

She thought he meant the Humber for a moment, and recoiled from the idea of crossing that enormous span to the Lincolnshire shore, miles away. Then she realized that he must be talking about the Hull.

"It's up this way," he said. "You go over the North Bridge and turn right down Great Union Street, then take another right, I think. It's got a big sign outside."

"What exactly *is* it?" she asked.

"I'm not sure. Some sort of night shelter place, I think. You know, for winos and the homeless and all that."

She thanked him and went back to the car, but a car seemed altogether too hurried a way to approach this difficult next step, so she fed the meter and followed Albion Street in the direction of the river. The directions led her down to an area which seemed to have little life left in it, scraped bare of time and dotted with chain-link fencing and utilitarian warehouses. There was a welding yard and a post office depot, straddling a road that went nowhere. It was a bleak place. An old dock, decomposing deep down, cut in from the river but ending at the road, baffled, useless, and outdated. Beyond it was a brick building, the only one in view with any age to it. She judged it to be Victorian at the latest. There was a wooden sign on the front that said "The Drydock."

Cars were parked nose to tail down the side of the road. A camera crew were heading for the front door, carrying lights and a tripod. Something had happened here.

Ominously, there were three police cars right outside the door and as she stood there, disturbed and uncertain, a policeman walked out through the door and saw her.

"Can I help you?" he said. "You look a bit lost."

"I'm looking for someone," she said. "Has something happened?"

"Depends what you mean. Who are you looking for?"

"He's called Don Gilby. Do you know him?"

"Do I know Don Gilby? Oh, yes, I certainly do. He's the reason we're here."

Oh, shit, she thought. *I knew something was waiting to happen. Is it me? Have I pushed him over some sort of edge? If I'd shut up, he'd still be at Paull Holme.*

"What's he done?"

"Plenty."

"Is he inside?"

"No, if he was, I wouldn't be out here looking for him."

FIFTEEN

WHATEVER HAD HAPPENED, IT HAD HAPPENED HERE, AND ALL THESE policemen were here because of it. Not just the police. There were others, old men in suits, young men in jeans, coming in and out, pointing, discussing, looking up and down the road. A search was in progress, that was clear, and the object of the search was equally clear.

Somewhere in all this, Amy knew, lay the answer to the questions raised by Don's injury, by the deep division amongst the builders, and by Dennis's distrust. She stood there, needing to know yet unsure how to join in, then intuition took over. She put herself into his mind. Water. He would head for the water. To the right of the building, separating it from the mud-filled dock that gave it its name, was a chain-link fence. In the mud alongside, she spotted a fresh footprint. Another footprint pointed her down the side of the dock toward the river, where a stone seawall made up the river's edge, with the water a few feet below. The top of the seawall formed a narrow ledge, hard up against the back wall of the shelter. The remains of a great balk of timber, a cushioning fender for the ships that used to moor there, was still attached to it a few feet below the top and, sitting on it as though he did not greatly care whether its ancient fastenings buckled under his weight, was Don, with his feet dangling over the water.

"Oh, Christ," he said when he saw her. "Don't you ever give up?"

"They're all looking for you."

"And of course *you* found me."

"Look, Don. You can't stay here, can you?"

He looked down at the muddy water. "I can do anything I want."

"Tell me what happened. Please."

"Why the fuck should I? Do you know, I think I'd rather go in there and face them all."

Looking at his face—eyes blazing, anger overcoming his habitual need to turn the scar away from view—she knew he would force his way past her even if by doing so, he pushed her in. She backed away and followed him back through a gap in the fencing.

"I'll come with you," she called.

He hardly paused. "You might as well see the final act. I can't stop you, can I?"

There were two policemen standing by the door of the shelter when they came into view, and they both lunged for their walkie-talkies. Don went straight toward them with Amy trying to catch up. One began to head him off, thought better of it, and stepped back, but by that time, Don was in between them and through the door. Amy followed him into a large downstairs room full of people, saw a barrage of flashbulbs and, to her astonishment, heard the whole crowd of them burst into thunderous applause.

It was a big, basic dayroom, a place people would choose to sit only because the alternatives were much, much worse. The walls were pale pastel orange and festooned with posters about health care, welfare programs, and addiction services. Battered chairs had been pushed back against the wall. A table by the window carried the TV cameraman, shooting over the heads of the crowd that filled the entire room. Behind another table at the other end stood a small group of people, watching Don's entrance. There was a lean old man with long white hair, a woman wearing a heavy gold chain of office, and a tall policeman with the silver braid of high rank on his cap. Don was back-slapped through the crowd, past the other photographers to the front, where an older woman came forward and hugged him. She had his eyes and nose, and the way she led him to one side so that he could shelter his face as he chose proved she had to be his mother. Amy thought she was a good-looking woman, with a weather-beaten touch of the older Lauren Bacall about her. She'd have held her own next to Bogart. Then she realized with surprise that Peter Parrish was standing behind Don's mother. The man with the white hair held up a hand and everyone fell silent.

"It falls to me as chairman of the trustees of the Drydock Project," he said, "to welcome our good friend Don Gilby here today to receive our thanks and a gallantry award for the action he took here in this room three months ago. I know from his mother that he wants me to keep this short, but I also know there are many people here who would not be at all happy if we didn't express our gratitude properly."

Don was looking at the floor.

"On Saturday, August twelfth of last year, young Don was paying a visit to this building to see his mother, our own greatly respected Ellen. Now as you will know, Ellen does not like to turn anybody away from this project, but during the previous week she had encountered serious and continuing problems with a particular client who had a long and troubled past history. I am unable to say much about the man in question, Vincent Williams."

Vin, thought Amy. *Dennis's Vin.*

"Williams is currently in custody awaiting trial," the man went on, "although I am sure the management committee and trustees of this project would urge the authorities to take into account his history of mental health difficulties combined with substance abuse when they come to decide how to deal with him. However, I am told that he has decided to plead 'not guilty.' " He looked around the audience as if that fact freed him from the need to go any further with his plea for sympathy. "Suffice it to say that when Don arrived, the man had been asked to leave the premises and had apparently done so. We now know that he had not gone far."

Don gazed even more intently at the floor. Amy, desperate to hear the details, felt she had got everything about as wrong as possible, a clumsy interloper in someone else's world, someone else's affairs. Don's disappearance had nothing to do with her at all. If he was planning to come here all the time, why hadn't he asked the Hawk instead of getting her into trouble? She looked up and saw Don's mother staring at her, and looked quickly away because there was a challenge in that stare that didn't seem friendly. There were too many people in that room, closing in on her.

"The man in question, undoubtedly in a troubled state of mind, came across a group of council workmen farther down the road, dealing with a fallen tree. While they were distracted, he was apparently able to take from their vehicle a chain saw ..."

Amy's skin chilled. Two men near her were writing furiously in notebooks.

"... and make away with it before they realized it had gone. He returned at once to this building, started the saw and, it would appear, set upon the first person he saw, our well-loved colleague Sarah Mulvaney who, as we know and deeply regret, lost her life in the attack."

He was silent for a moment and Amy could see he was struggling to fight back tears.

"By the greatest of good fortune, as Williams was making for the stairs, Don happened to arrive in the building and, without any regard for his own personal safety, tackled the assailant, forcing him to the ground and taking the chain saw from him. At this point, roused by the noise, Ellen, who was entertaining Mr. Parrish in her office, came down the stairs and between them they were able to subdue the assailant. By this time, however, in the course of the struggle, Don had suffered severe injuries. He will bear the scars of those injuries for the rest of his life."

There was loud applause but still Don did not look up. *He* knows *that,* thought Amy. There was no need to say it. She saw Ellen staring at her son.

The speech continued in that manner for a little longer. Then came the presentation of the award, at which point Don had to get up and play his part, though he resisted all attempts to make him say something. He took some sort of plaque from the policeman, mumbled a "thank you" and something else Amy couldn't hear, then his mother, looking at him in concern, took his arm and led him upstairs. There was a chorus of worried noises in the room at which point the man with the white hair stood up again.

"Do help yourselves," he called. "There's a buffet laid out in the kitchen."

A young man pushed through the people toward Amy. He wore a

black jacket that owed its origins more to crude oil than to cowhide and he brandished a spiral-bound notebook at the ready.

"You the girlfriend?" he said.

"If that's a question it seems to be lacking a verb," said Amy. A flashbulb went off in her face.

"What's your name?"

"I'm *not* the girlfriend."

"What are you doing here, then?"

"I was just passing."

He laughed. "No one just happens to be passing this place. Tell us your name, anyway."

He wasn't local, Amy thought. His voice sounded more Midlands.

"Emma Bovary," she said.

He wrote it down. "Bove ... How do you spell that?"

"B–O–V–A–R–Y," she said helpfully.

"Are you proud of him?"

"I don't even know him," said Amy. "I was looking for the Job Center."

Someone took her by the arm and said firmly, "We need you upstairs."

Don's mother.

"Ha!" said the reporter triumphantly and another flashbulb went off.

As if Amy were under arrest, Ellen did not lessen her grip on her arm until they arrived at a room upstairs where Don sat at a table with a mug of tea, looking pale and exhausted.

"Why *did* you come?" he said to the mug. "I'm beginning to feel like I've got no private life as far as you're concerned."

"He needs leaving alone, love," said Ellen. "That's what he needs. Today's bad enough for him without you showing up."

"I didn't know anything about today," said Amy. "I wouldn't have intruded if I had."

Don thumped the table with his fist, spilling tea. Amy jumped. "You don't *need* to know. It's got nothing to do with you at all. You keep doing this. 'I didn't know.' That's what you keep saying. As if all I've got to do is tell you absolutely bloody everything about me, as if you've got some *right* to know so that then you can decide which bits are your business and which bits aren't. Why don't you just fuck off and—"

Which was when Amy, instead of getting angry as she normally would, burst unexpectedly into tears, thinking as she did, with peculiar clarity, *Damn—that's the second time he's got to me.*

Don didn't flinch but it wasn't in Ellen's nature to see somebody suffering and not do anything to help.

"Oh, come on now, love. Have a sit-down. Shall I get you a cuppa? There's a fresh pot."

"Don't fall for it," said Don, "she's just—"

"Shut it, Don," snapped Ellen. "Don't mind about him, love. Take a deep breath and just tell us, that's me and my unfeeling lout of a son over there, how you came to be here, because he wasn't exactly planning to shout it from the rooftops, you see?"

"B-but you've got the TV here and the press and—"

"*We* didn't get them. They just came. Someone told them and I'm sure I can guess who," said Ellen, grimly. "That's why the star of the show here did his vanishing trick at the crucial moment. So what brought *you* here?"

"I was told to come. I didn't plan it. I . . . Well, he said I'd lose my job unless I went and found Don and got him back and—"

"Who's '*he*'?" asked Ellen.

"Hawk. The foreman. He said I needn't bother coming back if I didn't find Don and it was all my fault. He said things had been all right before I arrived, so I went to look for him but he wasn't on the road and Hawk said I should come here if I couldn't find him and when I—"

"Hang on right there," said Ellen. She was lighting a cigarette, and Amy thought she would like to paint Don's mother entirely in diluted shades of tobacco juice, nicotine brown. Until that moment she had thought Ellen dyed her hair, but now she realized the yellow at the front was stained by the smoke.

"So, young man," Ellen went on when she'd taken a drag, "did you forget to tell the boss you were taking the day off?"

"He lets me work the hours I choose. Bloody Parrish knew, didn't he? He's here. I didn't want to have to tell everyone what was happening."

"He's not *bloody* Parrish. Don't start that again, and he's not your boss, is he? It's the foreman you have to ask." She looked at him judiciously and blew a very ragged smoke ring. "But I have a suspicion that it quite suited you to pick your moment so it looked like this poor lass had pushed you into walking out."

"It wasn't like that."

"Wasn't it?"

"Coincidence, that was all."

"I'll believe you. Thousands wouldn't." She straightened up. "Listen, you two, I'd better go and do a bit of pressing the flesh. Stay up here or come down. It's up to you."

In the silence after she had gone, Don continued to look at his mug, then eventually he said, "I didn't want the rest of them to know. I'm sorry the Hawk gave you a mouthful."

She shrugged.

It wasn't the time to ask about the division of opinion amongst the men of Paull Holme, much as she wanted to.

"That doesn't matter now. This is your day. Shouldn't you be downstairs?"

He just shook his head.

The speech downstairs had cleared Amy's head of the whirl of suspicion and fear instilled by Dennis. She looked across at Don and saw only the damage, the bravery, and the sweet potential for them both. Reaching across, she squeezed his good hand but got no response.

"What you did was great," she said gently. "I was so relieved. I thought the police were looking for you because you'd done something dreadful."

"Maybe I did," he replied, staring at their hands together on the table as if they had nothing to do with him, "but why would you have thought that?"

That was a mistake, she thought. She tried to pass it off. "I don't know. No real reason. The police were—"

"Because Dennis talked to you. That was it, wasn't it?"

"Dennis? Well, he only said ..." her voice trailed off.

"What did he say?" Don's voice was venomous.

He's entitled to sound like that, she thought. *If Dennis's mad, smashed nephew nearly killed him, he's allowed to be angry.*

"Nothing I took any notice of," she said firmly. "He's loyal to his family, that's all."

"Don't talk to him anymore, OK?" He took his hand away and scratched at the hard surface of the table with a finger. "It's all bullshit, though, isn't it?" His voice had changed, become less harsh.

"What is?"

"This whole award thing. I was shitting myself. There was nothing gallant about that."

"Being afraid makes it braver, not less brave."

"You'd know, would you?"

"No."

"I can't remember what I thought. There was him, that guy, and a hell of a mess and hell of a lot of noise. You know how much racket those saws make? The room was full of the smoke and the smell of it. That and blood. The woman was on the floor and there was blood all over everything. I didn't know what was going on. Do you know what I thought first?"

She shook her head.

"I thought, Mum's going to be really annoyed at all this mess. Then we were fighting and the saw was revving and first I had it, then he had it, then I had it again."

She kept silent waiting for him to finish.

"Everybody thinks I was protecting Mum and the others. Maybe I was just protecting me. What's brave about that? It was him or me. Gut reaction, nothing to do with heroism, and it didn't stop the woman dying."

Listening, Amy felt every word etching its way into her memory. Why did he say "the woman"? Why not "Sarah"? Did it make it easier?

"People love heroes," he went on. "If there isn't a real hero about, they'll invent one. They invented me. So can we stop talking about it now? Forever?"

"All right. Tell me something else, then. Were you coming back?"

He glanced half up at her. "To the job? Why do you ask?"

"I looked in your room. Just to see if you were there. It seemed to me that you'd taken a lot of stuff with you."

He laughed. He laughed in a straightforward way, the way you do when someone says something funny, not the way he'd laughed in the past, not to fend off anything.

"There's a washing machine here. One of those industrial ones. It gets my overalls clean."

"Yes, but there's something else. My book, Amelia's daybook. You took that, too." It occurred to her as she said it that there was another possibility: Dennis might have taken it. But Don was looking embarrassed.

"Yeah, sorry."

"Why?"

"I thought I might show it to my mother while I was here. Didn't get round to it though, what with all the commotion."

"You could have asked." *And I would have said no,* she thought. "I didn't come straight here," she said instead. "I went to the library first. I read a bit more of Amelia's journal. It's the bit where he's starting to paint her portrait."

"Ah."

"She doesn't like it. She gets really irritated with him because he keeps talking."

"No, she doesn't."

"What do you mean? I've just read it. That's what she says."

"I've just read it, too. It's not like that at all."

"In the *daybook*? You opened another page of the daybook?" She didn't say it, but her tone of voice implied the silent words *without asking me, without sharing it.* "There was an owl in your room," she added illogically.

"He's back, is he?" Don fidgeted. "Maybe I shouldn't have. I was angry. Anyway, it's not really yours, is it?"

"I'll hand it over to Parrish, don't you worry," she said bitterly. "I know I can't keep it. I just want to read it first. Well, are you going to tell me what it said?"

"You can read it now, if you like. You're better at it than I am. I might have got it wrong. There's no hurry, they'll be eating the sausage rolls downstairs for a while yet."

"Where is it?"

He got up from the table, went to a cupboard at the back of the room, and took out the daybook. He wiped the table with his sleeve and put it down in front of Amy, opening it carefully. "See what you make of this."

She had seen the start of this passage before. Indeed she had read it, revised and tidied up, only an hour or two earlier. She started to read.

"Out loud," said Don. "Please."

" 'A winter day after sunshine with north winds showing the places where the men have not yet done their proper job in the roof. Roused from sleep before sunrise by rain on my bed and set bowls in place to save the floor.'

"Yes. That's it. This is the same bit I read in the journal," she said excitedly. "The words are a bit different but it's about the same things. She finds him in the kitchen next. That's right. Listen."

She read again of Amelia's annoyance at finding the Dutchman in her kitchen, using her best pestle and mortar, then " '... I did give him the old mortar instead together with a full remonstrance at the spoiling of my best pestle but the fellow will but smile when I speak whatever it is that I say. It is most hard to be out of sorts for long with him. He has a wise face and a knowing eye.' "

Amy stopped reading and looked up at Don. "She didn't say that in the journal."

"Go on."

" 'Today he is to start, at my husband's command, on my portrait and I confess that I am nervous of how it will be to sit so long in his presence without making some mistake. My husband is to town to flog a dead horse with the Elder Brethren concerning his difficulties and Marvell has gone to challenge Gilby for the rights to claim Sunk Island, which all men say should be no man's but Crown land, being risen from the river by the grace of the Lord. I do not think one may draw a line between Marvell and Gilby in this, both being out for themselves in the matter and anxious to secure the island for no other benefit but their own.'

"Did you know there was a Gilby in it?" Amy asked Don.

"He was in Parliament, too. He's supposed to be a relation of ours."

"What's that all about?"

"Haven't a clue," he said. "Mum will know."

"I don't want you telling her about it."

"I already have."

"Have you?" She could feel her ownership of the daybook slipping away, which brought with it a desperate sense of loss. Amelia was hers, not theirs. "But isn't she on Parrish's side? She worked for him."

"She did more than that," he said. There was an edge of black night in his voice.

"Why do you say it like that?" she said.

"What do you mean?"

"You sounded angry."

"I don't like Parrish fawning over my mum, OK? My business. We'll show it to Parrish when we're ready. Mum's as interested as we are. Don't forget, it was her who typed out the journal. Go on."

" 'We did start upstairs this noon-time when Vanrin was quite ready, spilling much Venice turpentine on the new boards so that I gave instructions for a cloth to be brought to protect the wood, a vexing business. There is to be a contest as they tell me between Vanrin and Marvell, his picture of me ranged against Marvell's next verse, and I am to be the judge of it and the decider of the prize. He amuses me, this limner, being sharp of eye and quick of tongue. Nor does he know how to hold his tongue but does make very free with his thoughts on all matters. I shall stay dumb at all times, otherwise ill chance may . . .'

"End of the page," said Amy. "Can we open the next one?"

"Not without damaging it. I tried."

Amy weighed the fragile daybook in her hands. "We're going to have to be very careful of this."

"Too right you are," said Ellen, coming back in through the door, "otherwise, there'll be hell to pay. I'm not going to be answerable if you damage *that*. Let me see it." She took it and held it reverently in her hands, opening the pages no more than halfway. Amy's resentment vanished. This woman understood.

"You'll give it to him soon, won't you, love?" Ellen asked. Amy nodded.

"Do you know about Sunk Island?" asked Don. "He talks about it."

" 'Course I do. You should, too. I've told you the story. Come to think of it, you've been there enough times." She started pulling drawers open. "There's a map here somewhere. Have you seen it? Oh, here it is. Someone's pulled the cover off."

She spread it out on the table and jabbed a finger at a big bulge projecting from the north bank of the Humber.

"See it there? Before 1660 you wouldn't have. Didn't used to be there. It was just a mud bank at low tide, then something changed and it began drying out. You go there now and it's hard to believe it. Must be five miles long and a couple of miles wide, and there's just a couple of muddy old creeks that meet up round the back of it to show it was once an island. Do you see there's a house marked?"

Amy peered at the map. "The Old Hall?"

"That's it. It was a Gilby who built that. Colonel Anthony Gilby. Supposed to be some ancestor of ours. He got his hands on the whole thing, being a Member of Parliament you see, using his influence. There were two Members, him and Marvell, and they bloody hated each other. Marvell loathed the colonel so much he had a big fight with him once in the House of Commons. Got into loads of trouble for it, too. I reckon it was because the colonel got Sunk Island before Marvell grabbed it."

"So you know all about Marvell?" asked Amy.

Ellen stared at her in shock. "Where were you brought up? He's even had pubs named after him."

"I'm sorry. I'm not up on the history of Hull; I'm still learning."

"I'm not talking about the history of Hull, for God's sake. I'm talking about the history of *England*. Didn't you do English at school? Everybody knows about Marvell."

"So it is the same one: Andrew Marvell, the poet?"

"Of course it is."

SIXTEEN

Thursday, January 23rd, 1662

I BEGAN TO PAINT AMELIA DAHL ON AN OVERCAST THURSDAY AFTER-
noon, when the thin cloud was on fire with a glow of flattened sunlight. That light was god-given. It was a light you might get, with luck,
once or twice in a year, and it lasted only three hours before the kind
god who gave it took it back into his safekeeping. It filled the room
with soft, even definition, and I tried to commit to memory and to my
palette every nuance of its remarkable effect. What that light did was to
give me perfect tone and perfect detail. You cannot imagine the effect
of light such as that; when I was young, it would only have produced a
variety of despair in me knowing I could never capture its totality in
the time it would last. Now I am older, I know better. I already have
the index to that light in my memory, and I know how to capture certain key tones and textures, a notebook, if you like, for the rest of the
painting.

It almost made me want to paint a landscape. When I was woken
by all the noise no more than an hour after dawn, I went to the front of
the house where a queue of oxcarts waited. They were piled high with

earth, which men with long-handled spades were spreading across the ground. This required a deal of shouting. Piling fresh earth on a good field appeared to me an unprofitable way to spend money, but the lady wants her flat lawn, it seems.

She was watching from the window above, looking ready to leap down and grab a shovel herself if any of them made a mistake.

Needing a piss, I walked to one side of the hubbub to a place where a low hedge shielded me from view and let fly. Halfway through I looked up at the river and spied a ship. A large tub with masts and sails sat on the still water like no other ship in the history of ships, suspended in a new medium, a lake of yellow mercury, the ship itself as dense as if it were carved out of coal and so clear that every knothole in its planking could be descried despite the distance. I was so astounded that I peed on my boots and, an instant later, received a violent blow to the back of my head and a torrent of what could only have been abuse delivered in a strident female voice.

I turned and, in so doing, hosed the person who had administered the buffet with a last squirt of urine, entirely by accident. This served to increase the volume of her criticism somewhat. By her dress, her huge size, and her floured hands, I understood her to be the cook. She continued to upbraid me, trying to slap me again whilst I mimed incomprehension and dodged out of the way of her enormous hand. When she pointed at the plants I had so recently been watering and mimed eating, I made the mistake of laughing, which earned me another blow, propelling me into the row of vegetables and fueling her tirade still further. I was compelled in the end to take to my heels, neglecting to secure my member before so doing, and as a result I had to run the gauntlet of laughter and ribald cheering from the shovel brigade, though at the time I didn't understand the reason. All because of one small mistake, which meant I did not get another chance to look at the water until I was back at the front door.

Long ago, when I was starting out as an artist, I realized people will pay far more for a portrait than for a landscape. The only way to make landscapes pay is to etch them and sell as many prints as the market will bear. This was not a view for an etching. This light was made for painting but, though I had an unusual desire to capture that otherworldly river, I had an altogether stronger desire to wrestle with the image of Amelia Dahl in the room upstairs. That thought made me aware that the area around my yard, my pintle, my member, whatever you choose to call it, was somewhat cooler than it ought to have been, thereby explaining the raucous reaction of the shovel brigade. This was a timely discovery to make before coming into her presence, and I was able to secure myself in time. Half of me hoped she had not noticed my state of exposure from her window above, occupied, as she clearly was, by her vision of the perfect garden. The other half hoped she had.

The moment at which Mistress Amelia Dahl, the lady of the house, the proud possession of an autocratic husband, the fire and life of Paull Holme Manor, finally sat down in the chair was a moment I had been eagerly awaiting, a moment with the potential to change everything. What power is afforded the artist. As soon as a man starts to paint a woman, the usual conventions disappear. He has every right to stare at her, to walk around her, to touch her so as to adjust her posture. He is a painter. He can get away with almost anything in the course of practicing his art.

Not only that. Her beauty, her most precious possession, is in his hands. How can a woman see herself? Only in a mirror or in a painting. A mirror most decidedly does not tell her how the rest of the world sees her. It shows her transposed from side to side, and whatever tricks she may try with other mirrors subtly arranged at angles to each other, she can never catch herself properly the right way round. Does it make a difference? Yes, of course, it does. However pleased or displeased she may be at what she sees in the glass, it is not her as others see her.

Only in a painting can she hope to find that truth.

The truth is in the hands of the painter. She has delivered her most precious secret, the secret of what she truly looks like, into the hands of the painter and she is utterly beholden to him, in thrall for the entire time it takes to produce that painting. The painter is a priest. He is in charge of a mystery, which is perhaps why the process of painting takes on the character of the confessional. Leave a pretty woman hanging between heaven and hell, immobile in that chair in front of you, and within thirty minutes she will start to bare her soul. However haughty she may be at the start of it, she will need to get you on her side, to draw you in so that you are kind to her because she has no idea, sitting there, whether the paint going onto the hidden canvas is kind or unkind. All she knows is that the picture is a judgment. It is a judgment that will be seen not only by herself, but by everyone who comes into her house who will be paraded in front of it by her husband—not necessarily because he is proud of her but because he is proud of the picture, the artifact, and what it says about his ability to pay for such things. It will haunt her, this picture whose back she is staring past as she sits and sits and sits.

She sat there in front of me, and shed ten years of age and inner certainty immediately. I looked at her so hard that I found I could alter her face with the force of my gaze. I stared at her left eye, wondering how to do justice to its pure blue brightness, when her eyelid began to flutter. I transferred my gaze to the right eye, which was rendered a shade greener by the light reflecting from the wall, and its eyelid also blurred with irresistible movement. I ran my eyes, like the gentlest brush, slowly down the angle of her cheek to the very corner of that tremendous mouth and found the lips moistening for me. I came out from behind the easel made for me by the joiners on Marvell's say-so, and saw both eyes widen as I approached her. I was unable to resist taking her shoulders gently in my hands and moving them just a little round to the light and then just a little back again to where they had been before. When I took my hands away, she spoke. I have no idea what she said but it was obviously a question from the intonation. Probably something like, "Am I sitting wrong?"

It occurred to me with a huge sense of disappointment that this sitting could not follow its ideal course. If I couldn't understand her, what use could that confessional process be to me? When I painted Maria Trip, she talked her way out of her clothes in three sittings. All I had to do was make sympathetic noises when she told me of what her stepfather had tried to make her do with him in her mother's absence. Amelia gave a little gasping chuckle when she realized the pointlessness of what she had said, and put her hand to her mouth.

I smiled in response. "I wish I could speak your language, but alas, I am unlikely to learn it in the time available." It was a lie. English sounded barbarous to me. I had not the slightest wish to learn it. Dutch had been good enough until now.

She looked at me questioningly and, suddenly understanding what an interesting freedom this gave me, I said, "If I *could* speak English, I would sing your praises. I would tell you how the touch of light on your cheek is a rougher kiss than its beauty warrants. I would tell you how hard I will have to work to make the paint flow as smoothly as your skin, because I must break my habit and paint you as smoothly as a picture ever was painted. I would tell you how I am already quite convinced I have never seen such a fine-looking woman as you. If I could speak your language, that is what I would tell you."

She stared back at me with an expression that said she had understood more from the way I spoke than I had intended. I resolved to be more careful. I made my voice as flat as if I were ordering groceries, risking only the occasional glance at her while I studied my canvas.

"I know when you look at me, you see a man who appears to you to be of no consequence, but there are ten thousand women in Amsterdam who would give up everything for the privilege of sitting where you are sitting. I would not let a single one take your place. In all my life, I have never before had to rise to such a challenge. If I can do you justice, then your portrait will be a picture that all men will fall in love with as soon as they look at it."

I inspected the wooden panels on my easel with a measure of despair, wishing in a moment of weakness that they were, after all, canvas, and four times the size because there are things you can do with a brush and canvas that board will not allow. You can work your passion into the push and give of the canvas and leave on it the record of the raw emotion in your arm. My painting has for some years now been all about raw emotion, of troweling and pummeling the paint onto the canvas so that it becomes the undulating topography of my emotions. This board was a stiff substitute.

Her eyes followed me as I talked. I was arranging my palette, a job my students used to do for me, but here it required my fullest concentration. Dutch women are almost all the same color. They tend to the blue, gray shades as they get older, and when they're dead they go white, then eventually green like anybody else, but any of my students could put together a good enough palette without even seeing the client. What you need on your palette for a standard Dutch face is red lake, vermilion, red ochre and light ochre, umber, coal black, green earth, and one of the yellows. It goes without saying you also need an exceedingly fine lead white. I have always believed in the purity you achieve by keeping your pigments to a minimum. I find if I try to combine more than five or six of these, I begin to lose that perfect control. I was struggling more than usual because in Amsterdam, I know *exactly* what to expect when I start mixing, *exactly* how one pigment will mix with another. We had done well enough on our trip to York, but there was much I had to learn about the English versions of my colored friends. The ochres, in particular, were very grainy and did not mix easily. Even if I'd had my own studio available to me, it would have been a hard job. This woman in front of me was a true challenge. I began to experiment, talking the entire time.

"No, that's not it. That's the color for the clearest skin I have seen until now, but it is still twenty shades away from *your* color. I think I may have to mince you up and mix you into the oil. It's the only way to do it."

I got the base tone at least, by taking unheard-of liberties with that pigment mixture Lievens always liked to call nun's blush. I took an egg from the bowl I had requested, broke it, and stirred a little of the yolk into the mixture, working it until it ran like cream. Then I put brush to board and began to paint in the dead ground, the background color, to lay the foundations for the most exquisite construction I had yet attempted.

My stare now became a truly professional tool, with all my concentration focused on doing her justice. I could touch her with my eyes as if my gaze was a willow wand reaching across to dimple her skin.

"If we could talk, you and I, then I would ask you if there are many more like you in your family. Your mother must be a great beauty and your father the most handsome of men to have made you as you are."

She stared through me, oblivious. Thinking, no doubt, that I was speaking of the weather.

I had the dead color for her head done now, and normally I would have sent my sitter away for a while because the ground for the body could be put in without her once I had the outline right. She did not know that, so she could sit there for my pleasure alone. I painted in silence for some time, and now I had the excuse for my gaze to travel down her body. "Excuse" is perhaps the wrong word. It was an absolute necessity that I should study her body.

She wore a soft cloth, unlike anything they wear in Amsterdam, as sheer as silk but in texture more like cotton. It followed the demands of its weight. It rushed down from above, as if desperate to reach the floor, molding itself to her flesh. I had to get it right and if that meant studying it, then so be it. I could see the effect on her as my eyes fed on the adorable complexities of her breasts. I have always been fond of ample women with ample breasts, breasts to be played with, pillows of breasts, but one had to be silent in the presence of *these* breasts. They had a subtlety of form and they came to a focus, a point almost, not a blunt buffer. Saskia, Hennie, and even spiteful Geertge had admirable breasts, but they might have been a different part of the anatomy altogether compared to these. As I ran my eye backward and forward, I could see from the corner of my gaze that Amelia's color was rising with each pass, that her lips had parted slightly more, that her breath was coming faster, and that each time she exhaled a glaze of moisture appeared on those perfect lips.

"I expect you would like to know about the women in my own life," I said. "They usually ask, my sitters, those who don't know. I have been married only once. You would have liked Saskia. She had spirit enough for a room full of girls. When I met her, she could have made Job laugh. The flash in her eye could set off a cannon. We needed nobody else, we two, and time stood still for us in reverent silence when we were alone. She was my great love.

"What happened to her, do I hear you ask? Can you tell by my voice that something did happen? She died. Consumption consumed her and made her still prettier with its treacherous colors and I died with her because *all* of life changed. Every single bit of it. Someone loaded all the humor onto carts and took it away in the night. There was no joy anywhere. I painted the three worst pictures of my *life* that year, so bad that I cut them up and burnt them on the fire. I know the doctor thinks I killed her myself. He didn't say so, but he kept telling me to keep her away from the fumes. There was acid in the house, you see. For the etching. It is never very kind to the lungs."

I finished the dead color for the walls behind her and mixed up something that sufficed for her clothes.

"Saskia was rare. Do you know that? She was daring and brave and funny and respectable all at once. She came of good stock, you know, so all those tedious solid citizens would forgive her the odd bout of high jinks. By my nuptial relationship with her they would forgive me, too. Then she was dead, and I lost the goodwill that had come with her. I acted stupidly then. I turned for comfort to the nearest woman, a woman who had come into the house as a nurse, and she tried to take from me everything I had. Do you know that? No, of course you don't.

At least that part of my reputation is safe here. After that there was Hennie, and she is a dear heart and she puts up with me mostly, but I mourn the death of all the fun and all the love and all the joy. I mourn."

I woke up to myself eventually, realizing I had been standing there silent, doing nothing and staring into space for heaven knows how long. Amelia wore a strained expression, as if unsure whether to try to attract my attention. *My God,* I thought, remembering what I had done to her husband also.

"Finished," I said, gesturing for her to get up.

She understood and tried to stand, but her legs seemed to have gone to sleep and I held out a hand to her. I pulled her to her feet and she came fast out of the chair, close to me. I saw I still had not caught the full measure of her extraordinary face, so I put up a hand to warn her not to move.

"My hands must measure you. They must know you for the sake of the brushes," I said, and I ran my fingers down each side of her face, then backward and forward over her brow, softly stroking each cheek and brushing the warm, wet lips.

"What the hell do you think you're doing?" said a voice from the doorway.

SEVENTEEN

Wednesday, April 11, 2001

DON WAS WALKING FAST WITH HIS BAG OVER HIS SHOULDER AND Amy, skirting a puddle that he had strode right through, felt a physical tie between them tugging her in his wake, a tie that would start to ache if stretched too far. Anything could have been happening around him and she would have been oblivious. She tried to catch up, needing to be near him, wanting to talk, drawn after him by biological magnetism; her eyes were fixed on the way he walked, athletic and contained, prowling again. From here behind him, there was no sign of the damaged man to get in the way.

"If they'd given him a first name, I would have known," she said. "If Amelia had written *Andrew* Marvell. I felt such a fool when your mother said that. I did ask you, didn't I? You said he was a politician."

"He was. He was both."

She was beside him now, where she felt she belonged. They were walking up the side of the marina in the old docks.

"Let's get a drink," said Amy.

"Are you thirsty?"

"It's a sociable activity, Don. Sitting in the sun with a glass in your hand is not just about drinking. It's about watching the world go by together. It's about seeing and being seen. There's no hurry, is there? We've got as long as we want. The Hawk didn't set me a time limit on finding you."

What she wanted was to be with him, just the two of them, away from Paull Holme, away from anybody else they knew. She wanted to give the uncertain flame between them another chance to catch and burn bright.

"There's a place up here," he said. "It's old." The enthusiasm had vanished from his voice.

Seeing and being seen, she thought. *Was that a stupid thing to say?*

"Go on," she said. "Tell me what you know about Marvell."

"OK, I knew he was the same one, really. I wasn't thinking. Ellen says round here, people didn't even know he *was* a poet. At the time he was just a politician. All that poetry stuff only came out much later when the Victorians discovered him."

"How do you suddenly know all that?"

Don glanced at her, and she suspected for a moment that such information was currency to him, to be gathered, hoarded, and spent when it suited him to bring them closer.

"You took your time in the loo. I asked Ellen."

Relieved at the honesty of that reply, she let go of her suspicions.

"Does your mum know a lot about history?"

"Hull history mostly. She's mad about it. Reads everything. That's why she did all that work for Parrish. She's always borrowing bits and pieces from him. She does extra night shifts at the shelter. Doesn't need to. I mean, she's the boss, but she manages on a couple of hours sleep and reads the rest of the time. If it's quiet." He fell silent and she guessed he was thinking of a day when it hadn't been.

"So what else did she say?"

Don frowned. "He wasn't *just* a politician. He was a bit of a diplomat, maybe even a spy. Oh, and she said he was certainly a turncoat."

"Meaning?"

"Meaning he was on Cromwell's side right through the revolution. When the king came back, he persuaded everybody he'd always been a royalist to get elected to Parliament, but all the time, he was away on funny foreign trips, cloak-and-dagger stuff."

"What sort of stuff?"

"Don't know. Ask Ellen. Ask Parrish. He knows everything."

The Minerva was located on the end of the row of warehouses that flanked the old docks. It was long and thin and it protruded to face the Humber with a narrow bow-fronted prow, rounded off to split the cold winds that might tear in from the estuary.

Amy left Don at an outside table, away from the other drinkers, and went to get two beers. When she came back out, she could tell right away that the short respite they had enjoyed was already over. He was hunched in his chair, turned awkwardly away to the wall. The reason lay in the noisy family who had moved in to occupy the adjoining table. All brisk and smiling, she pushed past the family, their stroller, and their two quarreling toddlers, and put his glass down in front of him.

" 'To His Coy Mistress,' " she said. "I remembered. That's his big one, isn't it? I don't think I know any of the rest."

"That's the only one I know. It's the only one anybody knows, I think."

It was a good sign, she thought, that he took her offer of distraction eagerly. She craved a normal conversation with him, a conversation without an edge. A conversation that would answer this breathless expectation building in her.

"How does it go? Something about winged chariots?"

"That's it."

"If you know it, you tell me."

He laughed. It was a wonderful thing. The laughter opened the curtains behind his eyes. Until that moment all that had attracted her to him was dark. She knew that staying too long in the darkness would inevitably chill her; here at last was the chance of sunshine, of something more durable.

"If you think I'm going to spout love poems at you in public, you can think again. The general public might get the wrong idea."

"In private, then?"

"No. Then *you* might get the wrong idea." Amy felt a twinge of disappointment, but decided to let it go.

"So nobody knew he was a poet?"

"One or two of the old books mention it, but they just say things like, 'He also writes poems but they're very hard to understand.' My mum told me he worked for Milton. Did you know that?"

"John Milton? *Paradise Lost* Milton?"

"That's the one. Milton had some government job under Cromwell. Something to do with foreigners because he spoke lots of languages, and Marvell did, too."

"So Marvell became a poet because of that?"

"Who knows? Maybe."

"Go on. Remind me. How does the winged chariot one start?"

He smiled as if he was about to. He even opened his mouth to say something that could have been the first line, but the older of the two toddlers at the next table forestalled him. It was a boy of indeterminate age whose sole contribution to the high noise level at the next table had been to wail very loudly that its father had brought the wrong flavor chips. Now it came, or rather waddled because chips were clearly the main part of its diet, to their table in order to place on it the half-full plastic beaker it had been holding. The beaker was an unpleasant sight, containing a mush of some purple soft drink into which the child had crushed the rest of the packet of the wrong flavor of chips. Its parents were smiling indulgently, as though they expected Amy and Don to be impressed by this clever trick.

The child banged the mug down on the table with a challenging thump and stared at Amy, seemingly saying "Well? Want to make something of it?" Normally she loved children but she was prepared to make an exception for this one. She was facing the wrong way for the parents to see her face, so she narrowed her eyes and gave it a hard look. It stared back truculently, banging the mug so that liquefied chips splashed on Amy's knee, then it turned its gaze to Don.

Then it screamed.

She caught up with Don a hundred yards back down the dockside, but only by running as hard as she could.

"He only screamed because I trod on his foot," she panted.

"Balls. You were nowhere near his feet."

"He's just a kid. A horrible bloody kid at that. Forget it."

Don didn't even slow down; she was still half-running to keep up. "Listen to me," he said. "I make children scream. The sooner I get to grips with that the better. I make children scream and I always will. Can we go?"

"Go where?"

"Back to Paull Holme. Builders don't scream."

He said nothing all the way back and she could think of nothing to say.

At the house, he was out of the car and away before she'd got the handbrake on, and the Hawk swooped on her before she could go after him.

"You're back, then."

"Indubitably."

"Come again?"

"Yes, I'm back. I found him. He was—"

"I know where he bloody was."

"You do?" She looked at him indignantly. "You knew all the time?"

"No, I knew at four-fifteen when the evening paper was delivered." He thrust it at her.

"CHAIN-SAW HERO GETS AWARD" announced the front-page headline. She scanned down the paragraphs. The article more or less followed the lines of the speech. Then she saw the other photo, the one of her, with the caption that read "Mystery Girlfriend Emma Bovary." The copy said, "Friends were speculating on a romance between the injured hero and leggy blonde Emma Bovary, who refused to answer press questions at the award ceremony."

"Well?" said the Hawk, staring at her indignantly.

"Well, what?"

"Is it true?"

"I don't think that's any of your business."

She tried to walk away but he leapt in front of her. "Oh, yes, it is my business. It's very much my business."

"Look, Mr. Hawkins," she said, taking a deep breath. "He's an extraordinary guy but he's in a terrible state and I don't know if I have the time or the strength to nursemaid someone like that. I like my guys to be fully functional. Having said that, don't worry, I am *not* about to give him a hard time. He's doing that quite well enough himself."

"What the fuck are you on about?" said the Hawk, clearly mystified.

Amy did a lightning-fast review of all she had just said and began to suspect she had made a fool of herself again.

"Weren't you talking about the romance bit?"

"No, I bloody wasn't. I don't give a fuck about fucking romance. I was asking you about your *name,* because I can tell you here and now that if you're stringing me along with a false name for the tax people, I'll have you off this site before your feet touch the ground."

"I'm Amy Dale," she said. "What are you talking about? What name?"

The Hawk looked at the paper. "Here. It says you're called Emma something. Emma Bovary." He looked at her in surprise. "Don't laugh. It's no laughing matter."

She shook her head and walked away. It was too late to start work. Everybody else was downing tools and Amy, reluctant to talk to anyone, walked round to the far side of the house to find a quiet place. There, in an overgrown clump of rhododendron, was a brick-built arbor, sheltering an old bench. She sat down, unsettled by the day, staring moodily across the fields and wondering what kept her here in this pressure-cooker of a house where every conversation, every decision, seemed surrounded by perilous consequences. The car keys were in her pocket. It would take five minutes to throw her clothes in a bag, gather her brushes, and go. What kept her?

Don kept her.

A man approached, whistling. She curled herself up small, squashed in the corner of the seat, but it didn't hide her from Dennis, who came round the corner holding his old tray.

"Brought you a cuppa," he said.

"How did you know I was here?"

"Is that how you say thank you where you come from? I saw you from the window."

"And you thought I came out here because I needed a cup of tea?"

Dennis put the tray on the ground and sat down beside her. "No, as it happens, I came out here because I thought after the load of old crap you've been listening to today, you might just want to hear some truth."

"And how do you know I've been listening to a load of crap?"

"Because I can read, OK?" There was the same edge in his voice that she'd heard when he'd tried to lay claim to Amelia's book. "I read the evening paper. I know what they said at that bloody ceremony, and I know you were there because you're spread across page two in glorious black-and-white."

"All right, Dennis. Spit it out. What makes it a load of crap?"

"I'll tell you what I'll do. I'll go and get Vin's version, shall I? The way he told it to me when I saw him in the cells. It makes very convincing reading."

She shrugged her shoulders. "Just tell me."

"Vin's a truthful boy, Amy, always has been. That's part of his trouble. When the cops ask him what drug he's taking, he tells them. When they ask who he gets it from, he tells them that, too. It's cost him blood. Vin says he saw Don take the saw from the council truck." Dennis saw Amy stiffen and nodded emphatically. "That's right. *Don* took it. Vin followed him in. He saw the woman try to stop him and he saw what Don did to her with the chain saw. Then Vin says he saw red. He's not a strong lad but he went for Don, rushed him from behind, knocked him over, and got the saw off him. That's when Don got hurt, but then Don got it back and Vin reckons that would have been the end of him if the others hadn't come downstairs. That's the way Vin tells it, and you know what, Amy? I believe him. It's not just blood being thicker than water. You read it, and you'll believe him, too."

Dennis's voice had a growl of violent desperation in it, quite unlike anything she had heard from him before. This was Dennis with no holds barred, no disguises. Amy thought she wished she had never heard this Dennis. "Why would he do that?" she asked.

"Because he's got a black hole where his soul ought to be," said Dennis savagely. "He's as unstable as they come. It's all about Parrish and his mother. That winds him up so tight he goes manic, right out of his mind. He was after *them*. That was why he took the saw in there."

The information was more than Amy could take. "Leave me alone, Dennis," she said. "Just go."

"Will you read Vin's version?"

"Tomorrow," she said, more to get rid of him than anything else.

Dennis got up. "This isn't about me and Vin," he said. "I'm not telling you to score points. The lads don't know the half of this. I'm telling you to keep you safe, between you and me. Think about it."

He picked up the tray, the mugs of tea untouched, and walked away. Amy, deeply disturbed, stood up, too. Needing a change of scene, she headed down across the field toward the river; behind her, behind the thin wooden back wall of the shelter, Don uncoiled himself from the place where he had been hiding, shielded by the bushes, and watched her go through a crack in the planks.

Amy walked through the field trying to balance versions of the truth in her mind. Jealous Don, jealous Dennis. Dennis wanted Amelia's book. Don wanted … Don wanted what, exactly? Her? The book? She didn't know. Was Don just as interested as she was in getting at the old story, or was that just a tactic, a shared interest to make sure she believed him?

She jumped down the ha-ha's drop and skirted the meadow beyond until she arrived at rough scrubland bordering the river. Sitting on the bank, she looked along the shoreline. Seagulls were pecking and fighting over some dead thing on the edge of the ripples. A speedboat screamed, jumping and thumping over the estuary waves. It was far out from the shore, and the sound of its crashing lunges reached her so late that it seemed to be colliding with a solid, invisible ceiling every time it rose into the air. How far out was it? The world was full of questions, but this one provided a harmless distraction. What had she counted as a child between the lightning and the thunder? Seven seconds, she thought, seven seconds to a mile. There was only a second between the sight and the sound of the boat. A seventh of a mile, two hundred and fifty yards.

Ridiculous, she thought, it was much farther away than that. Then she realized that the crash could just as easily go with the impact before the one she had counted. There was no certainty to be found in anything. She switched her attention to what lay right in front of her, on the edge of the mud, where stumps of rotten wood stuck out, tracing the decayed framework of a landing stage. It dawned on her that she might well be looking at the very place where the painter, trying to come ashore, had fallen into the water. More questions. How long did wood endure? It seemed important. They'd replace a jetty if it rotted, wouldn't they? But would these big old timbers rot quickly? Could these have survived three hundred and forty years? Could they be the same ones?

Amy wanted this to be the spot, wanted to imagine the arrival of the rowing boat, the splash as the painter fell in and the laughter of Amelia and Marvell.

"It *is* the same place," said Don behind her.

"Don't do that," she said, whipping round.

"Don't frighten you?"

"No—don't read my mind. Why do you say that?"

"They're oak, those pilings. They may look rotten on the outside, but try to stick a knife in and it's like solid iron an inch under the surface."

"You tried?"

"Yes. I brought you this. Parrish left it for you. He was looking for you."

"This" was a fat envelope. It could wait.

"How did you know I was here?"

"I saw you walking down."

She guessed, quite wrongly, that he'd seen her from the window.

"I thought the Emma Bovary thing was pretty funny," he went on.

"Hallelujah. I'm glad someone's finally understood it. The Hawk thinks it's my alias for the Inland Revenue."

He smiled and the power of the smile pulled her a little nearer to his camp.

"How did you hear about it?"

"Some thoughtful person pinned a page from the paper on my door." He sat down, as she knew he would, on the concealing side, but he was close enough to her for a chemical, electrical magnetism to flicker unsettlingly.

"So this really might be where he came ashore?" she asked.

"The track down here runs in a little dip. It takes a lot of feet and a lot of years to do that. Now just imagine it." He held up his hand as if for silence. "I'll tell you what happened."

"All right."

"Amelia's up early and she looks out and sees that Dahl's ship has come in during the night. The *Godspeed*. She comes racing down here because she's dying to see her old man. Hasn't seen him for ages, can't wait to get her hands on the living, breathing flesh of him, horny as hell, I should think. Instead there's the little boat coming. Can you see it? Just out there. Two seamen rowing?"

"I see it."

"The catch is, it's got the wrong people in it. Not Dahl but friend Marvell, and I don't think she likes Marvell very much. Also there's this old man she's never seen before. How would you feel?"

"Disappointed."

"Like crying, I should think. Marvell skips onto the jetty, all teeth and pretty words. They don't notice the old bloke until he goes arse over tit into the water. There. Did you see it?"

"What a splash."

"That cheers up Amelia. Marvell thinks it's the funniest thing ever. But the laugh's on them really, isn't it?"

"Why?"

"Because they haven't a clue who he is," he said. "They have no idea that the man they're laughing at is the most famous painter in the world. Don't you think that's funny? I do. I think it's pretty funny when people can't see the plain truth right in front of their noses. What did Dennis tell you?"

The abrupt switch in subject caught her off balance.

"He said . . ."

"He said I had the saw and Mad Vin was trying to save them from me?"

She was forced to nod under the power of his gaze.

"And you believed him?" She stayed silent, dismayed by the rasp in his voice. No words came to her. "Did you believe his druggy nephew was telling the truth and I wasn't? Did you believe I wanted to kill my own mother? Don't you think it's a bit more likely that a deranged screwball with his veins full of heroin and a grudge against her might just have been the guilty party?"

"Of course I do." Her words were faint but his voice softened when he heard them.

"Amy, I tried to tell you not to talk to Dennis. I know he can be funny, but he's not what he seems. You shouldn't be alone with him."

"Come off it."

"I mean it. He's been inside."

"In prison? So? So have lots of people."

"Not for what he did. Young girls."

"How do you know?"

"Someone told me." He stared across the river. "He's trying to get close to you and I don't trust him one bit."

She didn't believe him, but both of them were looking for a way out of the conversation. Amy was still holding Parrish's envelope in her hand and Don looked down at it. "Do you want to have a look at that?" he asked. "He said it's something to do with Rembrandt."

The envelope had both their names on it, Amy and Don, an accidental intimacy that startled her so that she looked at him just as he looked back at her, straight into her eyes for a moment, his own eyes widening. She reached up, knowing the risk, and touched his cheek, his scarred cheek, and felt him flinch as she ran her fingers lightly across it, stroking the scar. The tips of her fingers tingled but, like an angler striking too early at the bite, she lost him. It was too much. He turned his head away.

Neither of them heard Peter Parrish approach and Parrish, seeing how it was between them, stopped in his tracks to give them space.

"Why don't we read it?" Don said, his voice thick.

"All right," she said, sitting up, hoping she could get back to that place he had just left. She took the top sheet of the stack. It was titled "Rembrandt's self-portraits. Notes to an illustrated lecture, Ferens Art Gallery, October 1979."

"Who was Alexander Brigham?" she asked.

"I haven't any idea. Why?"

"He gave a Rembrandt lecture, here in Hull."

"Then I suppose he's a Rembrandt expert."

"It was twenty-two years ago and he writes like an old man. I expect he's dead."

From behind them, Parrish's voice said, "He was a man who wore paisley scarves and talked in rather a high voice, who died five years ago, mostly of disappointment, I think."

"How long have you been standing there?" Amy asked, turning round to look at him and trying to remember what they'd been saying. Don sighed.

"I just arrived."

"What do you mean he died of disappointment?"

"Nobody ever took him seriously. You'll find out why if you read that."

"Well, I'm sitting comfortably if you want to begin," said Don. Peter Parrish sat down to join them.

Amy tried affecting an old man's voice but it only lasted a minute.

" 'It is my contention that the self-portraiture of the incomparable Rembrandt Harmenszoon van Rijn may be divided into three distinct periods, each marked, one might say, by a very particular state of mind. I am fully cognizant of the fact that many art experts may take issue with what I plan to say, but I believe you, the audience, should be the judge. Broadly speaking, and I shall come back to this in more detail later in the course of this lecture, the first period beginning in the artist's youthful Leiden years is characterized by a wish to see himself as rather more dashing and handsome than he actually was. Lights dim. First slide.' "

"What?" said Don.

"That's what's written here. 'Lights dim. First slide.' "

"We'll just have to imagine it," said Parrish. "Go on."

" *'Perhaps the exemplar of this period is the portrait dated sixteen hundred and twenty-nine and now in the Nuremberg Museum, of the young Rembrandt, aged twenty-two or twenty-three years old, adorned by a small piece of armor in the form of a gorget or neck guard, just the sort of fashionable accessory a young blade might have worn as an affectation. What do we see when we look at him? This Rembrandt is a bonny lad. An aristocrat, a sophisticate. He looks at us with one eyebrow raised a shade sardonically. He has a little quiff and a rather adorable look to him. This Rembrandt is indeed rather a one for the ladies, one might think. Pause. Await laughter.'* Good God, do you suppose anyone did laugh?"

"It was a long time ago," said Parrish. "We laughed at gentler jokes then."

"Where was I? *'This Rembrandt is a beau, a dandy, a youth to attract the fluttering sighs of the fairer sex. Do we believe it? We might be fooled, might we not, were there not another witness waiting in the wings, for Rembrandt was not alone in Leiden. Oh, no. He shared his studio with none other than the renowned Jan Lievens. Now, we have no way of telling after all this time what form the relationship between the two young men took, although we do have the words of a visitor, Constantijn Huygens, who says they were stubborn and arrogant young men, wonderful but difficult—a pair of right royal know-it-alls, too obsessed by their own brilliance to bother to learn from their elders. They have no time, he says, for the innocent pleasures of youth. They are like two old men. He wants them to relax a little, to ease up on their all-consuming art because their young bodies are being ruined by this sedentary occupation as they urge each other on. Mind you, Huygens has no trouble picking out the better of the two painters, no trouble at all. He sees with absolute clarity that the one who will go down in history is, pause, Lievens. Look around whimsically. Wait for laughter.'* "

Don snorted in irritation. Peter Parrish smiled.

" *'What we do not know, therefore, is whether, when Lievens painted Rembrandt, he was deliberately unkind, for there can be no doubt that his view of his colleague is altogether less dashing, much less attractive, a different man altogether. Lievens's version of the young Rembrandt resembles a turnip with a startled expression.'* "

Parrish laughed and Amy frowned at him.

"Hush. It doesn't say anything about laughing there. *'We see then that right through Rembrandt's early life, except when he is practicing some of his wilder expressions in the mirror, he takes care to paint himself in a very much more flattering light than a more dispassionate observer might choose to. We turn then to the middle period of his life, and here again we see a certain degree of self-gratification. I believe one can represent this period by another single exemplar. Slide. Pause. Here we see Rembrandt at the age of fifty-two, in the painting that now resides in New York in the remarkable Frick collection. What a fine fellow he is. There he sits, expansively, gazing at us with that impassive expression—and how magnificently he is dressed. That wonderful golden garment, almost a bodice, swathed across his manly chest. That magnificent cape, thrown over his shoulders. All false, all pretense. Do you know what they were? We do know. We have the information in the catalogues from the forced sales of his possessions just a year or two later. They are junk. They are old clothes he himself bought at auction as costumes for his painting but, my goodness, with his world falling in ruins around his ears, bankrupted by his collecting obsession and by the collapse of the Dutch financial system, the end of the tulip boom, the fellow still can't give up the pretense that he is a hugely successful painter. The only thing lacking in this portrait, the only part of the delusion he has abandoned, is the golden chain around the neck. The earlier portraits in this middle period of his life usually feature that golden chain. Its significance is immense. It is the chain that Rembrandt never owned, the chain he longed for. It is the chain of royal patronage that Peter Paul Rubens deservedly had and that many lesser painters of the time received from their royal sponsors, but Rembrandt never achieved such status. He spent his life longing for it on the one hand, and behaving in such an individual and, not to put too fine a point upon it, cantankerous manner that he denied himself the chance of ever receiving it. So the saddest thing, the very saddest thing, ladies and gentlemen, is that in the end he had to bestow it on himself, in paint. For that chain, ladies and gentlemen, existed only in paint. We know, again from the sales inventory when he was forced to give up that great house in Amsterdam's Breestraat and move to the squalor of the Jordaan district, that his golden chain was mere costume jewelry and probably looked finer in his painted rendition than it ever did in real life.'*"

For no reason she could name, Amy looked up across the vast, relentless river and found the power of its seaward push unsettling. A dinghy was scudding across it, two crew members hanging out on trapezes, and as she followed it, the boat abruptly capsized.

"Look," she said. "Are they all right?"

"That's what dinghy sailors do all the time," said Don, but they all watched until the little boat was upright again and scooting on its course. He turned to Peter Parrish. "Why don't you tell Amy about Marvell's father?"

Parrish looked at Don sharply and then at the little boat. "Oh, really? Well, it's true. His father died out there, you know." Amy thought she heard an odd inflection in his voice. "It's a dangerous beast, that river, as we know. Marvell's father was vicar of Winestead. You could see it from here if we were a bit higher up. It's a tiny little place. Just a few miles inland."

"What happened?"

"He was coming across the river with some woman, and the boatman was drunk. Apparently there was a sudden storm and that was that. Nothing was ever seen of them again."

"How old was his son?"

"A teenager, I think."

"What was all that stuff about him being some sort of secret agent? I couldn't remember," said Don.

Parrish shrugged. "The story goes that he was a bit of an expert on Holland, and as we kept having wars with the Dutch, he was backward and forward over there rather a lot. They always say he was a great patriot, but I'm not sure about that. I sometimes wonder whether he wasn't dead against the king even after the Restoration. Perhaps he was really plotting with the exiled republicans for another revolution."

"That's what Mum always says," Don said. "She gets all her opinions from you." It could have been a flattering statement but his tone undermined that possibility.

"Ellen's quite capable of making up her own opinions," Parrish retorted. "Maybe I got it from her." He seemed to have suddenly had enough. "I must get back. I'll see you tomorrow, I expect," and it was only after he had gone that Amy thought to wonder why he had been looking for her in the first place.

"You were a bit sharp with him," she said to Don.

"No, I wasn't."

"That's the way it sounded to me."

"Do me a favor. Listen, I've known him since I was five, right? He was always around. He's the one who pushed me through school. He never stops pushing."

"Perhaps you needed it. He seems such a kind man."

He shook his head as if her statement were an irritating fly.

"Now we're here by ourselves, will you tell me how that poem goes?" she asked.

"No. *Especially* now we're here by ourselves."

"Is it that powerful? I promise not to misunderstand you."

"I said no. I might misunderstand myself."

Abruptly, she wanted him again, wanted to knock down his barriers, but someone else was behind his eyes now. He stared at her as if he was studying her weaknesses. She wondered if she should run.

"Shall I read the next bit?" she said, and to her it seemed her voice sounded as if she had already been running.

"No, it's bloody boring," he said. "You've got Amelia's book, haven't you? Read that if you must read something."

Between them, they carefully separated another page and she enjoyed the conspiracy of their bent heads and their single purpose. She pored over what they revealed. "There's a poem," she said. "She's written out a poem."

"Can you read it?"

"Give me a minute." She studied it while he studied her.

"Did you like being called a leggy blonde?" he asked.

"I'm not answering that," she said. "I'm a modern, liberated woman, me. I don't accept any typecasting by chauvinistic men. Of course I liked it. Now let me concentrate."

Cars departed behind them on the evening run to the pub, disturbing the rooks in the trees. It was dusk and a bank of cloud somewhere beyond Hull was staging an unrealistic light show in purple and orange.

"OK," she said, "I think I've got it. It's much smaller writing than last time. As usual it starts halfway through a sentence, which is a little frustrating on account of what that sentence says."

She cleared her throat. "It says, '... *demanded to know, without once considering the likely truth of the situation, what it was that we did and the limner, divining Marvell's meaning though he had spoken in my own tongue did reply at length and in a way that seemed to me, even without understanding, to come it quite high. Marvell strove to interrupt him and I feared others in the household would hear, so to dissuade him from further discourse I told him I knew a verse of his by rote and would like to test it with him for accuracy. He was amused by this and bade me say it and I said it as I shall here write it down for use on another occasion.*' "

Amy stopped for a moment. "Wow," she said, "so this is a genuine Marvell poem."

"Read it."

> " 'Of a tall stature and sable hue
> Much like the son of Kish, that swarthy Jew,
> Twelve years complete he suffered in exile
> And kept his father's asses all the while.
> At length by wondrous impulse of fate
> The people called him home to mend the state
> And clothed him all from head to foot anew.
> Nor did he such small favors then disdain
> Who in his thirtieth year began to reign.
> Bishops and deans, pimps, peers and knights he made,
> Things highly fitting for a monarch's trade.
> With women, wine and viands of delight
> His jolly wastrels feast him day and night.' "

"What are viands?"

"Meat, I think," said Amy, "like the French."

"It's not very good poetry. More like doggerel, really. Go on."

She looked down at it. " 'When I had said it, he demanded to know who had told it me, but I would only say that it was a good poem though some might think it too cruel to our restored King. At that he blanched and I said I thought no more harm of him for it than he did of the limner for—' That's it. End of the page."

"It's blackmail, isn't it?" said Don, pleased. "There's some row between Marvell and our friend, and so she's stepped in to say she knows he's written this poem, which amounts to treason, doesn't it?"

"You're guessing. There's not much to go on."

"There's not much to go on right through this whole thing."

"I want to know what this contest is really all about. Amelia's judging Marvell and Rembrandt and she's giving a prize."

Don looked at the book. "The answer's probably in there somewhere."

"Don, do you really, really believe that we've got this right? That Rembrandt came here in real life? That he painted that sketch on the wall? That he fell into the mud?" It wasn't just a question about a long-dead painter, it was a question about where they stood, she and Don. Were they together, not just in this but in all the rest of it? She needed him to say yes.

He was silent for a while, staring out to where the dinghy had been. "My heart does some of the time," he said in the end, "but my head hasn't quite got there yet."

"What's the alternative if it's not him?" she demanded.

"That someone else came here calling himself van Rijn? Someone with the same surname. A pretty good painter who just never got to be famous. Maybe, having the same name, he lied a little. The whole thing could be just that, nothing more. Of course, if it *was* him, then that wall's worth a fortune. Pity we can't fit it into the back of your car."

Amy didn't want to be flippant and she really, really didn't want to believe Don's alternative. She looked back toward the house. "I expect they've all gone. Can I paint you right now?" she said. "I want to get on with it. Let's go upstairs."

"I don't know what this is about," he said, shaking his head; again, a stranger had taken over his voice. "Maybe you just have to have all these fantasies going in your life."

"What do you mean? What fantasies?"

"Rembrandt. Amelia. Me. What are you into, Amy? Is it just that life's too dull if you're not pulling the strings? What am I? Some stray dog you're rescuing?"

"Why would you think that?"

"Look at me. Look at the state I'm in."

"Balls. I think you look just fine."

"Oh, sure."

"You mustn't live like this, Don," she said. "Your scar's not pretty, but it's healing. It's not *you*. It's just an injury."

He was on his feet in a flash. "Fuck you," he said brutally. "I made a kid scream today. Remember that?"

EIGHTEEN

AFTER THE CARS HAD COME BACK FROM THE PUB, AFTER THE BOOK
had slipped from her hand, disturbing her just enough for her to turn
out the light, after slipping back again into the comfortable illusion that
she was asleep in a proper bed in a proper room, Amy woke abruptly
and totally, sitting up so fast that she bounced on the air mattress and almost fell over. Someone was dying. Someone right here with her in her
room. Waves of gasping distress poured out of the darkness as if the
time-soaked walls were exhaling something they had long ago sucked
in. Drawn-out sobs, quivering with insurmountable grief, assaulted her.
Shaken, she flailed around for the light, whacked the bulb with her
hand, and groped for the stiff switch.

There was only a wall to her right. She was alone. The sound was
coming from the other side of the wall. The sound was Don.

She got up and went to the door, realizing, just as she opened it,
that she was naked. She wrapped a towel round herself in case anyone
else was about, then she went through her door and stopped, irresolute,
outside Don's. She tapped quietly, but the noise continued, moan after

moan, smothering the sound of her knocking. Her first thought was to protect him from the others, to stop him before he woke someone who might be less gentle.

She turned the knob and pushed the door open. He was lying on his bed, twisting and turning, his eyes tight shut.

"Don?" she said. Nothing. She said it again a little louder. "Don? Wake up. It's Amy. It's all right."

As she bent down to touch his shoulder, he shot out one arm, hit her hard on the cheek, and sat up as she fell backward on the floor.

"Go away," he said. "Get away from me—"

"It's only me." She was trying to sound calm though her eyes were stinging with tears of pain. "It's Amy."

"Don't come near me. I'll have you. Get back." He drew in two or three harsh breaths and woke up fully, looking down at her. "What are you doing down there?" he said, confused.

"You knocked me over."

"Me? Why are you in here?"

"You were making terrible noises. I came to see if you were all right."

Don let out a long breath. "I didn't know I was making a noise. What sort of noise?"

"Dreadful moans. Were you dreaming?"

"It's my hand," he said. She didn't think he was telling the truth. "I get pains, I told you."

"Do you want the mirror?" If he needed a physical excuse for his distress, she was prepared to go along with that.

"That would be good." He still sounded like someone who had gone ten rounds in the ring.

She found it propped against the wall and brought it to the side of the bed.

"Shall I switch on the light?" she asked.

"No," he replied sharply. "Moonlight's enough."

She dragged up the chair and sat holding the mirror for him as he held his undamaged hand to it, flexing the fingers and staring at the reflection. He said nothing for a minute or two, then he let his hand drop and lay back on the bed.

She watched him, waiting, and in the end he said, "It wasn't that."

"What was it, then?"

"It was yesterday."

"That's no surprise."

"Have you ever seen something that's burned itself into your brain so deeply that whenever you shut your eyes it's there?"

"No."

"Each time you see it, your memory changes it just a bit."

"That's good, isn't it?"

"I don't know. I can't trust it anymore. I need to see it just the way it was."

"I understand."

"No, you don't. That stupid ceremony. That was for them, not for me. Back in the same room. Telling everyone how it was, but they haven't got a clue. They don't know what happened, do they? And they were trying to tell *me* what happened? Was that supposed to be *nice* for me?"

"Heroes. You said it yourself. They need heroes."

"Heroes? Maybe it was me who had the saw. Maybe *he* was trying to stop *me*."

She couldn't help it; she gasped. He looked at her sharply as if she had fallen into some sort of trap he had laid.

"We both know that's what he told them," he said challengingly. "But he's mad and bad, isn't he, so they don't believe him."

"They wouldn't, would they?"

"So where do you stand now, Amy. Are you going to go on listening to Dennis?"

He was watching her in the dark, waiting for an answer.

"Tell me about it, Don. I'll believe you if you just tell me."

It took him a long while, but finally he began to talk.

"The main thing was the smell. I hadn't smelt that smell since the day he . . . Since then."

"Haven't you been back there?"

"Yeah, I've been back there. It always smells of smoke and piss and disinfectant. They'd polished the floor for the event, that's what they'd done. And they'd polished it back then. It was just like being there again. Well, like it was before that bloody saw started up."

He was coming out of his trance, she thought. Talking was good.

"It won't last, will it?" she said, reasonably. "The memory is bound to resurface, but not like before, because it isn't real anymore. Maybe you should talk about it more."

"Who to?"

"Haven't you had any therapy?"

"Physiotherapy? Loads of it."

"No. Treatment for trauma."

"Head stuff? Someone saw me in hospital. She was useless. I couldn't trust her."

"You could trust *me*."

"There's only one person anyone can trust and that's themselves," he said. "I don't know you. I see you talking to Dennis and I just don't know you."

Sharp silence followed, filled with pain. "That thing you do with the mirror?" she asked to end it.

She could just see him nod in the moonlight.

"You said you look at your good hand and it fools your brain." Her voice sounded false to her. "When I first came in, you were holding up the wrong hand, your hurt hand. Why?"

He took the offer of truce. "Curiosity," he said quietly.

"What do you mean?"

"It stops the pain when I stare at my good hand, so I thought, would it make that one hurt if I stared at the ... the other one."

"Did it?"

"I never found out. You came in."

"If you let me paint you properly," she said, "you can look at the picture. You won't need a mirror. Will you let me?"

There was no answer but his breathing was easier in the silence that fell again. It didn't occur to her to move either toward him or away. She sat in the chair, listening to him breathing deeper and slower, falling asleep, as if she were a nurse with a dangerously ill patient. Time trickled away and there was the night and Don's breathing and no clue as to where it would end.

Amelia came into Amy's head and she knew Amelia must have been in this room. There was no room in her house she would not have been in. This tower was old when the rest of the house was new. What was it then? Servants' quarters or a storeroom perhaps? Amy tried her hardest to imagine Amelia in the darkness and found she could only imagine herself, in something vaguely old-fashioned, long and flowing.

At that moment, she wanted to believe in ghosts, to summon up Amelia. She tried to find fear inside herself, to generate that first shiver on which fear might catch and form, but fear wouldn't come. Half dreaming, she saw a woman in the room in a chair, and a man who was painting her, not onto canvas but directly onto her face, adjusting the color with tiny dabs at his palette until it flowed on invisibly. He stopped and held her face in his hands and worked the paint into her skin with his thumbs. Then she was the painter and Don was the subject and she was painting his injured face, and the contest was to make the scar disappear as she matched his skin with the oil paint. She put the palette down and knew that she needed to touch his face again, to run her fingers over his cheek and feel the ridge of the scar. *I must do that,* she thought, *then I will know how to paint it smooth again so I can paint him back to life.* The thought brought her back to full wakefulness. The moon was shining brightly on his face as he lay asleep. Carefully, she inched her way out of the room and came back with sketch pad and pencil, then began to draw him. There was nothing about him now that was wild or dangerous.

Looking at him asleep, Amy tried to suppress the awareness that part of her was enjoying the ambiguity, the frisson of danger. Dennis's warnings had only made Don more attractive to her—so long as she didn't have to know one way or the other. Annoyed at herself, she took up her pencil, but at the first attempt she got the proportions of his head all wrong, too short from top to bottom, and rubbed it out in irritation. The second time was better, everything in the right place and the right proportion, but it just wasn't Don; it was a sleeping cipher with a resemblance to Don, at best. She knew she hadn't been brave enough with the scar. It was neither one thing nor the other, merely a faint pucker down the line of his cheek.

Then she drew him older, trying to envisage the shape of the skull bones so she could shrink the flesh on them, imagining that glossy black hair graying and receding and the eyes turning watery. When she tried drawing herself next to him at the same age, the two pictures stayed resolutely apart on the page.

He groaned again, and she got up from her chair and reached out to touch his shoulder. She stroked his arm and he made a different sound now, a questioning sound, and she wanted to cup that damaged face in her hands, knowing she could soak up his pain and take it from him. Aching to get into bed with him, she knew all she had to do was let the towel fall and slide in next to his warm back, putting her arms around him to soothe him. The memory of the last time, of the perfect fit of their bodies, the dropping of the barriers, filled her so that reaching that place again was only a motion away. Then the owl hooted, right outside on the window, and in his sleep Don said, "I'll get you. I'll kill you," perfectly distinctly and the barriers stood between them in the dark, as real as steel.

Waking in her own bed as the very first light was creeping over the horizon, she knew she wouldn't get back to sleep so she put her overalls on and crept down to the dim kitchen to make herself tea. The house felt a different place, where there were no people around. It seemed a moment for her to take stock, but it was too confusing so she gave up and, mug of tea in hand, wandered around the deserted ground floor, glad to focus on something inanimate, predictable, taking it in at her own speed.

It wasn't the Dales who had closed up the old house ten years earlier, Parrish had told her. There hadn't been Dales at Paull Holme since 1928. Another family had lived there after them. The rooms that had not yet been touched revealed the 1950's fireplaces the new family had installed to reduce the coal bills, and the horrid wallpaper that covered the decaying plaster on the walls. For all that, with her eyes half closed, she could still feel back toward the seventeenth century, toward the strong woman who had first made this her house, her creation. She went up the stairs to do a tour of the first floor, where most of the work was going on, but there was less sense of a living house there. Almost every room was in the process of being stripped, except for one at the far end of the corridor, which was locked.

She went to the room where she and Don were working. The ceiling would take another five or six days, she thought, judging by what she'd done so far. The half-exposed painting on the wall caught her eye and she knelt down in front of it. The brown lines were faint, just legs, a skirt, and two pairs of feet, but it did seem they had a fine quality to them, an extraordinary economy of style. Was that just because of what she thought she knew? Running her finger over the plaster, she thought to herself that there were not many people who could claim to have touched an unknown work by Rembrandt. Then she looked at the barrier, the place where all those old layers of paint covered the top half of the picture, down to the horizontal division where the paneling had saved it. Amelia was hiding under there. Amelia's head, maybe Amelia's face. She felt the edge of paint with particular care. It had that texture possessed by the rough edge of an oyster shell, where the creature has also built up its coating layer by layer.

Seized by a sudden impulse, Amy went in search of a tool, and found just what she was looking for in an adjoining room: a paint scraper with a blade like a tiny scimitar, a curved blade on one side and an angled edge on the other. Back at the wall, she chose a spot halfway through the thickness of the paint and carefully pushed the point of the scraper up into it, working vertically upward from below. The paint's layers gradually separated under the pressure, and by carefully wriggling the blade from side to side, she found she could eventually push it all the way in. Only the wooden handle was sticking out at the bottom; with some trepidation, she twisted and levered it so that a sizable section of the layered paint buckled and separated from what lay below it. That made it easier.

In only a few minutes she had cleared a large area. The question now was whether she could safely go further. The other question, which struck her rather too late, was, what would Parrish say when he saw what she had done? It was already too late to worry about that, and in any case, she felt she had a right to do this, as if she were the guardian of the painting under the paint. Parrish would not cover it over again if he could only see what was there. At the very least, before that happened, she desperately wanted to see what Amelia looked like, because she was quite certain it *was* Amelia lurking under there, just as she was certain that a Dutch painter called van Rijn painted it and that there wasn't more than one van Rijn.

As she worked away at it, she kept thinking of Don and the previous night when it could all have been so simple. Amy wished she had simply got into bed with him and let their bodies do the talking. There was a Don she yearned for, a Don who had answered all her body's questions. The other Don, the darker Don, full of odd resentments, was only there if you talked him into being.

Forty minutes later, at about six-thirty, Amy was still squatting there, surrounded by a sea of paint fragments from an area of some six square feet that she had painstakingly levered, scraped, and peeled apart. Now only a thin layer of paint still covered the top part of the picture. Realizing how stiff she was, she got slowly to her feet as the door opened behind her.

Dennis peered in.

"Well, strike a light," he said. "What's happened here?"

"Nothing much."

He looked at the hole she'd made in the wall with awed disbelief. "Well, nothing that a year on a health farm and a team of top psychiatrists couldn't sort out. What did you do that for?"

"There's a picture underneath. Come and look," she said.

"What am I looking at?"

"A ghost," she said. "Amelia's ghost. The woman who made this house. Do you see her just starting to show through?"

"I see a wall."

"No," said Amy. "Look harder. Here and here. Follow the line up. Do you see now?"

"I think so."

Very faintly, where the paint still covering it was at its thinnest, the Dutchman's sepia lines were coming out to greet the day.

"You can see her body, Amelia's body, and part of her head, too."

"Look, kid. It's a very nice picture but the Hawk will do his nut when he sees that. So will old man Parrish. Do you want me to plop some plaster over that? Won't take me a moment to mix it up. The Hawk doesn't like holes in walls, particularly holes in walls caused by people of the wrong sex with aliases. If it was me he'd shave off my buttock hairs with a power sander."

Amy couldn't resist smiling. This was the Dennis she thought she knew.

"Have you got buttock hairs? Really?"

"Of course I have. It's a builder's natural defense against windchill caused by the cruel demands of fashion, dictating as it does that we expose the top three inches of the aforesaid buttocks while working. Would you like to see?" Dennis twirled around and started to undo his trousers.

"Probably not."

"Well, what about the plastering?"

"Thanks, Dennis. It's a kind offer, but I don't think so."

He looked at his watch. "I've got something to do," he said. "I've got a new trick. I'll pop back in afterward and see if you've aged enough to turn sensible."

She waved at him absently, still staring at the wall. Twenty minutes later, the peace of the house was destroyed by men's shouts and pounding feet on the stairs. Gengko flew past her, wild-eyed, when she went out on the landing.

"Stay there," he called back to her. "Don't come down."

Eric was close behind him and she blocked his way.

"What's going on?" she said.

He looked at her, white-faced and staring. "Bloody Dennis," he said. "He's bloody dead."

NINETEEN

Thursday, January 23rd, 1662

MARVELL HAD MARCHED INTO THE ROOM LIKE AN OFFICER OF THE
watch arresting some felon and I found, to my intense irritation, that I
could not easily face him down. He even used a Dutch expletive,
something I had not heard him do before, and he got it right, which
was worse.

"*Bij gans bloet dood*," he said, and that got my full attention. "By
Christ's bloody death, you are taking liberties, sir. That is your host's
wife you are touching."

"*Duizend pokken, Marvell*," I said, replying in kind. "A dozen
plagues on you. I am touching her face to learn its contours, the better
to paint it. That is what we have to do, us painters."

"Save your tales for the unweaned," he retorted. "I have been
painted three times and nobody ever felt the need to feel the contours
of my face."

"You have been painted by lesser painters, then," I said. "I am famous for the depth of my images. Your poems may float around in the
firmament of your own head, anchored to nothing but the frothings of

your mind. My art is rooted in the world outside it. I have to know the uttermost truth of the shapes that I paint."

"Well, I wonder," he said. "The painting will be the test of that. You fooled me in York, but I am less certain now that you are who you claim you are, van Rijn."

"What? I made no claims at all," I said. "I think you'll remember it was someone else entirely who named me."

"How do I know what you might have arranged with some passing countryman of yours?"

"You were there, sitting next to me on the bloody bench. How could I have?"

"I was . . . I was transported by my art," he said. "I was half a world away, walking the banks of the Nile, searching out the scenes of my poem. Anything might have happened in my absence."

"Oh, bollocks to your poem," I said. "I didn't fix up anything. I wish he'd never opened his vile mouth."

Amelia was standing by, looking extremely concerned. I noticed that as her color rose further it changed the focus of her face in a most interesting way, highlighting the cheekbones remarkably. I resolved to see if I could introduce that color into her cheeks next time she sat. She spoke to Marvell, and I would have given a hundred guilders to know what she said. It sounded light and conversational, and halfway through it assumed the quality of a recitation. The words she now spoke seemed to rhyme like verse. They were clearly familiar to Marvell, and he kept nodding and raising a hand as though to cut her off, but she, guileless, insisted on continuing. She said a final, sweet, barbed sentence that drained the rest of the color from his face. It was clear she had the upper hand. Marvell coughed to stall for time, turned to me, and said, "Mistress Dahl has explained that what happened here was of no import and that I may have misunderstood it. I am satisfied with her explanation. The matter need proceed no further."

Well, he might say that, but the embers in the furnace of my temper had been fanned into a good flame. He and I still had business with each other.

"I take it badly that you impugn my reputation, sir," I said. "Whatever you may think, the fact is I am known throughout the length and breadth of my country as the best of all the portrait painters."

"Your country is neither very long nor very broad," he said, "and you must think me very foolish indeed if you believe I have not made enquiries. We have a Dutchman at court now, a proper expert appointed Keeper of the King's Pictures. I sent for his views on the subject. Would you like to hear them?"

I don't mind admitting that news came as somewhat of a shock. Someone had buttered up the new king. Someone was in for a good shower of gold. I couldn't think of any Dutchmen I knew who deserved such an honor.

"He insists that our friend in York must be mistaken. He says there are two van Rijns in Amsterdam who paint. One is Gerrit van Rijn, who is twenty years old, which you, sir, clearly are not. The other is indeed the noted Rembrandt van Rijn, but I am told that he is known for never leaving his home and that, in any case, he is currently said to be busy rectifying a commission for the City Fathers. This van Rijn, I grant you, is indeed a most famous painter but my informant tells me he is undoubtedly in Amsterdam and certainly not here with us in England. As I say, you had an accomplice perhaps in York, someone out to persuade us your portraits are worth more than they really are."

"Who is this curious countryman of mine who utters this shit?" I asked.

"He is called van Ulenborch," said Marvell. "Do you know him?"

Van Ulenborch. The name made my heart spin and sink at the same time. My old friend's son. My old friend who brought me to Amsterdam, who put my pictures on sale and, above all, who introduced me to his even dearer young cousin Saskia. The son was nothing like the father. Mind you, I'd had my moments with both of them.

"He is a criminal," I said indignantly. "He sold fakes to Brandenburgh and had to go on the run. We would not have him in Amsterdam. He would have broken his father's heart. You should tell your king to watch out for him."

"Keep your advice to yourself," snapped Marvell. "I think the pot is calling the kettle black. His letter warns me that there is an old pupil of Rembrandt van Rijn who likes to borrow that signature for his own paintings. Maybe *that* is you. I have looked hard at your portrait of Dahl and while I admit it is competent, I do not discern in it any signs of greatness."

"That is a jobbing piece," I said, my blood truly up. "As workaday as your damned poems. No better than them, I concede, but I think that whereas they may be the best effort you ever make, Dahl's portrait is far from mine. Did you see what I had to paint it with? You decide who I am, Marvell. You judge me by this portrait in front of us now, no other. You hold yourself so high, but you could not create anything one hundredth so beautiful as this will be."

Amelia chose to intervene again and her intervention seemed to be a quotation, perhaps from the same poem as before. I caught the same sound at the start of it. She used the words as a whip to beat him back. Marvell gave her a vicious look, then crossed to the easel.

"Ridiculous," he said. "There is no skill in this, just blotches."

"Do you know *anything at all* about painting? This is the dead color, the base for everything that follows. This is no more than the equivalent of you cutting your sheet of paper to size. Come back in a few days and you'll see what a real portrait should be. Then you will admit you could never match it in verse."

"Our contest has begun in earnest, then. I doubt you, Dutchman. Only gentlemen have the sensitivity for true art. You are a peasant through and through."

"I told you before," I said, "I am not a peasant. My father was a miller. I am proud to be his son. Real blood ran through his veins, not the cousin-mated, strained-thin stuff of your gentlemen. I was raised as part of the real world around me, not forced to look at it through window glass, separated by the filter of gentility and clean linen. Listen, you fop, I have a talent that is made of wind and fire, not learned in some costly academy. I have heard what you claim to be verse, and I will paint you into the ground."

"The poem that is forming in my head will beat anything you can paint, Dutchman," said Marvell.

"We have a contest indeed, mister poet. I'll wager anything you like on it."

He laughed scornfully. "It is a shame you have nothing worth wagering."

"If you win, I shall paint the portraits you want for nothing. Amelia's portrait, Dahl's portrait, and your own portrait, too. If *I* win, you pay me treble for this painting alone."

That thwarted him. "How is it to be judged?" he demanded. "How can anyone choose between a picture and a poem?"

"Have you changed your mind? Do you not believe in a universal scale of artistry? I thought you claimed it would be self-evident. Simply choose a judge whose taste is beyond question."

"In Hull? Is there such a person?"

"In Paull Holme, if you wish," I said, nodding significantly toward Amelia. "You have said yourself that this house is her canvas, her great artistic endeavor. I see harmony all around me. I see evidence of a creative mind that understands the finer points of form and color."

"Her?" he said doubtfully. "Would that be suitable, I wonder . . ."

It must have been entirely obvious that we were discussing Amelia, for she gave him a look that could have fried bacon. Blow me down, he took the bait.

"Yes," he said, "it is true that she has some claim to artistry. She regards this house as a work of art rendered through color, shape, and texture. She also understands the beauty of the English tongue." He addressed her rapidly in that tongue. She raised an eyebrow and replied somewhat tersely.

"She accepts," he said. Then he bowed abruptly to Amelia and left the room as if he took with him all that mattered in it.

I whistled and looked at Amelia. "I don't know what it was you said at the start there," I remarked, "but I thank you for it. You put his tail between his legs."

She patently understood what I meant and gave me a delicious look of mischievous complicity. Was Marvell such a fool that he did not realize no woman could fail to give first prize to such a picture as I had in mind?

She came around to the easel then and inspected the dead ground I had painted, then she raised her eyes to study the wall behind and looked down at the color of her dress. Pointing at the empty space next to her in the picture, she raised her eyebrows in interrogation. I shrugged. I had not yet thought of how to fill that gap. There was a tall column behind me, made of a dark green ceramic, China work, I would judge. On it was a plant in a pot. She indicated it and held up her hands in pretty supplication and I saw how well it would fill the space, how neatly it would set off her color and the color of her dress.

I nodded. She did indeed have an eye, this woman.

After dining, I went up to my room at the top of the northern tower. I needed to think hard about what I would do. Amelia was in my mind and before my eyes, open or shut. In fact, that's an exaggeration. I should have had her and nothing but her on my mind. That's the way it *should* have been because, after all, I had held those superb shoulders in my hands that morning, I had stroked those angled cat's cheeks with impunity, I had been able to make those lips part just with my voice and my eyes. It proved one thing, one wonderful thing: I wasn't too old after all.

I suppose I should say that it was quite some time since I'd had an attractive woman on the end of my paintbrush and even longer since I'd had the opportunity to do anything about it. Somehow Hennie always managed to be somewhere close to hand when there was a girl sitting for her portrait. Any man knows the importance of casual encounters, those brief ambiguous, speculative looks from passing women in the street. You *know* when they've noticed you. There's a spark. There must come a moment, however, when that spark passes down a generation. I thought that moment might have come one morning last year, as I was walking down to see the progress of the Koenigsgraacht dredging. It was always interesting to see what came up in the buckets and shovels as they dug the great trench where the new canal was to be. As I was walking, I saw a beauty approaching, a woman of perhaps thirty but still oh, so sweet. From far away, long before I could make out her features, I spotted that confident sway, that sinuous thing they do with their whole bodies when they are supremely confident that the looks they draw will be entirely approving. When she got nearer I saw that her confidence was not misplaced and that she had a face to start a thousand cocks rising to crow. I gave her the look; of course I did. She looked back at me, then she looked again with that tiny hidden smile that hides an infinity of imaginative possibilities. For a moment I thought she must have a slight squint as the glance was off target and then, finally I realized with horror that instead of looking at me, she was looking at my son, Titus, walking next to me.

The strumpet.

My fingers' grip on the whole world seemed suddenly to have loosened. I was not wearing good clothes that day because I had come straight from my easel, and my hair was not brushed. Today proved all was not lost. Today proved the game was still in play. Today showed that that woman may well have had a squint. Amelia had given me back my rightful place in the world, so I should have been thinking about her hands and her face and her body and nothing else.

Instead I was brooding, in a thoroughly self-flagellating manner, on Marvell's communication from the black sheep van Ulenborch. The father, old man Ulenborch, hadn't always been whiter than white. He had been central to my life, the man who brought me into the artistic and social life of Amsterdam, who found buyers for my first paintings and sitters for my portraits. However, he had this unpleasant habit of demanding collateral for loans that I thought should have been straightforward family matters once I was married to his kin. He took paintings, my paintings, as security. Worse than that, he used to make rather a lot on the side, being rather fond of having copies done and flogging them in, shall we say, a somewhat dubious manner.

Worse still, at one point, let me see, twenty years ago or so, I was in hock to him for a rather sizable sum and I'd secured it with my etching plates, a hundred or more of them. Ulenborch, playing the game at both ends, borrowed the money he lent me from the Waterland Mennonites. He didn't make any conditions, and he didn't ask me, he just passed the plates straight on to them, bang. Well, they did what you'd expect, didn't they? They started printing off them. Of course, they didn't do it well and they didn't use the right paper or the right ink. I got the plates back fairly quickly, but for a couple of years after that, I couldn't sell an etching at a decent price because they'd flooded the market with their second-rate offerings. I was so cross I lost my temper entirely. They tell me I picked Ulenborch up by his collar, right off the ground, and shook him.

Marvell, with his sure touch in getting under my skin, had also reawakened the memory of the bloody City Fathers who had rubbed salt into the wounds of my bankruptcy. Amsterdam is a clannish place. Whom you're aligned with matters a great deal, and the people I knew had no real authority. When someone called in an old favor and got me on the list for the new Town Hall, I was already riding for a fall. They were waiting for me to stumble. First they gave the whole damned lot, eight bloody great paintings, to Flinck, who learnt every single thing he knew at my knee, and hadn't been above signing *his* student pieces with my name, come to that. By this time, Flinck had prostituted his art. He'd been good once, potentially great, but then off he went on his own and got all fashionable. He started using an absurd range of bright colors to please simpering nincompoops with deep wallets, with no knowledge of the subtlety of art.

Oh, yes, he became very fashionable indeed, but he lost that key to understanding how a painting will stand the test of time if you restrict your palette. A narrow range, that's what you need. You have to let the viewer's eye do the work and see the colors that are not really there. Anyone with any sense should understand that the viewer's imagination is the most powerful tool, and as soon as you merely *hint* at things, you bring the whole power of that tool into play.

I wondered if Marvell knew that. It surely applied to verse as much as to pictures.

I doubt it.

Flinck was given the entire job. Almost immediately, conveniently, or so it seemed at the time, he turned up his toes. Rumor had it that he ate a bad lobster at some smart party. That lobster did not die in vain.

Of course, this left the City Fathers in a quandary, so they divided the job among Lievens, Jordaens, and me. Lievens was somewhat truculent about it because he wanted the whole job. You have to understand that these paintings were specified down to almost the last detail. There is a type of Hollander who thinks it is not enough to be Dutch, who feels embarrassed that the Dutch are a bit of a mongrel breed. Such a type has to believe in a glorious past, so what did they do? They invented some glorious ancestors, the Batavians. Later on we applied the name to our Spice Island colonies, but these original Batavians were supposedly our forefathers in our own land. Myth has it that one of them, Julius Civilis, pushed out the Romans so, as everyone loves to be descended from heroes, he had to be the very first scene and they gave me that one.

I may have been a bit rash to do what I did, but I was particularly concerned not to proceed down the fashionable Flinck route. If Julius Civilis was anything, then he was clearly a bloody-minded barbarian through and through. You don't get the better of Romans by looking like a court-favorite milksop. My Civilis was the sort of man who could empty an inn with a single grunt. His empty eye socket was a hideous reminder of battle. You wouldn't cross this man, or at least not more than once.

I gave it a rough, tough texture because it was going to be very high up on the wall and smooth detail does not work when it's high up and badly lit. My paint reached down and grabbed the eyes however far away the viewer stood, but the City Fathers did not like that at all. In truth, they didn't like me, the way I lived with Hennie, or anything else I did, and I felt much the same way about them. My painting was earmarked for rejection before I ever picked up a palette. The canvas was destined to end its days as a cart cover if I was any judge.

Enough of that. I had a picture to paint and a contest to win. Amelia deserved my entire attention. Dahl was away again, which seemed an extraordinary waste of a wife, particularly such a wife as his. There were always servants around. The room in which I was painting her was far from private. My tower room was a different matter. No one came up here except me. You had to go out of the house and in through a separate door to get to the stairs, which were more of a ladder really. It was a strange arrangement, caused I suppose by the fact that the two towers, one at each end, predated the rest of the house by centuries. Suddenly I could see possibilities in that awkward layout. This room of mine offered a tolerable afternoon light through its windows. I wondered perhaps if I could find an urgent need to paint some quick studies, to try Amelia in various poses for which only the windows in my tower room could provide proper illumination. I knew how it would go then. There was nothing we might not do up here.

The following morning we were to continue with the painting. I had chosen to dine in my room when I learned that Marvell was planning to stay. He still tried to treat me as a man of no status and until I had leveled him with my portrait, I preferred to stay out of his way. I woke uncomfortably early knowing with certainty that I was in trouble. It was Amelia's superb skin. Without the purest of lead whites, I would never achieve the translucency that I could see in my mind's eye.

I would just have to make some.

There were snippets and off-cuts of roofing lead all around the outside of the house. I ransacked the larder, to the indignation of the cook, who kept trying to swat me with a ladle. None of the vinegar jars smelt anywhere near strong enough. Then, opening a large stoneware pot right at the back, my nostrils were wonderfully assailed by the biting, pungent odor I needed. The jar was full of eggs, a curious custom of the English perhaps, to pickle an egg, an item best eaten as fresh as possible. The cook tried to seize the jar with one hand while beating me with the other but I got clean away. Outside I borrowed a thin pan from the chicken house and then I set off for the horse's field. For the very best lead white, you need a fresh heap of horse manure, firm but hot, in which to bed your pan. Then you pour the vinegar over shavings of lead and, so long as you add further fresh manure, the magic happens. Pure white pigment begins to form under the effect of the heat and the special vapor. Marvell's snorting steed was in the field and I watched the damned thing for an eternity before it deigned to lift its tail and issue its brown bounty onto the grass. It was years since I'd done this, not since my Leiden days. It was quite a business, collecting that stuff between two roofing slates and stacking it where I wanted it, out of the way. In the end, I had just what I wanted, as white a white as any I have ever seen. Now the perfect finishing touch would be just the right oil, because the linseed I had was just a little bit too colored for my purpose.

I went inside and was trying out a mixture of ingredients on my palette when Amelia entered the room.

"Goot mornink," I said because I had learnt that much English already.

She raised her eyebrows in surprise and gave me such a smile as made me determined to learn more, then she said something. I was forced to shake my head to show I did not understand. She pointed, and I saw that the column and its flowerpot had been moved into place. It was perfect. She sat in the chair, and once more I had the delight of playing with her limbs, adjusting her shoulders and her hands and her arms just so. My heavens, it took a time to get right.

"I need oil of walnut," I said, and of course I used the Dutch word *Walnoot,* having no idea of the English. "That is what I need if I am to do you justice. This linseed is good but there is too much tint in it for the white I am seeking."

She looked baffled.

"Walnoot?" I said again, hoping perhaps the word sounded similar in her language. No response. I beckoned her out of her chair, mostly because it would be fun positioning her again, and, dabbing a brush on the wall next to the sketch I had already made there, drew what I thought was a fair image of a walnut.

She understood then. She said the word for me in English. "Worlnutt," she said. It was very nearly the same word, walnut, *walnoot.*

"Walnut," I repeated and she laughed and nodded, then affected puzzlement.

I showed her the linseed oil and said "Walnut" very emphatically. "I need good, clear walnut oil." I must say, she caught on quickly. She nodded and mimed someone mounting a horse and trotting off.

"Not me, please," I said, tapping my chest and shaking my head, and she laughed again. She went to the door and called out, then gave instructions to the girl who came.

"How long will it be?" I wondered aloud. "I cannot proceed properly until I have it. Will it be here tomorrow?"

She caught the sense of my question, beckoned me to the window and, pointing at the sun, mimed one passage across the sky. One day. After that we mimed as furiously as children playing a guessing game. I eventually showed her that I could not paint without the oil but that there was something else we might do in the time available.

"I wish to do some sketches of you," I said, miming drawing, then I pointed up toward my room. "In the tower, where there is just the right light. Yes?" I drew windows in the air and walked my fingers up imaginary stairs. "Will you come with me?" I had my charcoal sticks and paper from York. I picked those up and made to leave with her.

There was a moment when she might have shied at the fence, the moment when we came to the tower doorway and she knew for certain, after the ambiguities of the mime, just where we were heading. My heart was in my mouth because if she, finding that improper, had turned back, then I don't think I could easily have made up the lost ground.

She did pause for a moment. She looked at the stairway and at me with a quizzical expression, then she began to climb up in front of me.

TWENTY

Thursday, April 12, 2001

THE SAW WAS STILL HOWLING ITS SONG OF SAVAGE TRIUMPH. AROUND it, a horrified half-circle of builders stood well back, dressed, half-dressed, or just wrapped in towels. Eric was poised on the balls of his feet, swaying as if his brain told him to go nearer and his eyes told him not to. Gengko was moving very slowly closer, taking trepidatious, tightrope-walker steps. At the center of the tableau, Don knelt on the ground facing them, with Dennis slumped across his lap. Don's hands and Dennis's chest were uniformly soaked in the bright arterial blood that had pumped Dennis's life out of the great wound gouged into his neck. Amy pushed through the middle of them and, finding she could not stop, walked toward Don and Dennis's cradled body, breaking the spell of stillness.

Don looked slowly up and met her eyes. "Tell them to turn that thing off," he shouted above the noise of the saw.

She turned, pointed at the saw's switch, and Gengko, moving carefully to avoid the puddles of blood, pushed the button that let the saw spin down from fury to resentment to sullen silence.

In the absence of noise, Dennis's body became more real, more destabilizing.

"We'll call an ambulance," she said, looking away.

"What's the point?"

Gengko came to her side, bent down, and lifted Dennis from Don's lap, laying him on the ground to one side. "Get a blanket," he called, and they covered Dennis over. For a few seconds, his body was just a neat mound of cream wool until the scarlet evidence of death soaked through into their sight, widening as the blanket molded itself to his wound. She concentrated on Don then, inspecting his face, but could tell nothing from it. He stared back at her as if he expected her to have some answer, then he turned away and walked back into the house.

They had all edged in closer now. Nobody asked what had happened. It was too obvious.

"Bloody stupid tricks," Eric muttered.

"Who saw it?" demanded Tel as if only that information, that act of witness, would make it real.

Nobody volunteered.

"Don, I guess," said Gengko.

Later, after the car park had filled up with the official attendants of disaster, after the scene-of-crime officers and the coroner's men had measured and photographed and taken the body away, after the Hawk, coming in late from a night spent in town, had wreaked indiscriminate verbal revenge on all of them simply for being there, it was Gengko who told them all that Don hadn't seen it, either. Amy had gone to look for him when the arrival of the police had broken the spell that kept them all standing round the blanket as if holding a vigil. All she had found in his room was the bloodstained overalls he had been wearing, in a heap in the middle of his floor. Later, and time had stopped so she had no idea if it was ten minutes or an hour, Gengko came into the kitchen where they were all sitting in silence drinking endless mugs of tea.

"I found him," he said, "down by the river. Fucking state of shock, he's in. He'll come along when he's ready."

"What did he say?" asked Jo-Jo. "Did he tell you what happened?"

Gengko shrugged. "Not a lot. Said he looked out the window, saw Dennis switch the saw on, went down to stop him. But by that time it was all over. He was in a heap on the ground."

"And that's it, is it? He wasn't down there with him?" There was an insinuating edge to Jo-Jo's voice.

One or two of the men glanced up sharply. Gengko swiveled round to look at Jo-Jo. The air in the room, suffocating a moment before, became charged.

"He didn't maybe just happen to push him, did he? Just a little bit maybe? He—"

Tel jumped to his feet, his mug smashing on the floor, and pulled back his fist. Gengko took a step forward to get in between them, arms raised to ward them off. At that moment, the door opened and a policeman appeared in the doorway.

"Looking for Donald Gilby," he said. "Is he here?" He looked again at the tableau of frozen figures. "Something going on here, is there?" he asked. "Something troubling you gentlemen?"

"I'll get him for you," said Amy, suddenly desperate to get out of that room. "Ten minutes. I'll be back in ten minutes."

Three minutes to walk down to the river, three minutes to walk back, leaving four minutes to sort out the ferment in her mind, to address the unthinkable made brutally thinkable by Jo-Jo's words. Things like that didn't happen in real life. . . .

Once she was in the lower field she could see Don ahead, standing on the bank just above the landing stage. She wondered what expression she would see when she saw him face-to-face. What would Don's portrait tell her now? Uneasy at the thought of taking him by surprise, she turned away, heading for the bank twenty yards to one side of him. There was nobody else in sight. Dennis's warning hung in the air around her, his voice clamoring in her ears. For a moment she was poised to run away, then Don turned to look at her and, seeing the tear tracks down his cheeks and the swollen red of his eyes, she ran toward him instead. With her arms around him, holding him tight, she let go of herself and sobbed out her horror and her fears but most of all her relief until she felt his hand stroking her hair, stroking her calm again. His tears were the sign she needed to show that Jo-Jo was wrong.

"They want to talk to you," she said when she could.

"Who do?" he said, drawing away and holding her at arm's length.

"The police."

For a moment, his eyes widened with an expression she hadn't seen before. "Well, I'm used to that," he replied. "I'll go back in a while." He let her go.

"They want you now. I said I'd get you."

His head jerked round but he thought better of whatever he had been about to say. "All right then, I'm coming."

The whole morning was taken up with statements and the minutiae of death. There was no work going on. Amy went up to her room, unable to settle. She was fiddling with her sketch pad when she heard footsteps approaching her door. There was a knock, and she opened it to find a policewoman standing there.

"Amy Dale?"

"Yes."

"WPC Percival. Can I come in?"

"Of course you can."

Amy, feeling suddenly nervous, looked around the room at her dearth of furniture. "Sit down," she said, indicating the chair. "I'll sit on the bed."

The sketch pad was lying on the chair and she went to take it away, but the policewoman, picking it up to hand it to her, looked at the drawing of Don. "Is that Mr. Gilby?" she said. "Particular friend of yours, is he?"

"No, not really. Well, I don't know. I've only been here a few days. I've talked to him quite a lot, I suppose, being right next door, and we're working in the same room." *I'm talking too much,* thought Amy, and she stopped. *Why does that uniform make me feel guilty?*

"Do you mind if I ask you a couple of questions?"

"Of course."

"I don't think we need a formal statement or anything at this stage, but it has been put to us that you might have had something to do with this morning's incident."

"What? I wasn't even there. I was inside. I was down in the—"

"Yes, I know. I don't mean it like that."

"Oh. What *do* you mean?"

"It's been put to us that Mr. Greener might have been trying to impress you with his stunts."

"Mr. Greener?"

"Dennis Greener?" WPC Percival looked at her curiously. "The man who died."

Death had brought Dennis a dignity he would have hated.

"Of course. Sorry, we all knew him as Dennis the Menace."

The policewoman frowned. "In what sense was he a menace?"

"It was what he called himself. It was a joke. Anyway, who on earth said he was trying to impress me?"

"Do you think it might be true?"

"No. At least I don't think so. He used to do those horrible tricks before I showed up."

WPC Percival looked uncomfortable. "Did he ... do you think he might have been attracted to you?"

"Oh, what? Look, he was a nice man, very funny." Don's accusation stalked around in the back of her mind. She pushed it aside. "He was thirty years older than me and he knew it. He wasn't kidding himself. You know how it is? I'm sure you've experienced it loads of times. You can tell instantly, can't you? You know when some old man forgets his age and thinks he's love's young dream. He wasn't like that."

"Don't tell me," the other woman said. "You should see what the uniform does to them. So he wasn't an old lecher?"

"Not for a moment."

"It doesn't mean he wasn't trying to impress you."

"No, it doesn't, but I think he was trying to impress everybody. He cast himself as the court jester. It was his moment of glory. Macho rubbish. I wish he hadn't." She felt tears coming.

"I'm sorry, I had to ask."

"Can you tell me who's been saying these things?"

"No, I can't. Someone who thought it mattered," said the policewoman, getting to her feet to go, but then, as if she couldn't stop herself, her eyes drifted across to Don's picture on the pad. "Nothing else you want to tell us, is there?"

Amy closed her eyes. There was so much she wanted to tell someone. At that moment she wanted to pour out all the muddy whirlpool of doubt swirling around her head. The chain saw, droning an evil harmony to this morning's violence. The triangle of Dennis, Don, and Vin. The look in Don's eyes. She wanted to confess it all, but she wanted to tell it to someone who would listen and smile and tell her it was nothing to worry about, that it was all imagination, not someone who would take notes and, possibly, action.

"No," she said. It made no sense to raise doubts. "I suppose ... I suppose you couldn't tell me something about him, could you. About Dennis?"

"What sort of something?"

"Someone told me he had a record, a criminal record. I don't want to think of him like that. Can you tell me if it's true?"

"I can't help you there," said the policewoman firmly.

When she had gone, Amy crossed to the window but down there, right in the middle of her view, was the saw bench. Feeling trapped by the walls and the window she took the pad and went downstairs and out into the yard at the back, hoping to get away from all the people, all the searching looks. Instead she found Gengko, glaring up at the sun as if it had no right to be shining.

"You all right?" he asked. She shook her head.

"Police seen you?"

"Yes."

There was a short silence while he studied her. "That stuff with Jo-Jo," he said in the end. "You didn't say anything, did you?"

"No."

"It's our business, all that. It's not for anybody else's ears, right?"

"You don't believe it, do you, Gengko?"

"That Don pushed Dennis?" He looked at her somberly then shook his head. "Why would he do that? Listen, kid, Dennis was his very own accident, just waiting to happen. Go easy on Don. He's had a hard time." He stopped talking as a policeman walked out into the yard, looked round, and went back inside. "I hope they do, too," he said.

Amy went for a walk, but grief and doubt make poor company and she took in very little of the countryside around her. She followed the road the other way, where it turned inland away from the Humber; after half an hour's walking she turned and retraced her steps to the point where she could just see the house away across the fields. There she sat on a wall and remembered Dennis and his rubber ducks and wondered if he would still be alive if she hadn't happened along that road that day.

It occurred to her that her life was dominated by hidden faces. Amelia hiding her face behind the plaster, just a fraction of an inch out of reach of her sight. Don hiding his face at every opportunity, unable to accept that the sight of him could please her, scar or no scar. In her sketch pad, she had drawn him with his eyes closed, with no clue as to whether darkness or light ruled behind them. Rubbing them out, she penciled wide-open eyes in their place, the look she had seen most recently when she'd told him the police wanted to talk to him. His expression made her shiver. She quickly rubbed those out, too, and drew the closed eyelids back over them to make them go away.

Sitting there on the wall, with the sun coming out to warm her face, she shivered and resolved to take control. First there was Vin's account of what had happened. She had promised Dennis she would read it; so long as she could find it, that was what she would do. It would clear her mind. More important, it would clear Don, too, free him of all the suspicion people had put in her mind. Her soul was dancing in the flames with Don and whether she liked it or not, it was beyond her control. She needed to believe in him. It was the first time she had ever got out of bed with a man feeling shaken to the core by what they had done together. She wanted very much to be in that bed with him again, not just in the dark, but to wake up with him in daylight, to gaze at each other with nothing in the way. It should be the right Don, a Don who wanted the light on, who wasn't scarred inside and out. A Don who was good for her and for himself. She wanted a man whose eyes didn't change so much, a man who could look straight at her. She wanted a Don whose picture could plausibly exist on the same page as hers.

"Bugger," she said, getting up to walk back to whatever Paull Holme Manor now held for her.

Back on her gloomy landing, she saw Don's door was open wide and the room empty, so she turned and entered his bedroom as if that might somehow make everything clearer, looking at the chair and the bed as if they held the answer. Looking at the bed, remembering the feeling of him against her, she suddenly knew she had lied to Dennis, that she was in far deeper than her knees.

Belatedly, it came to her that the solution might lie in her own hands, in her brush and her palette, by painting Don either into her life or out of it. A picture was a two-way transaction. She could show him the version she saw, the one she wanted to be with, and then see if he could be that man. That was what she had to do, to coax him into accepting the way he looked to her and to the world. Looking around, she knew this was the right place to do it, next to that bed with its memories and its promise. What had this tower room been? she wondered again. A defense post? A storeroom? Had people lived here, loved here? Had passion ever had the chance to soak into these old stone walls? It was Don's own separate space, apart from the house that had been built on to it. No normal rules would apply here. It made an unlikely studio, this room, but that was just what it was going to be.

There was a note pushed under her own door. Peter Parrish was downstairs and would like to see her.

It was only when she pushed open the door of the room where she had been working that she remembered what she had done to the wall in that far-off time just a few hours before.

Don was sitting on a box, his back half turned to Parrish, who was standing with his hands clasped behind him, gazing at the wall. The noise of the door opening seemed to break a long silence.

"Hello," said Parrish. "I'm glad to see you. Are you managing?"

"So far," said Amy.

"Mr. Hawkins and I have put our heads together and we've decided it might be best for everyone if work carries on as usual. There'll be plenty of time to talk later. Is that all right with you?"

Amy nodded.

Parrish indicated the great hole Amy had made in the plaster. "I see you've been a touch impulsive," he said. "I'm glad you stopped where you did."

Don got up from his box and went back to work. Every piece of paneling was being taken off now, after careful labeling to make sure each went back in exactly the right place. He was easing out the pins that held the frames of the panels together, using long-nosed pliers like a surgical instrument to avoid damage, pretending not to listen.

"I was really careful," she replied. "There's no harm done. I just wanted to show you it was possible, so you didn't cover it all up again."

"Careful?" Parrish said with an unexpected touch of sharpness in his voice. "We had a plan for this room, young woman. It did not involve knocking half the wall down. We would have recorded what was there, then we would have put the paneling back over it and started researching the history a little more. Then and only then would we have made a proper decision about preservation. Do you understand?"

"Yes," said Amy meekly, understanding that this was his way of distracting himself.

"I mean it wasn't *going* anywhere, was it? There was no real urgency. Now what are we going to do? It certainly can't be left like that."

"Can't you get someone in to uncover the rest of it?"

"Have you any idea how tight the budget is for all this?"

"I'll pay for it if you like," she said.

His voice softened then. "You have no idea how much work like that costs. I suppose we'll have to get *some* sort of conservation done. I know what you think, but it's not Rembrandt. You should get that out of your head. It's just a doodle," he added. "A very high-class doodle, I know. Some workman was enjoying himself."

"The limner," said Don quietly.

"Oh, yes," said Parrish, "the mysterious limner. I grant you that. You're right; I looked it up. So, there was a portrait painter and maybe he did this, but that doesn't mean a great deal. Look, we have to go about this a different way, do you understand? This is architectural detective work, a form of archaeology. That means we look for certainty, not wild theory. We carefully explore what is here, and we interfere with it only when we're quite certain we're doing the right thing."

A voice sounded in Amy's head. "The Hawk will do his nut ... so will old man Parrish." Dennis, alive, here, this morning. She closed her eyes and sighed.

Parrish pursed his lips. "Oh, dear. I know I shouldn't add fuel to the flames, but I did make a call to a friend on your behalf."

"What about?"

"Wait a minute," said Parrish, and he went to the door and looked out. "Just checking for Mr. Hawkins," he said. "He doesn't like me wasting your time, even though it is meant to be *my* time. I like to stay on the right side of the Hawk." He had allowed complicity to reenter the conversation, and Amy was deeply grateful.

"Tell us," she said.

"I have a friend at the Victoria and Albert Museum," he said. "I asked him to look at the Vertue notebooks for me. After all, that's the main source on this business. It turns out it's a bit more complicated than I thought. Is this an absurd time to be discussing this?"

"No. I think it's a very good time." Don was still working but she knew he was listening.

Parrish opened his case and drew out a sheet of paper. "Now, there's the business of the date. Do you remember? Rembrandt was supposed to have dated one of his Yorkshire pictures 1662 slash 1661, according to Vertue. That's what really seems to make a nonsense of the whole thing. I told you, didn't I, 1662, fair enough. Rembrandt could have been anywhere in the first few months. There's no record. But 1661 is a different kettle of fish. We know he was in Amsterdam pretty much all year. It doesn't add up. Or so everyone thought."

"What's changed?" asked Amy.

"Well, I think I've been rather clever," said Parrish. "I've been reading my old favorite Samuel Pepys again lately. The whole diary, in full. A million words or more. Wonderful stuff. There's nothing like it. Well, I suppose you might say our own Amelia comes closest, but you know she never really lets her inner feelings out, does she? With Pepys, of course, he was writing in code, in shorthand, and when things got a bit steamy, he used all these Spanish and French words to cover his tracks on the rude stuff. Old Amelia was a bit too upright for that, eh?"

Amy just nodded.

"The point is I suddenly realized Pepys does his dates like that, too—1662 *over* '61, like a fraction, so I looked it up and guess what? It doesn't mean what everybody thinks."

"So what does it mean?"

"It's all about the New Year," explained Parrish. He stopped for a moment as footsteps sounded in the corridor but they passed by and went down the stairs. "Until the middle of the seventeenth century, the new year didn't start on January first. It started on Lady Day, which is March twenty-fifth. The *year* didn't change until then. Then they modernized it you see, so that the new year began in January. Of course it took a few years for everyone to get used to that, so just for a while they used this formula, like a fraction, sixty-two over sixty-one. It doesn't mean two whole years. It means a very precise time period between January first, 1662 and March twenty-fourth of the *same year*. Now, that removes one key objection, because we have absolutely no evidence that Rembrandt was at home in Amsterdam during that time. It also means that if our friend *did* paint a picture in Yorkshire, then he painted it during a very particular period of less than twelve weeks."

"That's good," said Amy.

"Aha, it gets better yet. You see, my friend at the V and A says there's something else that's interesting about the Rembrandt passage in Vertue. There were ten George Vertue notebooks, and they're all in his own handwriting. Except for the first one."

Parrish was growing more and more animated, striding backward and forward wagging his finger like the gifted amateur detective about to unmask the villain at the end of an old movie. He seemed to have forgotten everything else. Don had paused and was looking round at him.

"It's the first notebook that has all the Rembrandt stuff in it, the story about Laroon and the detailed description of the Yorkshire painting. Apparently it's not always terribly clear in the notebooks whether Vertue has actually *seen* the pictures or whether somebody else has just told him about them, but in this case it's quite blindingly obvious."

He waited for them to ask why and when neither of them did, he was forced to go on.

"Something happened to the first notebook. Maybe it got wet or the mice attacked it, I don't know, but somebody else wrote it out all over again in different handwriting. My pal thinks it was probably one of Vertue's assistants. They tended to have young chaps around them doing the donkey work, these chaps. Wish it was still like that. Now quite clearly, this man couldn't be entirely trusted because he made lots of mistakes, so poor old George had to go right through the whole shebang all over again, correcting it. By the time he got round to it, it was probably a year or two later, do you see? By that time, he'd had a chance to go to see some of the pictures he'd only *heard* about before, so he could update what he'd written. The end product of this is that I think we'll carry on taking off the paneling for the time being, and you, Amy, I want you to come down to London with me. Hello, Mr. Hawkins, how is it going?"

The Hawk had come into the room halfway through the last sentence. "Didn't hear any work going on, Mr. Parrish. Thought I'd better take a look under the circumstances. You going to London?"

"Tomorrow. Just a day trip. We have to touch base with the people holding the purse strings, you know. There's a possibility of some charitable funding."

"I heard you say you were taking her." The Hawk nodded toward Amy.

"That's right. She has some work to do, checking similar designs and so forth. Room one seven, you know, the one with only the fragments left."

"Whatever you say. There's no overtime for travel." The Hawk didn't look unhappy about having Amy out of his hair for a day. He slipped out as abruptly as he had come in.

"Oh dear," said Parrish. "I *was* meaning to ask you. Meant to talk to you yesterday. Now I've landed you in it. Do you mind?"

"I'm a little bemused," said Amy. "Am I really coming?"

"Well, I'd like you to have a look at the records of contemporary decoration. We've got to come up with some good ideas in the other rooms. I'm driving down. Pick you up at six?"

"*Six?* In the morning?"

"My meeting's at nine-thirty. I'll be finished by lunchtime."

Why not, she thought. *Better than being here all day.* "All right, then. But he's gone now. You can finish what you were telling us."

"Oh yes, George Vertue. My friend says you just know when you look at the way he's corrected the notebook, he's been to see the pictures in the interim. There's a *certainty* that comes out of the handwriting."

"Are you saying he's changed the details of the Yorkshire picture?"

"Yes, exactly that. There was all sorts of stuff about the signature and the date and what was painted on the frame, and he's amended it all. He must have seen it and he must have believed it was genuine."

"So what exactly does it say?" asked Don.

"Oh, I don't know. He didn't tell me that. Anyway, we can discuss it on the journey, Amelia."

"That's *Amy.*"

"Oh, yes, of course. Now, Don, how's it going with the paneling?"

"Slowly," said Don. "This one's come completely apart. I'm labeling them like you said. I'm taking them from the left, as you see, so I thought tomorrow, after they've been cleaned up, I'd start putting them back in from the right so there's never more than a couple of sections out at any one time."

"Very good, except that doesn't help us sort out what we're going to do with Amy's revelation here." Parrish was looking at the legs painted on the wall. The light had changed during the time they had been talking, and the top part of the picture was showing itself a little more clearly through the remaining paint.

He bent down and looked at the next section, where Don had just taken the adjoining panel away. It, too, was covered in dust and cobwebs; he brushed it off with his hand.

"Ah," he said.

"What is it?" Amy took a step toward him.

"I almost hate to say it," he said, "but we appear to have another picture."

"Where?" Don had joined them like a terrier at a foxhole.

"It's very small. Do you see?"

There was a pale brown blob on the wall under the grime, not much more than an inch across.

"It looks like a stain."

"It's not a stain, Amy," said Parrish, staring at it. "It's quite definitely a painting of a walnut, and it's really rather good. Another little Paull Holme mystery to solve." He turned to Don. "Let's hold off putting any of the paneling back on, shall we? We'll make a decision later." He looked at his watch. "I must go," he said. "Six o' clock tomorrow, then?"

Amy groaned. "If we must."

TWENTY-ONE

Friday, April 13, 2001

AMY HAD ALREADY BEEN UP FOR AN HOUR BEFORE PETER PARRISH collected her the following morning. She had used the time to search Dennis's room, moving as quietly as she could. It shouldn't have taken long, because he had so few possessions, but that didn't stop tears coming to her eyes at the sight of what he did have. There was a wedding photo of a much younger, dashing Dennis in naval uniform, an unexpected prayer book and, in amongst the rubber ducks, a small stuffed teddy bear. In his worn shoulder bag she found a cardboard folder that had "Vin Williams" written on it in felt-tip lettering. She opened it expectantly, but all she found inside was a list of prison visiting times and a copy of the newspaper article about Don's award ceremony. Loose in the bottom of the bag she found a small square of yellow paper with a paper clip still on it. "Vin Williams. Statement made to Dennis Greener" was written neatly on it, but there was no sign of the document to which it had once been attached.

It was only when she had sat on Dennis's chair for a while, looking around the room, that she realized something else was missing. There was no sign of Dennis's old wooden tray.

In the car, Parrish tried, in an awkward way, to say the right things about Dennis but he clearly had hardly known him at all. Amy knew there was something else he wanted to say to her but couldn't quite bring himself to. Instead, all the way to London, he gave her a long lecture on vernacular architecture in East Yorkshire. Parts of this, the human parts, were fascinating—but that left a great deal that wasn't. Parrish drove fast and surprisingly well. Amy would have pinned him as a nice old ditherer but he carved through the traffic quite ruthlessly, the result of which was that they were in the middle of London by nine o'clock.

"What exactly do you want me to do?" asked Amy.

"I'll drop you at the Victoria and Albert. Go through the museum to the National Art Library. Ask for Tony Jones. He knows you're coming. He'll fix you up with a temporary reader's card and he's got some stuff together for you to have a look at. Shouldn't take too long. It's just drawings and pictures."

"Of what?"

"Oh, you know. Interiors. Other decorated ceilings of the period. I want you to get the general idea of how they looked. He'll copy a few of them, so choose the ones you think come closest to the style we've got. I'll come and pick you up when I've finished. About half-past one?"

At the V & A, Tony Jones proved to be a man pressed from the same mold as Peter Parrish, though rather better groomed; gratifyingly, he knew all about her. The Art Library had a lofty air of studious elegance, and she was glad to be a welcomed insider. Otherwise, she thought, it might have felt like a very exclusive club.

Arcane knowledge was required. Each desk was fitted with a hinged piece of wood, which folded down. Amy fiddled with one surreptitiously but could find no apparent purpose for it, and when she looked around at the intent art students who surrounded her, she couldn't see anyone else using them.

However intimidating, it was certainly a beautiful library. The desks were of polished wood and black leather, with old-fashioned numbers for each seat and a bronze reading lamp with a green shade. A strip of carpet up the middle of the room helped to hush the footfalls of any who might dare to walk noisily. There was a high balcony above; an arcade of arched windows looked out into a garden. She looked assiduously through the material Tony Jones brought out for her, a little disturbed by the responsibility she'd suddenly been given for the future decoration of Paull Holme Manor. At twelve o'clock, she gave a selection of designs to him for photocopying. When she put them down on the desk, he said, "Oh. By the way, Peter mentioned you also wanted to see this," and handed her a book.

She took it back to her desk, a little annoyed because she thought she had finished and had been hoping for time to look round the museum before Peter returned. The book had a gray cover bearing a white label, which read, "Walpole Society Volume 18 1929-30." Inside it was all text and no pictures. Her heart sank, then she remembered where she had heard about the Walpole Society before and a strange thrill passed right through her. A note inside the cover confirmed her memory, saying that the Walpole Society had been instituted in 1911 and that one of the main obligations laid upon it had been the publication of the manuscript notebooks of George Vertue. A slip of paper had been inserted into the pages. She opened the book at the place and found she was looking at a page of irregular printing, interspersed with footnote numbers. She scanned down and found what she had hoped would be there: *"Renbrant van Rhine was in England liv'd at Hull in Yorkshire (reported by old Laroon who in his youth knew Renbrant at York) where he painted several Gentlemen and sea faring mens pictures. One of them is in the possession of . . ."* She stopped reading and stared at the page until her vision focused entirely on the words that followed, while the rest of the page dissolved into a white whirlpool.

When Peter Parrish arrived an hour later, she was still studying the book, having composed more than a page of notes.

"We finished early, thank the Lord," he whispered, bending over her. "How about you? Shall we go and have lunch?"

"Come and sit down for a minute," she said. "There's something here you really have to look at."

He pulled his glasses from his breast pocket, put them on, and immediately adopted that head-tilted-back look of the person who is about to study something. "Is that one of the Vertue notebooks you've got there?" he whispered. "Oh, good. I rather hoped you'd be finished in time to have a look. Did you find it interesting?"

"Yes, I did," she answered. "So will you. As you said, this is a later copy, which Vertue corrected. It's all about this one particular portrait." She looked at him. "You have to concentrate on this."

"Oh, I am," he replied quickly, though he looked a little mystified. "As it first appeared in the notebook," she explained, "it said this portrait is in the possession of a sea captain with the gentleman's name on the frame together with Rembrandt's name, except he spelled it Renbrant, with an 'n.' Then there's all the business about the date and the place and that funny way the year's written. Vertue's corrections aren't the most interesting part, except you really do get the feeling he's seen the picture since he first wrote about it. He says it doesn't say 'York' on the frame after all."

"Jolly good," whispered Parrish, "but that's rather a shame from the point of view of your theory, isn't it?"

Amy looked at him, savoring the moment. "I've left out the best bit," she said quietly.

"What's that?"

"The name of the sea captain."

"Someone we know?"

"Oh, yes. Take a look."

Amy pointed at the page and Peter Parrish craned over her to look. Then, in his amazement, he spoke the name aloud. "Dahl." Everybody in the library turned round in indignation as if that were the worst four-letter word they had ever heard.

Lunch, by mutual consent, was a sandwich because they both wanted to get back on the road north.

In the car, Parrish said, "I'm so glad you spotted that."

"Had you never looked at it?"

"Years ago, I suppose, before I ever knew anything about the history of the Dales of Paull Holme. 'Dahl' wouldn't have meant anything to me then, you see."

He darted into a gap in the fast lane and earned a horn blast from the Audi coming up behind.

"Silly bugger," he said. "Could have fitted a double-decker bus in there."

"So long as it was doing ninety-five," murmured Amy. "Why *did* the later 'Dales' leave?"

"One of those First World War things, I think. The sons got killed in the trenches. The parents stayed there until they were too old to look after it. Sold up in the thirties. I suppose you must be a cousin or something?"

"A few times removed, I expect. So, if there had been a portrait of old man Dahl, it could be anywhere."

"Well, I was just thinking about that. They sold a few bits and pieces—we've got the catalogue somewhere—but a lot of it stayed with the house, you know. It's itemized in the deed of sale. So either way, if the picture was still there in the thirties, there ought to be a record of it."

"Are you turning into a believer?"

Parrish smiled. "Not yet. However, I do think we should keep all this absolutely to ourselves. It might all sound very silly to anyone else. We can let Ellen in on it, of course. We must tell her. I've never kept anything from Ellen."

"I'd like to know about her," said Amy. "You've got a lot of time for her, haven't you?"

"Marvelous woman," said Parrish. "Entirely self-educated, did you know that? Brought up Don by herself after her husband died. I did everything I could to help. I knew her, you see, ever since they got married. Used to go fishing with Gil, Don's dad."

"What happened to Gil?"

It took Parrish a moment to reply. "Well ... it was pretty bad. He was drowned. He was fishing in the Humber late at night. He used to like to go out in the dark. They think a ship ran him down."

"Oh, no."

"They found bits of wood from his boat with red lead paint on them, completely shattered. It must have been hit by something big."

"I had no idea. How old was Don?"

"About five or six."

Amy remembered Don talking about Marvell's father, Don reading out the inscriptions on the gravestones, telling her how the corpses washed up at Paull, failing to say anything at all about his own father. She tried hard to remember what she had said, and prayed it had been nothing flippant.

"Did they ... did they find the body?"

"Yes, it washed up at last, like they do."

"Was that at Paull?"

Parrish shot her a startled look. "Yes, I think it probably was, come to think of it. It's twenty years ago now."

"And then?"

"What do you mean?"

"You and them."

"I did what I could."

Amy knew the interviewer's trick of keeping quiet, of letting the silence stretch out until the other one had to fill it, so she kept silent until in the end he had to speak.

"I had a very soft spot for her, you know."

She waited.

"I really adored her," Parrish said. "She's such an extraordinary person."

"Do you still?"

"I think I won't answer that one, if you don't mind."

Shall I push it? wondered Amy. *Of course I shall.*

"Why didn't you two ever get together?"

"Did I say we didn't?" retorted Parrish. "Well, it's true we've lived separately of course."

"That seems sad."

"It was . . . it was difficult."

Then he glanced at her and cleared his throat and she thought, *here we go. He's been trying to bring this up all day.*

"The thing is, Amy, Ellen's very worried about Don."

"I'm sure she is."

"No, it's not just the injuries. There's more to it than that." Parrish switched on the wipers as the car in front sprayed windshield-washer fluid back at them, straight over its roof. "You wouldn't know he was the same person since the attack."

"It's not at all surprising, is it? Not really."

"Well, of course not, but Ellen says she doesn't feel it's just the trauma. She's worried that it goes right down to the *core* of him somehow. Don was just a bit vain before the attack. He liked to look good, you know? He worked out in the gym. Had some really stunning girlfriends, too."

"I'm sure he did."

He blinked at her. "Ellen says his image of himself has been shattered. She deals with people in trouble, day in, day out, and she says you can very often get to a point where their self-esteem was destroyed and everything else in their life went to pieces as a result. She sees it happening to him, and she's scared stiff of the way he's going."

"There's something I'd like to ask you," she said.

"Yes?"

"You were there, weren't you, in the Drydock, when it all happened?"

"Yes, I was."

"There seems to be a difference of opinion over what actually happened. I don't really know what *did* happen."

"I'm not sure anyone does," said Parrish, and she knew that it was going to cost him something to tell her. "I had to go over it all again and again. You know, for police statements and so on. It's so hard to be a witness when you're not quite sure what you remember and what you added afterward."

"Do you mind telling me?"

He took a moment and she knew he would rather not have to.

"I was first down there when we heard the noise. Ellen was behind me. He'd already attacked Sarah."

"Who had? Vin?"

"Yes. She was on the floor." His voice trailed off for a moment. "It was the most terrible sight. By that time, Don had got the chain saw from him, but this other man was still fighting to get it back. That was when Don got hurt, while they were fighting, because the blade was flailing around all over the place. Then I think Don must have turned it off because the noise just suddenly stopped, thank God, and we all piled on top of the man."

"What sort of state was Don in?"

"Absolutely awful. Then he fainted. I'm sorry, I hate to talk about it."

He'd said enough. She'd been hoping for certainty, for a witness who had seen Don take the saw from Vin, someone who could swing the balance decisively against the horrible worm of doubt Dennis had introduced, but there was nothing even approaching certainty in what Parrish had just said.

"Do you think he's capable of violence? I don't mean self-defense; I mean real violence."

He didn't answer for a long time, overtaking a long chain of trucks, then as he moved back into the middle lane, he said, "Maybe we all are. My advice would be, don't ever provoke him far enough to find out."

"Did you know Dennis Greener was Vin's uncle?"

He looked at her in astonishment. "No. Is that right? How extraordinary."

She changed tack. "So Ellen's worried. What's it got to do with me?"

"Ah." Parrish drummed his fingers on the steering wheel and made an unnecessary meal of checking his mirror and looking over his shoulder before overtaking the truck in front. "Ellen's a bit ... well, I suppose you might say she's a bit concerned about your effect on Don."

"I've only met her once for about five minutes."

"Yes, she said."

"I must have made an incredibly bad impression."

"Oh, no, not at all. An impression, yes. A powerful impression, I think, but not necessarily a bad one."

"So why is she worried?"

"Well, for one thing, she ... Oh, dear. Well, she thinks Don might be ... I don't know what the expression is these days."

"He might fancy me?"

"Oh, that's a little earthy, isn't it? I think she meant something just a shade more spiritual. She thinks he might be *falling* for you." Parrish glanced across at her and hurried on, "Then on top of that, she thinks you might be somebody who feels sorry for people in trouble."

"Is that such a bad thing?"

"It depends why you're doing it, at least that's what Ellen would say. She says some people need the self-gratification, the warm glow they derive from doing some good, but then they move on. She says she thinks if that happened to Don now it might be the final nail in his coffin."

If only it were that simple, thought Amy. "All right," she said, "I'll tell you how it is and you can decide what to tell Ellen."

"Agreed."

"People shy away from so many things. If you have a death in the family, or you've got cancer or something, people prefer to pretend it's not happening so they don't have to talk to you about it. Me, I talk. If someone's got a problem, I talk, and most people are pleased to be talked to. Don's not. Don's got an awkward streak."

"You haven't known him for as long as we have." It was a mild reproof but it came from a mild man and it hit her harder for it.

"Sorry, am I wrong?"

"I think you'd be worrying Ellen if she could hear you now. She would say it's what *he* needs that matters, not what *you* think he needs."

"Just between us, Mr. Parrish, can I tell you what I'm going to try to do?"

"So long as you don't call me Mr. Parrish. Peter is fine."

"Peter. I think I'm trying to paint Don back to life."

"Good heavens. That sounds a little grandiose. What do you mean?"

"It's *not*. All I mean is that I'm going to paint his portrait as I see him, so maybe he'll be able to see that he's not some kind of freak. I want to give him back a face he can live with."

"Are you good at portraits?"

"It's what I do. Ceilings are a sideline."

"And if you succeed, what then?"

"If I succeed, then Ellen has nothing to worry about. He'll be looking the world in the face again."

"And if you don't? She's afraid that when you go, you'll take part of him with you, and he hasn't got very much to spare."

"That doesn't sound like the Don I know," said Amy. "The future is still over the hill, isn't it?" She found herself unwilling to be drawn any further on exactly how she felt.

There was another question Amy wanted to ask but she didn't know if she dared. She looked out of the windshield at the oncoming traffic. *If two of the next ten cars are blue, I'll ask it,* she thought. Two of them were.

"Was it Don who stopped you and Ellen getting together?"

"Why do you ask? Come to that, why do you think I might answer?"

"It's for me," she said. "For my peace of mind. I keep seeing someone there who frightens me a bit. He seems to be very jealous."

"Is he?" said Parrish, without apparent surprise. "Of who?"

"Of some of the other builders," Amy said with deliberate vagueness.

"You might expect that, I suppose," replied Parrish, "considering that he's low on self-esteem and you're a very pretty girl."

Amy tried saying nothing again.

"You're right, of course," said Parrish after a while. "It was Don who kept Ellen and me apart. I played it all wrong. He found us... Well, he came in at a bad moment when he was still pretty tiny... After that he'd get furious if we showed any affection when he was there. He'd throw a real tantrum. You can't blame him."

"And that kept you apart?"

"Sounds silly, doesn't it? You'd have to be there to understand. It got rather extreme at times. Ellen had to put him first, I quite understood that."

"You poor man."

"I think perhaps you should save your sympathy for Don. Can you imagine what it must have been like for him yesterday?" said Parrish thoughtfully. "He was the first one there, wasn't he? It *would* have to be a saw again. That was cruel."

"Yes, it must have brought back some vicious memories. I should have stayed there today. I could have helped."

"Amy, I'm not such an old idiot as I may look. I've known that boy for many years. You were best out of the way. He'll have been a bear with a sore head all day. By tonight, with a bit of luck, he'll be looking for distraction and human company, and I have something in mind."

"What is it?"

"You'll see. It involves the three of us and, though I hate to say it, your friend Rembrandt because, I have to confess, you've finally managed to shake my disbelief, enough at least, to suggest we go hunting."

"For the picture? You mean there was stuff like that still in the house?"

Parrish gave Amy a crafty look. "I wondered when you'd get round to asking about that."

"Well?"

"We put a lot of it away for safekeeping. It's in room one eight."

"What?"

"When we took over the house, they'd left all manner of bits and pieces upstairs, downstairs, in the attic, in the outhouses, wherever you looked. We pulled out all the stuff that might be worth saving and put it in room one eight."

"Is that the locked room?"

"That's it. First floor, far end from your tower. It's a great big room and we're due to do it last."

"What's in it?"

"Junk. It's absolutely crammed. We *have* to keep it locked, you know. There's something about builders. They seem to think anything lying around is fair game."

"I've noticed."

"That's why I'm a bit worried about this Rembrandt idea getting out. There are one or two who would have that door off at the hinges in no time if they thought there might be a quick profit to be made on the other side."

"But with what we've just found out, it is in fact quite within the bounds of possibility," she said slowly, "that there is an unknown Rembrandt portrait in room one eight."

"Unless, of course, we burned it."

She looked at him in horror. "Is that possible?"

"There were a few pictures that were so far gone, there was nothing else we could do. Just broken frames and torn, dirty canvas. Nothing of merit," he said. There was a short silence. "I devoutly hope," he added less certainly.

"So shall we go scavenging in room one eight?" she said gleefully.

"I don't think we have any choice, do you? I really hope that I know enough about art not to have looked at a Rembrandt and failed to spot that it was anything special. However, I just might have."

"So tonight, we'll go and look?"

"You, me, and Don. Getting back to Don, whatever Ellen may think, I think he needs you right now and I don't think you'll let him down, will you? But then in the course of all this, you've somehow managed to avoid telling me what you feel about him."

She considered evasion, but in that confessional car, with this concerned man next to her, there was no room for a glib reply. There was no place for precise honesty, either, because she found she didn't know the answer.

"I ... I like him," she said, "a lot." Was that true? "At least, I find him really attractive."

Parrish was silent, apparently concentrating on his driving.

"No, more than that. Overwhelming, really," she went on. "But I'm not sure it could ever go anywhere."

"Unless he learns to like himself again," the man next to her offered.

"Yes, maybe."

"The injuries don't make any difference?"

"No," she said, "not the ones on the outside, not at all. Only the ones on the inside."

"Then I think you must paint his portrait."

TWENTY-TWO

Friday, January 24th, 1662

BEYOND MY MOST PRIVATE DREAMS, AMELIA HAD AGREED TO COME to my room. I gallantly stood aside and ushered her up the steep staircase before me, then climbed up close behind her, catching a delightful glance at a shapely leg and yearning to see more. Sadly, having twenty-five years on me, she scampered up that staircase at double my speed and disappeared from view. At the top of the first flight, the stairs opened onto an empty space, filling the whole tower, full of spider-webs and rat droppings. I was accustomed to it by now but I wondered if she had ever been here before. This part of the house, so much older and harder than the rest, seemed entirely outside her world, but she did not hesitate for a moment and was up the second stairs before I reached the top of the first.

My room was ready. In preparation, I had pulled the coverings tidily over the palliasse that passed as my mattress, and swept the worst of the dust out onto the landing. I caught up with her at the door, where she was quivering like a bird unsure whether to step into the trap.

I offered her my most reassuring smile and a sweeping bow, which at least had the effect of making her laugh, and said, "After you, madam. My superb studio is entirely at your disposal."

She inclined her head and stepped inside. My heart beat a little faster.

I folded a pillow cloth into four and set it on the chair for her, and she sat down carefully, looking all around her. It struck me again that it might be the first time she had seen it. What reason would she have had to come here before?

Seeking to hide behind artistic purpose, I picked up the board I had prepared as backing to my paper and set to in charcoal. It isn't my preferred medium for sketching, being too prone to snap just at the moment when the passion starts driving the process and the fingers lose all reserve, but the alternative was a brush and some sort of pale ochre, which felt too restrictive. I knew I would not want to stop to charge up the brush, needing the freedom to prowl the room, searching for my quarry in hidden angles. Free to say anything I wanted, I assumed my most neutral voice and said, "The curve of your neck is designed for a man's lips. Did you know that? I'm sure you did. I hope Dahl's lips are as soft on your skin as you deserve."

She glanced at me as though to apologize for not understanding and, once again, I found in her complete incomprehension a thrilling range of possibilities.

"I wish my lips could taste it. I know how to make a woman sigh with the pleasure of the caress. You would bend your neck to open more of your sweet skin to me if I were to try that, my beauty."

My voice was having the same effect that my gaze and my brush had had on our previous encounter. I could see Amelia relaxing into the smooth flow of words, I could see the blood flow nearer to the surface of her skin as my words caressed her. I moved behind her and she turned her head sharply to see where I had gone but I motioned her back to her position.

"Just another sketch," I said, "to capture the line of your shoulders. I need all aspects of you at their best, the entire contour of your body at the moment it is flushed with the full power of your female desire. Only then does your flesh fill and soften and take on that extreme degree of perfect beauty that I know you to possess. I would paint you as if you had just finished a long, sweet act of love, then all who look at your picture will feel a deep stirring in them as they linger on you."

She did not like me talking to her from behind. She fidgeted.

I moved closer to her and looked down on her from just behind her head. The clothes she wore—I don't know what you would call the upper half, a bodice perhaps—were made slightly loose by her posture and to my delight, I found that from my position, I could see down the gap between cloth and flesh and there, in that private place, were her breasts, pushing out, open to my gaze almost to their very tips where the cloth clung to them and hung sheer.

"On my soul's ease," I said, "what a wonderful sight. I must paint you naked to paint you as you truly are. If your nipples are half as delicious as the rest of your breasts, then I think you take the prize for any woman I have ever painted. You are truly glorious."

Without turning round, she pulled her bodice tighter around her as if I had suddenly gone too far. She hunched forward away from my gaze, while a pink blush spread across the cheek that I could see.

A horrible certainty spread through me.

"You have understood every word I have said," I muttered, my voice trembling.

"Yes, I regret to tell you that I have," she answered in Dutch, perfect Dutch, coarsely accented like a sailor's, but undeniably the Dutch of someone who had spoken the language in everyday life.

Everything I had been saying to her in the sure knowledge that she did *not* understand exploded in my ears.

"I would not have ... everyone told me ... I mean, I had no idea you spoke my language."

"It is a secret I am entrusting to you as a hostage for the secrets you have been unwittingly entrusting to me," she said—a stern speech to hear at such a moment.

I walked slowly round in front of her and met her gaze. With her color heightened, she was even more lovely.

"My husband has no idea that I speak your language, and he must have no idea or the consequences will be dreadful. The same goes for Marvell. He will only use the fact to his advantage as he uses all facts that come his way."

Pressing her on this secret seemed altogether safer than having to revisit all I had said before.

"You will have to tell me why. A blind man may stumble into holes others would easily avoid."

"I don't have to tell you anything, but I will tell you enough to stop you asking more."

I sat down on the other chair, astonished, intrigued, and, unusual for me, deeply embarrassed.

"I met my husband on his ship," she said, "returning from Batavia. Have you been to Batavia?"

"I have never been anywhere," I said. "Not until I came here."

"But you know of it?"

"Our Spice Islands? Most certainly. Down at the docks there is always talk of the latest cargo to arrive, the latest passengers to leave, the latest lists of those whom disease and hazard have killed there. I have never had the slightest desire to go."

"They are the jewel of your empire," she said, "more beautiful than you can know if you have only seen this muddy river and its Dutch cousin. The sea there is not brown; it is a turquoise necklace on the sand's white neck. All the wonders of nature are to be found there."

"You liked it there?"

"I hated it," she said with vehemence.

"Why?"

She hesitated. "I am placing my whole life in your hands by even hinting at this."

"I seem to have put my life in yours quite by chance also. We are safe with one another if we hold a knife to each other's throat."

"I was a year in Batavia, a whole terrible year, stranded. I learnt my Dutch there and wish I had not."

"How did you come to that?"

"I took ship to marry the man I had loved since we played together at twelve years old. My parents were both dead. I had some money but no great dowry, and he sent for me to come to him. Between my ship's leaving the cold north and its arriving in the warm south, a fever took him and instead of his face, waiting eagerly for me on the quay, there was a cold letter to freeze my heart. I was in a place stranger than any I had ever imagined, prepared in no way whatsoever for a life alone there, and knowing nobody. I was desolate. He had been a month dead before I came and was already entirely forgotten. Intending to make my life there, I had no money for a passage home. The captain of the ship that brought me was ready enough to take me back but there had been," she hesitated a moment, "some difficulties on the passage out which made me reluctant to accept. On the way out, at least I had the protection of a husband known to be waiting for me. On the way back, alone, I would have been at great risk. Only three ships came in the next few weeks and though I haunted the docks, visiting each captain in turn, I found nobody kind enough to take me home on trust."

I knew to my cost how dedicated my fellow man can be to the coin that he clutches in his grasp. "There was nobody in the town to help you?"

"I don't wish to speak harshly of your fellow countrymen, but the women closed their doors to me. I did not then speak the language and could not make myself plain to them. None of them were prepared to have me in their houses."

Well, I knew why, of course. No Dutch dumpling in her right mind would have let her sleep under the same roof. There wasn't a red-blooded man on earth who, knowing Amelia lay alone nearby, would not have been driven by the hot itch to try his luck on a nocturnal visit.

"Only one other person offered assistance. It seemed impossible for me to accept. He was a man by himself, another of your countrymen. He came from Dordrecht. He had a plantation. I could not go to his house alone...."

"But in the end you did," said I, with a sudden insight into the nature of this story.

Amelia looked down at the floor and her voice dropped so that I had to lean toward her to hear it.

"I had spent all the money I had. I ate almost nothing and lived in a foul room. I sold the few things I had to sell and then when I was in despair, he came and offered me the post of housekeeper. I thought it must be better than dying on the dockside."

"Was it?"

"No, it was not."

"Tell me the end of the story then, if the middle is too hard."

"The end? After nearly one long year, he died."

"And how was that year?"

She looked at me in a way I had never been looked at before. It was as much as I could do not to try to capture it. It had sex and steel in it, fire and deep weariness.

"We came to a way of being in which the price he demanded was one that I was just prepared to pay."

"How did he die?"

"He died of Batavia. Something bit him. Not me, though I had often considered it. The bite worsened, then he suffered an apoplexy and lay in his bed without the power to speak. I consigned his body to the garden boy for burial, took my clothes and all the money I could find in the house—which I considered was at least what he owed me for the yearlong insult—and I went again to the docks. There I found, perhaps by Providence, Dahl and his ship, newly come to Batavia for the first time, loaded with cargo and now preparing to sail. I asked him for help, showed him the shine of my money, and bought a passage back. He told me that Hull in England was his home port and it seemed infinitely close to home when compared to where I had been."

"And on the journey you turned from passenger to wife?"

"We took the first step in that direction. I was wounded and scared and he was calm and kind. I told him an untruth because I had to, saying I had been very ill in Batavia, prostrated by a fever for weeks almost from the day of my arrival, and therefore had no knowledge of the country worth speaking of. I had met no one and seen nothing, I said, save my room and its walls. There was another passenger on board and of course, he told the story at second hand, exaggerated out of recognition, of the strange foreign woman who had so scandalized all right-thinking society by her loose behavior. Dahl asked me if I knew this woman and I repeated that I knew nothing of the country. By good fortune, the passenger did not know the name of this person whose story he magnified with such relish. Yet I have to say that I still live in some anxiety that one day someone may come here who knew of me then."

I regarded her in an entirely new light. She was not the innocent I had thought, not the ripe plum, heavy with inexperience, ready to fall into my hands.

"You understand now why I cannot be heard to speak your language. The matter of how I came to learn it would be quite impossible to explain."

"Well, yes, I understand." There was a lot I did not understand still.

I no longer understood anything about the potential of the situation between us, of why she was in this room with me at all. I had thought it was I who was making up the rules of this game. I now had an unnerving feeling it might have been her all the time.

"I have to ask you," I said. "All these words I have spoken, these dangerous and foolish words which I believed were for myself alone, intended to fill the silence of the room. Will you tell me whether these words were unwelcome to you?"

She looked straight at me again and I saw, to my enormous surprise, a look of suppressed excitement on her face.

"There is not a woman born," she said, "who does not wish to know how men see her, and the truth is very hard to discover by enquiry, when mere gallantry may explain everything. You have given me the rare chance to hear thoughts you would never have spoken otherwise. Here in Paull Holme, I am what I have to be, a demure and dutiful wife. Do not mistake me. Underneath that appearance, I am of Viking stock. Do you know what that means?"

"That you'll hit me with an ax if I annoy you?"

"Possibly. I recommend you don't take the risk. It was Viking blood that took me half across the world after the man I loved. It was Viking blood that allowed me to survive all that followed. In a private world," here she glanced around the old tower room, "in this *private* world, which has no connection to what life may be in the rest of the house, I can speak and be as I truly am. I am an artist, too, in my heart. Does that surprise you?"

"No. I can see it in this house. You have a painter's eye for color and detail."

"Oh, indeed," she said sharply. "If I start on *that* one, you may be dead of old age before I stop." She frowned. "I am a woman, and women's art is not to be taken seriously, it seems. I would paint if I were *allowed*. I would write if that were thought a suitable activity. I would certainly write better than our friend Marvell. I have channeled all my art into my house because my husband has strong ideas on what is and is not proper. That is to be my achievement, it seems. Indeed it may be my only achievement if there is to be no family." She seemed to remember herself then. "In short, the answer to your question is this: What woman would not thrill to be so looked upon, so described by a man who, as he has told me, has made the most careful inspection of so many, many women?"

"Outside this room, there is your husband and he is a fellow to be reckoned with."

"My husband is a sailor, with all that entails," she said dryly. "There is an English expression," she said the word for me, "a fumbler? You have no word quite like it that I know."

"And it means?"

"It means the sort of man who has no children even though he is married."

"We have a wide range of words for that," I said, "but it depends what it is that afflicts him. To choose the right word, I would have to know more. Like a play, it is a question of whether the performance is unable to reach its final scene, or whether it reaches that point but in so doing fails to inspire any reaction in its audience. Perhaps it may even be a question of whether the leading actor collapses before making his entrance."

"Whatever it is," she said, "it is not the fault of the audience."

"I was certain of that. No normal man could fail to be stirred. When you reminded me that your husband is a sailor, did you perhaps mean that he prefers a male audience?"

"Oh, no," she said, startled. Then she gave a little giggle, a delightful lapse into conspiracy. "I simply meant he is all bustle and orders. There is never more than that. Normal men are in short supply in these parts."

"Marvell is a normal man. I detect that he pants after you," I said, watching for her reaction.

"Marvell is not in any way normal," she said calmly. "Marvell seeks to disguise his intentions always, cloaking all his actions in layers of mystery. Marvell is political and diplomatic and he finds any excuse to be in this house. Sometimes it is his lighthouse plan, sometimes it is his intrigue against his fellow Parliamentarian. At the moment it is you. Mr. van Rijn," she said, looking at me as if she could hold sugar in her lips and never make it wet. "The real prize in this contest of yours is not the fee for the painting."

"What is it, then?"

"It is here before your eyes. It is me."

"He hasn't told *me* that."

"No, of course not. He would certainly hope you might not realize the precise prize you could claim."

God's teeth. She looked at me while she was saying that as if she were discussing a flower show. "The contest gives him an excuse to do something he could not otherwise do," she continued. "It gives him an excuse to write a love poem for me, about me, directed at me, without seeming improper. Do you understand?"

"I'm starting to. He wants to woo you with a poem under cover of our wager. From what I've heard of his poetry so far, you're not in much danger."

"Danger?" she said mockingly. "And am I in danger from you?"

I had now entirely lost the day's initiative. The blind innocence that I had relied upon had dissipated, or rather it had never been there, which I had finally come to realize. A new sense of excitement now washed over me. This was to be a contest under new and wild rules.

"That depends on whether you accept that you are the prize. Perhaps I will let my painting decide that issue," I said. "After all, I believe that, if it is possible to compare these things, I am a far greater painter than he will ever be a poet."

"I shall be what I please, prize or not. Don't underestimate the power of his pen. From time to time he shows true talent. His pen against your brush, a duel of artists."

"A duel in which the winner takes you?"

She smiled, a smile that was for herself, not for me. "There is my own artistry to consider, too. The winner must also rival my own skills to be considered a worthy victor."

"But the prize . . ."

"No picture or poem shall blow me off the course I shall choose. That course, for the moment, is my business."

"The future is uncertain," I said.

"Yes," she said, "that is usually the best thing about it. Now, have you drawn enough?"

"No," I said. "One favor, and then we are done for the day and you can go back to being the demure mistress of Paull Holme. I want you to think about a proposition, to think hard and let me know your answer tomorrow. I think you are a woman who sees beyond all pretense and who understands the value of the pure portrait, the portrait that goes to the heart of everything. The pure portrait is bound to contain the truth of the painter and the painted. It cannot lie."

"So what do you want?"

"I want you to let me paint you as you really are."

TWENTY-THREE

Friday, April 13, 2001

DON CAME TO HIS DOOR WHEN AMY KNOCKED. PARRISH WAS RIGHT. He took her in his arms and held her without a word being spoken between them.

"How's it been?" she said. The house was hushed and heavy in the aftermath of all that had happened.

"We've had them all through here today—police, health and safety, council, insurance, everybody. They've got the Hawk downtown answering questions. They asked me a few more questions, that's all."

"The police?"

"Yeah. Jo-Jo's been leading them astray. I've sorted him out." He was clenching and opening his good hand, as if trying to get rid of an ache. "I don't want to keep going over it."

"You didn't fight, did you?"

"We had a difference of opinion," he said grimly. "My opinion proved persuasive." He moved aside to let her into the room.

She shook her head, knowing this was not the time for what would follow. There were other ways they could be close. "Peter Parrish requests the pleasure of your company downstairs. We're going hunting in room one eight."

"For?"

"Rembrandt's portrait of Captain Dahl, as listed in the Vertue diaries."

She told him all she had found out on the way down and he was as excited as she was, sharing it as she had hoped. At the far end of the corridor, Parrish had unlocked the door to his storeroom. There were two large windows, but evening was drawing on outside and it was lit only by the high, harsh light of a single bare bulb. The room was stacked three-quarters full with the detritus of an old house: chairs; curtain rods; boxes of decaying books; rolled-up, dust-laden, insect-infested carpets; broken candlesticks; bundles of ancient magazines, held by string; and a large brass telescope, badly dented, on a mahogany tripod. To Amy at that moment, thinking how much Dennis would have liked to have been let loose in here, it seemed only a small respite from the horrors of the previous day.

"The pictures are mostly at the back," said Parrish, "but I've got something I'd like to read to you first. I think it sets the scene. Why don't you take a pew." He looked around. "Not that there's a chair in here that one would entrust one's bottom to. How about the window seat?"

Amy sat in the window. Don pulled out a wooden box and sat on that in a dark corner while Parrish opened a folder.

"I had a quick look at the rest of your mother's transcripts," Parrish said to Don. "This is the material that wasn't quite so relevant to the structure of the house as such, but I found this." He looked down. "It's dated the twenty-fourth of January, 1662."

He was intent on taking them into another world, which was precisely where Amy wanted to be. Don sat impassively in his corner.

"You've got more of Amelia's journal?" asked Amy. "Not just the bits about the building?"

"Oh, yes, Ellen typed out the whole thing for me. Didn't I say?"

"No, you didn't. Can I borrow it?"

She could hardly believe it had been sitting there all the time without her knowing. No more stolen moments in the Hull archives, queuing for a machine, struggling with the script to glimpse a day at a time.

"Of course you can. I'll bring it in for you. There's a whole lot more." He was holding a single sheet in his hand. "Are you ready?"

They both nodded.

"Here it goes. *'I confess I am more and more vexed with the limner who does go out of his way each day to distemper me. I will sit for the picture because it will please my dear husband but for no other reason, and I shall not tell my husband on his return what lengths this does put me to, lest he break in pieces with the limner who will be soon gone when the picture is made. He is a corpulent and ill-favoured man, of gouty visage, who prates incessantly in his ugly and incomprehensible tongue. I fear he is an incontinent rogue.'* " Parrish looked up. "That doesn't mean what you might think, by the way. *'Incontinent'* meant someone who wasn't exactly a saint, sexually speaking."

"What does 'gouty' mean?" asked Amy.

"Sort of swollen, puffy."

"She doesn't exactly like our painter, does she?" Don said.

"It fits your man, though," answered Parrish. "Think of those later self-portraits. Corpulent and gouty sounds about right."

"Does incontinent sound right, too?" Amy asked.

Parrish raised an eyebrow. "Rembrandt? I rather think so. He was a lusty man. After Saskia died he couldn't keep his hands off the housekeepers. It got him into no small amount of trouble. Do you know about Geertge?"

"No."

"Geertge Dircx, the trumpeter's widow. She was quite attractive in her chubby little way, judging from his pictures. When Saskia died, little Titus was only a year old and she was his nurse. Pretty soon she was sharing her bed with Rembrandt. He got a bit carried away and gave her some of Saskia's jewelry." He stopped. "Am I just droning on or do you want to hear all this?"

"We want to hear," said Don from his corner. Amy suddenly found tears in her eyes and hoped they couldn't see.

"Anyway, with Geertge promoted to bedmate, he hired another woman to do the household stuff, and that was Hendrickje Stoffels. Have you heard of her?"

"I've seen the portraits," said Amy. "The one with the woman holding her skirts up in the river, that's meant to be her, isn't it?"

" 'A woman bathing,' yes, supposedly. He went out of his way to make her beautiful in that bulky way of his, didn't he? You can tell he liked her a lot. Hendrickje was a good egg, much better than Geertge. Anyway, all three of them were living together under the same roof, and when Geertge saw his attentions were waning, she took him to court. He'd given her Saskia's ring and she said that proved he'd agreed to marry her."

"Did she win?" Amy asked.

"To start with, yes. The court awarded her lifelong support. Then, I'm afraid, we have to see old Remmy in a rather poor light for what happened next. He didn't want to shell out cash for years to come, so he got her sent to prison on some trumped-up charge—in fact, not just a prison, but a terrible place, a madhouse more or less. She spent five years in there before her friends got her out. He still owed her money when he died."

"He wasn't a nice man, then," Don said.

"Who knows," said Parrish. "Perhaps she had it coming. She sounds pretty terrible. Not at all like Hendrickje. Now *there* was a woman who stood by her man. When Rembrandt went bust, she stuck it out. She and Titus even went into business to sell his paintings when he was banned from doing it himself."

"Why did he go bust?" Don asked.

"He stopped being fashionable. People didn't like the way he painted anymore. Can you imagine it? Long, long sittings, immensely thick paint, unfashionably thick, built up in layers so that it stuck out like a sculpture. The paint that runs down like dung, that's what they called it. Ironic, isn't it? All the things that killed off his trade were the very same things that eventually got him recognized as one of the best there's ever been. Of course it was too late to give him any pleasure, poor old boy. But I think there was more to it than that," said Parrish. "There was his grandiosity. He thought great paintings should be worth a great price so he'd go to auctions and pay insane prices for Old Masters just to show how much they *should* be worth. Then again, he was also an inveterate collector of absolutely anything old and interesting—he was buying stuff left, right, and center. Most of all though, he bought a very pricey house on Breestraat that he couldn't really afford, using borrowed money. Of course, when his reputation started going down-hill, his creditors wanted their money back."

Don frowned. "Couldn't he have sold some of those Old Masters?"

Parrish snapped his fingers. "Now! This is where it gets interesting. Have you read that thing I gave you, the transcript of the talk at the Ferens? You know, the Brigham lecture?"

"Bits of it," said Amy, who had forgotten all about it.

"He says all of this has a simple explanation. Yes, of course Rembrandt could have sold those pictures, *normally*. He might not have got the inflated prices he paid for them but he'd have done all right. No, he was as unlucky as it gets because if you look at the dates, which very few art historians seem to have bothered to do, all this comes in the wake of the collapse of the Dutch tulip boom. You know about the tulip boom?"

"Yes," said Amy.

"Not really," said Don.

"Do you want the one-minute version? Tulips were brought back from far-off lands. They had that odd quality that makes people behave in a daft way when they see something new. You could breed them to make fantastic multicolored offspring and, of course, you could then divide their bulbs and make your fortune the following year when those grew. Supposedly. All those silly speculators bet their shirts on a few bulbs and when the bubble burst they were ruined overnight. So what happened? They couldn't afford to have their portraits painted anymore and they started unloading everything they had for sale— houses, pictures, the whole lot. Prices plummeted. Poor old Rembrandt was doing his best to sell his possessions but there weren't any buyers. That part's all documented. He got back a tenth of what he paid for some of those pictures, and of course the house itself wasn't worth a fraction of what he'd bought it for. So, bankruptcy came along and cut him to the bone."

He fell silent. The turn of phrase brought Dennis abruptly back into Amy's mind. Perhaps the same thing happened to Parrish because he frowned and carried on.

"I was just thinking how it must have been, moving from glamorous Breestraat into the Jordaan. Twenty years earlier, the Jordaan was just a boggy mess of dykes and ditches on the edge of one of the big canals. They built the streets on the dykes. Nothing fancy. Then they moved all the unwanted industries out there, the smelly ones like tanneries and sugar factories. After that they moved in the immigrants— the Sephardic Jews from Spain, craftsmen from Belgium and France, then the Ashkenazi Jews from Eastern Europe. I can't help thinking he probably liked it there. The houses were little, jerry-built rabbit warrens but the people were much more his sort, you know, artistic renegades."

"So his life changed, did it?" Don asked.

"Oh, yes. So did his painting. Something happened to him around about then, from the early 1660's. He became less pompous, more honest—in his pictures at least."

"What do you mean?"

"Those later ones are his greatest self-portraits by far. After 1662, that's when you get the real honesty, the unvarnished truth, age and self-knowledge staring you in the eyes."

"Because he went bankrupt?"

"What else do we know that could possibly explain it?"

A contest, thought Amy, but she could not say the words out loud. A contest that took place right here under this roof. A contest between a great painter and a great poet for the approval of a beautiful woman, in which her beauty was the raw material. With a thrilling surge of certainty she knew what the prize must have been.

Parrish looked at them. "That's about it. That's our man. Are you ready to go looking for him?"

"Where do we start?" asked Don while Amy rolled this new idea around her mind.

"There are some pictures stacked up against the wall behind the commode. I think there are more in the middle of this lot. There was a big tea chest, I remember. It's full of them." He glanced at each of them in turn. "Be careful. If there *is* something here, remember this might represent the art find of the millennium."

"Which has, after all, only just started," said Don, getting up.

"Of *any* millennium, then," said Parrish. "I'm serious."

"So you believe in all this now, do you?" asked Don.

"I'll suspend disbelief," said Parrish, "for as long as there's a chance of finding something in here."

The pictures by the wall were a disappointment: a misty Scottish mountain scene with a stag proudly waiting to be shot, an appallingly sentimental Victorian scene of a mother comforting a sick child, and an amateur view of the Humber. After that, they started moving furniture. The tea chest proved to be right in the middle of the stack and very hard indeed to get at. It took all three of them tugging to move the chest out of the awkward position it was in, jammed between a pine cupboard and a splintered bookcase. There were several pictures in it, wrapped in old curtains. Peter Parrish lifted out the first one and unwrapped it carefully. It was not at all what they wanted to see—some sort of framed proclamation of good service to one Richard Bolitho, dated 1955. The second was just a frame and a backing board, with nothing else to it at all. The rest were all Victorian.

"Are you *sure* there aren't any others?" Amy asked.

"Pretty sure, I'm afraid," said Parrish.

"Nothing in the attic?"

"Definitely not," said Parrish. "That was emptied completely because they had to strip the roof. Most of this came from up there."

"Perhaps they sold it," said Don, disappointed.

"Oh, yes, that's possible. I did pull out those sale catalogues I mentioned, and the bill of sale for the house. There *are* a couple of suspects. Let's see now." He ruffled through his folder. "Here's the auction catalogue. 'J.J. Metcalfe and Sons, August eleventh, 1933. The major part of the contents of Paull Holme Manor, late the property of Major Reginald Dale MC.' Stacks of furniture, various outside effects, and the pictures. There's a few Dutch items, a van Goyen. Gosh, someone's penciled in the price it sold for: seven hundred and forty guineas. That's a serious picture for the time. Then there's what it calls a small landscape by Jacob van Ruisdael, who was pretty much a direct contemporary of our man. Nine hundred and twenty guineas, that one. I wonder if it could be the same one that's in the Ferens now? Beautiful picture of a wood and a cornfield. There's even a Constable sketch, 'Somerset Cottage with Figures.' Nothing else that sounds remotely like Rembrandt."

"There would be two portraits, wouldn't there?" Amy said. "The one Vertue saw of Dahl himself and the one we know he was painting of Amelia."

"If he ever finished it," said Parrish. "From the sound of the journal, she might not have let him. Let's look at the other one, the bill of sale for the house. This is it." He held up a thin gray booklet, opened it, and leafed through.

"It's a funny old mixture of stuff. Carpets and curtains, fair enough. A string of horses and a Chevrolet horse trailer. All sorts of outside equipment. Now, here are the pictures. 'Lady sitting on chair. Signed P. Cullingford. Eight feet by four feet.' That's not it. 'Head of old man with red cap. Two feet by two feet.' How about that?"

"Dahl wasn't that old, was he?" said Amy.

"We don't know."

"Yes, we do," said Amy and, getting a sudden nudge from Don, realized it was only because of the daybook that they knew it. "No, we don't," she added.

"Actually, come to think of it, we do know about *that* picture because it *was* here and it's gone off for conservation. Late eighteenth century, I believe," said Parrish. "Ah, wait a moment. What about this? 'Pair of companion portraits. Gentleman and lady. On oak boards. Eighteen inches by twenty-two. Poor condition.' "

"No artist's name?" asked Amy.

"Nothing else. That's all it says." Parrish was clearly excited. "Think about it a moment. It's a pair, and they're the same size so the chances are they really were a pair, painted together. Not only that but they're on oak panels, not canvas."

"Did Rembrandt paint on wood panels?" Don was on his feet and looking over Parrish's shoulder at the catalogue.

"He certainly did early on, but I think he always used canvas in his later years."

"Perhaps he had no choice," suggested Amy. "Perhaps oak was all there was here. I mean if he *did* come to Hull, would he have brought all his tools with him?"

"Oh, I should think so," said Parrish. "Aren't artists rather pernickety about that sort of thing? He would have come prepared, surely? He wouldn't have arrived empty-handed."

"Yes, but it could be him, couldn't it? Two portraits, a gentleman and a lady. Where are they?"

Parrish put the piece of paper down and stared around him. The pictures they had unwrapped were propped against the remains of a wooden rocking horse.

"I haven't a clue," he said, then he stiffened and snapped his fingers. "Yes, I have. Good God, how stupid."

"What?" asked Amy and Don together.

"Use your eyes," said Parrish. "One of them's right in front of us."

Amy looked around. She could see nothing.

"Where?" she demanded.

"Eighteen inches by twenty-two," said Parrish. "I'll get a tape measure, but that looks pretty close. Oak panels, and we didn't give it a second look."

He was pointing at the picture they had already discarded, the one that consisted only of a frame and a backing board.

"It didn't occur to me," he said, picking it up and turning it to the light. "It's not just a backing board. Look at it closely. Do you see? The wood's been really carefully jointed together."

Amy was on her feet, too, now.

"Better than that," she said. "It's been prepared. Look at the little hollows, where the grain's uneven. There's traces of something in there."

"You're right," said Parrish. "What is it? Gesso? Some sort of smoothing layer. They used size, didn't they? Boiled-up rabbit glue. That's what it is."

"For Christ's sake. That's it? I can't bear it," said Don. "Are you telling me that *thing* is a Rembrandt, and all we've got left are a few specks of bloody undercoat?"

"Maybe," said Parrish. "I'm no expert, but it could easily be seventeenth century. That frame is carved wood. Look at the curve on it; it's beautiful. Oh, and look at this."

There were two tiny holes in the bottom of the frame.

"There's been a nameplate on this at some point. Do you know, that could be the plate that old Vertue saw, couldn't it? The one that said all those things about the date and the place and Dahl's name." Parrish now sounded very like a convert.

"The nameplate might have dropped off," suggested Amy. "Look in the tea chest."

There was nothing to be found there, and they searched as much of the room as they could get at between the array of objects filling it.

"I think that plate's been missing for a long time," said Don, peering at the holes. "They're full of old dirt. If the screws had come out recently, they'd be cleaner."

"Can I hold it?" asked Amy.

"Of course," said Parrish. "It can't really come to any more harm than it already has."

Amy held it out at arm's length, willing it to tell her something, trying hard to see the ghost of a face in its dark surface. For a moment she felt it was trying to communicate. A half-formed idea came into her mind and then fled again before she could seize it. She felt as if she had held this picture in her hands before.

"You know, one thing I do remember from art history," she said, "is that lots of pictures have needed serious restoration because they were painted with bad quality oil and pigment. Supposing this is the earthly remains of Dahl's picture and supposing Rembrandt did paint it, he might have been improvising, mightn't he? If he didn't have any canvas and he had to use wood, maybe he didn't have his paints with him, either. Maybe he had to use second-rate supplies and it has literally all dropped off."

"Very ingenious," said Parrish, "but you make it sound like he was on the run."

"Perhaps he was. You said yourself that he hadn't been having an easy time of it."

"Stop taking it so bloody calmly, you two," said Don. "Look at that. Just boards. All the rest of it, all the beauty, all the skill completely gone. Dust. Rembrandt dust on the floor. Swept up and thrown out. I can't bear it. Isn't there anything you can do? They x-ray old pictures, don't they? Then you can see what's underneath."

"Don, this one doesn't need an X ray," said Parrish gently. "That *is* the underneath. I will do something, though. There's somebody at the Ferens who knows a thing or two about old frames and wooden panels. I'll ask them to have a look at it. Then at least we might know whether it's the right age."

"Will you tell them anything about it?"

"Perish the thought. I don't want to be laughed at any more than I can help. I'll just say we found it here and wondered how old it was."

"If it *is* Dahl," said Amy, looking at the picture, again with that feeling that she was missing something, "that still leaves Amelia." She looked round the room. "It's only seventy years ago, isn't it? The catalogue, I mean. They wouldn't have kept one picture and not the other, would they? I'm sure she's here somewhere."

They had another look to be quite sure. Amy realized she had passed the last five minutes without thinking of Dennis at all. Then there was no good reason to go on searching, no reason not to go back out into the house and confront the grief that had crept into the corridors to fill their throats.

TWENTY-FOUR

THERE HAD BEEN A MOMENT ON THE TOWER'S DARK LANDING WHEN they might have gone in through the same bedroom door, but it was past before either of them could overcome their uncertainty, and they went their separate ways to their separate beds. In the night, it was Dennis who came to Amy, walking into her dreams with a tray of tea in his hands and a rictus grin on his face, then falling apart in two halves as he laid it down. She reared up out of sleep in her cold bed in her cold room, sobbing, then lay back on the pillow and let quiet tears flow, crying silently as she had not cried since childhood. Afterward, when the exhaustion of her tears dumped her back into sleep, kinder variations of Dennis continued to keep her company, and when she woke up in the early morning, she was fooled for a moment into believing that his death had also been part of the dream.

She left her bed as if the dreams and the sorrow were a snake coiled on her mattress. Convinced that the world should look significantly different after all that had happened, she went to the window and looked out into the faint dawn light. Below and left, amongst the huts, bright tape around the saw bench caught her eye. There was a man standing by it, staring at it.

Don.

He stood still, looking hard at the place of Dennis's death, mercifully indistinct in the dawn distance. Watching him, she felt a longing, a need to go straight down there with open arms and lead him away from the savage place where he had cradled his accuser. Then she remembered once again that she had promised Dennis she would read Vin's account, Vin's missing account. Betraying thoughts slipped into her mind despite herself, each one pulling another after it. Don and Dennis. Don and Vin. Vin, who insisted it was Don who had the saw. Parrish and Ellen had been upstairs together. Don had been jealous of Parrish. Don had been jealous of Dennis. Jealousy and saws.

"Oh, come on," she said to herself out loud. "Forget it. That's not what happened," but the thought wouldn't go away completely however hard she wished it.

She stared at Don then, looking for an omen. If he turned away before she could count to ten, all would be well. At seven she slowed down her count. She reached twelve before he turned but another sign came, so unexpected that she chose to regard it as a superior omen to her count. He dropped his head as if in prayer, crossed himself, and turned to walk back to the house. Astonished by the gesture, she took it as proof that he was grieving for Dennis.

There was no work that day. "Don't think it's a bloody holiday," the Hawk said as he paced from room to room, face dark with fury. "I'm not bloody paying you. Ask the tossers out there if you want your money." The tossers out there were two tough women from Health and Safety who had shut down the site until some breaches of the regulations were set right.

Amy sat in her room, trying to work on her portrait of Don. She was sketching the outline of his face onto the canvas before she began to paint but it was proving hard. Somewhere behind the image, she kept discovering an unsettling ambiguity. Full-face, he always looked like a "wanted" poster. She tried the half-profile favoring his undamaged cheek but it reeked of compromise. The scar would have to be within the focus of the picture but, oppressed by the problems that raised, she left it to last and worked on his forehead, eyes, and nose instead. In outline, without color and highlights, she found she was still only able to draw eyes that frightened her, blank eyes, eyes that fueled her doubts.

Early in the afternoon, WPC Percival knocked at her door again.

"Miss Dale?"

"Hello."

"I see you're drawing Mr. Gilby again." She was looking at the easel.

"Oh, yes, I am. He's not an easy subject."

"A bit of a hero, I understand."

"That's right."

"You asked me a question last time we met," said the policewoman. Amy noticed how tired she looked.

"Did I?" She couldn't remember asking any questions.

"It was one I couldn't answer, and I shouldn't be answering now."

Belatedly, Amy understood what she meant. Dennis's criminal record. "Don't," she said. "I've changed my mind. I think I'd rather not know." Whatever Dennis might have done, she knew she would rather be able to dismiss it as youthful error, paid for in full. It would be harder to know the facts.

The other woman raised her eyebrows. "Really? I only wanted to say you didn't need to worry. He had a drunk-and-disorderly when he was nineteen, and that was it."

Around teatime, Don knocked on the door and brought in a tray of sandwiches and beer.

"I thought you might be hungry," he said.

Amy shrugged, staring at him.

"Why did you tell me Dennis had a record?" she demanded.

"That's what I heard."

"Who from?"

"I don't know. One of the lads."

"Well, just for the record, he didn't. Come to that, why did you tell the police Dennis was showing off to me?"

He didn't try to deny it. "Because I think he was," he said.

"Because he fancied me?"

"Yeah, maybe. Whatever."

"Don't be so casual, Don. It's crap. Dennis was just a nice old man and we had some good laughs together, that's all."

"If you say so."

"I do say so."

"All right," he said. "I'm sorry. I suppose I got it all a bit out of proportion. Let's not argue over the poor old sod." He smiled at her. For a moment the reflex turned the scar into something nearer a laughter line. His smile exorcised all the ghosts of doubt and fear inside her and melted her.

"I'm sorry, too," she said. "I had a horrible night."

"I know. So did I." He came to her and kissed her gently on the forehead. "Have a sandwich."

"Thanks," she said and reached out to take one. Her hand stopped in midair. "The tray," she said.

"Yeah?"

"That's Dennis's."

Don shrugged. "It's a tray, that's all."

"You took it. You went to Dennis's room?"

"It was lying around. I think it was in the kitchen. He must have left it there. I didn't know it was his."

Amy looked at the tray, wanting to believe him, noting its age, and remembering that Dennis had been pleased with his purloined antique. She was unable to bear the thought that Don might have raided a dead man's room.

"Do you want some escapism?" he asked. "We could read some more of the daybook."

Escapism was exactly what she wanted. "Yes," she said, "why not? But you have to read it to me for a change."

"Why's that?"

"Because we're going to do it in your room and I'm going to be painting you while you do it."

"I can't read her writing, you know that."

"But you can read the journal, can't you? The one Ellen typed out?"

"All right. Where is it?"

"I've got it in my bag."

Parrish had lent it to them as he had promised. It was another exercise book, matching the one he had first loaned to Amy. The same typed pages were stuck into it, but there were many more of them so that the whole book bulged with the extra load it contained.

Another sea fog had rolled in up the Humber on a wisp of east wind. Somewhere out on the water a steel cow was bellowing for its lost calf. The fog drifted in through gaps in the tower windows, causing Amy to shiver. It coalesced into a misty rain that might have been sent to wash away the residue of Dennis's death.

In Don's room, she set the table light to make useful shadows and, by its light, he read slowly and carefully.

"All right. She says, *'I will confide in this my most private Journal which is not to be read by any other but me, that it is only in the cause of obeying the express directions of my husband that I continue to endure the indignities forced upon me by this Dutch ape. He has once again insisted that the sketches for this day's painting must be made in his midden of a chamber where the stench of him lies thick in the air.'* What's a midden?"

"It's a farmer's dunghill, isn't it?"

"She really doesn't like him, does she?"

"That's what she *says*. Go on. Don't stop there." Amy couldn't get it, couldn't find the balance of color, light, and shadow to make the scar work as she wanted.

"OK. '*. . . the stench of him lies thick in the air. The reading room wherein I have sat for the painting thus far is a fair room where the servants may pass to and fro and have some knowledge of what may come about within. This vile room is far from aid were aid to be required. The limner insists that the men who fix the paneling in the reading room do prevent and interfere with our business there and for the matter of the sketching, this room wherein he resides has a quality which suits his task best but I am not fond of this tower which is not a gracious place for people to inhabit and—'* "

Amy stopped drawing. "The tower? This is all happening in the tower, for God's sake. He's got her up in his room and it's in the tower. It's this room, Don. She's talking about *this room*." She felt the roots of her hair prickling. There was a foghorn moan from the river.

"Not necessarily. There are three floors and there's two rooms on this floor, for a start."

"No. Listen, that's not right. There are no windows lower down, just slits. This is the only floor with light coming in."

"It is now. Remember, there were two old towers then, weren't there? Not just this one. Parrish says they built the new part of the house between the towers. All right, the other one fell down, but when this was written they were both standing. How do you know it wasn't that one?"

"It just wasn't, Don, believe me." She had never been so certain of anything. "I'm a painter, too. I know. The other tower would have got the wrong light. This is the one. This one gets the light you want."

"The windows could have been north, south, or east in that tower; you don't know."

"He was drawing her in this room, right here, where I'm painting you. It had to be here because he wanted the light."

"Amy, come on. The light's got nothing to do with it. It wasn't because of the light that he had her up in his room. He was after her, wasn't he? That's why he wanted her out of the way of the servants. He wanted to have his wicked way with her."

"All right, maybe that was what it was. It *was* here, though, I just know it." She knew it in the same way she knew the nature of the prize Amelia had offered her two rival suitors. "Either way, think about it, Don. Rembrandt was here, in this room, with Amelia, doing God knows what."

"You think."

"I know."

"What did *you* say to the police, Amy?"

She took advantage of the lift of his head to sketch rapidly, trying to capture the rare moment of his keen, direct look, before the meaning of his question hit her.

"Why do you ask?"

"Fair's fair. You've been giving *me* the third degree."

"Nothing. I told them he wasn't after me. I said he was showing off to everybody, not just me."

"Was that all?"

"Yes."

She could have challenged him, demanded to know what he meant, but she was trying to paint his eyes and, once again, what she saw in those eyes was not the Don she wanted to see.

Before either of them could say anything else, and to Amy's relief, someone shouted for them. She followed Don out of the room and found Sandy standing peering through the gap in the wall.

"We're having a bit of a drink," he said. "A wake, you might say. Down the pub. Leaving in ten minutes."

"I'll pass on that one," Don said.

"No, you won't, mate," said Sandy firmly. "Did I give the impression it was voluntary?"

It was a cheerless evening. Some of them did their best to tell Dennis's jokes, but nobody could do it the same way he could. Amy, stuck at the crowded pub table a long way from Don, watched him when she could, seeing him reply in monosyllables whenever someone tried to draw him into conversation. She did her best for a couple of hours as darkness settled around the pub and seeped in around the door. When she returned from a trip to the loo, she saw that Don had gone.

"Coming into town, love?" asked Tel. "We're taking Gengko for a tandoori."

"No, thanks," she said.

"Go on. Go and find him. Someone's got to get that guy straightened out," he said.

"That might be beyond me."

There had been a brief downpour while they were inside, turning the road into a black mirror of the pub lights. With a final flurry of drizzle, the rain blew away as she stepped outside, and she went to stand on the seawall. That first day she had seen this place, brought here by Dennis, seemed impossibly long ago. What had happened to her since then? Where had her independence gone, her control over her own life? Looking up at the sky without any intention for once of seeking an omen, one came despite that. Raising her head to look at the high moon, she saw in the direction of the river mouth that the rain and the bright moonlight had combined to make a great arch in the sky, glistening in graduated bands of silver-gray, a rainbow of the night sky with one end, she judged, meeting the earth on the rise that marked Paull Holme Manor. It shimmered there in the sky for a few more seconds, then faded like a beautiful dream as the rain-spray in the air drifted onward, out of the moonlight.

I'll never ask for another sign, she said to herself, *not if this one tells the truth.* What was that truth? If gold was buried at the foot of the daytime rainbow, then surely what lay at the end of this nighttime miracle must be even better. Wondering, she watched lights flashing on the Humber buoys and listened to the sounds of the ships out on the water, then she started up the road, eastward to the old house, going back to face some music to which she no longer knew the tune. Weary through and through, what she most wanted to do was to put it all out of her mind and curl up with Amelia's journal, to *be* Amelia for a little while and not herself. She wanted to find out what happened next in someone else's life, not her own. She wanted to prove to herself that Amelia had thought better of the painter than she dared say in words her husband might read.

What happened next in her own life was that, walking down that dark road, a greater darkness loomed up to her right, with moonlight catching pale stones in front of it. Amy was not frightened of very much, but she had forgotten Paull church and its graveyard. Her legs stopped walking of their own accord and she stood rooted to the road just short of the graveyard. Somewhere in the space between her imagination and the thick night, Dennis's shadow walked near her. The sense that he was in some way really there was so strong that, for a moment, she thought she could see his ghost moving among the gravestones, a light flickering in the deep blackness. *Those who die for the sake of a joke don't haunt us,* she thought, *only those who meet a darker end, so why would he be here?* She knew that if something was there, there was no joke on its lips. Her promise came knocking again, her promise to read Vin's missing account, missing from Dennis's room, where Dennis's tray had also gone missing. That was when all her suppressed doubts about Don came together in a chilling core of fear, as a figure coalesced out of that darkness, moving toward her from amongst the graves.

TWENTY-FIVE

Friday, January 24th, 1662

IN THE DARK, PAULL CHURCH SMELLED OF DEATH. WHEN A BUILD-
ing burns, the smell may remain for years, but there was something else
in the wind as well, as rank and rotten as the crawling contents of an
opened grave. It was to be a night of corpses.

I am approaching an age where the desires of the flesh will eventually stiffen the member a little less often, and I understand in myself the
urgent need to dance the double dance with a few more young partners
before that moment comes but, by Christ's death blood, this is different. This woman commands and compels me and could make me do
anything to have her. In my foolishness I thought I could lead her blind-
folded to that sweet, wet moment and now I find she has been leading
me by the nose the entire time. She is her own woman and I must play
her game by unfamiliar rules. To lose the opportunity of opening her is
unthinkable. To lose it by artistic failure to that prating Marvell would
be unbearable.

When I left the house, I was groaning with desire. To have her there
in my room, to talk to her as I had and discover she had understood

every naked word was not to be endured. Me, not in command, told I was a contestant in a covert duel, poem versus portrait, and for what prize? For her? Was that what she meant? Marvell meant it, but did she? I told her that I wished to paint her as she really was, and what did she do? She just gave me a melting, secret smile before she retreated down the stairs. All the rest of that day, I studied my sketches and drew her as Bathsheba, naked on the bed, the first thin Bathsheba I have ever drawn, but *I could not get it right,* could not get the feel for that flesh. Every inch of my body knows the curves of normal women, of Dutch women, of big women. To teach my brushes I needed to feel that narrow waist with my fingers, because those fingers would not believe what my brain was telling them about the shape of her. It was a half-Dutch, half-Amelia Bathsheba who emerged from that muddle, a Bathsheba whose husband would have survived because David would have walked straight past her without a second look. I gave up, and proceeded downstairs to see if there was any Genever to be found. There, I caught the briefest sight of someone leaving by the front door, just a glimpse of a figure disappearing. It was Amelia.

I followed her outside but she was gone like a wraith into the darkness. I went carefully along the track after her and the moon showed her to me by the white of her dress, moving through the saplings they have planted by the lane and then on down the lane. She was farther ahead of me now but I could see her clearly because the clouds had blown past the moon and she shone in its light.

Some pale bird, which might have been an owl, glided over me and shrieked once. On the river to my left there was a dim lantern, moving along high up off the water and a cast of the moon, showing silver sails, painted a ship for me. The creak of its rigging and the rattle of ropes in its blocks carried across the water. I could hear Amelia's footsteps, so I walked with care lest she should also hear mine. I could think of nowhere she might be going so recklessly into the night, alone. The village? Why? Then I considered that perhaps she had word her husband was returning from the city and she was on the road to meet him. I dismissed that as absurd immediately. Knowing something of Dahl, I could be quite sure he would take it very amiss to find his wife trudging in dangerous darkness.

Some way down that hard, cratered road, I tripped and lay winded.

When I got to my feet again, I could no longer see her moon-white shape ahead. The lane was in plain view all the way to the village and so should she have been, but she was not. That was when the church showed itself against the silver river, and I knew that she could only have turned into the churchyard. In another minute, I was at the gate myself and almost called her to avoid alarm, but I was too uncertain of her purposes to take that risk, so I crept in at the gate, not without a small feeling of fear.

The church was a ruin, its walls alone standing, and it was not a comforting place to be. Against the sky I could see some of the burnt rafters were still in place, but moonlight showed me the pile of rubble and wrecked woodwork that filled the nave. And that smell assailed me, charred wood and something horrid, long dead.

I stood undecided, ready to flee, when I heard quiet voices beyond the building; two, a man and a woman. There were bushes concealing the corner of the church toward my right, but it was cast in moon shadow, so I crept round the corner between the bushes, making no more noise than a field mouse. Ahead, by the boundary of the church-yard, in amongst the farthest gravestones, I saw a bench with two figures sitting upon it, close but not touching. The nearer was undoubtedly Amelia and in another breath, when I heard his voice, I knew that the farther was Marvell, and I wished him dead. The smell was stronger here than ever. Something dead was very close, immediately upwind of me.

In the clean air beyond, Marvell was arguing, urging something. Amelia was amused but confidently assertive of a counterview. This exchange lasted some time and seemed to end in compromise. An agreement of some sort was reached, and when Marvell appeared to continue to press a further point, Amelia, one hand raised, subdued him with peremptory ease. Then Amelia withdrew a little and half turned toward him. Marvell sat more upright and cleared his throat.

Oh, poxes, I thought, *he's going to bloody read her his bloody poem. He's finished it, or at least he has a draft to try out on her. He's trying to win the competition in advance.*

A silence fell and he began. I strained my ears to make sense of it to absolutely no avail. All I can say for sure is that it started with a singu-larly ugly word, "Hadwyburt." I said that to myself a few times as he banged on, so that I could attempt to find its meaning later, though whom could I ask? Neither Amelia nor Marvell, for sure. By the holes in Christ's side, that man couldn't deliver a poem calmly; he had to wave his hands about and let his voice wander up and down all the registers known to man. It was a profoundly horrible experience, but I realized to my alarm that Amelia did not seem to share that view. The moon showed me her profile, and she seemed fascinated by what he had to say.

When their silhouettes closed to only a hand-span apart, I thought it time to intervene. Groping around me, I found a lump of masonry within my reach fallen from the church wall, which I seized and chucked off to one side. It bounced off a gravestone with a satisfying crash, and brought Marvell to an abrupt halt.

They both said something at once, questioning, equally alarmed. Marvell got to his feet, then sat down again. Pleased with my success, I chucked another lump into the bushes beyond. They were both on their feet now. I didn't know whether they feared it was Dahl or a corpse crawling from an open grave. I didn't have to do anything else, because the owl did it for me. From somewhere up in the remains of the tower came a wailing scream of perfectly human misery. Marvell called out a challenge. The owl chose not to answer. Amelia now seemed to be giggling. Marvell made some sharp rebuke, which she did not like at all. She said something dismissive on a very final falling cadence and then got up, walked to the other end of the church, and vanished around it. In a few more seconds, I heard her at the gate and then her footsteps faded up the road toward the house.

Marvell called after her, "Amelia, Amelia." He crumpled his poem in sudden fury and hurled it away. Then he turned and came straight toward me. I shrank down into my bush. He took the road to the village, where I thought perhaps he had left his horse, and I waited a long time in my bush to make quite sure that he had gone. When I was certain that I was finally alone, I emerged and stepped straight into the source of the smell, which rose, appallingly redoubled, as my foot burst through the swollen, slimy, crunching thing. It had probably been a dog. It was now all over my foot. I found clean grass, as far away from the foul thing as possible, and wiped my shoe again and again. This had the effect of making the grass stink as badly as my shoe, without any apparent countereffect on the shoe.

Casting around for anything that might help, I found the crumpled paper Marvell had thrown away and considered using that to rub my shoe before deciding it might have some other more important purpose. Smoothing it out, I folded it and put it in my pocket.

I tried everything that graveyard had to offer, until it gradually dawned on me that only a prolonged soaking stood any chance of getting rid of the smell, and with the umber Humber not much more than a field's width away, there was no shortage of water in the vicinity. I put the stinking shoe back on my foot and headed across the fields for the river. The tide was in, and there was a stony spit jutting into the water, with tiny waves washing over it. Standing on the flattest stone I could find, I pulled off my shoe, narrowly avoiding tumbling into the water as I did so, bent down, and swished it in the ripples. The moon sailed out of the clouds and in its light I saw a bundle in the water, bobbing sluggishly in to the beach. Buoyed by the hope that it might be a parcel of scrubbing brushes and soap sent to me on the tide by a sympathetic creator, I set off toward it and realized on closer approach that it was something even better. A corpse. A corpse with shoes on. The creator has a sense of humor, it would seem.

You might think I was no better off, exchanging animal putrefaction for its human equivalent, but the corpse had no smell. I will not dwell on the state of the thing. Probably it had not been in the water more than two or three days, but that was enough. The shoes came off a bit too easily is all I will say. They were simple leather buckets, not at all unlike my own, and they pinched a bit but that was quite possibly only because they were wet. The fellow, because the gaping trousers showed despite the fishes' nibbling that a fellow it was, had a belt with a purse on it, for which he clearly had no more need. Having no money of my own, it seemed entirely reasonable to check it for any contents.

I was very careful indeed about twisting the catch to open his purse, and my care was rewarded: Inside, there were six gold coins and four rix-dollars besides. However he had happened to end up in the river, it was no footpad who tipped him in there, that was clear.

There was a large log higher up that beach and I sat on it, looking at the fellow bumping around there in the shallows, thinking how much I would like to draw him. I have painted dead bodies on several occasions. I still have a collection of pickled arms and legs, dissected and opened out by van Wesel, who knew all there is to know about what makes our limbs move. You might even say that I owe my early success in Amsterdam to a dead body. A man called Pieterszoon asked me to paint him when I was new there. When he was made Professor of Anatomy of the Amsterdam surgeons' guild, he thought the world would be grateful if he arranged to leave behind a portrait of himself as paragon. I don't think he knew half what van Wesel knew about what matters under the skin, but he wanted to show just how much he could lord it over his colleagues, so the portrait had to be of him instructing them—performing a dissection, no less. He even wanted me to paint it during the course of a genuine dissection. Those things were bear-garden events. They happened at rare intervals and the public flocked to them. Imagine it: The doctors would be down there on the stage, snipping and cutting, and the public would be drinking and eating and carousing high up on the banks of seats, with hardly a clue what was happening but cheering every time something got snipped off or a new organ was displayed.

When it went on display, the crowds flocked to it as if seeing a painting of a dead man's guts was nearly as good as seeing the real thing. After that the commissions poured in. I suppose that was why I decided to stay in Amsterdam, when I had at least half a mind to go back to Leiden.

It may seem a strange train of thought while I was staring in the darkness at a floating corpse, but it had a great deal to do with the competition facing me, a competition I was now utterly determined to win.

Something like despair hit me on that cold log, where I sat with my feet in a dead man's shoes. Marvell was ahead of me in the competition already, and time was running out. I knew I would not be happy unless the picture that emerged from the next few frantic days was the best I had ever done.

It would have to be different from all that had gone before it.

I walked back to Paull Holme in shoes that squished on my feet at each step, wondering whether this whole contest might not just be a camouflage for an affair already in progress between Amelia and Marvell. It requires a certain mettle for a woman to attend an assignation in a graveyard at night. I felt the poem in my pocket and fretted on the meaning of "hadwyburt" and how I might safely discover it. Arriving at the house, I climbed the steep stair to my tower room and opened its door to find it ablaze with candlesticks everywhere, as bright as day. Amelia stood up from where she had been sitting on my bed and said, "Is this bright enough for you to work?" Then reached behind her, unclasped the cotton gown that was all she wore, and let it drop to the floor, a goddess in the candlelight.

TWENTY-SIX

Saturday, April 14, 2001

THE SHAPE AMONG THE TOMBSTONES SPOKE TO AMY IN DON'S VOICE. She was still afraid, but the words that came out of the graveyard darkness took away her fear:

> " *'Had we but World enough, and Time,*
> *This coyness Lady were no crime.'* "

"*Don.* Is that you? What are you trying to do to me?"

He came into plain view from between two graves, silver-faced in the moonlight. "I was heading home and I knew you'd come."

"Bastard. Were you trying to scare me?"

"I didn't want you to see me. Then I did."

"Why?"

"I want to talk to you properly and I couldn't in the pub. If you were feeling anything like I was, I knew you would walk back."

Did she trust him? She wanted to very much. Underneath it all, at some fundamental level, it had become impossible for her to believe that someone she longed for so much could be capable of harm. Surely not harm to *her,* at least. She wasn't scared anymore, couldn't be after hearing those words. The poem seemed to tip the scales toward gentleness.

"Those lines. That was Marvell's poem, wasn't it? 'To His Coy Mistress.' "

"I can say it to you in the dark. I can do a lot of things in the dark."

"Can you say the rest of it?"

"Oh, yes. I think so."

"Will you say it for me now?"

"Here?"

"Here."

"There are some other things I want to tell you, Amy. Why don't we go back?"

"I'm not ready to go back. You started the poem here. This is where I want to hear the rest of it."

"All right," he said. "Let's go round the other side. It's quieter."

"It's not exactly noisy here."

"There's the road. I don't want cars interrupting me."

Amy almost pointed out that you could lie down for a five-minute nap in the middle of this road and have a very fair chance of survival, but she didn't want to spoil the mood.

"All right. Maybe we'll find a flat gravestone."

There was no need. There was a brand-new bench at the far side of the graveyard. In the moonlight, Amy saw it had a brass plate screwed to its back, in memory of some newly-dead parishioner, no doubt. They sat down at either end and there would have been space for a third person between them.

"There are two things I need to tell you," he said quietly. "Amelia's daybook. I think we—"

"Can I hear the poem first?" she said gently.

She could see him looking at her in the moonlight, and that was it, that was the moment at which she knew just how to paint him, not in daylight but just like that with the scar like a splash of silver on his cheek, war paint for a night god, and the eyes masked in darkness—the treacherous, ambiguous eyes bypassed.

"Stay just like that," she said, drinking in every detail of the way he looked. "I've got you. I've finally got you."

As if he knew what she had in mind, he said, "I saw a moonbow tonight."

"You saw it, too," she said, delighted. "Is that what you call it? It was extraordinary."

"It's what *I* call it. I don't know if it even has a name. I didn't know there was such a thing."

"Did you know that was what I was thinking about?"

"Was it?"

"That's how I'll paint you. The moon beau."

"Does that mean you'll paint me in the dark?"

"Maybe. Come on, the poem."

She was expecting to be disappointed, expecting the same halting delivery he had given to his reading from Amelia's daybook. What she got was measured, practiced, and as keenly felt as if the poet himself had been sitting on that bench.

He started again from the beginning.

> *"Had we but World enough, and Time,*
> *This coyness Lady were no crime.*
> *We would sit down, and think which way*
> *To walk, and pass our long Loves Day.*
> *Thou by the* Indian Ganges *side*
> *Should'st rubies find. I by the Tide*
> *Of* Humber *would complain. I would*
> *Love you ten years before the Flood;*
> *And you should if you please refuse*
> *Till the Conversion of the* Jews.
> *My vegetable Love should grow*
> *Vaster than Empires, and more slow.*
> *An hundred years should go to praise*
> *Thine Eyes, and on thy Forehead Gaze;*
> *Two hundred to adore each Breast,*
> *But thirty thousand to the rest.*
> *An Age at least to every part,*
> *And the last Age should show your Heart.*
> *For Lady you deserve this State;*
> *Nor would I love at lower rate."*

Above their heads, somewhere up in the tower, an owl hooted. Don stopped.

"That's not all of it, is it?" Amy asked, not wanting him to.

"No, far from it. Are you sure you want to hear it all?"

"Every word. 'By the tide of Humber.' I can't think of a better place to hear it." Amy shuffled along the bench next to him and laid her head on his shoulder. His arm slowly came around her shoulders after a moment's hesitation.

"Ready?" he asked.

"Yes."

> *"But at my back I alwaies hear*
> *Time's wingèd Chariot hurrying near:*
> *And yonder all before us lye*
> *Desarts of vast eternity.*
> *Thy Beauty shall no more be found,*
> *Nor, in thy marble Vault, shall sound*
> *My ecchoing Song: then Worms shall try*
> *That long preserv'd virginity:*
> *And your quaint Honour turn to dust,*
> *And into ashes all my Lust.*
> *The Grave's a fine and private place,*
> *But none I think do there embrace.*
>
> *Now therefore, while the youthful hew*
> *Sits on thy skin like morning dew,*
> *And while thy willing Soul transpires*
> *At every pore with instant Fires,*
> *Now let us sport us while we may,*
> *And now, like am'rous birds of prey,*
> *Rather at once our Time devour,*
> *Than languish in his slow-chapt pow'r.*
> *Let us roll all our Strength, and all*
> *Our sweetness, up into one Ball:*
> *And tear our Pleasures with rough strife*
> *Thorough the Iron gates of Life.*
> *Thus, though we cannot make our Sun*
> *Stand still, yet we will make him run."*

He fell silent, his hand stroking her shoulder. His hand. His damaged hand.

"That is the most powerful poem I know," he said, "but I don't think you need telling. You should have read it to me."

"No, we all need telling. Life's not a dress rehearsal. It's easy to forget." She smiled in the darkness. "I'm a painter to the depths of my soul and I don't think the best words in the world can touch the best picture, but that poem comes close."

They kissed, then stopped and looked at each other in the moonlight. She heard a car coming up the road from the village. The waves of the poem, carried on the tide of his voice, still washed over her. In that quiet place, staring at him, her doubts disappeared entirely.

"Do you know," she said from a center of deep peace, "it seems so stupid now."

"Tell me."

"Out there on the road, I was frightened."

"What of? Ghosts?"

"Of ghosts and of you."

"Me? Why would you be frightened of me?"

"I felt Dennis there. I let my imagination run away with me. I thought he was telling me something."

"I don't get it." He sat more upright. "What was he telling you?"

When she'd started to tell him it had been an intimate disclosure of an absurd thought. Now it was too late to stop, and his response, the stiffening of his body and his voice, made her wish she had never started.

"I imagined it."

"What was it?"

I'll get it out of the way, then we can laugh, she decided. She tried to convey the absurdity of it with her voice, "I thought maybe he was telling me you pushed him into the saw."

The car came past, its headlights spraying through the bushes and lighting his face as he stared at her, and in his eyes for just a fraction of a second, she thought she saw that same stark, savage look she had seen before, the look the field mouse sees as the hawk takes it. Then the darkness slid back in the car's wake and it was just Don staring at her curiously.

"Not again. First Jo-Jo, now you," he said, his voice back to normal. "It's just nonsense."

His eyes were soft now. "I know it is."

"Why did you think it?"

"I don't know. Just something that happened in the dark."

"Like you said, he was just a nice old guy."

"I saw you out there this morning, standing by the saw."

"What did you think I was doing, checking out the scene of the crime in case I'd slipped up?"

"You crossed yourself. I didn't know you were religious."

"Superstitious. Everyone believes in something, don't they? I wouldn't like to say what it is."

She needed to get back to safer ground. "Forget it. What about Marvell's poem?"

"What about it?"

"Well, who did he write it to?"

"I don't know."

"It was to a special woman, wasn't it?"

"Perhaps it was just a poem for the sake of it, not *to* anyone."

"No. That poem wasn't written in a vacuum. That was for real. Can't you tell?"

"Yes, I suppose so."

"I think it was written to Amelia."

He laughed and tousled her hair with his hand.

"You," he said. "I don't know. If it didn't happen at Paull Holme then it's not real to you, is it? You want it all to be about Rembrandt and Amelia."

She batted his hand away. "There was a contest. Amelia says so. It was between Rembrandt and Marvell, between a picture and a poem, and she had to judge it. I think maybe that was the poem, and I'll tell you something else: I think *she* was the prize."

"That's just wild guesswork," he said. "I'm pretty sure Amelia loathed the painter."

"No," said Amy. "Only in the journal. Anyway, what did you want to say? You said you had something to tell me."

"Oh, yes, I do." He thought for a minute. "Look, it's about the daybook. I think it's time to give it to Peter Parrish."

Amy stiffened. "Why? We're still reading it."

"When you were in your room, I decided I'd read another page."

"By yourself? Without me there?"

"I know. I was ... I was feeling angry. I found the rest of the pages are much more stuck together than the ones we've opened so far. You know how it's all balled up at the bottom corner? It's not nearly so easy from here on. I got one more open, but the corner came completely apart. We're going to ruin it if we go on the way we are."

Paull Holme without the gradual revelations of the daybook seemed a bleaker place to Amy.

"Are you sure?"

"Am I sure that's the right thing to do? Yes."

She recognized there was truth in what he was saying, even if she resented his trying to make the decision for her. "Did you read that page?"

"Yes. That's why I know what Amelia really thought."

"No," said Amy, more alarmed that she might be wrong about Amelia than she had been at the prospect of handing over the book.

"Don't worry," said Don. "I knew you'd want to know what it said, so I wrote it all down."

He took out of his pocket a tiny flashlight and a folded piece of paper, and straightened it out.

"It's dated Monday, January twenty-seventh. Listen to this: *'Today has brought more indignity than I have ever had to suffer in my life before. The limner, in setting the final touches to his work, did require that I attend upon him to see it in its fulfillment. For that purpose alone I took myself to his room, where otherwise nothing he might say would prevail upon me to go, to satisfy myself that the work was such that would please my husband on his return. This, despite the state of disgust with which the man fills me at his loutish bearing, foul smell and goaty aspect. It has been a constant burden to counterfeit pleasure during the unendurable hours the work has taken. I will not dwell on what now took place, but to say that at the moment when I cast my eyes upon the work and was searching for a way of speaking that would convey my deep distaste at it, the limner hazarded a move of such unwarranted familiarity that I was rendered incapable of resistance to it. In this most awkward moment I was delivered by the Providential return of my dear husband, one entire day before he was expected, brought early, I think, by Marvell's urging who, dear friend that he is, did foresee the danger so that my husband, upon entering the ...'* That's it, that's where the page ends. The next one's stuck like glue."

"Oh, God. Can you imagine it?" said Amy, distraught. "What happened? Dahl walked in on them, just as the painter grabbed her. Why does she suddenly hate him? She didn't hate him before." She didn't want Amelia to hate him now.

"Let's go and find out," Don answered. "It should be in the one my mum typed out, shouldn't it? It should be in the journal. She would have considered it a bit more and written it out neatly. Have you still got it?"

"Yes, it's in my room. But it's the cleaned-up version for Dahl's eyes." Half of her wanted to say let's go, but the other half wanted to stay and see if she could recapture that simple powerful feeling the poem had produced. "Is there any rush?" she asked.

"Only that there's one more thing I want to show you back there at the house."

"Which is?"

"I can tell you what colors he used for Amelia's portrait."

That made her move.

At the house, he took her first to the room where they were both working and turned on the light. The last panel he had taken off had revealed the usual expanse of gray cobwebs, but since she had been in the room, he had wiped the cobwebs away.

"There," he said, "as bright as day."

In the top left-hand corner of the exposed rectangle of old plaster, obscured partly by the panel still in place to the left and partly by the thick paintwork above, were a series of bright splashes, crescents of color.

"What do you think?" he asked, kneeling down in front of them.

She stared at them, then reached out to touch them.

"He cleaned his brushes on the wall," she said. "Look at the colors. Red, pink, yellow—and look at this one, the purest flesh tone. I'll tell you something. When we look at that paint there, we're looking at the color of Amelia's skin."

He had brought this as a gift to her to match the daybook. It made them equal partners in the matter for the very first time.

"Can you be sure?" he asked. "Why the wall? It seems like vandalism."

"He was carried away, Don. The painting occupied him totally. Maybe he'd dropped his rag. The wall was the nearest thing, and there was no time to lose. The picture in his head was burning its way onto his easel, don't you see?" *The way Don's picture is doing to me,* she thought.

"Anyway," she added more prosaically, "they were halfway through putting the paneling in the room, weren't they? He knew it would be covered up. It didn't matter where he wiped his brushes."

She stood and reached down toward the wall.

"He would have been standing here."

"Not sitting down?"

"No, I don't think so. The marks would be lower, wouldn't they? Do you see, all he had to do was just turn to the wall and wipe them up and down. Don, I'm standing exactly where he did, and this is where I'm going to stand to paint your picture, too."

"So where was she?"

"I'll tell you in daylight. Somewhere just about there. Listen, do you mind starting early tomorrow?"

"How early is early?"

"Half past six. In here. Just so I can get the basics right."

"I thought you said you didn't need me for this picture."

"I might not once I get going. Only for the start and finish. You know, a lot of the time it's just a matter of getting the right thing in the right place."

"And the right place is where he painted her?"

"That's not what I meant, but can you think of a better one?"

"No."

"I'll go and get the journal," said Amy. "Let's find out what happened."

They sat on the floor in that big, harshly lit room and she read what Amelia's journal had to say about Monday, January the twenty-seventh, 1662, and the day that followed.

———

"IT'S ALMOST WORD FOR WORD THE SAME," SAID AMY, SCANNING the first page in disappointment. " *'This day has brought more indignity . . . the state of disgust . . .'* She calls him *'slovenly, ugly, plebeian.'* Oh, yes, she says, *'he has in a small succession of days turned the clothing my husband has, of his good heart, given to him into the most filthy of rags, all fouled with paint and I know not what else.'* Then it's the same again down to where her husband comes in. *'. . . So that my husband on entering the chamber put all at a wonderful loss, occasioning great alarm in the limner and great sorrow in me that he should see me so demeaned. He dealt the limner a blow with his stick across the top of his head which brought him low and then did sweep his works to the ground. At first he seemed struck quite mute but then grew increasingly out of order, his voice coming back to him and did reproach the limner most bitterly, saying he would be driven from the house and set into the first ship that could be found. Marvell took the limner away, saying he would see to all, and then my husband fell to reproaching of me so that I was hard put to defend myself against him though I foreswore any inconstancy on my own part. He took himself to another chamber and I to our marriage chamber where I found myself considerably out of sorts and in consequence I could not sleep all night.'*

"That's the end of that entry, then it's the following day, Tuesday the twenty-eighth. She says, *'I have resolved to show this, my Journal to my husband that he may see through my eyes what I have been put to by this limner, whom he brought first to our house, and that I have done nothing but what my husband instructed in the matter. I have resolved also that I will reveal to him even my own daybook which he knows nothing of before now so that he may see clear what thoughts sprung from my head at first thinking on to the page. In this, it is my hope that he will see how once the limner did amuse me and then did soon disgust me and how I tried all ways to cover this from my husband so as to fulfil the task he had put the limner to perform. The limner is gone from here with Marvell to the port to take ship. His room is to be smoked clean and his daubs to be covered entirely with panels. The work he has finished hangs in the balance. My husband's first inclination was to have it burned on the fire but he owns that the merit of a work may sometimes exceed the purpose of he who performed it. I however cannot look upon it without a shiver of disgust.'* " Amy leafed through the next few pages. "Not another word about it. A bit more about Marvell, then she starts banging on about how dreadful the builders are. Would you believe it?"

"What exactly about Marvell?"

"It's in March. *'Marvell came by boat to bid farewell and joined ship in the stream for the United Provinces where he says he must away with a most high mission to perform.'* Not a lot more." She went on leafing rapidly through the pages. "The house gets finished, then a storm blows some tiles off. Oh wait, listen to this: *'The twenty-third day of April. It is clear to me this day that my husband's greatest hope is fulfilled and that I am with child. When he returns from his voyage, I will tell him and all will be well between us again. That is my most devout hope.'* Well, well. Dahl's going to be a daddy at last."

"That's your ancestry, Amy. Don't forget, those are your genes. God, I wonder where that picture is."

"Not here, not in the house. Maybe not even in existence anymore. Perhaps it was burned after all. Perhaps all the paint just came off, the same way it did with Dahl's."

"No, that can't be right," Don said. "Look at the wall. That's the paint he used for the second picture, Amelia's picture. It's still on the wall, isn't it? It would still be on the picture."

They both knelt down again to examine the streaks of pigment.

"Tomorrow, I'll take that next panel off," said Don, "then we'll see all the colors he used. I bet there's more."

"Tomorrow's Sunday. Don't we get one day a week off?"

"We're working Sundays now. The Hawk spread the word. There's lost time to make up."

It was a bleak thought to Amy. *Dennis dies and all it amounts to is more overtime.*

She had to hammer on Don's door at six-thirty next morning, even though she had spent half the night awake, working on the composition, sketching, mixing narrow palettes of blacks, blues, and grays for the effect she wanted.

She put a chair where the dawn light from the windows struck it just right, and stood next to the old brush marks on the wall.

"That's where she was and this is where he was," she said. "I wish I could paint like him as well as stand like him."

"I thought you might come in last night," he said. "Why didn't you?" There it was again, for just a moment. That look she couldn't bear.

"I was tired," she said. "Too much going on." She had thought of him just beyond the wall during her moments of wakefulness, and had almost gone to him but in the dark, the doubt had gained the upper hand over the passion. "You could have come to me."

"You might have thought I was coming to murder you."

She couldn't bear that look.

"Close your eyes," she said in a moment of inspiration. "Keep them closed. I need to do them later."

That was the way. She worked rapidly away until she was happy with the pale paint outline on her canvas.

"All right," she said in the end. "You can take a break."

He opened his eyes, stood up from the chair, and eyed the back of the canvas uneasily. She realized just how reluctant he was to see what she had done.

"Come on," she said, "have a look. It's nothing at this stage. Just outlines, that's all."

He came around behind her, suspicious at first, then clearly relieved and interested.

"What's that?" he said, pointing.

"It's going to be the bench in the graveyard."

"And those are gravestones?"

"That's it."

"Cheerful."

"You wait. It's all a matter of how the moonlight works. I'm going to do a bit more to it. Why don't you get us some breakfast?"

"Orders, orders."

"Yup. My order is a bacon sandwich and strong coffee with two sugars."

He laughed and her heart soared at the sound.

At eight-thirty, the Hawk opened the door.

"Is that work for me you're doing on that easel?" he said. "Or is it something else? Because if it's something else, I'm not paying."

"I'll start now."

"You do that."

Amy climbed the scaffolding to carry on where she had left off, and Don started on the next panel. Fifteen minutes later, Parrish arrived.

"Good morning, you two."

"Good morning. What are you doing here on a Sunday?" Amy asked him.

"The same as you. Overtime," said Parrish, "except I don't get paid for it. I have a meeting with your Mr. Hawkins. How's it . . . My word, what have we here?"

He went straight to the brush strokes on the wall.

"More of your painter's work?" he asked Amy.

"I think so, don't you? Someone who knows ought to take a look at that."

"Yes," said Parrish, "particularly when I tell you that the word on the oak panels from the other painting is that they are almost certainly seventeenth century, and what's on them is an animal size of exactly the right sort made from, amongst other things, boiled rabbit skins. It was certainly a seventeenth-century painting. There's no doubt."

"There's also no doubt that what we've got here is seventeenth-century paint. It's behind the paneling, so it has to be, right?" said Amy.

"Well, yes, indeed. Now my man who knows says those panels are very much the size and shape used by the only known Hull painter of the time, Nathaniel Wilkinson, so he's wondering if our mystery painter might not be Wilkinson. There's very little of his work surviving, and one would have to say it isn't terrifically good."

Don was carefully pulling the framing for the next panel away from the wall, and they could see more streaks of darker-colored paint behind it.

"Terribly exciting," said Parrish. "Reminds me of that story of Heron's. Did you ever hear it?"

"Patrick Heron? The painter?" Amy asked.

"Yes, he was down in the south of France after the war and he came round a bed on the coast road and he suddenly realized he was looking at a Matisse painting—the, er ... I think it was 'Route sur le Cap d'Antibes.' There it was, just as Matisse painted it. Anyway, Heron realized he could get himself into the exact same position that Matisse had painted it from, pressed almost up against the rock face. While he was standing there, for some unknown reason, he lifted up the vegetation that was growing all over the rock and there, caught in a little crack, were all these palette scrapings. The very colors Matisse had used, still there after twenty or thirty years."

"Twenty or thirty?" said Amy. "That's nothing. These are, what, three hundred and forty years old?"

"Remarkable. It would be wonderful to know for certain who we're dealing with, wouldn't it?" said Parrish.

"Amy," said Don, "why don't you take Mr. Parrish up to your room and show him the box and what was in it?"

"What?" said Amy, stung by the sharp tone in his voice and aghast at the way he was forcing her hand.

"Please?" said Don. "Will you just do it my way?"

"What's this box?" said Parrish, so she had no choice but to take him up the stairs.

"Is he all right?" asked Parrish when they were out of earshot.

"That's the real reason I looked in. Ellen asked me to. She's very concerned."

"Mr. Parrish, I—"

"Peter, remember."

"Peter, I don't know anymore. Sometimes I'm close to him and sometimes he frightens the hell out of me."

She was expecting Parrish to be concerned and reassuring. She wanted him to tell her that was absurd. Instead he looked at her in silence for a moment, then said, very quietly, "I know what you mean."

"Do you?"

"I couldn't say anything to Ellen, of course, but yes, I do. To be quite honest, most of the time I think of him as a desperately hurt young man, but every now and then I wonder."

"What do you wonder?"

He shook his head as if he'd gone too far.

"You must tell me," she insisted. "What do you wonder?"

"If he's been doing the hurting."

There it was, out between them, first Dennis, then Parrish.

"I shouldn't have said that." He sounded tired. "Don't take any notice of it. You have to make up your own mind."

She nodded. Up in her room, she showed Parrish the box and the fragile book inside it and read him a little of what it said. He was gratifyingly astonished.

"My goodness," he said, "what a find. And you say it's different from the journal?"

"It's what she *really* thought," she explained. "It's got the story of the painter in it, but it's not in a good state. I think it's going to need a lot of work to get the pages apart safely."

"Oh, don't worry," said Parrish, taking it in his hands as if it were holy. "It's going to get that, all right. I'm amazed. When did you find it?"

"The other day. I was waiting for the right opportunity to tell you."

Back downstairs, Don had the panel completely off; they could see the full extent of the painter's palette, swept clear of cobwebs. Parrish, highly excited, left them to telephone his friend, and as soon as they were alone, Amy rounded on Don.

"Why did you talk to me like that?" she demanded. "I felt really insulted."

Something in the way he looked made her stop.

"What?" she said.

"I had to get him out of the room, that's all. I couldn't think of another way."

"Why?"

"Because of what I could see behind the panel."

"Brush strokes?" she said. "He's seen them, anyway."

Don crossed over to his bag and pulled something out.

"Not brush strokes," he said. "This."

It was a sheaf of folded paper, and Amy felt a rush of excitement as she recognized the age, the texture, and the color.

"What is it?" she demanded.

"We'll have to see," said Don, "but I've got a pretty good idea that it's what Amelia Dahl *really* wrote in her daybook."

TWENTY-SEVEN

I HAVE LOST THE SUSTAINING BELIEF THAT I AM YOUNG. IT IS A SLEN-
der thing, belief, and its disappearance has hurled me headlong into the
ranks of the old.

This discontinuity, this business of going away and coming back
again, is extraordinarily dangerous. I was wise not to try it until now
because it obliges you to look at everything afresh. I have studied myself
in the mirror day after day after day from the moment I first began to
paint, but the same face has always stared back at me, the changes in it
too small to see, slower than the hour hand of a clock.

Not now. The face I saw in the mirror this morning was thirty
years older than the one I expected.

It is time for an act of bravery so I am standing before a great canvas again in my own studio, with my own maulstick and my own
brushes. The mirror is set up and all is ready but I am not sure where to
start.

Hennie and Titus were glad to have me back—until, that is, I began to impose my will on the house and they politely but firmly told

me they had done very well without me, had even got on a little more
smoothly in my absence. They had certainly, they both said pointedly,
spent far less money than usual. I submitted rather too easily because I
had been three entire days at sea on that heaving tub. The captain, may
sharks devour him, already had my gold coins off me by force even
though I know Marvell had paid my passage in Hull with Dahl's
money.

How did I come to be in that boat? By the basest of actions.

When I entered my tower room to find it ablaze with candlelight,
and Amelia sitting there; when she stood up, asked if it was bright
enough, then let her dress fall to the floor, an exultant rush made every
organ in my body swell to bursting; I knew where we two were going
now. She stood there, studying her effect on me, not in any sly way—
more like a feral animal judging her situation and mine and seeking
some advantage under the natural rules that transcend our brittle human codes. If I had any knowledge of the future, then I would have
thrown her out, dowsed the candles, and gone to bed, but when Priapus
is in the ascendant, there is no sense to be found in men.

I stared at her, drinking her in, understanding in a rush just how
her shoulders sloped into her breasts, how the ribs narrowed to a tiny
waist, how the small stomach rounded perfectly down to a delicate
mound of Venus between thighs that Michelangelo gave only to boys.
It became clear to me for the first time that it is the frame and not
the flesh that matters, that I had spent years painting women who
were too fat, and that what was now in front of me was as near to perfection as I would ever be able to imagine again, and do you know
what else?

For the first time in my life I worried about my belly, my thighs,
that wattle hanging under my chin that grew gradually more promi-
nent. Against the flesh of the women I had known until now, they were
a matching cushion. Not here.

"What is this?" I asked her.

She looked down at herself then up again and smiled. "It appears
to be me," she said. "Is that not what you wanted?"

I took an involuntary step toward her but she held up a hand, still
smiling, damn her.

"No," she said. "You may touch me with your eyes only tonight.

The contest is on and this may help you win it. Marvell knows me well already. It is only fair that I let you see me as you asked, as I really am."

Marvell knows me well? What did *that* mean? It could not mean what I feared, because what would be the point of the contest if it did?

"I will draw you now," I said, "but that may not be enough."

"We will see," she answered. "My husband will be five more days away."

The only way I could keep my hands and my raving mind in check was to draw just a part here, or there, the way the parts of her aligned. She let me hold up a candle and inspect her minutely with it. I needed to see those places that had a form I had never quite painted before, the lower bulge of each breast and how it met the ribs below leaving no hidden fold, the muscle sheet at the inner summit of her thighs, and the wonder that lay between. The sweet smell of her caused my head to swim as I made my tour of inspection, and I sighed with desire.

What would happen, I wondered, if I simply put the candle down and took hold of her? There she was, there I was, and there was the bed. It was not respect for her rules, or for her wishes, which seemed to me to be a little different from her rules. There was enough doubt there to leave the outcome uncertain. My lust was such that her rules had no sway over me at all, nor perhaps her wishes. It was Marvell. It was the contest. It was my certainty that my picture could beat his poem, that this was the competition my entire life had been heading toward, and that if the prize was taken too early, the matter could never reach that point of judgment.

It came close, though, and she knew it. She was enjoying this. She was aroused, but whether by me or by the power she wielded over me in that room, I could not tell.

I moved around behind her. Crossing her arms and putting her hands on her shoulders, she looked back at me and she was fully cognizant of the effect that had. I knew I could paint her for the rest of my life.

This was no Amsterdam burgher's wife with aged crannies to catch the candles and illuminate all the interesting hints of morbidity. This woman was all about smoothness, about the light that glowed through that perfect skin. She was translucent, and I would fix her shape on my flat board by my utter skill in flesh tones and in the play of light, not by the depth of my paint. She would live forever in my painting and I *would win*. It was not just Marvell I had to beat after all. There was her sense of her own artistry to take into account. I had to be worthy of *her*.

I crept in close to look at her earlobe, fighting the impulse to drop everything in my hands. She moved, not me. She moved slightly back and her neck met my face and my lips but the lightning crackle of that touch lasted no time at all. She stepped away, bent down, giving me another pose that would only have done for the most lewd of my etchings, slipped on that damned self-satisfied cotton robe, and went to the door.

"In the morning then?" she said. "Downstairs?"

The smile on her face as she left seemed to carry no other implication than that she was pleased with herself.

When she had gone, I strode up and down amazed and in the hot grip of the most anxious and unsettling lust I could ever remember. Marvell must not win. In my pocket was the paper he had balled and thrown away. I took it and smoothed it, looking at it in the candlelight. I did not understand a word but I could now see that it started with three separate words where I had heard one, "Had we but ..." What was I up against? Were these hieroglyphic scratches of any artistic merit? Not knowing the scale of my task, I decided, would simply spur me on.

The next morning Amelia was her other self. Cool, gracious, not understanding a word I said, with servants constantly passing through the room. I had a tantrum when it became clear the carpenters fully intended to keep installing the paneling while I worked. They had already covered half the wall. My walnut had gone, and the sketch I had done of the two Dahls looking at his portrait was half covered over. I made a point of standing close to the wall, closer than I would have liked, to prevent them working right behind me and so, frustrated in their task, they left with ill grace.

Amelia sat there, demure and lovely, as pure as a nun, bewildering. Now I had every excuse to touch her, to arrange her, and I contrived a pose that was what you might expect in all respects but two. I tilted her head a little more to one side than might have been considered the normal mode, because I knew what was happening here was far from normal. It had a suggestion of the coquette but more of a suggestion of somebody who was on wry and knowing terms with the world. Then there was the mouth. Relaxed, closed, it was no good. I used my fingers, molding her mouth just so.

"Like you were kissing," I said, and she pretended not to understand, which simply gave me the chance to touch her lips all over again.

Although it is me who says it, I excelled that first day. By the end of it, what was taking shape on the board already had a shimmering beauty to it. It was the way a half-sighted old man would have seen Amelia, or a lover looking through tears. I would not let her see yet.

That night, I fretted in my room, hoping she would come back with her candles, but she did not. Instead, thrice-damned Marvell came to the house and I heard them out on the terrace talking and laughing. Marvell and Amelia with no chaperon. I could have gone down to spoil their fun, but instead I watched and bided my time, ready to appear between them if he dared to read her any more poems.

The second day got the picture to that point where bad painters stop and good painters start. Inch by inch, I was breathing life into that face on the board. The door was kept open throughout as servants brought us jugs of this and plates of that. At the end of the day, she closed the door and murmured, "May I see it?"

"No," I said. "It is not yet you. It only has the promise of you. It may never be you. All hangs in the balance. What is greatest is achieved only by the greatest risk."

When it began to grow dark, I walked to the church and did a lightning-fast sketch of its broken bones against the sky. I thought by this I would have an excuse for happening upon that crumpled poem, on the back of which, because paper is paper and not to be wasted, I now made a second sketch of the aspect from the river side. When I got back to the tower, with no expectation of anything, I saw a tiny dancing light at my window and sprang up the stairs to find that same phalanx of candles and Amelia waiting, composed and with the look of the Sphinx about her.

"Where were you?" she asked.

"At the church, drawing it," I replied.

"May I see?"

"Of course," and I gave her the second sketch, poem side upward.

She looked at the paper in open surprise, then turned it and studied the sketch, nodding. Without any other response, she turned it back again and I saw her lips moving as she read. "Where did you find this?"

"In the graveyard, all crumpled in a ball. It was useful. Why, what is it?"

"Marvell's first attempt at his entry in our contest," she said straight away.

"How did it get there?" I asked.

"It is a first rough try," she said. "I expect it angered him. Imperfection of any sort does do that to him."

"Will you tell me what it says?" I asked.

"It is a man entreating a woman to waste no time in loving him because all flesh rots and we do not have an eternity before us," she said.

"And is it done well?"

"It is done half well. I have found fault with it and suggested some improvement. He says in a day or two it will be better."

"You would help him win the contest?"

"Listen, Dutchman, I will help you, too, if I think your picture lacking. Have you not understood at all? We must all three strive for the very highest achievement in this."

Her eyes outshone the candles and I had a glimpse of a deeper mystery than I could fathom. I looked at the paper again.

"But he has thrown it away. How can he write it again?"

"He carries it in his head. Now, enough of Marvell, unless you are prepared to haul up the white flag already. Do you need to draw me again?"

"More than ever."

"Why?"

She was taunting me, the damned woman. She was ready for it, because she was wearing that same cotton garment again, the dress that I knew could drop to the floor with a twitch of her fingers.

"Because I can't touch you. My eyes can measure you as best they can, but it is my fingers that hold the brush and it is my fingers that are best qualified to capture the real Amelia. My eyes must work five times as hard as my fingers for the same effect."

She nodded and the cotton crumpled to the floor again, and in soft yellow candlelight she could have been carved from butter. It might have been what I most wanted but it was torture.

"Read me the poem," I said.

"You won't understand it," she said. "Why?"

"I can hear its rhythm at least," I replied. I wanted her mind somewhere else, to recapture that transported air she had displayed last time.

She began to read and, of course, it made no sense, but it made sense to her. It made a terrible and sensual sense. As she read it in a low and husky voice, I could hear it reaching inside her. It was like watching someone else make love to her. A faint flush spread over her face and I moved closer to examine her expression, the expression of someone starting to feel the first fluttering promise of the climax to come. Damned poem. I tried to get that expression, tried and failed because when I had barely begun she broke off from the poem and said, "Now. Now you can touch me. Just my breasts, that is all," and went back to start it all over again at the beginning: "Had we but ..."

Oh, I touched her. I ran my professional artist's hands over and around those perfect breasts and her eyes half closed and her voice slurred and God almighty, I wished that vain bastard Marvell had written another fifty stanzas because she came to the end, stopped, opened her eyes wide, and stepped back from me.

"Tomorrow then," she said, dressed, and was gone.

I was up at first light that day and I worked and worked at the dress and the line of her breasts and the soft skin of her neck until I knew I needed her there for the final seduction of the face. When the door opened, it was not Amelia but Marvell who entered. Before I could stop him he walked hurriedly behind me to study the picture.

He whistled. "Extraordinary," he said. "Remarkable. One would think you had known her for years, old man."

"Not so old."

"That look on her face. However did you catch that look?" he said. "I know it well but I did not think she wore it more generally."

"I paint what I see," I said tersely. "That is what I see when she looks at me."

"Is it now? And how far from completion is your portrait?"

"It may be finished tonight," I said, "or again, it may not."

"I have to go to the town on Trinity House business," he said pompously as if I should fall to my knees in awe. "I will be back at dusk. I very much look forward to seeing it." He went as far as the door. "Oh, and by that time I expect to have my own entry in our contest ready. I will write a fair version of it in town today, and I have a Dutch version for your ears, too, so that you may understand and accept the judge's decision."

"I am writing one in English myself," I said.

That stopped him. "In English? How can you? You don't speak the language."

"I listen. I pick up words here and there."

"Why don't you write it in Dutch? You would find it hard enough to write a poem in a language you *do* know."

"No, I am happy in English," I said. "I have the first line and I think it sounds very fair."

"Let me hear it."

I struck a declamatory pose. "Had I but vurld enuff ant time," I said and he swore an oath, slammed the door, and left.

Amelia arrived a minute later and closed the door behind her. "What did you say to Marvell?" she asked. "He rushed past me and galloped his horse straight over the new grass."

"I can't think," I said. "Perhaps he smelled his flesh starting to rot."

It was a harmless enough start to the day, just my bit of fun, but that was not how Marvell saw it, not at all.

It was some time since I had painted such a small portrait, and its completion, as a result, leapt up on me quite unexpectedly. In the late afternoon, I made a tiny adjustment to the corner of Amelia's right eye, touched in a little white highlight on the side of her nose, and stood back to see that it was done. By heavens, if I'd painted at that speed for the past few years, I would have been a whole lot richer.

"You may get up," I said and she went through the pretense, because the door was open, of not quite being sure what I said.

I went to close it. "It is time for you to see," I told her. "I want you to get up and I will lead you round to it with your eyes closed. All right?"

"Yes," she said. She was in my power again.

I took her small soft hand and led her round to the front of the easel.

"You may open your eyes very slowly," I said.

I watched her face as they opened and saw the dawning wonder and the faint flush. "Am I like that?" she said. "Do you see me like that? Am I so beautiful?"

"At least."

"My lips look wet to the touch. Are they wet? Is it the paint that's not yet dry?"

"They will still look wet when the paint is dry. Do I win?"

She looked at me, open and moved and vulnerable, a woman to whom one huge tribute had been paid, knowing another was on its way.

"It beats his first effort," she said, "but will it beat his second?"

"No poem he writes can diminish what I have done," I said. "I know you, Amelia, as well as anyone can know you in so brief a time. I claim the first part of my prize."

I was close to her, and reached out, took her head between my hands, and kissed her on the mouth. She seemed to move toward me in response, but before the matter was entirely beyond doubt, the door crashed open. Amelia sprang back, screamed something that started with "Save me," and Dahl, accompanied by Marvell, rushed in through the door and laid about me with his stick.

So there I was at the moment of certain victory, beaten and aching, ejected from that house after a night locked into my room by Dahl and jeered at by Marvell. All the next morning I was kept there with neither food nor drink however much I shouted from the window and in the afternoon, bloody Marvell came to tell me my fate.

"You're to be put on a ship, old man," he said. "There's a cart to take you to Hull and two men to make sure you don't stray."

"What is happening downstairs?" I said.

"Downstairs. Should I tell you?"

"If you don't, I may succeed in making Dahl understand there were two entries in our competition."

"She has told him everything," said Marvell. "She has told him that she only consented to the portrait to please him and that she found you a repulsive and vexatious rogue from the first."

"She did not," I exclaimed.

"Oh, but she did," said Marvell. "It was only her natural sweetness and kindness that let you suppose she looked on you with any favor."

"You say that because you want her. It is not true. I shall tell Dahl about your poem."

He laughed. "You! Tell Dahl? How? His Dutch is not up to that, I promise you." He put his face close to mine. "If you open your mouth I will have you whipped."

"You can try."

He gave me a sour look. "It will be the ruin of Amelia. That might make you pause."

"What you claim is not true," I said, because it struck at something so near my very center that I knew I must deny it. "She did not find me repulsive. These are the words of a jealous man. I have been with her. Just the two of us together. I know how she was with me."

"You do not have to take my word," he said. "She keeps a journal in which she writes her daily thoughts. She has now shown that journal to her husband to prove to him the truth."

"To defend herself! Did he know she kept the journal?"

Marvell nodded, then smiled a cruel smile. "He did."

"So of course she would tell the story in it that he would like to read."

I had fallen into Marvell's trap. Now he sprung it.

"Stop fooling yourself, you filthy old man. What Dahl did not know was that she kept a daybook also, a rough notebook for when those thoughts arose. He had no knowledge of it. Now she has shown him that, too. He is quite persuaded. Would you like to hear what she said about you? What she really thought? Oh, I know how she sometimes likes to lead men on. She probably made you feel you were a god, did she not? She loves the game, does Amelia. She would have taken you to the edge of heaven, then delighted in casting you down to hell. She despised you, old man. Let me tell you what she wrote."

I did not assent but he told me anyway.

Oh, Lord. There then came to me as I listened that savage moment when a man is forced to see himself through someone else's eyes and may never look at himself in the same way again. I need this good mirror and this canvas in front of me now to search this face of mine to see if it is really true that all the parts I thought I knew have fled. Young Rembrandt, are you gone? Were you ever there? The boy I knew who's in me still is no longer there for other eyes to see. Is there nothing of him left in this old flesh? I fear this glass because what I see in it may lead me to despair. What I thought might be the finest flowering of my manhood in that attic room has turned out to be its epitaph. I will remember her words, her bloody words, until the day I die.

I NEED TO PAINT MYSELF AGAIN, TO INSPECT MYSELF WITH NEW EYES and record any change I find. At Paull Holme I painted the best portrait I will ever paint and it has been debased by circumstance into a tawdry thing. For all I know, it may already be ashes on Dahl's fire. I would have brought it with me if I could. Why did she play such a game? She had me fooled. It was all to spur Marvell and his poem, and probably his hands and possibly his prick by now. All a vicious game.

It should not matter what others think of what I paint. There is that tale I often told my pupils when they asked what was great art, the old tale of the young Apelles, who wanted to be reckoned the best painter in the world but knew that the reputation of Protogenes stood in his way. He sailed to Rhodes to see the other artist for himself, and found him not at home. When asked by one who was there to leave his name, he took a brush and simply painted the finest of fine lines across a board that stood upon an easel. Protogenes, returning, saw the line and knew who his visitor must be, but took up his brush and painted a thinner line down the middle of the first. Apelles returned with Protogenes once more away and divided that line in turn by a line so thin that it brought the contest to an immediate end.

It haunts me now as I stand here before my empty canvas. There is another tale of a simple proof of artistry from three centuries ago, when the Pope sent out an emissary to find a painter fit for St. Peter's. The messenger came to Giotto, having collected sample works from many others on the way. Asked for a picture to take away, Giotto simply took a brush and with a twist of his wrist, painted a perfect circle in one movement. The messenger, failing to see the point, took it with him in anger, but the Pope understood Giotto's message straight away and knew him for the best artist in Italy.

I stare at myself in the glass and a man I have never seen stares back and the honesty with which he looks at me is a lesson to me. This gaze of his strips me to my bones. They are the bones of an old man who had not learned to welcome age. Now I *will* welcome it. My years have made me the best painter the world has seen, and I will show them that. I pick up my brush and with no effort at all, I describe the lines of two perfect circles on the canvas as the background. When people look at this, with the honest old man looking back, staring out to challenge them, backed by those great circles, they will know me for what I am.

TWENTY-EIGHT

Sunday, April 15, 2001

THERE WAS A PROBLEM WITH THE DOOR FOR THE REST OF THAT DAY. Either that or a problem with the frame, depending on whether you believed Tel or the Hawk. Either way, they spent a great deal of time discussing it, and then a great deal more time trying to fix it, meaning that there were people coming and going through the room right until the evening. Amy might have been pleased to know that Amelia and the painter had experienced an identical problem in that same room with the servants passing through but, not knowing, all she felt was extreme frustration that the folded papers from behind the panel had to remain hidden, and undiscussed. Something happened in the forced silence. A fresh complicity grew up between her and Don; shared looks, a shared excitement, building and building.

When the Hawk finally looked at his watch, grunted, and said they were finished for the day, Don was out of the room in an instant, muttering "Your room, five minutes" to Amy as he passed. She ran upstairs after him, changed quickly, and threw a cloth over the painting on her easel as he arrived at the door. He came in carrying two mugs and four cans of beer on the tray, Dennis's tray, but that seemed nothing but old history now. What lay before them pushed everything else to the back of her mind.

"Are you ready to read it?" he asked.

"More than ready," she said. "Think what it must mean. She took these pages out of the daybook. She hid them behind the panels so that nobody would find them. That could only have been because what's in them is the truth and she couldn't let anybody else see it, ever."

"I suppose it would have been easy enough before the paneling was finished," Don suggested. "Safer maybe than burning them, because someone might have caught her halfway through."

"How could she take the sheets out of the daybook without Dahl noticing there was a gap?"

"Easy," said Don. "I had a look at it before we gave it to Parrish. It's bound in sets of sheets, four at a time folded over double to make eight pages for each set. There were eleven of those sets all stitched together. Eleven's an odd number, isn't it? There must have been twelve originally. She cut this set out really carefully, then she must have written it all out again in the rest of the book so that she could tell a different story, as if she'd written it that way from the start. Dahl would have to believe her, wouldn't he? These were supposed to be her first rough notes."

"I'll read it, shall I?"

"Go on." He poured them both a beer.

"All right. This first page is dated Friday, January the twenty-fourth. Here goes: '*This night, I acquiesced to the limner's wish to draw me as I truly am, without which, he says, he cannot expect to capture my nature with his brush. He was amazed by what I did, and I was moved that he, who has seen so many women, so many rich beauties and painted so many of them as naked as they were born, was struck into a state of ecstasy. Despite his age, being of greater years than Marvell, he maintains a manly gravity and thereto a quality I fear Marvell does not possess of utter dedication to his art, where Marvell spreads himself thin between his venal politicking, his grand projects, and his poetry. For all that, Marvell has excelled himself with his verse though I have chid him for some ugly rhyming and the childlike brickbats it does cast against the art of painting. He says he will amend this to my suggestion and the result will be the greater for my complaint. The limner, in the practice of his art, acquires a purpose which diminishes his years and shapes his features almost to nobility. I find myself moved toward him so that Marvell's intended prize may well be his instead and I shall take great pleasure from it. Marvell will be here when the limner is gone should I award also a second prize.' "*

She looked at Don. "I think I'm right about the prize, don't you?"

He nodded. "You need to know who won it."

"You do, too, surely."

"It's not *my* genes that are in question."

"What? My God." She really hadn't thought of it before. A woman conceives at just that moment, a woman whose husband has not until then given her a child. A woman who was her ancestor. A painter or a poet? Whose genes lived on in her? She knew who she wanted it to be.

"It must be Rembrandt, mustn't it?" she said. "I mean, I don't write poetry."

"That's no argument. They were both creative people."

"Chalk and cheese," she said. "They're not the same at all. A portrait has to tell the truth. Poetry gets away with whatever it wants."

She turned eagerly back to the papers. "It's the next day, Saturday. *'A day of abstinence from pleasures of the contest. Marvell did ask me to join him once more at the church but I find in myself no desire to do so, knowing he wishes the prize before the course is run and being no longer so certain that he is the leader in my own affections. The other has known many women, esteems all women high, and understands well the ways in which a woman may best be pleased. That time in which he thought I did not cog his meaning whilst he spoke his mind in utter freedom to me was among the most pleasurable I can recall. This is folly perhaps and when my man returns, then that must mark the end of it, but we will have a winner before that time and I shall carry the remembrance of this contest to the end of my days.'* Well, now, there's a woman to reckon with."

"Poor bloke," said Don. "Old Dahl, I mean. She took him for a ride, didn't she? I wouldn't have stood for that."

"And you think he didn't enjoy it?"

"Not in the end, no. I mean, we already know what happened, don't we? How much more is there?"

"One last day. A really short bit. Monday. *'This bids to be the end of all and I am a cursed fool to let that happen in the main house that would have been safely accomplished and more besides in the tower. Van Rijn has wrought a marvel, the best painting he says that he has ever done, one to which I cannot put forward any suggestion of improvement. On seeing it before me I was so stirred by the mirror of myself in his eyes that I acted with no caution and am paying the price for it. Marvell is deep in this. He has brought my man early from town, knowing his advantage in this game was disappeared. I have affirmed because I must that I am wronged in this matter and have suffered foul indignity from the Hollander and said plainly that I find him a dog and a rogue and no gentleman at all but did not like to speak of it before for fear the painting which was my husband's deepest desire would not be done for it. The limner is to go at once and Marvell is elevated in my husband's esteem so that no doubt my safety will be assigned to his hands in days to come. This page ends and all will be writ anew.'* And that's it. Finish. Just blank sheets after that. God, how could she?"

"She had to, didn't she?" Don said as if it were obvious. "What else could she do?"

"How did it make him feel, do you think? There he was, with her in his grasp and it all falls apart on him."

"Did he know? That's the question," said Don. "Did she tell him she was covering up or did she let him go thinking it had all been some sort of game?"

"Games. I think that was what Amelia was all about. She was looking after herself, wasn't she? I'm not sure I like her very much."

Don gave her a look she couldn't fathom. "Those are your genes, too, Amy." Then he turned back to the sheets of paper. "What shall we do with this?"

"We can't keep it, can we? I mean, when this job's over, we'd be fighting over custody."

"Oh, I see. You're going off, are you?"

"Well, I won't be staying here, will I?" She didn't know. At that moment she couldn't imagine either leaving him or staying with him.

"You don't have to go," he said and there was a moment when she saw lover's eyes looking back at her.

"Whatever happens, I think we have to give it to Parrish," she said, "but first we should write out what we think it all means so that he really understands and doesn't just lock it away in some dusty drawer."

"What will we say?"

"Just what we know for sure." She ticked the points off on her fingers. "That a Dutch painter called van Rijn, who was certainly taken for Rembrandt by others he met here, came to Paull Holme. That he competed for the favors of Amelia Dahl with Andrew Marvell. That van Rijn was sent away in disgrace having painted what he thought was his best-ever picture, and that Amelia faked entries in her daybook to persuade her husband she had always found the painter repulsive."

"Poor old bastard," Don said. "His prize snatched away and his nose rubbed in the dirt. What did it do to him?" He stopped. "Why are you looking like that?" he asked.

"Because I've just remembered what that man—what's he called? that man Brigham—said in his lecture."

"Which was?"

"Wait. Let me check." She skimmed through the papers. "Yes, that's it. He says the final phase of Rembrandt's self-portraiture was the greatest by far. He says a great change comes after 1662. There's a famous self-portrait in Kenwood House, the best of the lot, according to him. 'Suddenly we see complete honesty.' Isn't that the point Parrish made? He says Rembrandt's a pauper, Hendrickje is dying, and in the middle of it all the man is brought face-to-face with himself and somehow triumphs."

"I wish I could see that portrait."

"The one at Kenwood? I have. It really is great. There are these two huge circles on the wall behind him. I don't know what they mean, but you can see in his eyes that *he* does. Somehow he's saying, I may not be Rembrandt the young and beautiful anymore. I may not be Rembrandt the middle-aged, rich, and successful. I am Rembrandt the old and my age does not matter a fart because I am the greatest painter on God's earth."

"I will see it."

"But listen, Don. *We* know what happened, don't we? We know what changed his life. It was what happened here."

He looked at her as if he was unsure whether to trust her intuition, then he nodded. "Yes, I suppose it was."

"Don, I would so love to see Amelia's portrait. I suppose it's gone. Well, maybe it's time to accept that and concentrate on another picture. I'm going to get on with yours now." *I can't do anything about the dead,* she was thinking, *but maybe I can still do something about the living, about who this man in front of me really is and how I can decide.*

"Do you want me here for it?"

"No, not at the moment."

"I'm going to have one final look in that storeroom. I'll see if I can persuade Parrish to lend me the keys."

He didn't reappear until late, tired and empty-handed.

"It's very dusty in there," he said, and pulled out a handkerchief to blow his nose. "It's definitely not in there. It's not anywhere in the house." He looked toward her easel. "May I see it now?"

"No."

"Why not?"

Because so much seems to depend on it, she thought. "Because I'm going to work on it until I drop," she said, "and in the morning, when it's finished, you can see it." He gave a sideways smile as he left, still turning his cheek a little away. She hardly noticed it now.

Amy worked all that night. She was using acrylics so that they would dry fast, and at four in the morning, she finally had the Don she most wanted in front of her, a Don who could stare back at her with an open face. She looked at that Don for a long time, loving him in that form and imagining painting her own face next to his. She sat down on the bed to stare at it, and suddenly noticed two torn scraps of paper on the floor. Each irregular piece was perhaps two inches square and the handwriting on them showed just a few words from each line, a phrase or less.

"... Drydock. I often ..." was one, and underneath it, "... looked upset an ..." Turning over the other scrap, she read, "... expression in his ..." across the center of it.

The expression in his eyes. There was no doubt whose eyes the fragmented sentences referred to or where these scraps had come from. Vin's statement, torn up and pulled out of Don's pocket with his handkerchief.

And why not? Why shouldn't he have got rid of something so

hurtful, so wrong? Against that, how had he known it was there? So much for finding the tray in the kitchen. She hated the idea of Don pillaging Dennis's room, hated it and went on hating it while she sat on the bed trying to grope her way through all the conflicting shards of this man who still held her heart captive. Then, because she knew she had a choice to make and could think of only one way to bring matters to a conclusion, she picked up her brush again.

It was a clear bright morning with a breeze from the southeast bringing the mud and salt smell of the Humber across the grass in front of the house. As soon as it was light, she set up her easel down by the river, near the remains of the old landing stage, and hung a cloth over the finished portrait. She made coffee and toast, then woke Don, watching him while he dressed. She knew that in the next act of their play she would finally see him for what he was, one way or the other, and then her choice would be clear, to stay or to turn and walk away. In a few minutes' time, that decision would be made.

"This is it," she said, loading up the tray. "We'll have breakfast down there. Are you ready?"

"Not really." They were both nervous.

At the landing stage, he looked at the shrouded portrait as if he wanted to tear the cloth off it. "Not yet," she said.

She poured coffee, but her hands were shaking and she spilled it on the tray, wiping it away with her fingers. She looked down at the mess then up at Don, about to speak. He forestalled her, tearing his eyes away from the covered easel and saying, "I've got something for you first."

She had spread a rug over the bank and they sat on it side by side.

"He might have left from here, mightn't he?" Don asked.

"No. It said he left from the port."

"But he sailed past, and he would have looked across at the house, looking for her, wouldn't he?"

"I don't know," she said. "After all that, she was probably the last person he wanted to see."

"I have something else for you. It rounds it off, maybe," and he handed her a piece of old paper, folded in two.

"You can decide what to do with this," he said. "If you choose to keep it, that's completely up to you."

"What is it?"

"You tell me. I think it's probably the first version of Marvell's poem. I don't know how it got there, but it was behind the panel with the daybook pages. I kept it."

"Marvell's first draft? 'To His Coy Mistress'?"

"This version's called 'To my Coy Lady.' It's different. Read it out."

She took the heavy paper, thick and still surprisingly soft. The ink was quite black, protected perhaps by the darkness behind the panel. Someone had scribbled a rough sketch on the back of it, a sketch of a church.

She read,

> " 'Had we but World enough, and Time,
> This coyness Lady were sublime.
> Your Youth and Beauty for their part
> Would long outlive the limner's art.
> No need for painted artifice
> When Age could not impair that face.
> Thou by the Asian Tigris' side
> Shouldst Emeralds find; I by the Tide
> Of Humber would complain. I would
> Love you ten years before the Flood;
> And you should, if you please, abstain
> Until that Flood should come again.
> But at my back I always fear
> Time's quick carriage hurrying near:
> And yonder all before us lye
> Desarts of vast eternity.
> The Grave's a cold and dismal place
> And none I know there do embrace.' "

"I think it was better the second time round," said Don, smiling, and at the sight of that smile she wanted to abandon her plan.

"Did he read it to her? He must have done, then she hid it. That means there are only four people who have ever heard it." Including van Rijn, there had been five, but she could not have known that.

"Now the picture?" asked Don, looking at the shrouded easel.

"No, not yet," said Amy slowly, staring at the ground. "One more revelation first, I think. Don, don't you still wish we could see Amelia's painting?"

"You know I do. It's unfinished business. I'd give anything to see it."

"I know where it is." She spoke in a half-whisper.

He shook his head in disbelief and stared at her.

"Where? How can you?"

"I've only just realized," she said, "just a minute or two ago."

"Come on, tell me."

"On one condition."

"Which is?"

"When I show you your picture, I will know something from your response. I will know whether we have a future together. When I know, I will either stay or I will turn and walk away. My car's all packed up. If I do go, don't try to stop me."

He looked shocked. "You're serious," he said.

"Never more so."

"I don't understand, and I don't like it."

"You don't have to understand. I will know if I can be with you. It's as simple as that."

"Amy, you do *want* to be with me, don't you?"

"Oh, yes. I just don't know if it's possible."

He looked at the easel again. "It's all down to that picture? I think these are higher stakes than I care to accept."

"There's no real choice, Don. If you don't want to see the painting, I'm going anyway. Take it or leave it. The outcome will be the same, but you'll never know about Amelia's portrait."

She was on fire with certainty and he could see it.

"I'll take it," he said in the end.

"Good."

"So, where's Amelia's portrait? Let's go and see it first."

"We don't have to," she replied. "It's here."

He looked around them. "No, it's not." Then he looked at the covered easel.

"Not that one," she said. "Funny, isn't it? Preconceptions change everything. We've been looking for a painting. You know what paintings look like. They hang on the wall, they're vertical. We should have been looking for something horizontal. Something, what was it? Twenty-two inches by eighteen? A tray is horizontal. A tray is about that size."

He looked slowly down at the wooden tray on the ground, Dennis's heavy wooden tray with the ornate curved edges and, tipping the coffee mugs off it, he tilted it up to stand vertically. It was the exact match of the framed board they had found in the storeroom, the sad remains of Dahl's portrait. In complete wonder, he turned it round and they both stared at the surface, encrusted with dirt and old coffee stains.

"There's something under there," he said. "This time it's not just wood."

Where Amy had rubbed the spilled coffee with her finger, a glimpse of pale pink had appeared. He rubbed more of the dirt away, but she stopped him. *How Dennis would have loved to know,* she thought. *Maybe I'm doing this as much for Dennis as for me.*

"Later," she said. "Now it's time for you to see what I've done."

She went to stand behind the easel so that she could watch his face. He looked hard at her, trying to divine her intentions, then reached out and pulled away the cloth.

She was praying that she would see surprise, innocent bafflement—that he would turn to her with a smile and a question, unable to recognize himself in what she had done. For a moment he looked simply pleased. The portrait was all in silver-gray, and the Don who looked back at him was sitting half-turned on a graveyard bench, with the moonlight on one cheek and the shining scar adding a line of quicksilver to the other. It defined and hardened him, a being from another world, a hero of starlight and shadows. The man in the picture looked superb, made complete by his scar. The man in the picture was Don as Amy wanted him to be—except for his eyes.

The eyes in the portrait were cold and savage, the eyes that flashed from that other Don.

In the moment when Don looked at the expression in those painted eyes, in that brief unguarded moment, his face changed and his own eyes took on the cold, destructive rage of recognition, an unmistakable knowledge of what the portrait meant. In that moment Amy knew she had the answer she least wanted, turned, and began to walk back to the house, filled with a sudden fear that he might, after all, come after her.

"Amy," he called, "you've got this all wrong. Amy, stop. I didn't do it. I need you.

"You've got Marvell's blood, not Rembrandt's," he said desperately. "That's not me."

She turned and took one slow step back toward him, then another and another, looking into his eyes, searching his face, then she bent down, picked up the tray, and strode away. She was halfway back before she dared look round. There was no sign of him on the bank, though a small copse of trees blocked part of the view. The house was still asleep when she arrived there, and she stood undecided, holding the tray that was no longer a tray. Then she took pencil and paper from her car, crossed to the saw bench and, as if it were an offering for dead Dennis, she laid the tray on its bed, wrote a note to Peter Parrish suggesting he have it carefully cleaned, and turned to leave.

The hand that grabbed her forearm hurt her so badly that she cried out. Another hand, part of a hand, came across her mouth. Don, panting hard, was behind her, holding her so tight she couldn't breathe. She tried to kick back at his ankles, but his feet danced away from her as he dragged her off balance along to the end of the saw bench. He let go of her mouth for a second, and she got out another yell before she heard the rising whine next to her as the blade began to spin faster and faster. He hit her and she fell forward over the bench, toward the accelerating blade, trying to get her hand round something she could hold onto. All she could reach were the metal rollers and they spun from under her clutching fingers. She could hear Don sobbing, and above that, someone farther off, shouting. Suddenly, when she expected to feel its teeth bite into her, the power to the saw was shut off, its brake came on, and the blade slowed rapidly.

From a window in the house, Tel shouted at her, "Come on, Amy, run. This way," while Gengko erupted from the front door, racing toward them across the gravel. She ran to meet him and he stood shielding her, but Don hadn't moved.

"You're safe now," said Gengko breathlessly. "We were keeping an eye out, just in case. Tel cut the mains. What's that crazy bastard doing now?"

Don was still by the saw, smashing something down on the slowing blade, again and again. It was Dennis's tray, Rembrandt's greatest work, reduced to matchwood.

EPILOGUE

London, Saturday, June 16, 2001

ON A WARM AFTERNOON IN EARLY SUMMER, AMY WALKED TO HAMP-
stead Heath, an envelope crumpled in the pocket of her jeans, on her
way to a date. Their meeting place was the house in front of her, and
she made straight for the front door. She smiled at the uniformed attendant inside and, although she had never been there before, she headed
instinctively to the left, quite certain that she could find him with no
outside help. She turned left again into one of the wings jutting out
from the house, a high, crimson room with damask wall hangings and
there, just by the door, he was waiting patiently, gazing at her, a little
defiant, a little grumpy even, as if she had disappointed him.

"Hello," she said softly, "I'm sorry I took so long."

He stared unblinkingly at her, a white linen cap on his head,
blurred maulstick and palette in his left hand, and the sectors of two
great circles on the wall behind him. "Portrait of the Artist" said the
plate on the frame, "Rembrandt van Rijn." She drank him in. His
clothes were simple, his long gray hair bunched under his cap, but the
lighting contrived to highlight the size of his nose. There was no vanity

in evidence anywhere in the portrait. She felt a need to apologize for the painting in whose destruction she had played an accidental part, the painting she had felt with her fingers and never seen, the painting into which this man in front of her had poured all his art and remaining fire of youth.

Behind Amy, two middle-aged couples stood staring at the picture. "There's a new theory," said one of the men in a thin, petulant voice. "It's one I rather like. It holds that the circles, do you see, the circles on the wall *behind* him function as a symbol of his greatness. It refers to the story of Apelles, do you see? Apelles showed his rival that he was the world's best painter by drawing two perfect circles just so. I like to think that's what Rembrandt is saying, too."

Amy glanced round, irritated, and saw the young attendant who stood behind them. He had a ponytail and a nice face and, as she caught his eye, he winked at her. When the others had gone, striding into the next room expounding some equally dogmatic opinion, he took a step nearer, glanced at the picture, and remarked in an amused voice, "Wrong story."

"Was it?"

"He meant Giotto, not Apelles. You'd be amazed how much crap I hear in here."

Amy looked at the portrait again. "Do you know much about it?"

"I work here because of it," said the man. "It's why I applied for the job. The Turner and the Franz Hals are fine in their own way, but this is the one. This is the pride of Kenwood House."

"What year was it painted?"

"In the 1660's. Some say '62, others say it was a year or two later. Just look at him. Isn't that the most honest look you ever saw?"

"I think it was 1662," she said.

"Well, something's happened to him. Something's brought him face-to-face with himself. Hendrickje, his mistress, she died in '63. They think she caught the plague. Perhaps it was that."

"No," she said definitely. "It happened before that."

"His son died, too. The old man had six years by himself after that. Poor as a church mouse. Living off charity. But just look at that. Poverty didn't matter. He was painting better than ever and he knew it."

"So is that what the circles mean?"

"Yes. He changed the picture, you know. I've seen the X rays."

"How?"

"First time round, it showed him working away on a canvas, then he changed his mind. He put his hand on his hip, got rid of the canvas. But I don't think that's the main thing."

"Which is?"

The attendant was standing right beside her now infecting her with his enthusiasm. "He switched the picture round. His brushes and his palette and that stick, he put them in the other hand, his *left* hand."

"Fantastic," said Amy, and the young man next to her looked at her sharply.

"Are you making fun of me?"

"No. Of course I'm not. I understand exactly what you mean."

"Really? You'll be the first one."

"He's not looking in a mirror anymore, is he?" said Amy. "That's the point. He's turned himself the right way round. This picture isn't for him. It's not the way he sees himself; it's for the world. It's his statement. He's saying, This is what you see when you look at Rembrandt, take me as you find me."

"*Yes,*" said the man. "You *do* understand. Remember the circles, Giotto's circles? He's saying, I may be an old man now, but don't mess with me because I'm one hell of a painter. My name's Paul, by the way. I'd like to tell you more about it, but that's my boss in the doorway and he thinks I'm chatting you up. I finish in half an hour. I could tell you the rest of it then."

"No," she said, "I'll tell *you* the rest of it. I'll tell you how he came to paint this picture. It's time someone else knew. I'll be sitting outside on the grass, somewhere by the lake."

She sat down to wait for him on a grassy bank and looked at her watch. Three hours before she had to be at work at the wine bar. It wasn't really work, just the way she made her money, the way she paid for the paint and the canvas that occupied her right through the day, every day. She stared at the flowers and the lake for a long while, then, feeling for the envelope in her back pocket, she took it out. It had arrived that morning in delayed response to the letter she had written to Paull Holme Manor. Gengko had the neat, laborious handwriting of a fifteen-year-old, and he hadn't wasted any words.

"Your letter to Mr. Parrish came my way," it said. "He's in hospital. It was touch and go but he's on the mend. Don laid into him, did him some damage before we stopped him. They've put Don where they put the crazies. The cops say Dennis was right. Come back and see us. Love and kisses, Gengko."

Staring at the letter, she knew Don had been a dangerous illusion, and that what she really mourned was the beauty he had destroyed. At the bottom of the page Gengko had added an afterthought: "P.S. Next time, pick someone simpler."

Across the grass, far away, she saw Paul looking for her. Good advice, she thought, and wondered whether to wave.

AFTERWORD

Readers may wish to know what evidence there is to support the idea that Rembrandt might have come to Hull in the early 1660's. He was indeed a notorious stick-in-the-mud, "too busy to travel," and initially the idea seems absurd.

Interested in what happens to men who find aging hard to accept, I was looking at Rembrandt's changing view of himself over the years and began to read everything I could find about his life. I first came across a reference to Hull in Christopher White's excellent biography. Discussing the four English views drawn by Rembrandt around 1640, he explains them convincingly as probably based on the work of another artist. Then he goes on to describe as "more inexplicable" George Vertue's remark that Rembrandt visited Hull in 1661 or '62, saying that while there was no evidence to render this impossible, there was also no shred of confirmation and that Vertue was relying on the testimony of someone who was only nine years old at the time.

The idea delighted me. Rembrandt in Hull of all places. I went to look at the Walpole Society transcription of the Vertue diaries and the entry is indeed just as I have reproduced it. There, in the reading room in the Victoria and Albert, I felt the skin on the back of my neck start to prickle. It seems to me that you cannot read the amendments Vertue made to that part of his diary, correcting the words transcribed by someone else, without getting a strong feeling that Vertue did indeed see a painting of a Yorkshire seafaring man and that he believed that what he saw was indeed a genuine Rembrandt. Vertue in turn believed it was worth recording the story told to him by Marcellus Laroon, even though Laroon was only a child at the time. That Laroon should turn out to be a famous engraver himself is an interesting coincidence.

The more I looked at Rembrandt's personal circumstances, the aftereffects of his bankruptcy, his dispute over the Julius Civilis picture, and his low output of dated works for some months at that time, the more possible the story seemed. It was then, on a visit to Hull, that I first saw the Sheahan history of Hull, predating the Walpole Society publication of Vertue by half a century, and found the same story in that book, again reproduced here exactly as printed.

Van Loon's strange book, purporting to be the diaries of Rembrandt's doctor, really exists and does contain the passage quoted that details the Hull trip with its diversion via Sweden.

Vertue named Dahl as the owner of one of the Yorkshire portraits, apparently a man of substance connected with the sea. Dahl should have existed in the archives if the story was to stand up. I visited the Ferens Gallery and discussed the matter with Ann Bukantas, the keeper of fine art, discovering to my surprise that she was on the same trail, with a thick folder of material. We agreed that Dahl should appear somewhere in the records but he resolutely did not. The Hull archivists helped me all they could. Hull Trinity House, an ancient corporation with ancient shipping records and somewhat Masonic ways, was less helpful, charging me for a reply each time they said that no, they had no answer to my latest question. However, it struck me, late in the day, that Dahl might be spelled in many different ways, as names were rendered phonetically at the time. My skin prickled all over again when I found a Mr. Daril, living on the banks of the Humber and engaged in various large transactions at just the right time. Daril, I felt oddly sure, was the Dahl who had the Rembrandt portrait. I took the liberty of transferring him from the south bank to the north because in the village of Paull and the relic of Paull Holme tower I had found the landscape in which I wanted to set the story.

The moment when I thought of bringing Hull's Member of Parliament into the story was one of pure serendipity combined with blessed ignorance. At that stage in the plot I needed a cosmopolitan Hull-dweller, someone who, in a short peace between the Dutch wars, might speak Dutch. Searching a list of MPs, I was utterly astonished to find that one of Hull's two MPs at the time was Andrew Marvell, a Dutch speaker and a Dutch expert, apt to disappear to Holland on unexplained missions for his diplomatic masters.

Finally and above all, I found myself wondering about the change in the nature of Rembrandt's self-portraits in this final phase of uncompromising honesty. The dates fitted perfectly and, having developed a great affection for the crusty old man, I had no choice but to tell this story.

WILL DAVENPORT

ABOUT THE AUTHOR

WILL DAVENPORT lives in Devon, England, where he is at work on his next novel of suspense, *The Chantry,* which Bantam will publish in 2004.